walk of
fame

SHARON KRUM

 St. Martin's Griffin ⚔ New York

www.stmartins.com

ISBN 0-312-27310-X (hc)
ISBN 0-312-31632-1 (pbk)

First published in Great Britain by Quartet Books Limited
A member of the Namara Group

First St. Martin's Griffin Edition: July 2003

10   9   8   7   6   5   4   3   2   1

For Paula and Joseph Krum

Acknowledgements

Heartfelt thanks, giant bouquets and obscenely delicious chocolates to the following: my fabulous agent, Barbara Zitwer, my equally fab and inspired editor, Michael Connor, and Elizabeth Beier, for her enthusiastic support from the first page.

Thanks also to Henry Krum and Lauren Berkowitz for their encouragement, love, and the divine Joshua.

And last and definitely not least, my cheer squad across two continents: Cindy Berg, Pamela Haber, Kim Huey-Steiner, Sandra Lee, Jo McKenna, Patrice Murphy, John Romais, and Norman Steiner, whose unstinting friendship made this book happen.

'I must have fame! Fame!'

John Wilkes Booth, Abraham Lincoln's Assassin

Chapter 1

Just to set the record straight, I am not a loser. I mean, I was not a
loser. I mean, I was not a person losing at the game of life, at that
time, on the day that she called. Rather, I was, I believe, like most
of us at certain times, lost, which is not the same as lacking in life
skills. Lost, I have come to know, is a beast of an entirely different
nature. And being lost in life is not something to be dismissed as
mere geographical detour.

I don't remember taking a wrong turn anywhere; I can't recall
stopping at a gas station asking for directions, only to ignore them.
But since my wife had left me for my best friend (I know. And you
thought it only happened in soap operas. Well, so did I!), I was
feeling rather depressed and punch drunk for weeks at a clip, like
waking up every morning as if you had attended a really wild
party the night before.

Not that I was ever one for wild parties, which, if I remember
correctly now, may have been itemized there on her shopping list
of complaints about me. I was, I think, to be accurate, just going
about my business, through the motions, a fully fledged, card-
carrying member of the rat race with many, I repeat many,
endearing, if hidden, qualities. They were just not on public display
at the time, due to the circumstances.

This does not in any way make me the aforementioned loser,
despite what the media later suggested facetiously across their inky
pages and color screens. I was, I must insist, merely lost, floating

1

spirit-like in that netherworld in which you watch everyone but belong to no one, impatient for what's coming next, fearing it all the more.

But on the day that she called me, the day I now regard as D-Day, it didn't help matters that I was reading a new and particularly fine biography of Abraham Lincoln and had, just as the subway pulled into my stop, finished the chapter on his assassination.

As historical assassinations go, it was, frankly, the most exciting I have ever come across – no easy task when you have stiff competition from guys like Brutus murdering Julius Caesar, and Attila the Hun killing his own brother to get to the throne. (Talk about sibling rivalry. Talk about me being glad I'm an only child.)

So as I stepped out into the Wall Street subway station only hours before she called, my juices were flowing hot, red hot, hot like sex hot, thanks to John Wilkes Booth and the shot he fired, the shot that changed my country forever.

I know. You can't believe history can be sexy. You can't believe how it turns me on. Well, trust me. It does. Give me the right leader, give me the right century, and I can get, well, never mind what I can get.

Now please understand, I am not a bloodhound. I did not, I would like to point out, enjoy reading of the violence, the blood-bath, of Lincoln suffering for hours after Booth pulled the trigger. What I did relish was the drama. I mean, how can you not, even if you are no way near the history junkie I am?

Just look what we have here. It's fantastic. One President, a.k.a. Honest Abe, with the radical idea of uniting the country and abolishing slavery. One Shakespearean actor, John Wilkes Booth, who before playing his final role of assassin, had performed in *Romeo and Juliet*, *The Merchant of Venice*, *Julius Caesar*, *Hamlet* and *Macbeth*. In the 1860s Wilkes was an actor in demand. And handsome. A handsome actor in demand. You know what that means. Yep, women in hoop skirts were hitting on him left and right. To translate into today's terms, this guy was like Tom Cruise in a waistcoat and buckled shoes.

So now Tom Wilkes Cruise Booth has a slight problem with Honest Abe. Well, who doesn't hate politicians? Take a number and get in line. But Booth, whose only hobby outside of the theater was spying for the Confederacy, resolved that Abe had to be, ahem, dealt with. Now, I don't know about you, but if I was planning to bump someone off, someone famous, someone, say, who lived in the White House, I would do it quietly, in the dead of night, with a big ski mask over my head.

I wouldn't wait until my prey was at the theater, seated in front of 1,000 people, watching a play, and then emerge from the shadows to pump a bullet into the back of his head. And I wouldn't then dive from the presidential balcony into the crowd, stab a few more people (as one does in times of stress), then stare directly into the audience, making it oh so easy for them later to identify me to the police. (I would, however, like Booth, subsequently run like the devil from the scene. I think that was a smart move.)

So now out of the station and walking to work, I paid no attention to the thousands of office drones marching in step with me, lost completely in my own thoughts. I simply could not believe the audacity of Booth committing his crime so publicly, making no attempt to shield his identity from anyone. But then, that's actors for you. It's always *me, me, me. Look at me, everyone! I'm killing the President!* Booth's ego, his vanity, made it so simple for the police to find him. (And shoot him.) Actors! And here we are anointing them, worshipping them as gods, when in truth they can't step out of the spotlight for two minutes to pass Assassination 101. This, I believe, should be taken as a sign.

So seated at my desk, a mere two hours before she called, I was still obsessing over Booth. What if I were Booth? What if I, shy, retiring, Tom Webster, formerly of Houston, now of New York City, had shot Lincoln in identical fashion? Would anyone have recognized my face, had I jumped over the balcony into the orchestra pit? Would anyone be able to say to detectives arriving at the scene, yes, Captain, I am absolutely sure it was Tom Webster, I would know his face anywhere.

I concluded, much to my horror, that while everyone in the room had recognized Booth, I would have gotten away with Lincoln's murder. Nobody would have identified me, not in 1865 and not now. I didn't register on anyone's radar, except maybe Mom's. I used to register on Elizabeth's sonar screen, she's the wife who left me for my best friend (I know, you still can't believe it), but that was over. Truth was, I belonged to nobody, I was nobody. I know I sound very hard on myself, but that was where my head was then.

Before the call.

The bottom of the pit where I chose to reside then wasn't all self-inflicted, you know. Elizabeth had a lot to do with my shrinking ego. After ten years of a marriage I felt was running quite nicely thank you, she packed her bags and announced that I was dull, we were dull, life was dull. She needed excitement and I wasn't excitement. She needed a man who was dynamic and would take charge, and I was, apparently, none of those things.

'Tom, you prefer your books to me. You never take me anywhere. You never want to go out. And you never...'

You know what's coming, don't you? She declared I was mechanical in bed (I'm not – I do want to emphasize this point to you), and simply couldn't spend one more night under our roof, living our routine existence.

'Can we talk about this?' I asked, as she had never mentioned her unhappiness to me before.

'Oh, now you want to talk! It's a bit late after ten years of giving all your attention to those damn history books of yours, Tom.'

I was shocked. Elizabeth never said damn.

She then announced she would not be home for dinner, for that evening she planned to move into Jake's apartment. Jake. Jake Gissing, my best friend. Shall I mention his role in my life again or has it sunk in already? I was completely dumbfounded.

'You're leaving me for Jake?'

'I'm sorry, Tom, I know it must be a shock.'

'Shock! Shock! Try earthquake, Elizabeth. Try El Niño. Forget shock. When did this happen, you and Jake?'

'See, see, Tom, that's exactly what I am talking about. It's been going on for months, Tom. Jake and I have been... you know... interested in each other for, well, a while now, Tom. And any other husband would have noticed. Except of course if they were too busy buried in books about Alexander the Great.'

'But you loved that about me.'

'Maybe once. But not anymore, Tom.'

She explained, because it was understandable her leaving might anger me and she feared I might do something vindictive, she had instructed the bank to perform this financial headlock on our accounts, freezing them to arctic temperatures.

Why she did this I'm still not certain, but I suspect she was prompted by all those soppy TV movies she loved where men seek revenge on women who leave them by cutting off their credit cards, strangling their ability to shop. This of course had the effect of giving me little room to maneuver when it came to money, beyond my own paycheck, and may go some way to explain to both yourself and myself why what happened next happened next.

Even for a mild-mannered guy like me, to find your wife has been cheating can lead to thoughts of an Attila-inspired slaying of a rival. To discover she is entangled with the one person you trusted above all others, your best buddy, causes all the organs inside your body to spontaneously combust. The day she left, I felt like one of those Indy 500 drivers whose car suddenly hits the wall and bursts into flames. As the crowd looks on in horror, he runs from the car screaming in pain while emergency workers douse him in foam. Only in my case there was no foam, no rush to help, no trip to the hospital. It was just me, alone, sitting in a burning car.

Having been declared bland on the inside, I was plunged somewhat into a world without hope. (This still did not make me a loser. Merely lost.) My inside was, I always believed, my best feature. My outside was not, which is why I worked so prodigiously on the inside to compensate.

True, Elizabeth described me as cuddly (when she still loved me), which is an overemployed euphemism for tubby and amiable. But here's the bald truth. I am what you might call nondescript. Plainish, shortish and chubbyish, with thinning hair. Not (I believed then) someone you would remember if I ran into a theater and shot the President in front of you.

And yet, while nobody had ever used the word handsome when speaking of me, I was not offended. I had secretly come to like my appearance, a firm believer in the Napoleon syndrome, which dictates that men who are short and round on the outside are all marauding generals somewhere on the inside.

You see, one thing history has taught me is that planning a successful invasion in life does not require looks, height or muscles, which is very comforting, seeing as I possess none of them. Rather, you need a strategy, an army, maps, some cannons, guns, more cannons, big bullets, more guns and, if possible, the personality of a megalomaniac. So if I could develop the latter and get my hands on the former, I could turn this country into Tommerica within days. And I still might, so you can stop laughing now. Invading and then ruling a superpower against its will remains on my list of things to do, once I get my personal life sorted out.

Elizabeth's leaving and the depression I experienced in its wake all occurred one year ago now – Before She Called. How interesting that on the precise day of the call, it was John Wilkes Booth who was uppermost in my thoughts. In fact by noon the idea that I was a complete zero, a nonentity (Elizabeth's parting shots rang loudly), became a song I couldn't stop singing, and I called Jake at his hedge-fund management firm for support.

Yes, that is the guy who stole my wife (which we shall get to in a moment), and I asked for his take on the matter.

'Do you know, if I had shot Lincoln I never would have been caught.'

'What? What are you talking about now?'

'I think my life is over, Jake.'

'Because of Abraham Lincoln?'

'Exactly.'

'You're losing it, Tom.'

'That's what I called to tell you. I think Elizabeth was right. I am boring. My life has lost its way, or I have lost my way in life, or. . .'

'Oh, Jesus, Tom, what brought this on? You were fine yesterday. What the hell happened between then and now?'

'Nothing specific. It's just, you know, it's a year now since Elizabeth left, I'm alone, women aren't exactly lining up to date me, and I've started thinking there must be a reason. I push a pen all day, maybe I do read too much, maybe I have no personality left. You know what I thought on the way to work this morning?'

'Try me.'

'That if I assassinated Lincoln in cold blood, in front of 1,000 people the way Wilkes did, and even if everyone got a sensational look at me, nobody would recognize me. I am forty-three years old and have failed to make a dent in anyone's life.'

'Jesus. Fine. Okay. Just chill, buddy. Now. You know what I think? I think somebody should put down the history books and watch some more baseball, that's what I think.'

So Jake tried to change the topic to the Yankees game, but I wouldn't let it go, which is weird for me, because the only other thing I can talk about all day after history is baseball. Instead, kindly (and probably somewhat guiltily), he spent the next ten minutes massaging my ego and promising me I was still a very interesting guy.

Witty, thoughtful, supremely knowledgeable about the Roman army and American baseball (not a lot of people can pull that off, I have to admit) and most understanding, even forgiving, when it came to losing my wife to him.

Other men, he reminded me, would have been far more violent and far less resigned. In short, I was the proud owner of many redeeming features. Instantly I felt my ego sit up from its prone position. As for my fears about living an uneventful, routine existence, Jake insisted that everyone over forty complained their lives had become full of obligations and devoid of meaning, and I was, if it were any consolation, hardly alone. (Except I was alone.)

'And what about your friend Simon? Look at him, Tom. His life is worse than yours. Much worse.'

'That's supposed to make me feel better? I am supposed to compare my life with a guy doing eight years in prison?'

'Why not?'

'Why not? I am not a crook, Jake!'

'Tom, are you going to talk about the game or not?'

'Not.'

'Well, that's it then. I'm going to check the market.'

And he hung up. I was then depressed once more, after a temporary interlude of joy. My thoughts turned to lunch and whether that day would yield egg salad or ham on rye. The phone rang again, and I knew it was Jake, who always calls back minutes after hanging up with all sorts of amendments to our conversation.

'You know what I'm thinking now?' I said. 'Even if Bigfoot had shot Lincoln, they would find him before me, and nobody knows what he looks like except for his feet.'

'Tom Webster please,' said a young female voice which definitely did not belong to Jake.

'Oh, I'm sorry. I thought you were someone else.'

I felt like a complete idiot.

'This is Tom Webster.'

'Mr Webster, is this a good time?' she asked.

What a question that one was. Is this a good time? Any phone call that distracted me from my job deciphering the movements of those overpaid, oversexed stock traders on Wall Street was always a good time. But this phone call was, you see, not a minor diversion. Boy, did this one come out of left field.

Without exaggeration, her call was one that would, immutably, change my life. And I might add, now thoroughly convinced that I could murder honest Abe and escape with my life, boy, did I suddenly feel the pressing need to spice up my pathetic existence.

Boy Oh Boy Oh Boy Oh Boy.

Chapter 2

On the day of the call, I was, and continue to be, actually, a columnist for the money magazine *The Capitalist*. You have probably seen *The Capitalist* on the newsstand or read it at your dentist, but if not, let me give you the lowdown in twenty-five words or less. *The Capitalist*'s guiding principle was this: millionaires, billionaires and zillionaires – how they got that way, how they stay that way, how you can join their club.

My column, 'The Insider' (page fifty-four, small byline at the bottom), was not exactly the highlight of the magazine, but not the lowlight either. Each week in 800 words I was required to deconstruct the economic indicators artificially inflated and then deflated by the United States government every week. I then had to explain to our cigar-chomping readers how these numbers would impact on their gargantuan stock holdings.

This was, to say the least, a challenging assignment (one I inherited the day after the previous columnist suffered a fatal heart attack – yes, you read right, I got promoted based not on talent but on a funeral), as nobody knows anything about how Wall Street works, least of all me.

I mean, you would think I do, armed with an economics degree from Yale, but after ten years of watching the Street work, I confess, I haven't got a clue. I can, however, bluff brilliantly, which is a gift I didn't know I had until tested. The only thing I can say with any confidence is that everything is speculation. Washington thinks what it says about interest rates matters but it doesn't, and it's all irrelevant anyway, because Bill Gates owns all the money.

I bet you're wondering what I am doing in this job. Well, so am I. There is not a general or king in sight, and these twenty-first-century titans of industry you read about are hardly of interest to me. Well, for this state of affairs you can blame my father, may he rest in peace. I do. I desperately wanted to study history, but a scan of the Houston employment section revealed no call for historians, and Dad, being an accountant, suggested I study economics.

'It's important to be secure in life, son. If you can read numbers, you will always have a job.'

And so here I am, writing for and about people who make more money than I or you ever will. And, let's be honest, anyone who pays more in taxes than most of us earn should be despised, and, I might add, mocked at every opportunity. I had been informed, however, that unbridled envy is not one of the hall-marks of quality journalism, and, being a quality guy, was eternally vigilant that such sentiments never sneaked into my column. But they did sneak into my comments around the office – well, our comments actually, us being the entire staff, editors, reporters, artists, even receptionists.

Truth is, and you might as well hear it from me, every employee of a publication that covers the financial world despises their subject matter. Dissecting how rich guys continue to get richer while you never do is a strange profession indeed. But it does make for one harmonious office environment. Unified antipathy for the rich was the glue that bonded our little newsroom together.

Nor were we partisan in any way. We were equal-opportunity haters. We hated those who got rich by dint of hard work, we hated those who inherited their fortunes. It didn't matter how you got it, it was more that you had it and we didn't. That was the rule, and you couldn't bend it for anyone, even friends.

Friends, say, like Simon Burke, a Yalie who graduated in my year and immediately landed a job as a broker in a large white-shoe firm on Wall Street, courtesy of his family connections. Twenty years after we left Yale, Simon's annual income looked like one of those lottery jackpots everyone drives across state lines to enter.

Though I hated him for it (office rules), I had to be nice to him, because I needed him. When you write a column every week, trust me, you run out of fresh ideas pretty quick. So I used Simon, along with anyone else I had gone to college with, as a source when I need to quote someone from the street. My column was proof it's not what you know (as I said, I know nothing), but who you know, and what they know, that's important.

So Simon would appear in my columns as 'Simon Burke, senior stock trader at T—, tells me that if the Fed cuts interest rates, internet stocks are going to balloon 20 percent next quarter', stuff as tedious as that. I loathed calling him because just to talk to him reminded me how poor I was by comparison, but he always took my call. He had an ego the size of Texas, and lerved seeing his name in print. Well, um, he did.

That was before he was charged and imprisoned for insider-trading, which, after golf and cheating on your wife, is still the sport of choice on Wall Street. After he was indicted, he saw his name move from my column to the cover of the magazine (along with his picture), and that he wasn't quite so thrilled about.

By contrast, Louis was beside himself with joy. Louis Goldberg is my editor, and nothing boosts the magazine's (and his) circulation like a scandal. Louis wanted me to go to prison to interview him, but I declined, citing a conflict of interest. I did, however, venture upstate a few weeks after the trial to visit. Simon entered our little meeting room wearing an orange uniform so bright it looked as if it was nuclear-powered. It was certainly a step down from Armani, but other than the utter lack of sartorial style Simon appeared to be doing quite well, all things considered.

He missed his business lunches, his kids and sex, which, he confessed, he was having with his wife and his secretary until the arrest. But most of all he missed the power of being a player.

'They don't care that I made millions on Wall Street. I'm just another mouth to feed until I make parole.'

He explained that, just like in the real world, a class hierarchy exists in prison, dictated not by whether your parents arrived on the *Mayflower*, but rather by how heinous your sins were seen to be. For the sin of being white and rich, and his crime being an insatiable desire to get even richer, he was treated with contempt by his fellow inmates, except for one bank robber, with whom he played basketball every day.

He was most upset by this state of affairs, while I, to be honest with you, felt their behavior entirely appropriate. I liked it that Simon was incarcerated. I earn $70,000 a year before taxes, so I felt it appropriate and consistent with our office policy that he was being punished for earning too much money. True, his doing time meant I lost a valuable source, but if anyone was ever going to teach Simon Burke humility, I could think of nothing better than an exercise yard full of men who think interior decorating begins and ends with Miss January.

Chapter 3

When Elizabeth left me, her primary complaint was that over the years I had reworked my personality from endearing and dependable to stuck in a rut and lifeless. You might interpret this as my being a loser, the press certainly did, but I don't.

Still, I admit to feeling crushed after her pronouncement, and not without cause. Was I not a good conversationalist? All married couples run out of things to talk about eventually, but I rose to the occasion whenever called. I believed myself to be an even-tempered, faithful husband, something, frankly, a lot of women would kill for. And I should like to repeat again, for those of you who might have missed it earlier, I am not boring in bed. Sure, we were down to, you know, three or four times a month, but those liaisons were not, I can report, lacking in passion.

Elizabeth was right about one thing. I might have a slight problem living in the twentieth century. It's true. Since childhood I have considered all our great advances as a global community – the motorcar, the computer, space travel – completely devoid of appeal. The latter in particular was a major embarrassment for my family, for NASA was practically in our backyard. All I can say about the activities of our famed space agency is this: rockets, shmockets. I hate the future and have no desire to move there. If requested to participate in an experiment involving time travel granting me leave to move permanently to a prior century, I would be packed yesterday.

I never professed any love for the twentieth century and the fact we now have to live in the twenty-first makes me completely crazy. My passion – okay, obsession – is the study of those who lived in epochs before our own. Days I lovingly refer to as the Good Old Days. Really good old days, when people bickered at dinner parties over whether the earth was flat or round, and rather than hire a broker to shore up the deal, pillaging and plundering were the only way to acquire land in Europe.

I see now this may have been my undoing. People who harbor a voracious appetite for history, and spend all their free time reading it, may find themselves at a later date accused of being a lousy husband. In addition, you may be charged with never taking your spouse anywhere, never initiating new and varied positions in the bedroom, and spending too much time buying and reading books about Egyptian queens and fifteenth-century French kings. In fact, you might be accused of doing nothing other than going to work by day and reading historical biography by night, which, I have since learned, will give your best friend enough time to steal your wife from right under your nose.

Now, I never advertised myself as Mr Excitement when we wed, but I thought my very lack of flash was part of the appeal. Since then I have learned women want you to remain the man they married, but they don't. They want you to become more interesting over time, when in fact you can become only less, as the mystery leaves the room and familiarity creeps in.

As they say in New York, Go figure.

Elizabeth and I didn't speak after her dramatic departure, not that I didn't try. I tried many times, but she insisted it would be better if we didn't communicate.

'There's nothing to discuss, Tom. I've made my decision, and it would only be degrading for both of us to hear you beg me to come back.'

Begging aside, this was a ridiculous edict, considering I still spoke to Jake every day and she was now in his apartment. But Elizabeth can be very stubborn, and whenever I called, she grunted and then passed him the phone.

I know. You cannot for the life of you understand why Jake is still my best friend after stealing my wife. I'll tell you. We met in the second grade in Houston. We were swapping baseball cards at recess and you know what a bonding experience that is for six-year-old boys. From that day we were inseparable. We went on to play Little League together, smoke our first cigarettes together, read our first *Playboy* together, share a room at Yale, and then an apartment in New York, where we moved after graduation to make the money we heard was there for the picking, except, wouldn't you know, it didn't pick us.

We were in fact about to pack it in and go back to Houston when I met Elizabeth at a party thrown by a colleague at my old job, which was actually three jobs before the one I have now. I was working at a small newspaper, I mean four pages small, that covered the bond market. I had worked at a high-flying Wall Street investment house straight after college, but was told politely by my supervisor that I wasn't aggressive enough, and they would not be renewing my contract. He softened the blow by complimenting me on writing fine reports, and suggested business journalism. So I took my lack of competitiveness, my expert ability at writing boring reports, and moved over to the four pages that made up *Bonds Weekly*. He was indeed right, I thrived. My skill at turning boring reports into boring articles was duly noted. Tom Webster business writer was born.

Elizabeth was friends with the wife of the colleague throwing the party, and she threw us together the minute I walked in the door, because we are both Texans. You must meet Elizabeth! She's from Dallas! she insisted, as if birth in the same state was a good reason to meet someone.

As it turned out, Elizabeth was born in Dallas, but left before she was out of diapers. She moved with her family through a bunch of states the way army brats do, covering some twelve cities before landing in New York to go to teachers' college. That was it for her. She hasn't left the city since, nor does she intend to. And it's not that she thinks New York is the greatest thing since sliced bread, because she certainly complained enough about the place. It's the legacy of being an army kid. She just can't pack up her stuff one more time. If she had gone to college in Bosnia, she would still be there too.

So you see, by the time we met, Elizabeth was as Texan as I am

British. She had no trace of an accent left, she didn't ride horses, she didn't like barbecue... heck, she didn't have big hair. All the Texas had been bled out of her good and proper, and once that was established, we had to find other things to talk about.

So I asked her what she did. You know, your standard question. When she told me she was a history teacher, I thought I had died and gone to heaven. A woman who loved history. There is a God. We talked about what she taught, I talked about what I read. My interests ran more to invading generals, hers to benevolent queens, but aside from the difference (it's only testosterone, anyway) I finally found a woman who understood my obsession. I mean, she knew what the Magna Carta was. Most women thought it was a sports car. And she told me her hobby outside of teaching history was making quilts, so at the time I saw her as a modern-day Betsy Ross, and, boy, that really turned me on. Little did I know one day Betsy would turn into Lucrezia Borgia.

When I went home that first night I couldn't stop thinking about her. She wasn't beautiful in the way I'm used to women being beautiful, because if you are from Texas you have very high standards (hey, Farrah Fawcett is from Texas), but she had spunk.

She was also shorter than me (v. important for guys) and, heck, as they say at home, we just darn clicked. Maybe now that I think about it, marrying someone who is your mirror image, which seemed like such a good idea at the time, can be too much of a good idea. Maybe opposites are happier because loving someone you can't always read keeps a relationship fresh, and similarities invite boredom to move in.

But at the time we loved that we had so much in common. Well, I did anyway. Maybe she married me because at the time she was thirty and still single, and wanted to get a move on. Women do panic at that age. But, no, I can't reduce ten years of what I thought was a happy union to that. No, sir. Truth was, we started dating and fell in love, and I know this because we said things like 'I love you' to each other, which surely proves something. We were just comfortable together. She wasn't a big talker, and didn't expect me to be. (Although I did find out she could pack a wallop in a fight if she chose.)

We read history at night and she quilted and prepared lesson plans, and Friday evenings we had dinner at our local Chinese restaurant. We tried for a baby but it didn't work out, and we both made our peace with it. She taught kids all day, so I don't think she was desperate to come home to more. As I saw it, our only big gulf was baseball, which she didn't like, but what woman has ever cared about the game like us guys? It's not their fault. I think it's biological. They just don't have the baseball gene.

So I told Jake I wasn't going back home, because of Elizabeth. Of course, as we were inseparable, he cancelled his plans to leave New York too. After Elizabeth and I married, we did not become a couple so much as a triple. Jake, a bachelor, accompanied us everywhere, even on vacations, and she didn't seem to mind at all.

Now I think if he had made his intentions known earlier that he intended to bed my wife, perhaps I would have nixed the joint vacations. I believe seeing Elizabeth in a bikini on a tropical island started things for him, while seeing me in swimming trunks with a spare tire around my midriff started things for her.

Whatever the trigger, I was so naïve and trusting it never occurred to me that allowing them to spend time together might result in their developing feelings for each other. I actually thought familiarity between a wife and her husband's best friend bred contempt. And while it does, her contempt, I later learned, was reserved for me.

But having invested far more time in my best friend than my wife, I did not abandon one because I was abandoned by the other. Jake felt the same way. Women found the decision to divide loyalties appalling, but men understood.

After they moved in together, Jake mumbled an apology and said something to me like, 'No hard feelings, Tom?', and I assured him there weren't, which is insane, right? But it was true. While I was very angry at her, I harbored no desire to kill him. I know what you're thinking. This guy is Cleopatra, queen of denial.

Maybe you have a point. I mean, I know Caesar would have stabbed Jake viciously within minutes of hearing the news. Henry VIII would have cut off his head. Attila the Hun would have ordered Jake disemboweled and then eaten his intestines for dinner. Compared to my heroes, I completely wimped out, but I could not face losing my wife and my best friend in the same week.

And, as I am often told, I'm a decent guy. Tom, you're a real Texas gentleman, they say. So when Jake apologized, like a real Southern gent, I let him shake my hand, then went home to my empty apartment to get on with my life.

Which, frankly, AC, After the Call, was something you will not believe when I tell you.

Chapter 4

I suspect you know by now my passion is history. Baseball too, but that is a love affair abridged by the seasons. Summer is boom time. Winter a bust. Studying history, by contrast, is a year-round activity. And thank God. Both before the call and after it, history saved me. It had always afforded me the luxury of retreating from the world, but after the call a new, heightened urgency to study emerged.

I began to draw inspiration and solace from time's key players. Their struggles were my struggles, their strength gave me strength. And yes, their foibles and vanities, all mine as well. My specific interest involves individuals who have made their mark twice, finding fame in their lifetimes and then enduring in ours.

Cleopatra. Michelangelo. Alexander the Great. Henry VIII. Louis XIV. Put a number after somebody's name and I'm there. Since childhood I have been infatuated by those whose achievements reverberated across the centuries. To have one's name stand the test of time, one's exploits examined and scrutinized eons after they occurred, only then are you truly deserving of fame. Those individuals among us now famous for the stock fifteen minutes, I despair of.

Even fifteen years of fame is nothing to me. Fifteen hundred, now you're talking. I like my heroes long dead, buried in some far-off, inaccessible place, yet credited with exploits that send jaws to the floor. And toss in plenty of quid pro quo too, while you're there.

Something for something, thank you, not something for nothing, hear. If you invade Egypt or Persia and slaughter thousands in your wake, you deserve to be reviled yet recorded for posterity. But fame and recognition as reward for simply reading the news, appearing as a witness at a scandalous trial, how did we, when did we, allow this to happen?

It was a question I asked myself often when alone with my thoughts, which, after Elizabeth left, meant, well, nightly. Nor did I stumble upon an adequate response. But after the call, after her call, after she called, it was one riddle I was finally, confidently, able to answer.

The call came from a woman who introduced herself as Yancy. Weird name that, as if her parents meant to call her Nancy but couldn't quite figure out the spelling. Yancy informed me she was the assistant to Ms Jamie MacDowell, who was a woman, not a man, and don't you forget it.

Ms MacDowell, which Yancy pronounced Mzzzz MacDowell, was the editor of *The Vulture*, a super-slick glossy magazine that I remember Elizabeth used to read on occasion. The magazine's credo could be read on its masthead: '*The Vulture* – Picking Over the Bones of Contemporary Culture'.

Of course the word contemporary turned me off right away. Any culture that isn't dead isn't alive, if you know what I mean. To that end *The Vulture* was full of interviews with people I paid no attention to, namely movie stars so hot they were barely out of the oven, artists, singers, writers, politicians and a veritable chocolate-box assortment of those currently anointed to represent our creeping cultural advancement.

I recalled reading somewhere, probably the media section of *The Capitalist*, that competition with *The Vulture* had become fierce. While *The Vulture* was occupied picking over the bones of others, rival magazine editors wasted little time picking over theirs. One person with a good idea eventually gets clobbered by ten people whose only idea has been to plagiarize yours. For the uninitiated among you, this we call capitalism.

When this occurs, all editors resort to stunts to boost circulation, mine included. One tactic is to publish stories with misleading headlines, or tout an impending crisis or scandal that is usually quite tame. In the trade this is called 'food processing', and writers often find themselves under instruction from those better placed on the food chain to step into the reportorial kitchen. Putting an issue or personality in the blender and being told by an editor to 'turn it up to number ten' is not, I promise you, uncommon.

Thus celebrities married but a week find themselves 'considering divorce'. Billionaires who gave unlimited access to writers from *The Capitalist* often, I heard later, lived to regret it. You would too if an article supposedly about your rehabilitation as a business mogul after a stint inside for embezzlement used three pages to reconstruct your original crime, then as an afterthought mentioned how that life was behind you now.

BILL X TELLS HOW HE STOLE MILLIONS splashed atop Bill's face on our cover is going to sell far more magazines than I'M SORRY, I PROMISE I'LL NEVER DO IT AGAIN. You get the drift.

But *The Vulture* would boast it never resorted to those sorts of tactics. They were above it all, they were about 'serious' journalism. Except. Except in the past year, with rivals in the circulation war gaining an edge, *The Vulture* found itself forced to resort to the very tactics it once decried. *The Vulture* never considered this cheating, more a prescription of steroids for an athlete already naturally gifted. Myself, I thought a drug test would not be out of order, but found myself alone on this point.

To keep their athlete leading the race, in the last twelve months *The Vulture* had revived the ancient, though respected, magazine art of the undercover exposé. Pioneered by one Gloria Steinem, who infiltrated the Playboy Bunny Club in New York in 1961, then went on to write a searing article about Hef's playground, the practice, though it raises legal questions pertaining to privacy, does command respect.

Journalism 101 states that no interview subject acts naturally when placed under a microscope. Self-consciousness pervades every gesture, every thought. A true sense of a person and their ideas can be gleaned only when they are utterly unaware they are being observed. And thus, post-Gloria, magazines, and their electronic idiot cousin television, send reporters into doctors' offices masquerading as patients, government offices posing as welfare cheats, and movie sets impersonating personal assistants to bring home the dish.

The net result of all this blatantly fraudulent misrepresentation is twofold. First, the story published is more honest, revealing and compelling than what would otherwise be written. Second, the magazine always gets smacked with a giant lawsuit.

The Vulture apparently had smart and expensive lawyers on retainer, so focused on the former benefit and dismissed the latter. They had in recent months, I later learned, sent writers secretly into the neo-Nazi movement in New Jersey, a record company in Los Angeles and, my personal favorite, a call-girl service in Washington, DC. There a female reporter played receptionist for three months, booking girls named Buffy and Muffy and Sparkle on dates with senators and congressmen.

The fallout from that article, which revealed both Democratic and Republican politicians to be sexually deviant in equal measure, was immense. A number of divorce actions were filed as a result, so I am in two minds as to whether this particular ploy was as smart as it seemed. Exposing corruption is always to be encouraged. Breaking up families because Dad likes to be spanked after a hard day passing legislation is another matter. The stunt did, however, sell *The Vulture* by the truckload, a clear indication there was gold in them there hills. The people had voted. Let the mining continue.

'Mr Webster,' said Yancy.

'Yes. I'm here.'

'Ms MacDowell, who is the editor, as I told you, has asked me to call you to discuss a matter of the most intricate nature.'

'She has?'

'Yes.'

'Well, you have my undivided attention.'

And indeed she did.

'Ms MacDowell, however, does not wish to discuss this matter over the telephone. You understand, Mr Webster.'

'Of course,' I replied confidently, though I understood nothing of the sort.

'We realize you have a busy schedule, but she would like to meet with you this week if possible, to discuss "it".'

'It?'

'The matter.'

'Right. The matter.'

'How are you placed Friday?'

I could hear her turning pages in what I guessed was some gigantic calendar full of appointments that would have Mzzzz MacDowell discussing 'it' with others as well.

'I am busy every day this week,' I replied, lying like a rug. Two could play at this game. 'Wait, Yancy, a lunch with the chairman of Exxon has been canceled on Friday, so I do have a window.'

Another lie. I had never met the chairman of Exxon in my life, although I had purchased his gasoline at one time.

'Friday at one p.m. Does that help you any?'

Truth be told, I was always free for lunch, unless of course Jake called and we met for a bagel and cream cheese at the Blue Moon diner, perfectly situated halfway between his office and mine. However, the law in this game is that nobody must know this, particularly high-powered editors who call wanting to make your acquaintance. Amazingly, Yancy agreed to my suggestion.

Immediately I became way too excited. I was about to be taken to lunch by a socially prominent editor in a most public place. This must be big, I thought. This must be huge. This will make heads turn. This, I then learned, was not going to happen.

'Ms MacDowell is free Friday for lunch. You know where we are located, on Madison Avenue?'

'Yes,' I lied. I had no idea where their magazine was based, but figured this information was easily obtained.

'Excellent. Please come to reception at ten minutes before one, and ask for me, Yancy. I'll escort you to the private dining room where Ms MacDowell will receive you.'

I couldn't contain my disappointment.

'We are not going out?'

'Oh, Mr Webster, no, not in this case. What Ms MacDowell needs to discuss must be handled in secret. A restaurant would ruin things. People would see you.'

'Of course. People would see us.'

Apparently even Ms MacDowell had heard my life was in the pits and refused to be seen with me in public.

'All right then. Ten minutes to one. Friday.'

'Yancy. One question. Can you give me a sense of what this is about?'

'No.'

'Not a clue?'

'The fact is, Mr Webster, I can't tell you anything. The information superhighway is upon us you know. Never know who's out there. Never know who's listening.'

'That's true,' I agreed, trying to sound understanding. 'You never do.'

'Mr Webster, I think I should mention Ms MacDowell does not want you to discuss this with anybody.'

'Discuss what?'

'It.'

'It what?'

'Lunch. Your meeting.'

'But we haven't met yet.'

'Not a mention to anybody. Not even your best friend or your ex-wife.'

My jaw hit the floor. Actually it hit the desk, which interceded and cushioned the fall, but until that point it was heading for the floor.

'You know I have a best friend and an ex-wife?' I said, incredulous.

'Everybody does in New York, Mr Webster.'

'Not a word,' I promised, feeling faintly ridiculous, like a child playing spy.

Still, Yancy delivered her warning underlined with the suggestion of dire consequences, so I resolved to pay heed. I would not tell Elizabeth, which wouldn't be hard because she was not speaking to me. And I wouldn't tell Jake, because, well, he'd tell her. So whatever 'it' was, my lips were sealed. Even though we just met, I knew Yancy would approve.

That was a Tuesday. Between then and Friday I predicted two things were going to happen. Either I would die of curiosity and attend lunch in a wooden box with a wreath on top, or crack open the mystery using my natural guile and intelligence. But being Tom Webster, who was, at that time, lost in life, place and space, neither occurred.

Deadlines came and went. I thought about the call, then forgot about it, then thought about it again. Every time Jake and I spoke, I was just about to throw it into the conversation when something stopped me. I finally resolved it was a job offer. What else could it be? But then why the secrecy? Heck, I knew why. Mzzzz MacDowell had a reputation, and while she might want me on her team, she couldn't be seen breaking bread with the biggest idiot husband of all time, Tom Webster. Didn't you hear? Oh yes, he's the one who lost his wife to his best friend.

Frankly, I didn't blame her.

Finally Friday was upon me. Friday at one, she said. I donned my favorite suit, blue with the faint stripe of white, and headed to work. I'll be cool, I said to myself early that day. I'll be calm, sophisticated. I'll totally change her mind about me. Ms MacDowell will later tell Yancy I was a pleasure to dine with.

What a guy, that Tom Webster, she'll say. So witty, so conversant. We would discuss government policy and mergers and acquisitions, and I would impress her with my superior knowledge. Then I would brag about all the women I was taking out, leaving me so little time to decorate my apartment since my wife left.

I glanced at my watch every quarter-hour from nine to eleven. My colleagues all commented on my sartorial upgrade. Business lunch, I told them, and they nodded their understanding. Finally, my watch informed me it was time. Turning off my computer, I walked out of the building.

Chapter 5

She shook my hand with a firm grip. She asked me to call her Jamie, always a good sign. I suggested she call me Tom, even though she already had. We sat down to lunch in a dining room as big as a ship, sitting at one end of a table that could seat thirty.

I felt as if I was starring in one of those horror movies where the rain-soaked stranger appears in the dead of night after his car has broken down, then gets invited into a house you know is haunted. The stranger is given clean clothing, then asked to dine with a rich lonely widow. Together they eat at a long table laden with spooky candelabras. Except for the dripping candles and a hunchback lurking in the corner, that was the scene.

She was short, Elizabeth's height actually. I put her around forty. She wore extremely expensive clothes, Elizabeth would know the label for sure. She also wore very high-heeled shoes that went click-click-click as she walked. Her manner was warm but direct. A waiter wearing white gloves hovered over us. He offered wine, which she refused, pointing out it was bad form to drink before five.

'You cannot do anything after lunch with vintage Bordeaux running around the bloodstream,' she explained.

Really?

I, on the other hand, did not feel bound by any such ruling and indicated with a point of my index finger that Mr White Gloves fill up my glass. White Gloves served fish while we swapped meaningless patter about the weather. Ms MacDowell then threw a look to White Gloves, who instantly disappeared.

'Tom.'

'Ms MacDowell.'

'Please, it's Jamie.'

'I'm sorry. Jamie.'

'By the way, you're not related to the dictionary people, are you?''

'No,' I replied, although she was not the first to pose the question.

Not the first by a long shot. Often I was asked if I were connected to the people who wrote *Webster's Dictionary*. It was, I felt, a stupid question, but one for which, over the years, I had developed a pat reply.

'No, I'm not. But I do know a lot of words.'

She laughed politely, then lowered her voice.

'Tom, I'm not going to waste your time any further, I'll come straight to the point. I suspect you must be rather curious as to why I asked to meet with you.'

'I suspect you are right.'

'We here at *The Vulture* always pride ourselves in marking out new territory in quality journalism. You're familiar with the magazine, I take it?'

'Yes,' I lied.

'I must confess I don't read *The Capitalist* cover to cover, but my husband does and he tells me it's a very fine magazine.'

'Thank you, I'll tell my editor.'

'How is Louis?''

She knew Louis? I guess all the editors in this town knew each other. Maybe there was an editors' club.

'You know. The same.' Which was actually the truth. I didn't know Louis well, but he seemed the same when I saw him walking through the building that morning.

'Recently we started sending some of our writers into certain, how shall I phrase this, "situations" undercover. This is not, I want to point out, fraudulent in any way, though we have attracted some lawsuits.'

'I have heard about those.'

'The point is, to get access to people and places we are often denied takes some maneuvering. It also in my opinion gives readers a much better story than that acquired through other means.'

'By other means I assume you mean with the subject's permission.'

She smiled. I understood the point she was driving around and she understood that I understood.

'Truth is paramount in journalism, Tom. When subjects are aware they are being observed for the purpose of public consumption at a later date, truth is the first element that flies out the window.'

'And?'

'This is where you come in.'

Finally, we were getting somewhere. Jamie leaned closer to me. She smiled again. It was the kind of smile tinged with evil and raised eyebrows, the kind I believe Bloody Mary adopted as she explained to the heretics they were about to be burned at the stake.

'Please don't take offense, but you're an average guy, aren't you, Tom?'

'Excuse me. Average?'

'Correct.'

'Relative to who?'

'Well, the greater population of men.'

'I'm not sure. Define your terms.'

'You work hard, love sports, you're separated from your wife.'

This was the dictionary definition of average?

'And you are having a mid-life crisis.'

'I am. You're sure about this?'

'Statistically yes. Our market research is rarely incorrect. All men hit forty and spin out. Some make a lot of noise doing it – you know, fast cars, affairs, hang-gliding, that sort of thing. Others prefer to go off into a corner and break down quietly. Like you.'

I felt overwhelmed by the need to stop this character assassination and salvage the shred of my reputation left untainted.

'I did go to Yale,' I pointed out indignantly, not that an Ivy League education inures one from mid-life hysteria.

'I know that, Tom. I'm not suggesting for a minute you are not intelligent, because clearly you are, but, Yale aside, you don't have many demands or impose them on others, do you?'

'I suppose not.'

'I don't mean to offend you, Tom. Quite the contrary. I wish there were more men like you on the planet. I just think, unlike some of your gender, you live more – how shall I put this? – more quietly, more internally. For instance, I do know you read a lot of history.'

How the heck did she know any of this?

'Reading history qualifies me as an average Joe?'

'Yes and no,' she replied.

I couldn't quite figure out if I was offended or not by the conversation that far, but I decided to wait and let Ms MacDowell finish. Surely she didn't invite me to lunch to confirm what I had become convinced of that morning, that lackluster and personality-free were my new middle names.

White Gloves reappeared with a second course, which consisted of what I now can't remember. Our discussion comparing my averageness in proportion to other American males halted abruptly and turned to more small talk about the weather even though I thought we had already exhausted that route. Ms MacDowell shot White Gloves another stern look, and he bolted again.

'As I explained before, we are now focusing on publishing at least one undercover story per issue. Our research shows they press the right nerve with our readers. I'd like to hire you to write for us in a similar vein.'

So. This was it then. I admit I was flattered, immediately drowning in visions of buying a trenchcoat and enrolling in CIA-training school.

'I see.'

'Fame,' she said. 'Tom, I – we, we want you to explore the world of celebrity. What it is, how it changes you, everyone around you, what it costs, where you get it, and whether it is worth the price.'

'But I am not famous,' I shot back, confused.

'Precisely,' she said beaming. 'That, Tom, is exactly our point.'

'It is?'

'Absolutely. Tom, our culture is at the crossroads. The Internet can deliver news around the world at a speed unthinkable even five years ago. It used to be that everybody only wanted to become rich, but no more. Then they wanted to be powerful, until people realized attaining power and then maintaining it required a lot of work. Plus there were no guarantees millions knew your name. A lot of powerful rich individuals pull strings behind the scenes. We don't know who they are. But today, today all everybody wants is fame. Fame delivers money and power if you play all the angles, plus the added bonus of recognition. Tom, our cities are getting too big, and we are getting lost in them. Everybody feels dislocated. But if you are famous, everybody knows you. They love you. They write about you. What you had for breakfast, what your next move will be.'

'And?'

'And personally we think it's completely out of hand. Everyone is famous today, and for all the wrong reasons. May I remind you that a certain intern who dallied with a certain president now has her own talk show on MTV? Now, excuse my French, Tom, but when did a blow job in the Oval Office become a direct route to a career in broadcasting? Whatever happened to a college degree?'

Did she just say b. job? I think she did.

'I, I, I … see what you're saying,' I stammered.

'I know you do, Tom. No personal or professional achievement is necessary any more. You don't have to cure cancer, or run for office or add anything to the culture. Now you just work the system, hustle the media and achieve something overnight that used to take a lifetime.'

I certainly agreed wholeheartedly with her little lecture, but I still didn't get it.

'And my role in all of this would be?'

And then she told me. Ms MacDowell wanted to explore her theory that today fame can be manufactured as opposed to earned. The public appetite for the next big thing was hyper-ravenous. Feeding time at the zoo was no longer conducted at four-hourly intervals but around the clock. Your achievements could be minuscule but rival publishers would still compete to offer you a book deal. She wanted me, ordinary Tom, to star in an experiment.

I would seek to become famous and then write of the experience.

I would be given one month to engineer my ascent from the netherworld of nine to six to the hyper-fabulous world of celebrity. My mission was to put my name out there, not as the byline that I was, but a headline.

I had to do something, anything, that would make me famous, that would have people on the street recognize me, want my autograph, get me the best table in the kind of restaurant where the seating arrangements are more important than the food. Then, after finessing the deal, I was to pen my thoughts about being shot out of the cannon into celebrity heaven and receive $100,000 for my efforts. Half the cash would be delivered up front, the rest on completion.

'But you're asking me to involve myself in the very thing you just said you despise. Exactly what you think is wrong with the culture.'

'Absolutely,' said Jamie. 'But only for the purposes of illuminating our readers as to how utterly devoid of meaning celebrity is. It's just add water and stir now. Tom, listen to me. When convicted bank robbers beat out all other candidates for hosting jobs on quiz shows because viewers fell in love with them while they were on trial, I think we know the fall of Rome is imminent.'

I gave her points for her historical reference, which, clearly employed to impress me, had in fact succeeded. But was she not also being hypocritical?

'But fame is the driving force of your magazine,' I pushed her. 'You rely on famous people for your own stories, your covers.'

'Only the truly deserving, Tom. We haven't put anyone on the cover who hasn't been nominated for an Oscar or run for public office. We don't dally in the field of nobodies. Not like some publications I could mention.'

'And that makes it respectable?'

'Oh, yes.'

So there it was. She wanted me, Mr Average, repository of average looks, average clothes, average life, apparently having a mid-life crisis, to manufacture a stunt designed to surgically remove all traces of bland. As a journalist, I could appreciate the idea was a circulation booster. As Tom Webster, there was no way in this world, none, that I would ever take part in such foolishness. Just as I was about to tell her this and leave, she raised her hand like a traffic cop.

'I'm not finished, Tom. Please don't say anything yet. Obviously, if we give you only one month to pull this off, we are not expecting anything major. And in fact, that would be beside the point. Whatever you decide to do should really be totally unworthy of mass-media attention, and yet if I am right, and I know I am, you will have the press all over you like a bad rash.'

'I, I, I . . .'

The traffic cop hand-signal went up a second time.

'Give me an example, you are saying.'

I was? No, I wasn't. I was trying to tell her I thought she was a lunatic and I wanted to go back to the safe haven of my office, but she was unstoppable.

'Let me tell you some ideas I had. Say you hold up a bank to buy presents for war orphans. Or you streak at the baseball game. You do know the woman who streaked at the Cardinals game last month just got a pictorial in *Playboy*.' (Was he suggesting I streak to land in *Playgirl*? I would rather go to the Tower of London.) 'You might want to take out an ad proposing marriage to a newsreader. Any stunt to get people talking about you, writing about you. And if you want to break the law, we'll pay all the costs. Just find a new angle on overnight success. It's very simple really. Our theory, which we know you will prove, is that the system is so warped today, if you can do it, anyone can.'

If I can do it, anyone can? She just called me a big fat loser, didn't she? Yep, she did.

'May I speak now?'

'Certainly, Tom.'

'No.'

'No?'

'That's correct. No.'

'Ah, Tom. Of course. A thoughtful man like you cannot make rush decisions. You need to go away and think about this. Well, don't answer me now, then. Monday will be fine.'

'Excuse me, Jamie, but I can answer you now. My answer is no. I have listened to your offer, considered it, and while I can appreciate its inherent, ah, marketing value, I am not interested in turning myself into a public spectacle.'

'Tom. Tom. Tom. We here at *The Vulture* would never ask you to do that.'

'You're asking me to turn myself into a celebrity.'

'Indeed. And how terrible could that be? It's what everybody wants.'

'Well, I don't.'

'Of course you do, Tom. You just don't realize it yet.'

'I am sure there are plenty more average guys where I come from who would be more than willing to submit themselves to your idea.'

'Oh, sure, but we want you, Tom.'

'Why?'

She never answered me. Instead she launched into Phase Two of her plan. Death by Flattery.

'Tom, hear me out. You are forty-three years old. Alone. At home reading books about a lot of famous dead people. This is your chance to join their ranks.'

Oh, please. Me and Napoleon. Me and Alexander the Great. Mentioned in the same sentence in 100 years from now? I doubted it.

'Now I admit that, initially, whatever you do to engineer your fame will raise some eyebrows among friends and colleagues. But that is only temporary, Tom, and we know you have the strength of character to withstand it.'

I did?

'But you should also know that once you write your article for us, revealing that your fame was a hoax, done in the name of social science, done to hold a mirror to our shallowness, done to save our culture from sinking into the abyss, then, then, Tom, you will be hailed a genius. A hero, Tom. You will be congratulated on every street corner for your brilliance. You will be the Houdini of the new millennium.

'Of course, it might be uncomfortable for you at the start, when people are unaware of your true motives, but think how much better that will make your story. And remember, Tom, no pain, no gain.'

She was good, don't you think? I thought so, and the reason I thought so was I really warmed to the idea of being hailed a hero in the name of social science. Hell, look at my life. I was never going to be hailed a hero in the name of anything else. It was too late for me to embark on a career of pillaging and plundering the Persian Empire, discovering the New World or becoming an advisor to Louis XVI. Those heroes were already on the books.

This might be my last chance to make something of my life, make my mark. I would be remembered as that brilliant guy who showed us that Andy Warhol was wrong. Fifteen minutes of fame gained by being Madonna's chauffeur is not fame, it's garbage. It's worthless. But today, in the year 2000, he was actually famous. Famous like Ulysses S. Grant is famous. But for what? What did this guy add to our civilization?

Now I know driving Madonna to the Grammy's is probably not easy given the traffic, but it's not leading troops into the Civil War. Suddenly I could see what Jamie was saying, how we had lost sight of everything important. In fact, who could understand this better than me, the student of history? Nobody. So for a minute there I actually thought about saying yes. Thought that I could stop the onslaught of this madness. And then, mercifully, the minute passed.

'No. I'm sorry. I can't do it. I could lose my job. Right now it's all I have left.'

And this was when she played her last card. But what a card it was.

'If you do this, Tom, I guarantee it will make your wife crazy. Insane. You'd like that, wouldn't you, Tom? She won't be able to ignore you any longer, Tom. Everyone will be talking about you. She'll read about you in the papers, see your face everywhere. And it might start her thinking. Might make her miss you. You could win her back from your friend, Tom. Think about that. You will probably win her back.'

I would? I could? I could get her back from Jake? Now she was talking. I would be a famous hero, Jake would lose her, and he would see how it feels. See how it feels to be me before I became who I was going to become.

I felt the knees go first. This was a sure sign I might be weakening. The arms went next. I was weakening. I thought about the money too. I could sure use a hundred grand with all my accounts frozen. And I would be a hero of a kind, wouldn't I? Okay, fine, I wouldn't be mapping out a new frontier, but I would add something to the culture in the name of, well, culture. That wasn't nothing, was it?

I know what you're thinking. Amazing how you can rationalize anything if you want to. But let's face it. My life had gone to the dogs. In fact, dogs didn't want to live my life. Maybe this was the kick-start I needed for the new century. What did I have to lose? Yes, I would look a fool for a week or so, I might lose my job, my friends would think I needed to be committed, but then I would be a hero. The Houdini for the millennium, she said. And Elizabeth would not be able to ignore me. Now that was something I did not factor in half an hour ago. I could be a hero and a husband again, all thanks to this.

'Something small, right?'

Jamie beamed. She saw she had won. She continued beaming, and then started moaning. I know that moan. It sounded like we had just had sex.

'Tiny, Tom. Just tiny. Anything to launch you into the radar.'

'And if I fail at my mission?'

'Obviously we will pay you for your time, but, Tom, you won't fail. The system will see to that.'

As coffee was being sipped, Jamie explained we could not meet again. This was our first and final meeting until I handed in my efforts. A check and a contract would arrive via courier and I was to return the paperwork in the same manner. She signaled the lunch was over and she would walk me to the elevator. But I was not finished with her and asked she stay seated.

'Jamie, I have one question.'

She nodded. She knew.

'Why me? Of all the men in New York? How did you find me?'

'Simon Burke. Terrible business that, don't you think? He should never have gone to prison. I mean, who isn't insider-trading these days? Anyway, he suggested you.'

'He did?' I screamed.

'He and my husband, Roger, played golf together at our club in Connecticut. Anyway, when I hit on the idea of making someone famous overnight, I couldn't find anyone among my circle of friends who would qualify. Neither could Roger, or anyone on our staff. My husband then suggested Simon might know of a suitable candidate, someone on Wall Street. An Everyman. A worker bee. He called us from prison to suggest you were our guy. We did some digging on you, and well, you are our guy.'

I was really shocked Simon mentioned me.

'I thought Simon was a friend.'

'Are you upset, Tom?'

'No, just a little taken aback.'

'I understand,' she said, even though she clearly didn't.

'When Simon explained who you were and that you worked for *The Capitalist*, I felt we had hit pay dirt. Number one, you are separated, which means lonely, a nice starting point for the article. Believe me, once famous you will never lack for company again. Two, as a writer I assume you can work your thoughts into a sentence. Three, finance journalism is the anesthetic of the publishing world, so I knew you probably weren't much of a party animal.'

Hurt as I was, I couldn't disagree. Besides, Simon was in prison and already famous, well, infamous. Now I could show him. I could become famous too. And unlike Alexander the Great, I didn't have to embark on a three-year invasion of Mesopotamia to get my page in history. Do anything you can to seize the imagination of the public, Jamie insisted. Anything at all. You can keep your dignity, Tom, we don't need a scandal, just notoriety.

Now a big questioned loomed. What next? I cried out as I returned to *The Capitalist*. What next indeed?

Chapter 6

As a social experiment, Ms MacDowell's idea was not up there with the greats. She was no Pavlov, no Freud. She wasn't even Gloria Steinem. She was in fact as shallow and depraved as the people and practices she wanted to skewer. I regret now not quizzing her more on the logic of ridiculing and belittling the very same system of which she was part, but assume she must have resolved that moral dilemma previous to our lunch.

Worse, maybe she never had an ethical problem with the concept to begin with. It's all business, Tom, she said, just business. But unlike the writers who rode this racehorse before me, the undercover neo-Nazi and the receptionist in a whorehouse, who both attracted massive publicity in their wake, I was taking the entire charade one calculated step further.

My task, then, was not to be critical of the wave, but simply to ride it. The moral finger-pointing and excoriation would only come later, if it came at all. We appoint nonentities as gods, I can still hear her saying, and in a frenzy we worship them. Just prove me right, Tom, she said. Work it, baby. Work the system.

Time, of course, was of the essence. I had not the luxury of planning a detailed assault on the public at large. Unlike William the Conqueror, preparing for the Norman conquest, I had neither maps, plans nor an army to support me. My apartment would have to suffice as HQ. One month she had given me. This time frame suggested thirty possible attempts to find fame, of which only one would have to yield results.

I went home and microwaved some lasagna, then nestled into the lips. Possibly at this juncture I should explain. When Elizabeth and I married, we received as a gift, if you can call it that, a sofa in the shape of two giant lips. It was bright red velvet and possibly the most hideous thing we ever saw. While the original was designed by Salvador Dali and now lay in a museum somewhere, we owned the cheap imitation. A number of friends had banded together to purchase it, and Elizabeth and I did our best when it was delivered to look overjoyed. Or at least hide our shock. Over time it proved a terrible cross to bear. Neither small enough to hide in a closet nor fragile enough to break (like some ugly dishes we received), we covered it in Elizabeth's quilts and dutifully put it in our living room, where it sat like an eyesore for the ten years we were married.

When Elizabeth left, she removed most of our furniture, leaving those sorry lips for me. Suddenly alone in our apartment, I had taken to sitting on it, as it was, I confess, the only furniture I had left.

I turned on the television and caught the tail end of the news. Misery, politics, natural disasters, wars. Everyone was suffering except for stockbrokers, who seem only to grow richer by the minute. The inverse dynamic between the incomes of financiers and the rest of the population defies explanation. Still, somebody has to play with all the money, and they do seem to like the job.

And so the nightly news was where my journey began. Disaster makes headlines, does it not? When the forces of nature intersect with men trying to subdue them, drama results and the news crews appear. What if I were to survive a volcano eruption, a hurricane, a tidal wave?

What if I were to dive into violent seas to rescue a child, or throw myself on the mercy of a tree as the river rose around me? In theory this sounded perfect, in practice I was already screwed. The reason I like living in New York was the distinct lack of volcanoes, hurricanes and rising rivers in the immediate area. Encased in concrete from head to toe, New York is a city so allergic to nature it has even walled it off into a landmass commonly known as Central Park.

If you refused to interact with a blade of grass or a bug, aside from the roaches in your apartment and the rats in the subway, that privilege was yours for the taking. So the odds of finding said volcano, and my somehow spending the night in its core, then climbing out in the morning appeared rather scant. Ditto for hurricanes and blizzards.

I then explored air disasters for all but a minute before I discovered I was not about to board a plane in the next thirty days praying it would explode into flames so that I, ordinary Joe, could pull blond stewardesses out from the wreckage.

I pulled out a sheet of paper and began penning some options. Having abandoned natural and man-made disasters, my thoughts turned to crime. If I can't be a hero, I could be a villain. Though being a cad was antithetical to my nature, I was technically on assignment and so glimpsed room to maneuver.

White-collar crime was immediately eliminated due to the lengthy procedure required in setting up even the most substandard scam. Even if I got pointers from Simon, it could take years. Insider-trading is not all caviar and yachts on the Riviera at first. The glory comes later. Initially what is required is painstaking groundwork, encompassing bribery, blackmail, inside leaks and an offshore account to bury the evidence.

Following this, having the transactions uncovered and investigated takes months, possibly years. An arrest and trial could be delayed by shrewd lawyers, and then of course I would be expected to appeal. I suddenly realized how the wheels of justice turn incredibly slowly for the isolated few of us who break the law desperate to get caught.

Blue-collar crime seemed to make much more sense. A Yale graduate fleecing a multinational is not news, it's a rite of passage. A Yale graduate sticking up a bank is news at eleven. Yet robbing banks I dismissed immediately. Years of television and movies convinced me of the need for a gun, one thing I would have no idea of how to obtain, let alone fire. Even as a child water pistols were never my forte. Assuming I obtained a weapon, a getaway car would also appear necessary as opposed to waiting in the subway to make my escape.

Problem was, just as I always argued with Elizabeth over the intelligence of purchasing clothes for a special occasion and then never wearing them again, I did not want to waste money buying a car I would use only once and then abandon on the interstate.

Banks also suggested security guards, cameras, and once caught and convicted, I would no doubt be bunking down with Simon. My apartment is small and though Elizabeth took everything we purchased jointly, she did leave the lips. I never asked her why items we always considered ours were suddenly hers, but if she ever resumed speaking to me, I intended to.

Until that time I had rationalized the newly spare apartment by convincing myself it was not empty but post modern. I had read since Elizabeth's departure that in architectural circles, arbiters of taste praised spare interiors as clean, stylized and twenty-first century. I did not travel in those circles, however, and among those less in tune, that is to say my friends, I was only offered apologies because they assumed I had been burgled.

So while my furnishings were down to the bare necessities, at least the space was mine. I was not under any court order to share it with guys named Jimmy 'The Fish' or Vinnie 'The Weasel', or anyone who boasts an animal as a middle name. I could eat when I wished, not when a bell rang. I am no fashion plate, preferring brown corduroys and a tan jacket to anything Mr Brooks could tailor, but even I recoiled in horror at the thought of that lurid orange boiler suit that Simon wears.

The only scenario with promise, I felt, was Ms MacDowell's suggestion of a sympathy stick-up. I could arrive at a bank, barricade myself, the staff and customers inside, while ordering the delivery of bags of money. I would then tell everyone the cash was not for me but for the coffers of the New York Yankees.

I would announce I was an unemployed father of four and needed the money to buy seasons tickets for my kids. For a moment I actually convinced myself this idea was viable. You know as well as I that it's downright un-American not to take your kids to a ball game, and, costs being so prohibitive, bank robbery was, Your Honor, my last resort. But I didn't have kids, and when this vital information filtered down to the masses, instead of an understanding judge, only Jimmy 'The Weasel' awaited.

I lay down lengthways on the lips and continued to think. Still lurking in the corridors of crime, I settled on my next option, politics. Public office brings with it a certain cachet, a certain regard and a certain power which is certainly always abused.

I was not averse to being immersed in cachet, regard, power and its subsequent abuse, but never having even run for class president as a child, I had few skills necessary for the task. Nor did I have the money to mount a campaign, and I felt it might be too late in life to befriend Donald Trump.

The thorny issue of image would also arise. Ms MacDowell had now confirmed what Elizabeth said one year ago – that I did not register on the personality-o-meter. How would I get people to vote for me when I wouldn't even vote for myself? And then of course there was the subject of extramarital affairs, and my failure to have one.

Within minutes of announcing a run for office, male candidates are subjected to a thorough character screening by the press. Each is then found wanting in numerous departments, a lack of moral backbone usually the highlight. And then if he is even half a man, still breathing, even with the help of a ventilator, a buxom blond looking to regenerate her sputtering modeling career will emerge from the shadows to insist on a dalliance.

The candidate by then feigns shock, mock horror and finally an apology. And while his voting public feign shock, mock horror and finally forgive him, reality suggests that most males confronted by a buxom blond would also bed her in an instant. The ugly truth is, men may not like a candidate because of his views on social welfare or taxes, but we never deduct points for infidelity or hookers. Secretly we cheer them on, and while we claim it was their policy on immigration that won our hearts, it is their practice of serial adultery that wins our vote.

My own failure to practice infidelity even once during my marriage would foresee my downfall. Call me stupid, but call me faithful. I never cheated on Elizabeth, not that I hadn't thought about it. I had wants, but I lacked means.

When I first started at *The Capitalist* there was a temp by the name of Beth who smiled at me a lot, and I thought for a moment, she might, you know...Well, anyway she left and afterward I realized I was reading too much into it and she probably just smiled a lot.

So I realized, if I ran, a total dearth of women willing to regale my electorate with tales of naked romps could cost me male votes. Not to mention the humiliation I would suffer in admitting that in spite of my best efforts, I failed at Extramarital Affairs 101, the only compulsory freshman campaign subject. Oh, the shame, the indignity of it all. Better to remain a private citizen and keep the fantasy of infidelity alive than to become public property and admit you never slept around.

Dispensing with politics and crime, the luck of the gods was next considered. A lottery win would instantly confer fame and money, although the only people who ever win the lottery are assembly-line workers in Detroit. (And frankly, they deserve it more than me.)

Acting as a key witness at a trial could be counted on to provide a new image, though I lacked for associates currently under arrest whose crimes were so heinous they would make it onto Court TV. Streaking at the baseball? Not with this body. Winning an award? I was yet to make a movie or record a song. Hijack an airplane and demand a landing in Cuba? It was all the rage once, but why do it now? To see Cuba? Frankly I would rather go to a ball game. I fell asleep on the lips, still completely anonymous with no fame in sight.

One week came and went, and over the course of seven days my ideas became more and more lunatic. Crazed. Half-baked. The more I thought about it, subjecting myself to this ridiculous stunt, the more secure I became in the knowledge I would call Ms MacDowell and scuttle the deal. I had signed the contract and banked the money (which arrived the following day with terrifying efficiency), but now I wanted to unsign and unbank the cash.

She would understand. I changed my mind. I liked my life and didn't want to overhaul it, entirely believable. I practiced my speech. Ms MacDowell, you caught me at a weak moment, but on further reflection . . . Besides a flurry of reports on the budget were due in the next month and I would be overwhelmed deconstructing their meaning.

The decision was made and I announced to myself, completely relieved, the experiment was over before it began. I remember going to bed that night, excited to be sleeping anxiety-free for the first time in a week.

And then on that first night I slept soundly, an idea came to me. I had finally seized on the answer that for days had eluded me. Sports. Of course, it was sports. Hottest ticket to fame this side of the Equator and probably the other, though I had never visited.

But which sport? Truth was, I watched them all, but couldn't play any of them, so I wasn't about to be drafted onto any team. And then, just as furiously as the first, a second bell went off. I hit on a second plan so devious, so gloriously stupid, it had to work. Of course. You don't have to play any of them well, Tom, I told myself. In fact, if you fail, that's even better. Fail, Tom, fail.

Now this I could do. I had just failed at marriage, so found myself amply prepared to compete in the field of inspired defeat. It was seven a.m., a Saturday, I should have been sleeping in, but I was wired. Tom, I said, you are nothing short of Leonardo da Vinci, Michelangelo and Galileo all rolled into one. Finally I believed I had struck gold. Twenty-four karat, perfectly pure, precious metal.

So, light the flame, boys. Sydney, here I come.

Chapter 7

I had never overestimated, embellished or lived in denial about my physical capabilities. Some men are built for comfort, others for speed. I definitely fell into the former category, which clearly curtailed all my fantasies about life as a jock. Too short for football, too slow for ice hockey, too stiff for baseball and too white for basketball, I realized early in life, much to my sorrow, I was destined for the one playing field I could surely conquer.

The bleachers.

Watching others play sports you will never master is possibly the cruelest punishment ever inflicted on a man. The agony experienced as you witness men younger, fitter, more coordinated than you dribble, bat and volley their way into history eventually outstrips the initial ecstasy of marveling at their moves.

When you are a child you allow yourself the luxury of dreaming of a career in the Big Leagues. When you are an adult writing about government reports and your wife has left you for your best friend and your apartment has only one piece of furniture left, reality hits you in the solar plexus. It's at this juncture you reconcile yourself to the knowledge that baseball fantasy camp and not spring training is the only game awaiting your presence in Florida. And when you have to pay to play sport, as opposed to the sport paying you, well, folks, it's time to face facts. You can forget your face on the Wheaties box.

So I figured there must be thousands of men out there just like me. Everymen, as Jamie described me. Armchair athletes. Ordinary Joes. Plagued by mid-life crises and a distinct lack of muscle tone. For us, worse than baseball, basketball or even that lame British game cricket (which I have tried watching but fail to grasp – looks like baseball with tranquilizers to me), the Olympic Games was a truck of salt backing up into a gaping wound.

Sure, we watch the Games obsessively, but we can't relate. If anything, after the closing ceremony we became chronically depressed, broken from two weeks of witnessing athletes perform feats we never will. It was this sentiment, this loser-in-front-of-the-tube element, which I planned to exploit in pursuit of fame.

At every Games, the first athlete up to bat is the flame runner. Except for Barcelona, where a Spanish Robin Hood drew an arrow out of his pocket and set it alight, the usual drill involves some world-class athlete clutching the Olympic torch for dear life while he or she laps the stadium before lighting the flame.

This individual is the last in a long line of athletes who have transported the torch across field and stream and cliff and desert from its starting point in Athens to its eventual destination. This individual has the eyes of the world upon him or her as they triumphantly launch the opening of what we all know is a brutal competition to win at all costs.

This individual, I now believed, could be me.

My plan, which at the time I considered ingenious, would not on reflection prove so worthy of praise. The orgy of self-congratulation I threw myself and attended was not, I would see later, something Caligula would attend. Yet I am getting ahead of myself.

My ploy would consist of writing a letter to the Sydney 2000 Olympic Committee, bearing a novel suggestion.

Dear Sirs, it would say, re the Opening Ceremony and the torch-bearer job vacancy, why not flout tradition? Why not gives us Ordinary Joes a chance? I mean, heck, the Olympians get the rest of the Games to strut their stuff, I only want five measly minutes. Sure the bow and arrow theatrics we witnessed in Spain worked like a charm. Atlanta went one better with Muhammad Ali, although I personally would have preferred to see that tiny gymnast with the sprained ankle fly over a vault and light the torch, but it's over now, so forget I even mentioned it. Is it not incumbent upon you now in the new century to go one step further?

Then I would propose that I, a living, breathing example of Everyman – middle class, middle-aged, overweight and underfit – would run the flame on its last leg into the stadium. At the moment of conception and for a few hours thereafter, my idea appeared to hold some weight. I became overexcited, which should be read as a warning in itself. I grabbed pen and paper immediately and drafted a letter, which I later polished and repolished until in it you could see your own reflection. It was brief and to the point.

I offered my services as Olympic flame runner, in order to better relations between the athletes and spectators. Sure, Olympic athletes with their rippling muscles and washboard stomachs made us, the nobodies at home, feel proud, feel patriotic, but they also made us feel insecure. I, on the contrary, would allow all the nobodies at home to feel fantastic.

The arrival of the coach-potato flame runner in Sydney would be a first, a chance to make history, I urged. It might not be pretty, I warned them, but think of the publicity. I typed up my missive, contacted an Olympic hotline and was given an address for the Sydney organizers. I was, I believed, on my way.

As I saw it, my insta-fame stunt, slight and lacking in any intellectual substance, could not fail. The odds of the Sydney Committee inviting me to light the flame were clear. Zero. They may be planning the event on the other side of the planet and think crocodile wrestling is a sport, but they are not out to lunch.

The odds of the Committee writing a polite letter thanking me for the offer but pointing out the honor is usually reserved for an athlete from the host country blah, blah, blah, were meteoric. Thus armed with the letter proffering my services, and confident a reply would neatly dispense with them, I would then inform my colleagues in the media that the very people who preach peace, love, brotherhood and world records had broken my heart with their response.

This would be a story nobody could resist.

WORKING STIFF WHO BEGS TO RUN FLAME IS TURNED DOWN.

The media loves stories about ordinary people attempting

extraordinary things. Underdogs attempting to become overdogs. My plight, I hoped, would generate debate across the nation on the psychological damage inflicted on those who merely bear witness to the spectacle of human greatness without ever participating. Middle-aged bald guys would jump on my case and picket the Olympics. They would organize protests on my behalf. Larry King, I thought, here I come.

In a manner I now find entirely shocking, on Monday morning before jumping the subway to work, I casually waltzed to the post office and purchased enough stamps to send my letter across twenty-seven time zones. I then made a mental note to remember that day as one of the last I would walk the streets of New York unknown and unappreciated. In a matter of days, possibly one week, it would be, hey, there's that guy who wanted to light the Olympic flame!

And, hey, he's even shorter and fatter and nerdier than he looked on television last night! And I would counteract with, hey, pal, who now gets tables at restaurants that never admitted him before? And, hey, pal, who now gets women leaving him their phone numbers? (A lot of projection and wishful thinking going on here.)

And while we are on the subject, who has a book deal and a movie-of-the-week deal and who is a hero to millions of, well, guys who look just like him? Even though the subway car was crowded, at that instant I wanted to dance. Flush with excitement, I could feel fame inching nearer, even though I had, as Ms MacDowell ordered, done precisely nothing to warrant it. I had sent my name out there, and it was about to come back to me soaked and drenched and covered in hype.

Arriving at my desk, I noted the faces of all the characters who artfully blend into our office walls. The typists. The guys in graphics. The guys in charge. But most of all, the secretaries. Soon I would command their attention if they liked it or not. I liked it, Elizabeth would hate it, and, frankly, that would be all that mattered.

All morning while stewing over my column I indulged in fame fantasies, trying to consider the upheaval, the assault on my life. I only indulged in positive outcomes, scarcely giving a thought to the negative. But most of all I relished the fact that Elizabeth and

Jake and even Simon in jail would be forced to sit up and notice me, look at me differently, consider whether they had misjudged me. If there was a cost to this stunt, for this element alone, I was happy to pay.

The day wore on. My fantasies turned from color to black and white. I developed a pit in my stomach. Then it tripled in size. I cannot pinpoint when this occurred, except to say it was a creeping sensation at first that later enveloped me. Jake called and I was unusually abrupt with him. Instead of, Tom, this is going to be great, I suddenly heard a Greek chorus proclaiming, Tom, what in the name of Satan do you think you are doing?

Did I really want to make my mark in this world as the poster boy for inertia? To stand as a symbol for creeping middle age, passive participation in life? Could I really stand the social isolation I would suffer after proclaiming myself one of life's key losers?

It is one thing to accept your shortcomings, quite another to brag about and broadcast them. Vanity overwhelmed me. Finally the enormity of what I was attempting to do in the name of sociology began to sink in. Think icebergs and that big ship starting with T. I started to sweat. I realized I still had dreams of making it big the way my heroes had done. Sure, America and Europe had been mapped, but there must be some small islands in the Caribbean still undiscovered. I could buy a boat, sail by, plant a flag and join Columbus in the history books if I chose. I just had to find the time.

And there was another thing. I held a responsible job, in a stuffed-shirt, blue-blazer, white-collar establishment, and I did, let us not forget, attend Yale. My colleagues and professors and editors and even ex-wife for that matter might not appreciate the joke, let alone laugh at it. What if I was fired? Could Yale disown me? Would Simon re-establish contact once he was paroled?

These questions grew larger, the voices of retribution grew louder. For crying out loud, I was a grown man. This was truly ridiculous, even if it might make some salient point about the decline of our culture. Still, I resolved, let someone else make the point.

At that instant, I knew I wanted out. O-U-T. I have failed to invent a suitable stunt, Ms MacDowell, and on further reflection I have realized I am not your man. And about the money, that check for $50,000 that arrived the next day by courier (I had never been paid so fast by anyone – why?) I am happy to return it. Nervously, I stared at my watch. Seven p.m. I dialed *The Vulture*.

Yancy was not there. Ms MacDowell was in a meeting. I told a temp that I wished to speak to Ms MacDowell urgently. Not possible I was told. Not until tomorrow. Could I schedule an emergency meeting? I asked. What is this concerning? she replied. They would know, I explained.

She appeared to be satisfied and squeezed me in at noon the next day, for twenty minutes. There was still one more thing to do. I had to go back to the post office. Confident the building closed around eight, I chose the subway over a taxi and relaxed in the one space left in the car. The relief I felt defied description.

The decision to cancel the deal and return to the humdrum of my existence liberated me. I smiled for the first time that day. I resolved to call Jake when I got home and shoot the breeze, apologize for being short with him and feed him some excuse about the pressure of deadlines. I walked casually to the post office to find it had closed at seven-thirty.

Banging on the door like a maniac, a security guard came forward and motioned in the sign language we all use when separated by huge bullet-proof glass doors that the post office was closed. I then informed him also via sign language that this was an emergency. He opened the door to tell me he was closing it. Go figure.

'We're closed. Seven-thirty sharp.'

'This is an emergency,' I pleaded.

'I heard you. We open again tomorrow at eight a.m.'

'Look, I have to retrieve a letter I mailed today. They are probably sorting through my batch right now. This will take two minutes. Please let me speak to the manager.'

'Sorry, sir. Post office is closed.'

He locked the door in my face. Desperate, I went around the back and rapped on the windows through which I could see postal workers sorting mail. The manager motioned for me to go away. Back to the sign language, I explained I had to speak to him. Major emergency.

He signaled that I was to go to the back door, and I thanked him profusely by a sort of Kabuki performance of bowing and scraping, much to the amusement of the other employees. The door opened.

'Yes?'

'I know this might sound ridiculous, but I mailed a letter this morning which I have since realized cannot possibly go out. I must retrieve it. That's possible, right?'

'Wrong.'

'Wrong?'

'You heard me.'

'But it is in that room over there. I'm sure.'

'I'm sure it is too. But if I let every member of the public who changed their mind about sending mail waltz through here after hours I could hold a party.'

'But this is an emergency.'

'I'm sorry, sir, rules is rules.'

I wanted to point out that in fact the correct English was rules are rules, but thought better of it. Instead I pulled out my wallet and peeled off a twenty.

'Come this way, sir.'

We established the letter was in a bin marked International. There were around forty letters in there and until I found mine my heart beat so hard I thought everyone could hear it.

'I've got it,' I said, waving it about like a lottery winner.

'Good, follow me, please.'

The manager led me to the back door again.

'I can't thank you enough, sir,' I told him, extending my hand.

He shook it, then paused.

'You know, you don't have to tell me if you don't want to, but what was in the letter? Breaking up with a woman and change your mind?'

'Why do you say that?'

'Usually that's who rolls up here after hours trying to get back their mail. Men who write to women to dump them.'

'Really? I had no idea.'

'Yeah, all the time. We get at least three a week.'

'And women?'

'Not so many. My guess is women break up with men over the

telephone. They like the personal touch. Men use the post office.'

'And do you help them?'

'No. I have a strict policy. If you write to a woman to break her heart, you gotta take responsibility.'

'I was writing to the Sydney Olympic Committee offering my services to run the Olympic flame into the stadium in the year 2000.'

He tried to keep a straight face but couldn't control his eyes. They rolled like marbles.

'I wanted to do it in the name of all the people who normally never get to compete at the Games. Middle-aged, pudgy guys like me. But I found I am more vain than I realized and thought better of it.'

He scanned me from head to toe, taking in the paunch, saddlebags, wrinkles and distinct lack of conditioning.

'Maybe it was a good thing you took the letter back. I don't know if you are what they are looking for to do that flame-running thing. You know?'

Of course I knew, but I didn't need him to rub it in. But that's the problem with people today, even those guys down at the post office. Everyone's a critic.

Chapter 8

'Hello, Tom.'

'Ms MacDowell.'

'Please sit down.'

Notice how she didn't ask me to call her Jamie this time. I think she knew something was up.

I sat.

'How are you?'

Excellent question.

'Well, Ms MacDowell, I'm glad you asked how I am, because that is what I have come here to tell you.'

Like I said, she was way ahead of me.

'You're having second thoughts, aren't you?'

'Not having, Ms MacDowell. Had. Past tense. I had second thoughts and I believe they are the correct thoughts. I want out. I'm sorry for the inconvenience, but I am sure I was not the only candidate on your list. I am here to write you a check and return the money. I can't do it. I have thought about this long and hard. You have no idea the schemes and stunts I have considered and rejected. Ultimately, however, I found I am not interested in recognition without having earned it. I don't think I could live with the fact that I made it into the history books due to some clownish, infantile prank. My reputation as a serious writer would never be the same.'

Ms MacDowell forced her face to assume a veneer of calm, but

I could see the veins bulging in her neck. You can always manufacture social nicety, but you cannot dictate physiology.

'But that was the point, Tom. You understood that. You knew we were asking you to trade respectability for infamy. I thought, well, you seemed, when we last spoke, to have reconciled yourself to that fact. And remember there is an upside to all of this. We will reveal in the article your transformation was purely an intellectual exercise to prove a point. Nobody will think you a fool once they learn you engineered fame deliberately to test a theory. That must bring you some comfort.'

Yes, but not enough. Now let me out of this contract and this office.

'Ms MacDowell, if I succeed at what you are suggesting, of all the people who discover my name in the media, only a percentage of them will later read *The Vulture*. You know, and I have since realized, revealing my motives post the event will bring little relief. It's like newspapers who libel people in giant headlines on page one and then admit they were wrong in tiny print on page fifty. Nobody reads the apology. All they remember are the accusation and the headline.'

Now Ms MacDowell was smiling. She was Bloody Mary again, about to deliver the final crushing blow before she sent me to the axeman.

'It's too late, Tom.'

'Excuse me? I haven't done anything yet.'

'You took our money.'

'I'm here to return it.'

'We can't accept it.'

I hoped she was just teasing me before telling me she would accept the check, my sincere apologies, and she would be more than happy to go find another victim. I would even offer to recommend someone. Jake possibly. He might be enamored of the idea of a radical life change just as I had been.

'Tom. I don't think you understand what has happened since our meeting. All the pieces on the board, all the players on the field, they've been put into play. Advertising space has been sold on the strength of the story. The artists in graphics are working on layouts. I have commissioned other writers to pen pieces dissecting the culture of celebrity. I have a psychologist who will ruminate on what your future will be like. All these writers are working with you in mind. They have all been briefed considerably regarding you, your personality and your mission. And I might tell you, they think the ploy is a brilliant idea.'

This was cold comfort. A bunch of writers whom I had never met and a psychologist who had never had me on the couch for a day were already working on analyzing an event in my life yet to take place.

'Ms MacDowell, we're all adults here. I simply can't do this. Find someone else. I won't do this.'

'We'll sue you, Tom. It could get very nasty. We have a contract.'

'Contracts can be broken.'

'We will sue, Tom. If you think working for us will upend your life, try breaking our contract. We'll ruin you. We'll ruin your life. And you and I both know it's not such a great life to begin with.'

Meeeeeowwww. The claws were out.

Ms MacDowell looked at her watch. She informed me she had another meeting. The first law of getting out of uncomfortable situations in the workplace is to plead a meeting. Even I knew this trick. Then suddenly she altered her demeanor. This time she moved in reverse biological fashion from full-grown cat to helpless kitten. Her voice lowered to a whisper and she took my hand tenderly. Even though I was supremely aware of how fake the entire performance was, I fell for it anyway.

'I knew this might happen. I expected it. But, Tom, you cover the financial world. You more than anyone know that a deal is a deal. Too much has happened already. As my mother always says, Jamie, you can't unscramble an egg.'

'My mother says that too,' I replied.

'See, so you understand me. We understand each other. The eggs have been broken, Tom. The frying pan is heating up.'

It did not take a genius to realize the next words probably out of her mouth were something in the order of, 'All we need now is for you to jump in.' But she resisted saying it. Instead she motioned me to the door. 'I have the utmost confidence in you, Tom. I'm sure whatever you do will be done with integrity. Remember, it's not really happening to you. You will be able to disassociate yourself from it in the end. And whatever you do, it doesn't have to be huge. Just large enough to plant your name out there.'

'It sounds a lot easier than it actually is, Ms MacDowell.'

'Oh, Tom,' she said, admonishing me like a child. 'You did go to Yale. I know you can do it. We all do. *The Vulture* has great faith in you, Tom. Now, I have to go to a meeting, so why don't you go get famous!'

Chapter 9

I don't know how I got there, but suddenly I was on the street. I wanted to cry. My head hurt. I really wanted to cry. Like a baby. And then I saw it. Not that you could miss it. An enormous limousine, the kind with tinted windows, a minibar and a driver wearing a uniform. Only this limousine was longer. Larger. I guessed if you pushed back the seating there was probably a swimming pool beneath it.

A crowd had gathered around the car, even though it was empty. They kept approaching and peering in the windows. The driver, clearly enjoying himself, did his best to look like a CIA operative, standing to attention in his dark glasses, arms folded, alongside the car.

A policeman appeared and told the crowd to disperse. Police never learn that asking crowds to leave the scene of a crime, accident or even an empty limousine is simply an invitation for them to ignore you. Hell, no, they say. This is a free country. You don't own this street, Mr Policeman, buddy. If I wanna look, I'm gonna look. In fact if anything, the crowd only moves closer in an act of defiance.

'What's going on? Who's here?' I asked a young boy, probably fifteen or sixteen, standing next to me. He had a camera, so at first I took him for a tourist.

'Alexandra West. She's inside now but she's coming out soon.'

'Really?'

'Yeah. I got her autograph. Want to see?'

And before I could answer one way or the other, he thrust a piece of paper bearing her signature in my face. And all I could think was, big deal. My life is a wreck, how dare you be happy? How dare you meet Alexandra West, obtain her signature and generally enjoy your day. I hate you. Instead I smiled and told him I was impressed.

I think I should explain at this point that Alexandra West, though not my particular cup of tea, was, and still is, an immensely famous and buxom blond film actress. To be more precise, she was famous for being buxom, a feature she acquired apparently via some silicone and a surgeon. Never mind.

She was, even to the untrained eye, very pretty in a California beach babe sort of way. Again, not my taste, but highly profitable all the same. Unless you had been held captive by aliens or spent the last decade camping under a rock in the Australian outback, you no doubt were acquainted with Ms West.

Although there were no shortages of blond, busty women in the movies, she was clearly leader of the pack. At that moment I couldn't remember the name of the film that launched her into the stratosphere, but from what I could deduce, every film she had made since had been identical, only the names had been changed. Her specialty was disaster-movie damsels in distress, or else girl-friends of renegade cops who get kidnapped or girlfriends of drug lords who kidnap renegade cops. No matter what the storyline, Ms West always got naked after about half an hour. This was a tactical move designed to send teenage boys suffering from testosterone overload into a complete frenzy. It had the added effect of making her rich beyond most people's wildest dreams.

Calendars, fitness videos, books, apparently her adoring public had not yet reached their Alexandra West threshold. Whatever she marketed, they purchased by the truckload. Now I was about to glimpse her in the flesh, but first I had a question for the young man beside me.

'How did you all know that she would be here?'

'The network. We hear on the grapevine what her movements are going to be, then send it out over the network.'

'You mean the Internet?'

'No, the network. Her fan club network. Somebody always knows her movements.'

'Every day?'

'Yep.' He appeared particularly proud to be connected to whomever it was that followed her around and reported back to the hordes.

'So you came just to see her.'

'Yep.'

'Have you met her before?'

'Once. At a film premiere. I waited all day, but it was worth it. She signed my arm.'

I quickly glanced at both arms. They appeared clean and therefore I realized why he was back. Obviously hygiene triumphed over love and he washed her autograph off. Now he had returned to secure something more permanent.

Charlie, for that was his name, continued to explain that Ms West was upstairs at *The Vulture* doing an interview. This floored me. She was in the same offices I had just visited, but I had missed her. He further explained that word was Ms West was tired of playing the bimbo on screen, and wanted the public to see her in a new light. She was, so he said, really a serious and highly intelligent woman who was professionally sidetracked when her looks got in the way. That what was why, Charlie intoned, she was moving to New York, to work in the theater and independent film.

'She is?' I asked, incredulous.

Given that *The Vulture* would never be interested in somebody like Ms West as subject matter except as parody, I was intrigued.

'Yep. That's why she is here today. She's retooling her image. I heard they are going to do a big story on her. Might be a cover. I heard she's never making another disaster movie in her life.'

Charlie, it appeared, heard everything.

'You know she turned down $1 million to make *Die Now, Die Fast 7*? She said moving to New York is the start of a new chapter for her. She said she is going to show people she is more than just a body.'

'She said this to you?'

'No, she said this to her realtor, who was showing her

apartments on the East Side. He told the papers.'

'I see.'

'Personally I think it's only fair the world see the real Alexandra.'

'You do?'

'Sure. We know, her fans, we know she's really intelligent. It's about time other people saw it too.'

'And how do you know she is so smart?' I prodded.

'Just look at her. Can't you tell?'

Charlie was in love, that much was clear. Ah, the sweet crush of youth. In my day it was Farrah Fawcett, so I knew what he was going through. I also knew, though I didn't dare say, that he was living in fairyland. Having become besotted with a blank screen, he projected a personality where none existed. Yet Charlie was an adolescent, and that was his right. It was the adults in the crowd I worried about. As for Ms West, stories of actresses desperate to play Lady Macbeth when the entire world wants only to eat cheese-cake are a dime a dozen. Many, I was aware, think somehow packing their bags and moving east will be enough to erase the size of their breasts and copious bad movies from the public imagination.

I had no statistics on success or failure rates, but doubted the move had ever been of much assistance. Once filed under one letter of the alphabet in Hollywood, it probably would be difficult to move to another. And why bother? Ms West was clearly raking in millions. It seemed to me this was just another pathetic case of 'wanting to be taken seriously'. Well, I said to myself, she should have thought of that before having sex in a burning tower with her boyfriend in full view of the fire department in *Die Now, Die Fast 4*. Or was it *5*?

The whirring and clicking of cameras was incessant. I couldn't see her yet, but the noise signaled she was on her way. Alexandra! Alexandra! Over here! She stopped and smiled at the throng. They thrust scraps of paper in her face, and she dutifully signed them. At least she has manners, I thought. Men who had spent way too much in the gym stood by her side doing their best to look menacing. These were, Charlie informed me, her posse, her guards.

'They go everywhere with her.'

So did Charlie apparently, but I thought it best not to point that out.

At close range I can report she was indeed beautiful. Dazzling. Platinum-blond hair and blue eyes. The chest, as we had all gathered from the movies, was monstrous. She was wearing very tight clothes – a black leather dress, I recall. She swept into the car regally, like she was a head of state, and the door slammed. Fans began pounding on the windows. I was fascinated. The driver hit the floor hard and the car was away. The beefy guys jumped into a car behind and followed. While she played at actress, they played at being Secret Service. Most amusing.

I assumed now the fans, these grown men and women who were all truants from school or work, would then disperse and get back to their lives. I was wrong. Suddenly they all ran into the middle of the road to hail taxis. About a dozen skidded one behind the other to a stop. Everyone climbed in. These people seemed to have done this before.

'Charlie, what's happening now?'

'She's going to lunch at Café Pierre. We're going to wait for her there.'

'You know where she is going for lunch?'

'Sure. I told you. The network keeps us informed.'

He and a number of others piled into the last cab. He motioned for me to join them.

'There's room for one more in here,' he cried out. 'Come on.'

There was an urgency to their cries that I had previously witnessed only when ambulances arrive at a scene. Possibly armies during the Peloponnesian Wars acted the same way. But this militia of fans, this was an underworld I never imagined existed. Charlie waved his hands frantically.

'Are you coming?'

At that instant, curiosity took over. Maybe it was desperation. Depression. Shock. I was, I suddenly realized, still bound by the terms of my contract to *The Vulture*. My day was ruined. I couldn't go back to work. A power greater than I pulled me into the cab. I climbed in while Charlie leaned over to grab the door.

'Café Pierre,' he barked at the driver.

During the drive Charlie and his cohorts swapped stories of

previous sightings, gleanings from waiters and doormen, and the latest Alexandra West items in the gossip columns of the New York papers. They could never get enough of her. They knew where she bought her groceries in Los Angeles, who cut her hair, who broke her heart in high school, who took her to the prom.

In the taxi I learned she was currently single after a long-term relationship with an actor whose name I now forget who offloaded her for a singer. Or maybe a make-up artist. Maybe the boyfriend was a make-up artist. No matter. She had been devastated by the break-up, and they all felt her pain.

'She really wants to be married,' said one.

'She really wants a baby,' said another.

'She is so sick of men treating her like a Barbie doll,' said a third.

Never before had so many been on such intimate terms with someone they had never met. These people were crazy, I told myself. These people needed straitjackets ideally. But these people, I realized, had given me an idea.

Outside Café Pierre we repeated the scenario first performed in front of *The Vulture*. We waited outside while Ms West dined inside with a man in a very expensive Italian suit whom the fans insisted was her new agent. He had been appointed the task of steering her away from action adventure movies and toward Shakespeare and Chekhov. She was eating $40 pasta and we were eating hot-dogs bought from a vendor at the corner of the street.

The beefy guys, ever present and on guard outside, glared at us. I glared back, but they chose to ignore me. *I'm not like them*, I wanted to yell. But to all intents and purposes I was exactly like them. I was standing there, waiting, wasn't I? For what? I still didn't know exactly. But an idea was forming in my mind while I chewed on my hot dog.

Ms West, according to her devoted throng, was single. So was I. This woman made news wherever she went. Breakfast, lunch and dinner, an army followed her, the media swarmed about her. Could I, just once, take the place of the man inside and wine her and dine her? Ms MacDowell had instructed me to do something small. This was small. Well, smallish. Take a famous Hollywood bombshell to dinner, rely on the network to get my name out there, and watch the sparks fly.

There has long been an understanding among both historians

and the men in blue of the concept of guilt by association. Police believe if you keep company with criminals, the odds of you belonging to the same union are astonishingly high. Birds of a feather and all that. History teaches the same lesson. There were possibly some moral, upstanding members of the Borgia family living in Florence during the Renaissance, but they never received any credit for leading virtuous lives. With so many relatives, particularly the unbeatable brother-and-sister team of Cesare and Lucrezia, poisoning enemies, friends, wives and husbands left and right, the family reputation was cast. All Borgias were considered rotten to the core, and the nice, well-behaved ones were never given the benefit of the doubt.

Actually, all the Borgias were rotten to the core and there were no nice, well-behaved ones, but the theory still holds water. The reputations of those around you seal yours. If there existed a firm tradition of guilt by association, I thought, fame by association could not be far behind. Clearly if you stand under the sun long enough, you soak up the heat. I could go down for a minute in history as Alexandra West's date.

I could be like Prince Peter of Russia, married off as a teen to Catherine the Great. He was a 98-lb weakling who preferred his toy soldiers to his wife, which was just as well, because she was too busy amassing power to cook dinner for him anyway. No question history would have long forgotten this ineffectual Russian royal, but it hasn't. Why? Because he was married to *her*. We remember him because he rode the tail of her accomplishments. He was Peter the Weak, Catherine the Great's husband. Could I not be Tom, Alexandra the Great's date?

My mind was getting way ahead of me, but I let it examine the prospect. This was not damaging like the Olympic drama I cooked up, this could be fun. The only problem was, how could I make this happen? I had about as much chance of dating her as Charlie and all his desperate friends. Unless.

Unless I told the truth. Charlie and his buddies were, I would explain bluntly, let's face it, losers. I was not. I was in fact on a deeply penetrating and intellectual mission to sabotage my own private life in the name of social science. I would suggest to Ms West her complicity in this scheme would only enhance her own reputation. Revealed as a co-conspirator, she would later be lauded for allowing me, the writer, to exploit her fame. She could tell anyone who cared to listen that she felt her role in this game was pivotal in her own personal development. She chose to assist me to learn and comprehend the meaning of her own celebrity, which she now planned to discard in pursuit of a more pared-down existence.

I asked Charlie if he knew where Ms West was staying while in New York.

'At the Waldorf. She never stays anywhere else. She loves it there.'

'She does? How do you know?'

'Juanita said she is always saying how much she loves the place. The huge beds. The room service. She always leaves her a huge tip.'

'Juanita?'

'The room-service maid. Actually she is the head housekeeper, and personally supervises the cleaning of rooms of celebrities and politicians.'

'You know her?'

'I spoke to her yesterday. I left some flowers for Alexandra with Juanita. She promised to put them in her room.'

This staggered me. This kid, who clearly should have been in school learning history and geography and calculus, was befriending maids and room-service waiters in order to get one step closer to the object of his fantasies. I probed further. Juanita, I learned, worked the early shift, starting at six a.m. She was extremely punctual and, if you waited by the staff entrance at five of six, you could always catch her. If you gave her anything to pass on to your hero, a cash gratuity was always appreciated.

'So if I wanted to get a letter to Alexandra, I could trust Juanita to do it?'

'Absolutely,' said Charlie. 'Juanita is cool. Juanita rules.'

Suddenly I had the urge to go. Get off the street and return to work. I jumped in a cab and spent the rest of the afternoon penning a note to Ms West, asking that she dine with me but once, and never be obligated again. The rest, I explained, was up to me. I typed it out on official *Capitalist* letterhead, hoping that would impress her. This, I reminded myself, was the second letter I had written that week, the excruciating failure of the first still a vivid memory. I hit the subway. At home, I microwaved some lasagna, ate it on the lips, turned on the television and screened all my calls, not that I received any. When Jake didn't call it meant he and Elizabeth were out for dinner. Anyway, I went to bed early, intending to rise and intercept the wondrous Juanita.

As promised by Charlie, Juanita was on time. I had been given a vague description of her appearance. She had, apparently, dark hair and brown eyes, which meant she was any one of 10 million people in the New York metropolitan area. Still, she saw me hovering and guessed my purpose. It turned out she was an old hand at this stuff.

'Are you Juanita?'

'*Sí*,' she replied softly.

I pulled out the letter and a twenty.

'Could you deliver this to Alexandra West. She must read it. This is not a fan letter. This is urgent.'

She took the twenty and tucked it into her sleeve. She didn't buy the I'm-not-a-fan-line but didn't roll her eyes the way I would have if I were her.

'I promise to get it to her, *señor*,' she said. 'You can trust me.'

I had to. She smiled at me. She promised I could trust her. Charlie certainly did. I offered my thanks. I felt at that instant like a pathetic, middle-aged, desperate fool, and I realized Juanita probably thought the same.

Chapter 10

She was the object of a million male fantasies, my intended Ms West, but never featured in mine. Firstly, she was too blond, too tall, too plastic, a caricature of herself and her gender. She was also, I suspected, rather dim to boot. Not that I had ever conversed with her, but one can gauge these things from interviews, talk-show appearances, magazine covers and the like. It is not carved in stone that intellect has an inverse relationship to bust size, but in her case I suspected this equation might be mathematically sustainable.

Secondly, Ms West was far too twenty-first century for me. In other words, she was still alive. I have already confessed that, apart from Elizabeth and my mother, I like my women dead, preferably for hundreds of years. Some men go for older women, I like them ancient. Which explained why, for me, the prospect of dating Ms West actually held zero appeal. I looked at it purely from a business perspective. I had signed a contract, I was bound by its terms.

Still, if truth be told, when she actually responded to my missive, the electrical charge coursing through my veins had my body light up like a Christmas tree. Never mind which parts. Two days after I sent her my letter, she called me at *The Capitalist*. I am not making this up. Well, sort of. She did indeed call, although technically it was not her voice on the telephone.

It was deep and belonged to a man. A man who introduced himself as Michael Wilkes. He was the one anointed, I later learned, with the task of reinventing her image. Sitting at my desk, reading the *Wall Street Journal* at the time, distracted by an article on bond yields I neither understood nor cared to, to say I was caught off guard would be an understatement. After entrusting the fateful letter to smiling Juanita before dawn, I had concluded only moments later that Ms West, if she even read it, would toss it aside. I certainly would if I were her. And if she did consider my offer, would laugh it off and conclude the entire proposal was idiotic in the extreme. This was in fact my dream scenario. I still wanted out desperately. If Ms West ignored me, at least I would be able to reassure the vultures at *The Vulture* that I had done all I could.

'Mr Webster?'

'Yes.'

'Michael Wilkes.'

I racked my brains trying to remember where I had ever met a person with that name or that voice. Given that in the course of a normal working week I can speak to a number of business analysts, investors and dealers off the record, I assumed he was one of my more unmemorable and therefore useless contacts.

'I apologize, Mr Wilkes. I am sure we spoke a couple of weeks ago, but I just can't place you.'

'CC,' he said. 'I'm with CC.'

'Of course, CC.'

Except I didn't see, or have a clue either for that matter.

'The Communications Company. It's a mouthful, so we just use the initials. I mean, I do. It's actually my company. I'm the president.'

So the guy has his own company. Big deal. This is New York, pal. Everybody is president of something.

'I represent Alexandra West.'

That single line started my heart pumping furiously, while my voice reverse-broke and I found myself sounding thirteen again.

'You do?' I screeched.

'Yes. I'm handling all her media. Now that she is based in New York, she wanted someone on this coast who better understood her needs.'

'Of course,' I replied, curious as to precisely what those needs were.

'Mr Webster, I'll get – '

'Please, call me Tom.'

'Tom, I'll get straight to the point. We read your letter. I read it, Alexandra read it. We'd like to meet with you.'

They would? Really? At this stage I think I had slid off my swivel chair and was now almost face down on the floor. They wanted to meet me? They couldn't be serious. But, oh, yes, yes, they were.

'You read my letter, then?' I said, telling Mr Wilkes exactly what he had just told me. 'I, I, I thought if Ms West even read it, she would think it a hoax. Frankly, I'm staggered. I can't believe you called.'

'We have to read all the mail that comes directly to her, like yours. Nutcases, you know.'

'Nutcases?'

'Stalkers, weirdos. We sort through all of it to get a grip on exactly who is out there. The threatening ones are handed over to the FBI.'

'And the others?'

'We send them a standard thank-you note and an autographed photo.'

'I see. So you read my letter and decided I wasn't a candidate for a photograph or an FBI investigation.'

This was my attempt at humor.

'Right.'

'Well, that is a relief. I'd hate for grown men who talk into their shirtsleeves to have to waste their time tailing me.'

This was a second attempt at humor. He failed to emit the slightest chuckle, and I realized humor was the one sense he didn't possess. Probably just stuck to the basic five and skimped on the rest.

'We checked you out. It seems you're legit.'

I was? Thank God for that. They had me checked out? By whom? The thought of this was totally unnerving.

'Alexandra is staying at the Waldorf. You know where that is. Park Avenue and 48th Street.'

'Sure.'

'Could you drop by, say, around nine this evening?'

'Nine. Of course. Shall I . . . um . . . well . . . just come straight to her room?'

'No. Wait in the lobby. I'll be there and we will go up together.'

'How will I recognize you?'

'You won't. I'll recognize you.'

'You will?'

'Gotta go. Another call. Nine. In the lobby. Don't be late.'

He hung up. I slowly lowered the receiver. My jawbones unlocked and the lower half of my jaw came to rest on my chest. My respiration sped up to such a degree maybe I was fit enough to run the flame into the Sydney stadium after all. I did it. I did it. I actually did it. Jesus, I thought, this might really take off. Really happen. We would meet, eat and sacrifice ourselves at the altar of social science. I was going to date a movie star, that obscure object of desire, coveted by millions.

To be honest, I was mildly thrilled by the idea. All right, totally thrilled. I was also getting way ahead of myself. First, I had to meet the duo (whom I later learned were nicknamed Catwoman and the Riddler by competitors), and they had to approve my plan. Not unlike a company chairman hoping to convince the board to issue more shares, I would have to make a presentation to my intended. This to convince her of my suitability in taking the company, in this case her, even more public. I decided against the maps and flow-charts approach, opting instead for my best suit and tie. A haircut on the way home would not be out of order. But first I had to get through the rest of the day.

When suddenly confronted with the prospect of meeting the world's biggest bombshell, it does tend to distract you from all things mundane, such as, for example, your job. I walked through the rest of the day like an automaton. I was researching the sudden upswing in the bond market, a topic that lacked all the color, excitement and explosiveness of even one of Ms West's worst movies.

Instead I rehearsed our meeting over and over in my mind, and with each scenario became more convinced she was mine for the taking. I started to feel invincible, as one does when hypothetically playing out as opposed to experiencing situations in life. Now all my fears about the experiment subsided. Only hours before, I was praying she would ignore my missive and give me an out. Only hours before, I felt pathetic and embarrassed that I had sunk so low. No wonder Elizabeth left me, I chastised myself. If your spouse could even contemplate being used by a magazine like this there would be grounds for divorce. Some people sink into the pits, I thought, but this was the abyss.

But now the ridiculous possibility of taking Ms West to dinner had transformed into a realistic probability, I felt maybe I had been too hard on myself. Now I could see the upside of this, which was of course a meal with one of the world's most famous women, a little attention and, as Ms MacDowell suggested, a chance to make Elizabeth crazy with jealousy. Crazy. I could make Elizabeth crazy and mad. She could ignore me no longer. And that was just the downside of the upside. The upside of the upside was $100,000, and memories to kill for. Yes, folks, I dated her, I could say for decades after the event. We're no longer in touch, but once, once, I would boast, crossing my second and third fingers, once we were like *this*.

As the day drew to a close, Jake called. We discussed the usual topics that made up our daily conversation, baseball, the stock market, carefully steering clear of Elizabeth. It was a delicate dance we engaged in, but somehow we seemed to pull it off. I was at this point bursting to tell him about my rendezvous with the illustrious Ms West, but something kept me silent. Ms MacDowell had cautioned me against talking with anyone about the ruse, and I had indeed been paid handsomely to keep my mouth shut.

She explained, and I believed her reasoning had merit, that the reactions of those closest to you to your instant fame were crucial to the article. She suggested that colleagues, relatives and friends who considered you their personal ally would have interesting responses to the idea of now sharing you with the public at large. Some would resist it. Others would dismiss it. Jealousies would emerge. And then there were those, she indicated, who would wish to bask in reflected glory. For the fifteen minutes of fame I was grabbing, they would attempt to hijack at least five for themselves.

Instead, I tried valiantly to sound as routine as possible, which is insanely difficult when you are anything but. The best thing about the conversation was that it took place over the telephone, a device which covers a multitude of sins, facial expressions, lies and deceits. When you have known someone since the second grade, it is virtually impossible to fool them in the flesh. Had I been talking with Jake in person, he would have guessed something was amiss.

The telephone, however, accorded me a fantastic cover. I was bright and breezy, and he suspected nothing.

Then suddenly I panicked. In my euphoria over the call from Mr Wilkes, I had forgotten about the baseball. There was a ball game on television that night, and Jake and I always watch them together. As I have been banned from his apartment by my wife, the ritual is conducted at my place. The laws regarding this event are firmly set in concrete. He brings Chinese food, I supply the beer and we sit around, like guys do, conducting our own play by play. This means we yell at the screen, critique all the players and gripe about how much money they earn. We are highly dismissive of the network commentators and completely convinced that if they would only give us the job, the ratings would skyrocket. Between us there is nothing about baseball we don't know. Go on, ask me anything. I know the answer.

The fact was, the ritual was such a ritual we never even made plans anymore. Jake simply turned up at my apartment on game nights and we took it from there. So it was a godsend he even mentioned it as we finished our call.

'I'll see you later, then.'

He would? Oh, hell, the game. What in the name of God was I going to do? I wouldn't be home. I tried to stay calm.

'Jake, we can't do the game tonight.'

'Why not?'

I had to do some quick thinking on that one. Why not? Flipping through my excuses file in my brain, I settled on the best fallback, the work excuse.

'Didn't I tell you?'

'No. What?'

'Work. Louis wants me to cover the Annual General Meeting of Gen-Research shareholders. Thinks there might be a column in it.'

'Who are Gen-Research?'

'Small medical research company doing unbelievable stuff in the field of genetic engineering. Word is they are about to patent some new drug, and when they do, the stock will blast the roof off the building.'

'Never heard of them.'

'Me neither. But Louis assures me we will.'

Would we? I doubted it. A few days prior I had received notification of their general meeting by fax and, after perusing it, decided medical research was such a crapshoot I was not interested. I filed the fax under T for trash. Now this little upstart company had come to my rescue.

Of course, when the column failed to appear, I knew Jake would bring it up. He is very quick and never forgets a conversation. He is also extremely loyal and reads every word I publish. I would then use the second fallback I employ when money men I really do interview call to complain that their words of wisdom never appeared. Spiked, I tell them. Not my decision. Louis pulled it. Story wasn't sexy enough. Even columns today must be not only factual but sexy too. I'm not kidding.

That was Jake dealt with. I would deal with the problems that little lie would no doubt create later when they appeared. I told Jake I would tape the game, watch it later, and we could conduct the autopsy in the morning. He was most disappointed. He hated watching games alone. Elizabeth, I knew, would not watch with him because she never watched with me. She thought baseball was just a bunch of grown men in striped clothes being paid millions to hit a ball with a stick. Essentially, she was not wrong. But every time I tried to convince her baseball was more, oh, so much more, than overgrown children playing stickball, she left the room.

On the subway home I looked around the car in earnest. I knew something all these people heading home did not, that in but a few hours I would be meeting with a woman they had to pay to see. I had to stop myself from squealing. It's a weird sensation, that, feeling smug and nervous and superior and inferior all at the same time. On the street I headed for Tony the barber for a quick cut, then, once home, showered, drowned myself in aftershave and pulled out the number-one suit from the closet.

Every man has a number of suits in his possession prioritized on a scale of one to five. A suit coming in at number five on the scale indicates it is for everyday wear. Three means better occasions. Two means it was pretty expensive and is used only for job interviews, work interviews, funerals and weddings. The number-one suit, however, is in a league of its own. It's Italian, you paid way too much for it at the time and, when the credit card bill arrived,

71

rationalized the purchase by convincing yourself every man must own one designer suit in his lifetime.

I carefully pulled it off its hanger and put it on. Damn, expensive clothes feel good. I should wear this more often, I told myself. Leaving my building to hail a cab, my doorman, Hector, took in the new me. He smiled. You could see he was impressed. Have a good evening, sir, he said. Oh, Hector, I thought, from your lips to God's ears. Thank you, I replied, I intend to. What I really wanted to say was, *Hector, you have no idea where I am going from here.* I wanted to tell the cab driver all the way to the Waldorf. I wanted to tell the French tourists milling about the hotel lobby lugging cameras and shopping bags. But I didn't say a word. I sat quietly and, I hoped, coolly.

Then I saw them. Out of the corner of my eye, seated in a small group beside a giant vase of flowers near the elevators. Charlie and his friends. The throng of earlier had been reduced in size, and I guessed the cause was the call of duty, such as putting children to sleep or catching up on work missed during the day. Clutching pens and autograph books, the dedicated few had set up camp in the lobby, waiting for Ms West to pass by them on the way to yet another dinner or interview. I looked away, hoping they hadn't spotted me.

Excited and nervous, suddenly I had an out-of-body experience. I actually stepped outside myself and stared down at a man who looked remarkably like me wearing an Armani suit, sitting in the Waldorf lobby waiting to be received by a movie star.

Couples in dinner suits and evening gowns rushed past me to a fleet of waiting cars. Chaos reigned at the front desk, where a very noisy group of South Americans were checking in. From my feeble high-school Spanish I could ascertain that somebody's passport had gone astray. I looked at my watch every minute. At precisely nine o'clock I felt somebody's eyes were upon me. I tried searching through the crowd for a man I had never seen and barely spoken to, a task, I might add, that has its challenges. A short, squat man with blond hair in a navy-blue suit seemed to approach me so I stood up. We made eye contact but he walked right past me into the great beyond. I sat down again. Then a voice came from behind.

'Tom?'

I spun around. Standing there was a tall, lean, dark-haired man of impeccable grooming. The suit, the hair, the physique, everything was perfect. This man probably had a stairmaster, a treadmill and free weights at home. He certainly looked like it. But I couldn't get a really good fix on the guy, because he was wearing sunglasses. At nine o'clock at night, indoors. Sunglasses. We sized each other up as men do on first meetings. My earlier cockiness dissipated in an instant. I felt blindingly insecure.

'Mr Wilkes?'

He extended his hand and I shook it. Firm grip.

'Thanks for being on time. Nice to meet you.'

'Likewise.'

He smiled at me in an odd, strained manner, indicating, I supposed, that he was kindly disposed toward me. However, trying to communicate with someone who is wearing sunglasses at night in a closed room is both ridiculous and irritating. Either he didn't want to be recognized in my company, or he thought he was, as Elizabeth often said, too cool for school. By that she meant the ego was oversized, with no talent to match it. She used the phrase to describe the tenth-graders she taught, singling out individuals or cliques of students who were so consumed with wearing the right clothes and listening to the right music, the idea of coming to school to learn anything was completely alien to their hormonally challenged minds. At that instant, Mr Wilkes struck me as being too cool for school as well. I hoped the Armani suit would convince him I was also a player, rendering the shades unnecessary. But it was not to be.

'Shall we go up?'

'Sure.'

He was a man of few words, so I decided to follow his lead. As we walked to the elevators I attempted to shield myself from view of the fans. Once the doors closed I remarked on the presence of Charlie and company.

'They're harmless. They follow her everywhere. Kind of sad really, when grown men fixate like that.'

'It must drive her crazy. Doesn't Alexandra, I mean, Ms West, doesn't she mind?' I asked.

The elevator opened onto the penthouse floor.

'You can ask her yourself, Tom,' he said smiling.

I walked alongside Mr Wilkes to Ms West's room as if being escorted to the guillotine. The knot in my stomach had tripled in size. Mr Wilkes knocked softly and waited. I watched the doorknob turn at a 180-degree angle.

And there she was.

'And you must be Tom,' purred this Amazon with blond hair and shockingly white teeth who towered over me.

'I must be,' I replied.

Suddenly I understood how Mark Antony felt when he was introduced to Cleopatra for the very first time. Despite his best intentions, despite convincing himself she was a mindless vixen he would use and discard, it was in the end she who outwitted him. For her he abandoned reason for sex, power for love. He knew it was wrong. He knew it was foolish. And yet he couldn't help himself. This was me. This action-adventure damsel in distress had me in the palm of her hand. She ushered me into her suite and closed the door.

'Thanks for coming,' she purred.

'Thank you for seeing me,' I replied.

She motioned for me to sit down and then seated herself beside me. Mr Wilkes sat on the opposite sofa. She purred again. I swear it was purring. It had to be, for right at that moment, I, Tom Webster, rational thinker, amateur historian and economist from Yale, I wanted to climb right onto her lap.

'Drink?'

'No, thank you.'

'Oh, please, you must have something. Coffee, then?'

'No, really, I'm fine.'

Alexandra wanted to play the hostess with the mostest but I was too nervous to consider a beverage. She rose to pour herself a drink, a double vodka with a slice of lemon. She didn't offer Mr Wilkes anything, which I found kind of odd. Clutching her drink, she placed it on a table in front of us and sat down again. Alexandra nodded to Mr Wilkes, indicating it was his turn to do the talking.

'Tom, as I said on the phone, we read your letter. It intrigued me. Us. Both of us.'

'I'll be honest, I was surprised you called.'

'So you said.'

Alexandra smiled at me. In her own hyper-real, hyper-blond, hyper-endowed way, she was beautiful. High maintenance, I guessed, but also high wattage.

'We want to take you up on your offer.'

'You do? Really?'

At this point I was shocked they agreed to my proposal so rapidly. No pre-interview, no questions about my past, my job, my likes and dislikes. I could be a serial killer for all they knew. Suddenly after five minutes they wanted to strike a deal? I guessed in Hollywood people like to do business even more quickly than they do on Wall Street.

'You see, Alexandra isn't taken seriously out there.'

'Out where?'

'There.'

'Which is where?'

'Hollywood. New York. By people who matter.'

'Really?' I feigned surprise.

'She's made too many movies playing the dumb, blond, bimbo girlfriend, and nobody considers her for roles involving anything else.'

He had now mentioned the people 'out there' twice in the space of a minute. Whoever they were, I wanted to point out, they did not appear to be stupid. Looking as she did, could she really expect to be cast as Saint Joan? Maybe she thought so. Maybe this was the problem. Aspirations often exceed ability in life. In this she was not alone.

'She's moved east to retool her image. Get away from the Hollywood bump and grind. I, we, are going to reposition her, so that she can make a splash where it matters. Small independent movies, festival stuff. You follow?'

So she did want to play Saint Joan. Who wouldn't, of course? It's a role to die for. But last time I looked, Shaw had not written the character with somebody who could be on *Baywatch* in mind. Suddenly, Alexandra spoke.

'I know what you're thinking. That I asked for it. That if you play these kinds of parts, if you act the bimbo, you can't expect anything better.'

She looked me in the eye and I thought she might cry.

'Tom, I want better. And I'm not ashamed to go after what I want. I'm not stupid. I read books, you know.'

Yes, I thought, but there's books and there's books. Just because you read Jackie Collins on the red-eye, it doesn't make you Marie Curie.

'People assume if you look like this you don't have a brain. Well, I'm not like you, Yale and all, I know that. Okay, I didn't even finish high school, but I'm smart. I know I am. I'm sick to death of action adventure, I've had it with hanging out of buildings and jumping off burning boats. And I am never going to take my clothes off again. Ever. I'm only thirty-one. I can start over. Plenty of actresses have. Tom, I know my limitations. I don't expect to be up for A-list parts. Well, not yet. But my looks have always got in the way. Do you see?'

I certainly could see. At this point I thought it better not to suggest that some, if not all, of her current pain was self-inflicted. The chest enhancement, the willingness to play dumb, the over-dyed hair, none of this screamed Ethel Barrymore. Yet I felt sorry for her at that instant, sensing she had become trapped in a career that never led her where she presumed it might. Mr Wilkes allowed his client, overwrought by this little heart-wrenching performance, to rest and he took over.

'We think it would be good for Alexandra to date you. You're a serious, solid, grounded guy. Her last couple of boyfriends were, well, anyway, not like you.'

I didn't know whether this was a compliment or an insult. He still, by the way, was wearing his sunglasses.

'I'll be blunt, Tom. You want to use Alexandra to write your article. You need to hitch yourself to her, as you wrote in your letter, to experience a mild case of fame by association. I like that phrase, by the way.'

'Thank you.'

'Well, we'd like to use you as well. A night out with a pinstripe financial writer, a Yalie, would look good for us. You are the company you keep, Tom. You know that. If Alexandra is seen with you, your seriousness, your lack of pretension, they will rub off on her. People will say, hey, if that brainy guy from Yale is interested, maybe there is more to her. Maybe she is smart. Maybe there is something underneath all the blond hair. That's the kind of buzz we want to create right now.'

Thank God, I thought. They needed buzz, and I, the humble bumble-bee nerd from *The Capitalist* had flown in the window. This exploitative relationship was beneficial to both parties. Nobody was going to come away from this feeling cheated. Alexandra threw me another gigantic smile.

'So what do you think, Tom?' she purred. 'Do we have a deal?'

'I guess we do.'

'Right. So down to business,' said Mr Wilkes. 'This Saturday Alexandra has been invited to a film premiere for James Thurgood's new movie. It's his usual Eurocrap – you know, all art direction and costumes and no story – but who cares? He has his audiences and he always breaks even. He's an actors' director and we certainly need to connect with him. We think you should arrive with Alexandra in a limo, watch the film, drop in on the party, then have a late dinner. I'll let the press know Alex is coming with a mystery date, a new beau. That should get the hounds going. I'll tip them off about the restaurant too, so they can get some good snaps of you guys entering and exiting.'

Saturday? This Saturday? Couldn't we do this next month? Next year? Jesus, so soon? I started to squirm in my chair. I think I was sweating too, but I tried my damnedest to look calm and cool. Nodding furiously as he rattled off the arrangements, I finally interjected to ask what I should wear.

'That suit will be fine. In fact, if you have something even more somber, wear that. Pretend you are going to a funeral. We want you to look as serious as possible. Like you have no connection to the flash of the film world. Look like the banker you are.'

'But I am not a banker.'

'Whatever.'

Mr Wilkes looked at his watch. He motioned to Alexandra they had to get moving. She and I at this point had barely exchanged a few sentences. Mr Wilkes rose and prodded me to do likewise.

'I'll make all the arrangements. You just show up here around six on Saturday.'

'One question,' I asked.

'Shoot.'

'What do I answer when they ask how we met? I mean the press, when they ask how we know each other, what do I say?'

'Nothing.'

'Nothing?'

'Nothing.'

'Because?'

'It creates mystery. Keeps them guessing. If they ask, say you're not going to discuss how you met because it's private and you're a private guy. Grin a lot. The fact they are missing a huge part of the story will kill them and ensures they will keep after you. Just smile and say, no comment.'

Really? I was to say, no comment? Like I had been indicted just like Simon Burke and was being asked if I had anything to say about the charges?

Alexandra extended her hand. She thanked me for coming, told me not to worry, that everything would be fine and she would walk me through the night. Then, when she thought I wasn't looking, she shot a sharp look over in Mr Wilkes's direction. She walked me to the door while he stayed behind. He never took off those sunglasses either.

'See you at six, Tom.'

'Six on Saturday. I'll be here.'

And then I was back in the corridor, so long and wide, lined with velvet wallpaper and fire-red carpet. Catwoman and the Riddler repaired to their lair. I, meanwhile, walked out into the night as if injured by shelling. The sudden onset of a headache was overwhelming. It was a Wednesday then, and at midnight it would be Thursday. That gave me two and half days technically until Saturday night. I tried to remember all Mr Wilkes's instructions.

Downgrade from the number-one suit to the number-two. Watch the movie, hit the party, eat dinner. In the cab home, I was in shock, deep shock, the kind they admit you to hospital for. On Sunday morning the deed would be done. By Monday I would be part of the buzz, as Mr Wilkes had said. I wasn't having mere second thoughts, but third, fourth and tenth thoughts as well. Distinct problem was, it was now way too late to wriggle out of this one. Short of joining NASA and leaving on a Friday shuttle flight, I had to show up.

Then as the cab parked in front of my building, Mr Wilkes's ominous voice disappeared from my mind and in its place I heard hers. That little-girl voice, that purring sound she made even when she wasn't talking. Suddenly I thought, Tom, buddy, dating Alexandra West may not have been one of your initial goals in life, but on the other hand there are worse things that could happen to a guy.

Or are there?

Chapter 11

I slept fitfully that night. Waking every hour, I rose each time to see the moon recede a little more while the sun made its ascent. I was feeling sick again and I didn't know why. Hundreds of men would have killed to be in my position. Along with the prospect of an evening with the world's most desirable woman, I would be paid handsomely for my efforts. Even on Wall Street that kind of stock offering would be considered a sure thing, a good deal, money in the bank.

So why did I feel so torn? The deception was part of it. My inability to include Jake, my editors, anyone really, in on the scam gnawed at me. Their reactions to my new status were critical, and I was bound by silence in the name of science. The unmasking of my true intentions at experiment's end was bound to anger people, who would no doubt feel used and foolish. Tom, this is the point, Ms MacDowell was saying inside my head.

'If you can manufacture celebrity from nothing, disconnected from achievement, what is the value in effort, Tom? Where is the culture headed, Tom? Answer me, Tom? And I am asking these questions not to be cynical and sell magazines but because I genuinely care. Don't you see, Tom?'

That day in her office, I thought I did see. I thought the presentation she made at *The Vulture* was compelling and persuasive, and, aside from the wads of cash she was flashing in front of my eyes and the chance to drive Elizabeth crazy, relevant.

No more. Now at four a.m., and five a.m., and six a.m., I was staring at the ceiling working diligently on acquiring a stomach ulcer, trying to convince myself Saturday night was going to be an intellectual exercise in pursuit of truth and meaning. But I didn't buy it, and neither, I knew, did Ms West or Mr Wilkes. For all my insecurities and anxiety, there was only one thing I was sure of that night as I lay there in the dark. There was no turning back.

Completely exhausted, I dressed in the morning and went to work. I started taking note of everyone around me, and how they greeted me. Most nodded. Some grunted. All heads appeared to be buried in the *Wall Street Journal* or the *New York Times*, and occasionally the sound of tearing could be heard as they found articles of interest, that is to say, great stories they had not thought to report on themselves but were now bound to follow up. I did not have any close friends at work, initially a disappointment. In later years it came as somewhat of a relief. All the guys in my section were married with children. Their lives at work consisted of crunching numbers, attending the businesses lunches and swapping stories about their offspring.

Photographs of babies and teens cluttered their desks. As their children grew older they began to play-date each other, and many were enrolled in the same private schools. My colleagues often saw each other on weekends doing the rounds of the same birthday parties, or car-pooled to Little League. An invisible but keenly felt wall often separates parents from non-parents in the workplace, and when it became apparent that Elizabeth and I would not join the ranks of the former, the wall went up. This was not rudeness on their part, merely a tacit admission that we had little in common.

The 1990s, I noted, had ushered in a new age when it came to parenting, the golden era of the father. Men now attended births, devoured books on child psychology and bandied about words like developmental and dysfunctional when describing their progeny's progress. Many in my own office had entered this new age so completely they often sank into the netherworld of baby talk. They could be heard calling home during working hours to speak to their children in half-syllables or worse. Most of the time they sounded as if talking to a pet.

'Good boy,' they would cry when junior was put on the phone. 'Jamie go nap? Go nap now, Jamie,' 'Daddy say bye-bye. Daddy say ta-ta.' I have to tell you, watching financial experts, all graduates of excellent colleges, I might add, converse with their children in the same manner most of us reserve for a Labrador is terrifying.

But the infantile babble was adopted by all in the name of bonding and development and was therefore acceptable. I always secretly hoped that one day one of these fathers would place their child on hold to take a second call and forget to re-enter the adult world of spoken English in the rush. They would converse with a trader or arbitrageur entirely in baby talk.

'Billy wants takeover company? Bad boy. Bad boy. Not nice. Make nice with shareholders, no buy them out. Must go now, Billy. Phone ringing for Daddy.'

As the only man in my division without children, this had the effect of making me somewhat of a loner. Now separated, the situation had worsened. With no children I was an oddity. With no wife I was a pariah. Married men love to boast about their children and complain about their wives, in that order. Never mind that on surveys those same men indicate they are happily married, and, affairs notwithstanding, I believe that they are.

When women are not around, men enjoy nothing more than a simple game of spousal one-upmanship, in which husband after husband relates an anecdote in which their wives star as the villain. Insisting their other halves conspire to make their lives a living hell, they detail the injustice of having to take out the garbage during an NBA game, to mow the lawn, to separate the laundry and of being denied sex because Shirley was so tired after a day of looking after their children. This then expands into a keen discussion of what is it exactly that women do at home all day anyway, culminating in unanimous agreement that women do nothing but eat cookies and watch Oprah.

No longer could I join in these conversations, and I missed them. Ironically, one or two guys in the office envied me. They confessed they would love to come home to a house emptied of children and toys and nagging wives, where you could rule the television set and leave dirty dishes in the sink for a year if you wished. What I never said, what I couldn't explain, was that the grass was such a dark shade of green on my side of the fence it was approaching black. That being separated was lonely and hard, and not having to negotiate with anyone over your need to watch sports as opposed to her need for cheesy movies was not as exciting, as sustaining, as one might think. That even though you have the freedom to leave dishes in the sink you rarely do, for it was not liberating to have a kitchen full of cockroaches, merely unhygienic. And that hearing the words, 'Hi, honey, how was your day?' might drive you insane when it is the only phrase that has greeted you for twenty years, but not hearing it is worse.

So when I arrived for work on Thursday I was met with the usual smiles, grunts and nods that passed for morning greetings. I smiled, grunted and nodded back, for that was the rule. Then I buried myself in the day's papers, taking careful note of all business news large and small, but reading the gossip columns in the tabloids, something I never did. No mention of Ms West that day, but there was an item about James Thurgood's movie premiere, which suggested it was going to be an event bigger than big. There was much detail about catering and flowers and how much the studio was spending to launch what was in effect a small, independent film. Between the lines one could read the studio was hoping the prestige from the successful launch of that film would offset the snickers that greeted a recently released blockbuster. Thurgood was a boutique director who, as Mr Wilkes implied, never made major profits but had loyal audiences and a reputation among actors.

I had to write my column, but, utterly consumed with what was about to happen on Saturday, drew a complete blank for ideas. So I did what I always do when I have nothing new to say, I dusted off the trusty fallback topic of proposed government regulation of the Internet. If there is one thing my readers love passionately, it's the Internet. You know why, don't you? It's the only place left to make instant money. Think of it as Las Vegas for the Dow Jones set. You put your money down, you spin the website wheel and – whaddaya know? – the next day you wake up a millionaire. For these boys, the sexiest word today isn't orgasm, it's on-line.

I should add that the one thing my readers hate just as passionately is the federal government. They have long held the belief that government for the people, by the people, of the people is a lovely concept that should in fact be practiced on other people, preferably in countries far removed from the United States.

The US government, they believe, has unfettered, overreaching and sadistic powers, the most egregious of these being the control of large portions of their money. Pinstripes believe if you make bags of money, you should be allowed to hoard it in any manner you choose. Governments believe the more you earn, the more you should share, an idea pinstripes think is so unfair they are forced to establish trusts, shelters and residences in the Canary Islands, the sole purpose of which is to outwit the very people they elected to govern them.

So I scribbled off my standard 800 words, peppered with plenty of Wild West history thrown in for good measure. Watch out, I tell all those Internet cowboys, the sheriff is coming to town to lay down the law. Either you challenge him to a duel, or you get out of town. Then I threw in lots of references to Jesse James, Billy the Kid and Butch and Sundance, because Louis loves it when I do. He says all my Western stuff 'sexes up' the column, and if there is one thing I can do well, despite my wife's suggestions to the contrary, I can sex up a column.

In the midst of this Jake called. I knew he would, and he suggested lunch. I met him at the Blue Moon. Immediately he wanted to discuss the ball game, and I realized not only had I not watched it, I had not even checked the score. That gives some indication of how preoccupied I was with Ms West and our impending date. Burrowing through a bagel with cream cheese, Jake asked how the meeting went.

'Boring.'

'Those things always are. They should do something to liven them up. Entertainment or something.'

'At a general meeting?'

'Yeah, I don't know, singers or dancers. Anything to stop people going to sleep.'

'Jake, I'd write a column about it but even I am not that stupid.'

'Watch the game?'

'Got home too late.'

'I thought you were taping it.'

'I did, but when I got home I was dog tired and collapsed.'

'You work too hard.'

'And they don't pay me enough.'

'You and me both.'

We always agreed we were overworked and underpaid. We shared these sentiments at least once a day.

'So do you want me to tell you what happened?'

'No. You know I hate it when you give me a play by play. I promise I'll watch it tonight and we'll do the autopsy tomorrow.'

'Have it your way.'

Jake was a pretty easygoing guy. That's why I liked him. You could reason with him. You could ask him any favor and, unless it might end in a prison sentence, he would loyally carry it out. I'm sure if I asked for my wife back he would hand her over on a platter. So far I hadn't had the guts to ask.

Jake looked at his watch. I never knew why he was always so anxious to return to work on time. He was his own boss, and if he strolled in five or ten minutes late the only person who had the authority to punish him was Jake. Still, he had a thing about punctuality and who was I to argue. He leapt up and announced he had to leave.

'Speak to you later.'

'Sure.'

'You doing anything tonight?'

'No, going home. Watching the game.'

'Okay, call me when you finish it.'

'Roger.'

What was I going to say? The truth? Actually, Jake, I am going home to immerse myself in Alexandra West culture, so when I date her on Saturday night I will be ready. Oh, right. He would have called an institution and had me committed.

I finished my column and turned it over to the powers that be, the previously mentioned colleagues with children. Instead of going straight home, I sidetracked to my local video store, a man on a mission. I would be not be watching the game, for I had more urgent tasks at hand.

I realized I had never watched one of Alexandra's movies, and had better do so before our date. I doubted she would go to the reciprocal trouble of reading my columns, but she was a busy woman, with hairstyling and make-up probably occupying the better half of her day. I felt some homework was in order, and once inside Video Heaven casually cruised the aisles until I found Action/Adventure. I was shocked to discover she had in fact made what seemed like hundreds of movies. Probably only ten, but she had the aisle to herself. Her name was often bigger than the title, if that tells you anything.

She had, I learned, bestowed her acting talents on *The Devil and the Deep Blue Sea*, and its sequel, *The Devil Swims Deeper*. This presumably gave her plenty of opportunity to walk around in a bikini, and a later viewing confirmed my suspicions. In fact, even while scuba-diving to the depths of the Atlantic Ocean in search of buried treasure, Ms West dispensed with the legal requirement of a rubber suit (unlike her co-divers), and undertook her voyage to the bottom of the sea nearly naked but for some breathing tanks. All I can say is you had to be there. It was so bad it was good.

She had made other movies too, *Vixen*, *The Vixen Returns*, *Crusher*, *Crusher 2: Return from Beyond*, and, of course, the *Die Now, Die Fast* series, which earned her more money than even Simon Burke had swindled. I did not intend to watch them all, convinced one would suffice as an indication of her talents. I had her role down pat. She was the requisite bimbo girlfriend, a damsel in distress who needed a testosterone-charged he-man to rescue her. To thank him she paid with sex, which might on reflection have been a little hasty. A girl has to watch out for her reputation.

Plus I realized if I checked out more than one video from the West genre I might arouse the curiosity of the clerk, who at that moment had entered a zombie-like trance in front of a screen. He was watching a movie that was a pale imitation of *Jurassic Park*, clearly stitched together in the aftermath of the original's popularity. The dinosaurs looked fake and the storyline, from the five minutes I watched, didn't make sense. The clerk seemed not to care, he was transfixed. Approaching his counter, I decided to make conversation, hoping to distract him. My ploy failed miserably.

'What are you watching?'

'*Raptor Park*.'

'Any good?'

'Excellent, man. Totally excellent.'

He grabbed my video and scanned it across some device without appearing to take his eyes off the screen. I sighed one of those huge, king-size sighs of relief.

'Great movie,' he said.

'Looks like it.'

'I mean this one. *The Devil and the Deep Blue Sea*. Totally awesome. The special effects are incredible. And Alexandra West is such a babe.'

'Really?'

'Yeah. And you know what else? I heard she is throwing it all in to get serious. I'm bummed, man. She's the best.'

'Really? Well, you know, I'm only renting it because a friend's friend produced it and I thought before I meet him at a dinner party I better see it. I didn't even know who was in it.'

Sure, buddy. That's what they all say. Actually, I don't think the clerk heard any of my feeble attempt to deny knowledge of Ms West's existence. A dinosaur of dubious mechanical quality was eating a car and was now down to the tires. This was a moment not to be missed. He bagged my video and handed it over without his eyes leaving the screen.

'Have a nice day,' he said.

'You too,' I replied.

In the window reflection I could see the tires were now all but gone, and the car's inhabitants were shaking desperately behind bushes as the raptor of the title digested his dinner. Suddenly I realized I was hungry too, and rushed home to digest mine. Lasagna, of course.

In *The Devil and the Deep Blue Sea*, the plot can be summarized thus. Ms West, a.k.a. the devil of the title, teams up with a group of steroidal, Stallone-type scuba-divers who have discovered some buried treasure. Immediately word gets out that millions are to be found in Neptune's living room, an entire contingent of bad guys from various parts of globe suit up and attempt to go find it. Of course, a lot of them take only enough air to sustain them for an hour or so, failing to realize that oxygen under water is really quite important in that it assists in keeping you alive. So when they fail to find the loot off the bat and the search is extended, the bad guys drown.

Within minutes they are replaced by a second team of bad guys, who function as a sort of minor-league baseball team. Getting into the majors is their biggest goal, and they are oh so excited to be finally diving in the Atlantic equivalent of Yankee stadium. From the movie I learned that bad guys are evil and stupid in equal measure, so none figured out that death by drowning might be an option.

Meanwhile, a lot of explosions and car chases happened for reasons I did not understand. Bad guys who as children were probably scared of water and had to wear rubber rings in the pool do their dirty work on land and crash a lot of trucks in the process. Car crashes were intrinsic to the plot, and happened on land because, stupid as the movie was, nobody would believe a car crash at sea. During all this time Ms West was helping the good-guy divers prepare to go down and retrieve the treasure, while working undercover seducing the Don Corleone of the bad guys in order to get information from him. This involved sex, of course, and Ms West did not shy away from the camera, if you know what I mean. At this point I felt kind of weird, viewing her naked before we had dinner, whereas normally this situation occurs in the reverse. She was beautiful clothed and beautiful naked, although I guessed much credit went to her surgeon as well.

With a third team of bad guys up to bat and all bases loaded, the situation was grim. Suddenly a submarine appeared, which completely baffled me. The good guys were commandeering the vessel, and while they were all wearing these dinky sailor-type outfits, Ms West was wearing a bikini. Presumably one never knows when one will get a few minutes off for a bit of sunbathing on the ocean floor. There is a shower scene in the submarine where the walls steam up and Ms West has sex with her boyfriend while the crew threw each other knowing smirks in the control room. But the submarine trip is only an exploratory one, with the real party still to happen. When this does, good, bad and in-between guys duke it out at the bottom of the sea as Ms West hurriedly hauls cases of gold coins out of the wreckage and swims to the surface. She saves the day and, to reward her, her boyfriend has sex with her again, which is nice work if you can get it.

This movie, which I mentioned earlier, was so bad it was good. It was also so fantastically awful it made millions for everyone concerned. I thought about watching it again, hoping the plot would become more clear second time around, then realized the idea was hopeless. I could not decipher a story principally because there was none to be had. This was a film about flesh and fish, and, to their credit, the producers never suggested anything but.

Chapter 12

I remember little about the Friday preceding the date. I think the correct term is haze. Fog might work here too. Shell shock is another thought. I did discuss the ball game with Jake, that I remember, watching it after Ms West's efforts at playing the Little Mermaid had concluded. Even without a script the game had more action, excitement and genuine drama than *The Devil and the Deep Blue Sea* could have hoped for.

Sports truly are the ultimate movie if you think about it, for until the final siren you never know the ending. Even with the most complex films one can guess whodunnit, whodidit and whoisit pretty early on if you have half a brain. My favorite movies are always historical. *Spartacus*, which I could watch every day. Any version of *Cleopatra*, but particularly the one with Claudette Colbert.

Elizabeth preferred those soppy, girly Cinderella movies where the fated lovers hate each other but fall in love anyway and then have fantastic sex, following which the man proposes on one knee. She was not impressed that Thelma and Louise went over the canyon. She wanted them to go back home, divorce their good-for-nothing husbands and find men who wanted to love them just the way they were.

I do know that all day Friday I stared long and hard at my co-workers, trying to predict their reactions when I arrived Monday morning to punch the clock. In the intervening period of course

I would have escorted Alexandra to a movie premiere and, all things going according to plan, would be considered a beau of sorts.

The thought of their responses, which I guessed would range from horror to disbelief, filled me with flashes of glee, followed by prolonged moments of fear. You never know exactly what your co-workers think of you, for when they choose to discuss your virtues and faults, it's one party to which you never get invited. But I guessed they had me down as quiet, dependable Tom Webster, history buff and newly separated lonely guy. Tom was the guy in the office who always loaned you money for lunch if you were short and couldn't be bothered trekking to the bank. Tom was the guy who went to an Ivy League school like us, so for that reason alone he passes muster. Tom loved baseball, but basically Tom liked to keep to himself. Women on staff never flirt with Tom, for he doesn't have that kind of charisma they are drawn to.

I knew they would never see me as Charles the Bold, that French duke who spent all his days in the 1400s annexing Belgium. Now that must have been some day job. Nor did they see me as William the Conqueror, or Alexander the Great. I was just Tom the Okay, which I think says it all. Nobody looked at me and said, whoa, is that guy king material or what? What is he doing stuck in an office on Wall Street when he could be out invading Europe?

So come Monday they would, I expected, be somewhat relieved of their preconceptions surrounding Tom Webster. Whether I would be similarly relieved to have duped them remained to be seen.

Saturday morning began with a jog in Central Park. Now I never jog, strongly preferring to let others do the jogging for me. But I firmly ascribe to the credo better late than never, and while ten hours before a date was technically too late to try and undo damage wreaked by microwave lasagna and ballpark hot dogs, hope does spring eternal.

So I ran feebly around the park reservoir, overtaken at every turn by men older, younger, fitter and fatter than I, but all faster. When nobody was watching I slowed my jog to a crawl, a sad kind of semi-shuffle, hoping to buy time and pump some more air into my lungs. The minute another runner approached I resumed speed, hoping to fool them that I, like them, was a regular at this task.

The rest of the day passed interminably slowly. Jake and Elizabeth had gone to visit her parents in Philadelphia for the weekend, so I would not have to resort to lying to him about my whereabouts. I made the point of saying I intended to stay in and reread the new biography of Lincoln that I had loved. Jake knows when I love a book I can read it ten times over, so he bought my lie no problem.

In the afternoon, to kill time, I went to the supermarket in search of supplies. The entire practice of entering these cavernous institutions is still new to me, as Elizabeth always made clear that filling the refrigerator was her job. She enjoyed picking up groceries, while I never harbored a preference either way and was more than content to leave that politically incorrect wife role to her. Now I found myself pushing wayward, misbehaving carts down aisles that could double for bowling lanes, overwhelmed by choice after choice in every department. I have, however, learned to streamline my efforts somewhat by heading directly for the frozen-food section, which, might I suggest to searching women, is prime territory for meeting available men. Single, divorced and newly separated males congregate in frozen food, throwing each other sympathetic looks as we reach into the arctic display shelves to drag out identical precooked meals of chicken or lasagna. There is an understanding and bond between us that requires no language, no smile. Eye contact is enough, and volumes are spoken.

I showered again at four. Dressed in suit number two, the funeral suit, at five, and grabbed a cab at quarter of six. The day's activities had been so delineated by my watch I was disappointed I was merely going to a movie and not doing something more important, like supervising a military invasion. Whereas the early part of the day had been spent in emotional neverland, the ride to the Waldorf fixed that.

Waves of nausea overwhelmed me, and I became convinced I would vomit right there in the back seat. Donning more aftershave than usual, I noted I reeked of the stuff. Hopefully Ms West would be so drowned in perfume that our odors would cancel each other out. Think of the money, Tom, I said. Think of the money. Think of Elizabeth. This will make her so mad she will hate you but she won't ignore you. Not any more, buddy. Think that at best this could be fun, at worst a humiliation that will eventually be forgotten. Think that you are, above all this, conducting an exercise in the pursuit of truth. You are doing the culture a favor, Tom. A favor. Holding a mirror to their excesses, Tom. Think of the secretaries at *The Capitalist* on Monday who might pay you a little more attention. Think, Tom, I said. Think it all. And I did think it all. All the angles, all the outcomes, all the reasons I had undertaken this insane journey in the first place. The impulse to vomit then became overwhelming. Gastric juice began journeying up my esophagus, elevator fashion.

The cab left me at the Waldorf and I was back in the very same lobby where my journey began. Charlie and company were nowhere to be found, and I learned later they were at the movieplex awaiting the arrival of Ms West and her mystery date. They had arrived early to stake out a position behind the ropes and television cameras. It was said of them they were model fans, waiting patiently while passing the time swapping tales of celebrity sightings, displaying scrapbooks and playing cards. Into the elevator I went, pressing the button to her floor. This was it. This was really it. With bile in my throat, I knocked on the door.

Mr Wilkes ushered me in. He shook my hand, but it was the grip of jello, not of steel. I had felt previously I did not like him, but now I was sure. He was too slick, everything was too pat, the suit was too perfect, and overall he was too handsome. It wasn't just his hair, his entire body seemed to have been blown dry. He had this sort of evil smile that crept over his face while he was talking to you, indicating that he didn't believe for one minute what he was saying. Everything was an act, and he was probably a better actor than Alexandra could ever hope to be.

'Nice suit,' he said.

'Thank you.'

'Alexandra's getting dressed.'

'Great.'

At this point my height shrunk from five feet nine to two feet nine, not a particularly effective height from which to function. Despite feeling that in all ways Mr Wilkes was a sham, he made me feel totally insecure. I almost shook in his presence, something I am not particularly proud of.

'While we are waiting for her, I guess I should fill you in on tonight.'

'Great.'

I smiled awkwardly. All I could say was – Great. I sounded like a robot who had been programmed to answer one word.

'I called all the media, the tabs, the mags, TV. Well, actually they called me to confirm Alexandra was showing, and I didn't call them back, because you never do.'

'Great.'

'I made them wait a couple of hours, because you never want them to think you need them as much as they need you.'

'Great.'

'So I just called them all back, and told them she was showing, and yes, she was bringing a date. I pointed out you were just a friend, they didn't need to get themselves into a lather over it. Then...'

At this point his creepy smile stretched all the way to behind his ears.

'Then I told them all off the record about you.'

'Great... You did?'

'Well, you know, in my own way. In the way we agreed.'

'What way was that again?'

'Just that in fact you and Alexandra had been dating for some time, that you were more than a "friend", but that this relationship was very important to Alex because you weren't in the business. That you saw her as someone other than a sex symbol, that she really wanted to make it work and hoped the press would give her some breathing space. Because, you know, ten minutes after she says hello to a guy the tabs have her walking down the aisle.'

'So they think we are an item?'

'Let's just say I planted the idea in their stupid little brains.'

'But everything is off the record, right?'

Now the dastardly grin had stretched 360 degrees around his entire head.

'Oh, Tom. Maybe in your field, in the finance world, when people tell you things off the record, you don't print them. But the tabs, they will run with it like state troopers following a speeding car. They'll say sources told them, blah, blah, blah. Mr Sources is a very important person in the tabloid world.'

'Are you sure?'

'Am I sure? Sure I'm sure. This is my job, Tom, to keep Alex's name circulating.'

'But I got the impression she doesn't like her name circulating, as you say, given all the connotations.'

'Connotations, Tom?'

'You know. That she is a mindless sort of . . . bombshell.'

'Precisely, Tom. That's where you come in.'

And precisely that's where she came in. I stood up when she appeared, but that was all I could manage. Initially speech eluded me. She was wearing this glittery, spangly, blindingly bright miniskirt that appeared to be made of rhinestones or something similar. She wore extremely high heels, silver high heels, and a silvery T-shirt. She looked like a blond herring. For someone trying to recast her image, she was not, I thought, doing a very good job. Her hair had expanded, if that were humanly possible, to double in size. A hairdresser came out of her bedroom clutching a brush, and a make-up artist too. These people were never introduced to me. No matter, Alexandra rushed over to my side and kissed me hello. On the lips. Right on the lips.

'Hi, Tom.'

She was purring again.

'Hi,' I said, feeling like an idiot that I did not have anything more sophisticated to say.

'Nice suit. I like it. You smell nice too.'

Well, that was a plus. The overdose of aftershave had gone over well. I couldn't remember what brand I had used, but made a mental note to buy a case of it.

'You look beautiful,' I said. 'Very silver.'

'Dolce and Gabbana.'

Who? Isn't that a law firm?

'They are fashion designers,' said Wilkes, noting my blank response.

'It's from their last collection,' continued Alexandra. 'Fantastic collection too. They did the entire show in silver and black. They flew these pieces in from Milan for me for tonight.'

'They flew clothes in for you? Are you serious? It must have cost a fortune.'

Wilkes again intervened.

'They pick up the tab, Tom.'

'Excuse me?'

'Designers kill to dress celebrities like Alexandra. The publicity for them is unbelievable.'

'Are you saying that Alexandra didn't pay for these clothes, or to have them flown in?'

'Darling, I haven't paid for a stitch of clothing for ten years,' she boasted, pointing to her feet, snug in those silver heels. 'Even these Manolos are freebies.'

I now felt like a complete dope having committed the unpardonable sin of paying for the clothes I was wearing, donning navy instead of silver, and flat shoes instead of free stilettos. But I owned no suits in silver, and I wasn't really a high-heels kind of guy.

'Nervous?' she asked.

'I'd be lying if I said I wasn't.'

'Don't worry. These things are a snap. I do them all the time. Just think of tonight like dancing. I know the dance, so I'll lead. You follow. All you have to remember is not to step on my feet. When I say dip, you dip. When I say spin me around, you spin me around. That's all there is to it.'

I was actually impressed by her dance analogy. Maybe she really wasn't stupid, and I felt ashamed that I had written her off so quickly.

'That's a good analogy. I like it.'

'Thank you.' She seemed genuinely pleased that I commented on it.

'My mother was a dance freak. She and my dad used to go dancing every Saturday night. They don't anymore, not since her hip operation. Ballroom dancing. She was crazy about it. She sewed all the dresses herself and everything. She and my dad know all the steps, the tango, the samba. When I was little we would watch Fred Astaire–Ginger Rogers movies together.

'I have to be honest, I'm a lousy dancer.'

'Well, Tom, I may have to reconsider this entire deal, then.'

The woman had a sense of humor. I was kind of impressed.

'I'll tell you what. It's too late now to find a replacement, so even though you can't dance, I'll still take you to the premiere. Actually, I should put that another way. I'll still let you take me to the premiere. But don't do it again.'

The blond herring laughed out loud at her own comments. Mr Wilkes roared his approval in sync, as if he were hearing the greatest joke ever.

The phone rang and Mr Wilkes informed us the limousine had arrived. Alexandra sat back on the sofa while the hair and make-up people primped and prodded her one more time. She grabbed a bag of some description that was so small I wondered she even bothered, and threw another one of those eerily suspicious, knowing looks at Mr Wilkes.

'We're off. See you later, Michael. I'll talk to you tomorrow.'

Mr Wilkes, assuming the guise of a Cheshire Cat, said nothing, merely nodding in agreement. Alexandra then turned her attentions to me.

'Tom, shall we? It's time.'

That it was. It was time. Time to walk the long road toward Oz, or wherever I was headed, in pursuit of the fame which anointed Edward the Confessor, Ivan the Terrible, Caesar and Antony. Only I was not building an empire, invading a nation, leading a battalion. I was going to the movies. I was glad Edward, Ivan, Caesar and Antony were no longer living. They would have been appalled. I was.

In the elevator Alexandra suggested we hold hands when the doors opened. In fact she urged that we hold them all night, at the movie, at the party, at dinner. She said we should smile at each other a lot, but no other signs of physical affection, because that was tacky. She then admitted she didn't really think it bad, but Mr Wilkes did. He was of the opinion a serious financial writer would always be decorous in public, and any outward display of sexuality would be unprofessional and inappropriate.

Besides, I was supposed to be dating Alexandra for her prodigious mind, and kissing and such would yield no interest to me. I challenge anyone, however, to ride in a luxurious car, big enough to stage a tennis tournament in the back seat, with one of the world's biggest, brightest and, on that evening, most silver of actresses, and think about the federal deficit. Despite my best instincts, I was overwhelmed by the situation, and at that moment horrified that I was totally attracted to her.

When the elevator doors opened onto the lobby, I assumed the position as instructed. Overrun as usual with guests, staff and, on this evening, a bunch of overexcited thirteen-year-olds attending a barmitzvah, I reached out to hold Alexandra's hand. Even if she were nobody of consequence, her appearance would have made heads turn. But once the shock of recognition sank in, and it took no longer than a second, the lobby population were rendered speechless. The barmitzvah boy and his contingent whispered furiously among themselves, convinced they had died and gone to heaven. Murmurs followed us as we walked through the lobby.

'That's Alexandra West!'

'Is it?'

'No, it's not her. It's that other one. That other actress.'

'Yes, it is.'

'Isn't that . . .'

'Everyone, Alexandra West was just out here!'

'You just missed her.'

'No, I swear, I saw her with my own eyes.'

And then finally somebody took note of me.

'Who's that guy she's with?'

'No idea.'

We entered the limo with the voices trailing behind us. I asked Alexandra if that happened often. Only all the time, she shot back. People constantly talked about her within earshot, convinced she heard nothing. Nor were they gracious. Once they had secured her identity, women, she told me, often broke into discussions about whether she was better-looking in person, had put on weight, had surgery or dyed her hair. Many concluded she was not as beautiful in the flesh, a statement, she noted, they made with much joy. Conversation among men was more sexual in tone. A lot more sexual. She said one guy in Hollywood came up to her once at a party and said, riffing on Mae West, 'Hey, baby, this is not a pistol in my pocket, I really am happy to see you. Wanna go for a drive?'

'And did you go?' I asked.

'Are you kidding? He was a writer. What would be the point of that?'

The limousine was so large it could have solved New York's housing problem. I had seen these mobile monsters on the streets but had never been inside one. I asked Alexandra if she felt comfortable traveling this way. In fact I asked lots of questions of her on the way to the premiere, while she asked none of me. I found it odd she never mentioned the article I was writing for *The Vulture*. I found it strange she was not intrigued by the prospect of being an eyewitness to my life changing overnight. It seemed to me she thought my entire presence in her life on that night was a simple business transaction, and there was nothing left to say. Either that or she was collecting herself for the onslaught she knew was waiting for her at the other end. Dutifully she told me no, she thought the car was huge, but fans expected her to be larger than life in all areas of her existence, including arrivals and departures. It was a game she played, she said. Given the other things she'd endured since stardom hit, an oversized car was the least of the concessions required. I wanted to know what these other things were, but opted to save that question for later.

We turned the corner onto Broadway. Turning the limousine took quite a while, with the rear arriving about a day after the front. As we crawled along in heavy traffic, I could see people trying to look inside the car, their efforts thwarted by the tinted glass. We could see them, of course, a rather cruel game, but, Alexandra said, a necessary one.

'Nutcases. You never know who is out there. If we had clear windows and other cars could make us out, they would trail us in traffic forever.'

'Really?' I was incredulous.

'Oh, sure. When I'm driving in my car in LA, if I get spotted, guys follow me for miles. And men you wouldn't suspect either. Not just young guys, but men in suits, men with wedding rings, men who are pushing ninety and shouldn't be on the road anyway.'

'Doesn't it drive you crazy?'

'Once. But not anymore. You get used to it. You wear sunglasses.

You keep your eyes on the road and ignore it.'

I liked her. She was not overtly friendly toward me, but she was honest. Even in the little time I knew her, she was clearly more thoughtful than anyone had given her credit for, including me. She had, it seemed, made peace with her fate, the constant intrusions into her life, the fact that a life of celebrity was full of compromises, the loss of privacy to be stoically endured rather than railed against. While I was digesting all this, the car came to a sudden stop.

The driver, who thought he was a Pan Am pilot, sprinted around to open the door. I looked out of the window to see this crush of people, cameras, videos, fans, and lots of noise. Yelling. Screaming. More yelling. It was chaos. It was insane. I wanted to run and be sick. Alexandra turned to me. She didn't speak. She purred. Suddenly I was happy again.

'Just take my hand and walk me slowly down the carpet.'

There was carpet? Really? Carpet? Ohmigod.

'Don't say anything. Let me do all the talking. When the cameras hit you, smile big. Got it?'

'Yes,' I said, although I hadn't got anything, least of all this was happening to me, and not another person called Tom Webster.

I still don't remember how I got out of the car. I do know that Alexandra went first, and I followed. She grabbed my hand, and the flashbulbs were blinding. The last time I walked down a narrow carpet was at my wedding and we all know how that turned out. As fans threw autograph books and pens in Alexandra's face, and she stopped to accommodate photographers and TV crews, all I could hear were the murmurs again, although this time they were all focused on me. Clearly they knew who Alexandra was.

'Who's the guy?'

'Which guy?'

'The guy with her.'

'I have no clue.'

'I think it's her new boyfriend. I heard someone say it's her new boyfriend.'

'Him? She's dating him? He's so short.'

'That's him? That's the new boyfriend? Christ, look at him.'

We walked a ways along the carpet. I have never fallen into such deep shock while being completely conscious in all my life. Suddenly Alexandra and I stopped to talk to a television reporter. Wasting no time, the reporter cut to the chase.

'And can I ask who you are with, Alexandra?'

She shot me a loving smile. Really. A loving smile. If the press were surprised, you should have seen me.

'This is Tom,' she said.

'And does Tom have a last name?' asked the reporter, giggling.

'He sure does. It's Webster. Tom Webster.'

Still in shock, all I could manage was a feeble smile. No words. Any instant I was convinced I would collapse in a faint. The flashbulbs came in waves. The reporter suddenly became the center of a veritable journalistic huddle, in which many more had gathered. I searched the pack for any faces I might recognize, and was relieved I came up empty-handed. I did not see *über*-fan Charlie either, but I was certain he was there.

'He's just a friend,' she said, winking at them. And then, lowering her voice, she leaned into the pack.

'Please, guys. He's more than a friend but he's very private and I don't want to scare him off. He really didn't want to come tonight, but I begged him.'

The huddle nodded sympathetically.

'Alex, what are you wearing?' cried out a woman all in black standing right at the entrance to the cinema. She had a TV crew in tow.

'Dolce and Gabbana,' she purred, then twirled around to do a full 360.

'And what are you wearing, Tom?' she said to me.

What was I wearing, Tom? She already knew my name? Already what I was wearing was of consequence? I stared desperately at Alexandra.

'What are you wearing Tom?' she whispered frantically.

'I have no idea. I bought it with my wife on sale at Macy's.'

Well, you can imagine how hip that would have sounded on TV. Alexandra knew it too and jumped in before I could open my mouth.

'Tom is wearing Gucci.' She smiled, then pulled me forward to the next throng of reporters.

I hoped the Guccis didn't own a television set or subscribe to any newspapers. We continued into the cinema as other notables arrived and the pack abandoned us for the next wave.

'When you spoke to them just then, asking them to leave us alone, will they?' I asked.

'Are you kidding?' she said. 'I just did that to make sure the opposite happens. We will be all over the papers tomorrow. But that's what you want, right? That's what you need for your article.'

So she did remember I was writing an article. More credit to her. Not only beautiful, she was shrewd as well. Just how shrewd I would learn only later. At this point I had entered a state of delirium that people normally take drugs to induce. Coming into the darkened theater there was, I recall, a lot of air-kissing as Alexandra introduced me around. I shook a lot of hands and repeated my name so many times I sounded like a robot incorrectly wired. The lights went out and the movie began. We held hands, a factor everyone around us noted. I cannot tell you how distracted I was. I barely remember the movie, for I spent the next two hours digesting the first ten minutes of the evening.

It was beautifully shot, however, a period piece about unrequited love at the turn of the century. All the budget appeared to have gone on the costumes, and many women in the audience cried at the end, so I guess someone died but I couldn't say for sure. I have never been so inattentive at a movie in all my life, but I think it was the kind of film Elizabeth would have liked. When the lights went up I noticed Alexandra's eyes were dry.

'What did you think?' I asked her.

'Boring,' she whispered. 'Nearly fell into a coma. But that's his thing. Nothing ever happens in his movies except the women get to wear beautiful clothes. There's never a plot.'

'But I thought you wanted to work with him.'

'Oh, I do,' she said. 'Everyone does. If you even set foot in one of his movies you get nominated for an award.'

Now I understood. We rose, heading back outside. A number of media had left but the fans were just where we had left them. Suddenly I spotted Charlie. He looked directly at me, but it was not to acknowledge our previous meeting. It was the look of complete shock. The kind of look villagers in 450 AD had on their faces when they saw Attila the Hun coming up the hill.

I could see he was trying to put the pieces together, and I wanted to tell him there was no point, because they wouldn't fit. Instead I kept moving as Alexandra waved to the crowd, stopped in front of yet more cameras, this time to gush at how much she loved the movie.

'He's a genius. That's all I can say. His best movie yet. It'll break your heart. I couldn't stop crying at the end.'

My, she really was a good actress. She waved some more and I, suddenly overwhelmed by the situation, waved too. The Pan Am pilot put us back in the car. Next stop. The party. I lingered behind Alexandra as she walked in confidently to a restaurant in SoHo. She kissed everyone, introduced me as Tom Webster, a financial writer at *The Capitalist*, waited just long enough for it to register and then hauled me away, as we continued on her mission of meet and greet.

Sidling up to director James Thurgood, Alexandra gushed about the film, and he thanked her for attending the premiere. Under strict command to say nothing, I kept myself occupied drinking expensive champagne and nibbling little sandwiches that kept coming around. It became obvious early on the party had little to do with celebrating the release of a movie and everything to do with wheeling and dealing.

As a finance writer this I appreciated. Eavesdropping the odd conversation on budgets, overheads and star salaries, I found myself interested and wished I could join in. But Alexandra had me moving around the room with her so fast, I couldn't speak to anybody. We only stopped moving to pose for photographs. Finally Alexandra decreed we must leave and go on to dinner. She told me later she never stayed longer than one hour at those events because she didn't want to become overexposed. I wanted to point out that her entire career was a textbook exercise in overexposure, but thought better of it.

'Always leave them wanting more,' she said.

I made a note of it.

As we left the party, the fans were waiting outside. Alexandra signed autographs and seemed to revel in the attention. Then the most extraordinary thing happened. A woman came forward from the crowd and asked me for my autograph. She was furiously thrusting a pen into my sweaty palm when I threw Alexandra a desperate stare.

'What do I do?' I whispered.

'Sign it.'

'Why?'

She shrugged.

'Why not?'

To this day I still don't understand what made me do it. I signed her autograph book. 'Tom Webster,' that's all I wrote. Alexandra said later I should have written, 'Best wishes, Tom Webster,' but I felt enough damage had been done. Back in the limo I asked why they would have wanted my autograph.

'They had no clue who I was. I'm nobody.'

'Wrong, Tom. You're not nobody. You're with me. And I'm somebody. And now that makes you somebody too.'

Heaven help me. Ms MacDowell was right.

Chapter 13

I lost all track of time at this stage. I think now it was around ten p.m. but I couldn't be sure. I do know we arrived at a restaurant on Park Avenue and my hopes that we would enter quietly were dashed the minute the car pulled up to the entrance. A number of paparazzi and what Alexandra called videorazzi were waiting, and Charlie and company were there in full force. Didn't these people have lives? Day jobs? Husbands or wives? How could they simply follow stars from event to event?

More cameras. More flashbulbs. The maître d' bowed and scraped when we moved inside, a factor that made me distinctly uncomfortable. Life really was different once you had penetrated the celebrity stratosphere. People walked on their knees, instead of on their feet, around you. Nobody disagreed with you. Nothing was ever too much trouble. You could send dishes back to the kitchen as many times as you wished and waiters did not walk back to the chef with your food, they danced.

I was not naïve. I was aware this happened, but to witness and experience it at such proximity provides a new perspective on the fame game. To her credit, Alexandra did not abuse her power. She ordered wine and food and ate it without pause. I was still in such shock over the entire evening I cannot remember what I ordered or if I ate it. I do remember a slew of waiters hovering like bees, asking every thirty seconds if everything was all right. They seemed disappointed when we constantly reassured them it was.

They wanted to do more, and we wouldn't let them.

One thing I did learn that evening was, one of the immutable social laws of New York dining is never to stare at a celebrity. Once the arrival has been registered, you are never to look in the direction of the victim again. To do so would be a major faux pas, and the diners at this establishment would rather die a thousand deaths than be thought social misfits. Once the food arrived, we were left to our own devices. It was during this one-hour window that I decided to ask Alexandra a number of questions. Instead she beat me to the punch.

'How are you holding up?' she asked.

'How do you think?'

'Well, you were shell-shocked early on, but you seem to be doing fine now.'

'I don't feel fine.'

'Fake it. Everybody does. I'm not crazy about those premieres either. But you go, you smile, you take photos, you get the hell out of there.'

'And you go because...'

'If you go to their premieres, they owe you. Then they come to yours. And the more people at all the openings, the more press, the more buzz, you know... That's how it works.'

'Alexandra?'

'Yes.'

'I don't wish to be intrusive, but for the purposes of my article, I would like to ask you a couple of questions. Do you mind?'

'Shoot.'

Good. I had her attention. Now all I had to do was think of the questions. Earlier that day I had many. Now of course my mind was blank.

'I watched your movies, but in truth I haven't followed your career all that closely. I will of course be reading everything I can about you, but in twenty-five words or less, can you bring me up to speed?'

'Sure.'

The waiter arrived again to check that everything was to our satisfaction. I don't think he cared if it was or not, he just wanted another opportunity to stare at Alexandra in the flesh. He was doing a fine job of it too. But Alexandra indicated he could leave, and he nearly cried as he retreated.

'I was born in New Jersey. My parents are strictly blue collar. Dad works in a chemical plant. One sister, Alison. We don't get on that great. It's a long story. I won't bore you with it. I developed early. Like I was five feet nine when I was thirteen, and I felt like a freak. Physically everything happened early too. That's great now, but when I was a teenager I couldn't get a date. I was taller than all the boys, none of them wanted to go near me. I sat home a lot of Saturday nights. Nobody believes me, but it's true.'

'And you always wanted to be an actress?'

'Not at all. I still don't even know if I want to be one some days. What happened was I was shopping at a mall when a man approached me and asked if I was a model. I laughed at him, but he gave me his card and told me to call him.'

'And you called.'

'Not at first. Then I got my driver's license and wanted a car. My mom said if I wanted one I could work for one, they weren't a bank. Usual stuff parents say to kids to try and teach them that money doesn't grow on trees.'

'My parents did the same thing to me.'

'So I called the name on the card. I thought, modeling might be fun. It can't be worse than flipping burgers. Anyway, first came catalogues, parades at malls, then I went to New York one day to meet an agent at one of the big agencies, and they signed me, and that was it.'

'That was it?'

'Sort of. First they made me go on a diet. They told me to join a gym. They had me dye my hair much lighter so they could sell me as the California beach girl. I don't have that sophisticated New York look, you know, dark hair, dark eyes, so my agent suggested I move to LA, where I could make more money.'

'And school?'

'I dropped out in eleventh grade. I hated school and I was making so much money... I mean, how much money were you making in eleventh grade?'

'$60 a week bagging groceries.'

'Yeah, well I was making $1,000 a week.'

I dropped my fork. For that kind of money I would have dyed

my hair blond, dropped out of school, put on a bikini and moved to California too.

'So what else do you need to know?'

'What happened in Los Angeles?'

'My photos ran in *Los Angeles* magazine, and this acting agent called my modeling agent and asked if he could represent me.'

'Just like that? Why? How did he know you could act?'

'He didn't. He liked my pictures. That's how it works now.'

'I see.'

'So the acting agent started sending me on auditions, and I have to admit it was fun. I mean, I had done a couple of school plays so it wasn't like I didn't know anything about acting.'

Now I knew what I was dealing with. Alexandra was an actress who felt no shame about putting down the fact she played a pilgrim in the third-grade Thanksgiving concert on her résumé. More power to her.

'You learn your lines. You go in. You say them. And that's how it started. Of course, there is a lot of competition out there, you know.'

'How so?'

'Well, in my high school I was, and I am not being vain about this, I was the prettiest girl there. In Hollywood everyone is pretty. Eventually you have to find something that makes you stand out.'

'And you found . . . ?'

'I bleached my hair even more blond. I had some surgery. Big deal. Everybody does.'

'And I am assuming smaller parts led to bigger ones and then . . .'

'And then the whole world wants a piece of you. You wake up one day and you see your face on magazine covers, and producers offer you bags of money to be in their films and fan letters start arriving and, I don't know, it sort of happens to you without your permission almost.'

'But you seem to enjoy it.'

'Some days. I like making movies. I like making money. I'm not complaining. I get good service in places like this. I can travel. I can buy nice clothes. I bought my parents a house. The only thing that pisses me off is men.'

'Men?'

'Like when I fall in love with one, I never know if they love me or Alexandra West.'

'You make it sound like they are two separate people.'

'They are.'

Alexandra threw me a giant smile. It was soft and genuine, not like the one she plastered on for the media earlier.

'It's nice to talk to you, Tom. You're a good listener. Nobody really cares what I think or what I have to say. They just keep me moving around, shooting films, signing autographs. Men just want to fuck me. They never just want to talk.'

At this juncture I felt it best to say what was on my mind all along.

'Alexandra, you know, I mean, what I want to say is, well, the way you look, you know... the calendars, *Playboy* layouts, the movies...'

'I know. I created the monster and now I have to live with it. I understand that, but after ten years it starts to have its downside.'

'And that's why the move to New York?'

'That and I turned thirty last year.'

'I remember thirty. I was not thrilled about it. But let me tell you, forty is worse.'

'I hope to never get there.' She laughed. 'On my thirtieth birthday I woke up totally depressed. I thought, shit, my twenties are gone, what now? And that was it. I was bored. I wanted more. I know nobody thinks I can do Shakespeare, and I don't want to, but I knew if I ever wanted to do anything other than burning-building movies, I had to get out of LA. I am not going to feed you the usual bullshit about needing to stretch. I don't pretend to have Meryl Streep inside me busting to get let out. I just want a job that requires me to think a bit and wear a few more clothes. In LA they have me pegged as a mattress.'

'A mattress?'

'Model turned actress. Also known as a bimbo, a ditz, you know.'

I truly felt sorry for her. Honestly. She seemed to have a keen awareness of how she had exploited the system, but nevertheless wanted some breathing space.

I rose to go the bathroom. Once inside I was cornered by a man who introduced himself as Paul. Just Paul, Paul from a supermarket tabloid, *Celebrity Scene*. I think approaching people in bathrooms simply to shoot the breeze is uncalled for, but requesting an interview is downright rude. He wanted to know who I was, where I met her, how serious it was. I asked him if he always conducted his interviews at urinals. He answered he was operating under strict instructions to get a story, and cared little where the exchange took place. I asked him to leave. He refused. I informed him I would not say anything and he was wasting his time. He stayed. I said nothing. I returned to my table.

'I was just cornered in the bathroom by a reporter.'

'Oh, yeah, I should have warned you that might happen.'

'You're kidding, right?'

'No.'

'But it's so sick. In a bathroom?'

'Anywhere. They're real persistent. He'll probably follow you home.'

'Are you serious?'

'Serious as a heart attack. Tom, those guys are like roaches. They're everywhere and they never die.'

We rose and I was somewhat confused about the check. Did I pay? Did she pay? As it was, we left and nobody paid. Later I learned we had been comped, which meant given a free meal. In exchange, the restaurant called the media to inform them Alexandra was there, which meant their name splashed in news items around the country. You can't buy that kind of publicity, I was informed.

The limousine dropped us back at the Waldorf. I escorted her upstairs in full view of the lobby population which had somewhat decreased in size from earlier that evening. At the door to her suite she made it clear that I would not be invited inside.

'Tom, really, it was fun. You're a nice guy. Nice meeting you. Hope this helps your article. Send me a copy. Safe trip home, okay?'

And that was it. She went inside. I returned to the street, where six hours earlier this insanity had begun. A porter hailed me a cab. On the way home I was mute, even though the driver worked hard at making conversation.

Back inside my apartment I kicked off my shoes, tore off the jacket, loosened the tie. It went all right, I thought. I didn't make a complete fool of myself, did I? Not that I had much of a chance as I barely spoke to anyone. Thank God it's over. What now? Now, Tom? Now, I just wait for everybody's reaction, write the article, collect the money and get on with my life. Simple, but then not so. Oh, what a tangled web we weave, you know the rest.

Thankfully, the Sunday *New York Herald* made no mention of the premiere. In a supreme effort to compensate for the oversight, every other newspaper in town went berserk. My photograph was everywhere. I did not know this at first. I rose early, after a night of fitful sleep, and went to my local deli to buy the *Herald*, some milk, some bagels. The man behind the counter, a man, I might add, who has ignored me for years, stood to attention when I walked in, wished me a good morning and then winked. Winked. My God, what was happening? I grabbed the *Herald*, my purchases, and headed for the counter. He leaned over towards me.

'You don't want the other papers?' he asked.

'I don't want them. Why do you ask?'

'You're in them. It is you, isn't it?'

I dropped everything and ran to grab the other papers. Furiously turning pages, I finally landed on firm photographic evidence that the previous evening had not been a dream. There I was, arm in arm with Alexandra. Not only that, there were captions, stories about us, our relationship. I skimmed everything like a maniac, paid and rushed out and back into the safety of my apartment. And all I could think about at that instant, I have to admit was this: Tom, you don't take a bad photo.

I looked kind of okay... even, well, not handsome, but not ugly. Napoleonic. The photos were nice, given they were grainy and black and white. But my mood changed swiftly after I read the articles that accompanied the pictures. Not that they were bad, but they were nothing I expected. And when I say nothing, I mean nothing.

At least the *New York Review* spelled my name correctly. In a caption underneath our photograph, readers learned that sex symbol Alexandra West attended the premiere of James Thurgood's new movie with her 'main squeeze' Tom Webster, their words, not mine. That was it. But in a lengthy summary of the event alongside photos of the party a columnist explained to anyone who cared that I was a serious, highbrow financial writer, a Yalie who worked at *The Capitalist* and that Ms West and I had been an item for three months now. This was certainly news to me. Sources had told the columnist that we were 'serious', that Ms West told friends she was relieved to have finally met a man who saw beyond her body.

The *Sunday Dispatch*, however, went one better. Their sources had informed them that Ms West and I had been meeting furtively for six months no less, and that I was the key reason she had decamped to New York. Extracting much mileage out of our dissimilar appearances, the writer said our relationship was a classic Marilyn Monroe–Arthur Miller match-up. You know, beauty and the brains. The article suggested we were in fact the reincarnation of Marilyn and Arthur, and I must admit had it not been about me I would have found the article most entertaining. It never explained how we met, but confidently informed its readers I had told friends in the business world that no one understood the real Alexandra, who was highly intelligent and read voraciously. That I loved her for who she was, that our days were filled with deep discussions about politics and economics. I also apparently told my 'friends' that as soon as my divorce came through I intended to marry her. More news to me.

The *Sunday Observer* also went heavily on the Marilyn Monroe–Arthur Miller angle, and had even sidetracked into a little pop psychology. Their columnist suggested that it was understandable that the fantasy women of our culture tend to fall for serious guys like myself. She said Alexandra could trust no one anymore, but with me she felt safe. How she knew this I could not ascertain. In all, I had been described as strong, intelligent and serious. Clearly the fingerprints of Mr Wilkes were all over this, and I felt an arrest was in order. Still, if Alexandra's association with me had conferred upon her some of the serious, brooding, intelligent, silent qualities I was said to possess, I was only too happy to oblige. You are the company you keep, Tom, said Ms MacDowell.

While absorbing the insanity of the situation the phone rang. It was Jake.

'Tom, what the hell? Have you seen the papers? Can you

explain this to me? I'm in shock, buddy. Elizabeth nearly passed out. What the hell, Tom!'

I was delirious. Elizabeth knew. She saw the papers. Thank you, Alexandra. Your check is in the mail.

There was another call. I told Jake I would put him on hold and get back to him. It was Paul. The same Paul who cornered me in the bathroom the previous evening.

'Mr Webster, this is Paul. From *Celebrity Scene*. We met last night.'

'Paul, hi. I haven't forgotten meeting you but I am on another call.'

'Please, I need one minute. The papers went big today on you and Alexandra. I need a new angle. I just want to ask you some questions. Is it true you intend to marry her?'

'I'm on another call.'

'She says it is.'

'She? Who's she?'

'Alexandra, I just spoke to Michael Wilkes. He said you two were madly in love, that he had never seen Alexandra happier. He said he wouldn't confirm anything about a wedding, but suggested I call you.'

I nearly dropped the phone. Twenty-four hours ago I was her date. Twelve hours ago I was her beau. One hour ago I was her main squeeze. Now I was in love with her, and she with me.

'Paul, I have no comment about a wedding. No comment about anything.'

I hung up the phone, forgetting Jake was still waiting in shock on the other end. I grabbed my keys, turned off the lights and headed outside into the fresh air of Central Park to clear my brain. I could hear the phone ringing as I waited for the elevator. Now I was in love? I had really only loved one woman in my life, and she had broken my heart. Now I was in love again, a player in one of the most interesting celebrity match-ups since Miss Monroe and Mr Miller. Mr Wilkes was spreading the word she loved me. This was not part of our agreed plan, and I was not impressed. Particularly because I take the whole idea of love, its very nature, its practice, very, very, very seriously. I do not fall in love on a weekly basis. I do not give women false hope and fill their hearts with empty promises.

When I say I love you, it's because I truly mean it. And if I said it to Alexandra, I certainly wouldn't repeat it to a newspaper reporter. But once in print, an idea takes root in a way that is impossible to kill. I know that better than anybody. So here I was. In love with a movie star and readying myself to wed her. Do you, Tom, take Alexandra to be your lawfully wedded wife, to have and to hold, etc., etc., from this day forward? Even though I didn't remember it, this is what I apparently said.

I do.

Chapter 14

The fresh air felt wonderful. I was back at the site of my previous attempt to whip myself into shape, though this time I wisely chose to forgo the earlier humiliation of jogging. I walked around and around in circles, my mind racing. Chaos. I tried telling myself to relax and enjoy the ride. I tried telling myself this had not really happened to me, that it was merely a work obligation that would soon be terminated. Most of all I kept wondering how I could have been so stupid not to anticipate the fallout.

It now appeared I walked zombie-like through the entire ordeal, failing to make follow-up plans. The media wanted answers. Jake wanted answers. Colleagues would want them when I appeared at work. This was all well and good, except for one minor problem. I had no answers. Nothing smart and witty, no repartee honed in advance to brush off the incident, to confidently take it in my stride. Now I knew why Ms MacDowell was paying me $100,000. It wasn't for the article. It was for the pain and suffering and the time I would be doing on the couch. You've heard of milk money? Well, this was shrink money.

Two hours later I returned to my apartment, hoping to sit and brood on the big red lips. But there was the small issue of sneaking past my doorman first. No luck. Hector was waiting for me, beaming as if hooked up to a generator. He made it clear I would not be allowed to rush into the elevator as I planned.

'Mr Webster.'

'Hector.'

'Good morning.'

'Thank you. Good morning to you too.'

'Mr Webster?'

'Yes, Hector.'

'Some people came by. They wanted to talk to you. They had cameras.'

'I see.'

'Yes, Mr Webster. So I buzzed you, but you didn't answer.'

'I was out.'

'That's what I told them. But that's not all. Later I found a man out the front going through the garbage cans.'

'How sad.'

'No. No. He wasn't homeless. He was one of the ones with a camera. He was going through the trash. Your trash. He found an envelope addressed to you in one of the bags, and then went through the rest of the stuff like a scientist. You know, real careful.'

'And what did you do?'

'He was making a huge mess, Mr Webster, and I asked him to leave. He laughed at me. He said I would be interfering with his right to free speech if I tried to stop him looking through your trash.'

Oh, that was a good one. When you can't think of anything else to say, hide behind the First Amendment.

'He was with the press, I am assuming.'

'Yes, Mr Webster. I assumed so too.'

'Did he find anything?'

'Nothing. And he was mad. After he rebagged your trash I asked him what he was looking for.'

'And?'

'You'll never believe it, Mr Webster.'

'I won't?'

'No.'

'Well?'

'Condoms. He was looking for condoms.'

'What?????'

'He said they help him figure out where to wait. Where to wait for a photo. He said if they were in your trash, it meant that she

116

was sleeping at your place. Because there were none, it meant you were sleeping at hers.'

I cannot tell you how embarrassed and sickened I was at that moment to be having that particular conversation with Hector, one he would surely repeat to his wife, and from there I knew it would blanket their Brooklyn neighborhood.

'Hector. I am so sorry you had to deal with those people this morning.'

'Actually, Mr Webster, it was fine. The job, you know, the job gets kind of boring. This morning the time just flew.'

I'll bet it did. I guessed he had seen the papers. A quick glance behind his desk confirmed my suspicions. They were all there. One was even still open at the page which bore my photo.

'Hector?'

'Yes, sir.'

'If anyone else calls by, anyone, please tell them I am not home. Don't even buzz.'

'Of course not, sir.'

Well, this was new. He was calling me sir. Isn't that what everyone called King Henry VIII? Next thing he would be addressing me as Your Highness. What I didn't know then, but learned soon after, was that far from protecting me from the photographers who set up camp outside my front door, he had climbed into bed with them. Each had slipped him a 100 bucks and a business card. In return, if ever Ms West appeared at the building, he was to phone them. Now, I have no intrinsic problem with doormen moonlighting on the black market, except of course if they are trafficking in my affairs.

The answering machine was blinking furiously. I do not believe I received as many messages cumulatively in my entire life as I did that day. Many of them were from Jake, reporters from magazines, Jake again, my mother and even one from Ms MacDowell. No Elizabeth. Well, not yet. I was sure she would bite.

'Tom. It's Jamie. MacDowell. From *The Vulture*. I just wanted to call and say well done! Brilliant! You're a genius! Good work and congratulations. No need to call back.'

The rest were neither as brief nor as joyous. Everyone else was in a state of shock, and made no attempt to hide it. Jake's messages became more frantic with each call. Mom called to say friends in New York had called her to say my face was all over the papers, pictures of me with a movie star. My mom being of your classic variety, just wanted to know that I was all right. Call and let me know that you are okay, honey, she said. That Paul character left a message too.

Other reporters, some talking about money, big money, requested I talk to them exclusively about my relationship with Alexandra. Tabloid TV news shows left messages. It was astounding. I pulled the telephone out of the wall. I would not take any more calls that day, nor return any. Instead I would sit on the big red lips and sulk and brood and ask myself why I felt so awful when I should have been feeling fantastic. Resolving that the entire day should not go to waste, I grabbed a pen and paper and began writing down what I was feeling. These notes would be crucial, I told myself, when it came to writing my piece. When I was done I turned on the television.

Baseball. Thank God. It was a boring game but I watched it anyway. Despite my instructions, Hector buzzed me a number of times throughout the day, and I ignored him each and every time. Instead, all I could think about were condoms. Condoms, for godsakes. They were looking for proof we were having sex, so they could dutifully report it to their faithful readership. I was horrified. This much I thought, however. You may question their methods, but boy, they were good. Damned good. And fast too. I grabbed the notebook again and scribbled some lines about the incident with the trash. That would certainly add some kick to my piece. In fact, if nothing more shocking happened, and why would it, I'd use the frantic search for evidence of foreplay, afterplay and duringplay in my opening paragraph. Little did I know.

Chapter 15

I slept, if you can call it that. I showered, shaved and dressed for work the following day in my standard work uniform, beige pants, navy jacket, white shirt. I thought if I went through the motions as if it were simply another day, maybe it would be. On the subway I could not look anyone in the eye. Sadly, in New York, this is not difficult to achieve. Nobody looks at anyone anymore as we speed on underground, fearful a smile, a raised eyebrow, will be misconstrued and gunfire will result.

Normally I find the silence of morning rush hour rather depressing, that a group of people who all share the same city, same government, same mode of transportation, fear any human connection. That morning, however, I was thrilled that the specter of violence on the subway had risen so high over the years that nobody dared acknowledge my presence.

At *The Capitalist*, however, the subway scenario was not to be repeated. Was I more self-conscious that day, or was everybody looking at me differently? Probably both. Just take it all down, I told myself. It's all source material. The minute I walked through the security check I felt all eyes upon me. I uttered a few wimpish good mornings and raced to my desk. Even so, I could not miss my co-workers' reactions. The facial expressions were not the usual, oh-it's-Tom, it was, I-saw-you-in-the-paper-with-that-babe-and-I-*can't-believe-it*.

Everyone raised eyebrows, craned their necks, discreetly used their index fingers to point out I had arrived. Thankfully nobody spoke. Within minutes the entire editorial floor knew I was present, though not one word was uttered. Incredible what people can say in total silence.

The silence did not last. It was broken eventually by my desk neighbor, Frank Wicker-Smith III. I had long ago come to the conclusion Frank Wicker-Smith was the biggest WASP in America and after sitting next to him for three years I was without a doubt. Of him I knew this. He had married a perky blond of similar country-club background and had the requisite 2.4 children, one of which was Frank Wicker-Smith IV.

Frank lived in Connecticut, commuted to work by train and stuck to his own kind. We were cordial, but never more. Frank had gone to Harvard, which he declared, using various digs, was superior to Yale. I'm sure what he thought made it superior was the fact that he went there. Frank had this air about him, this born-to-rule superiority that Simon also displayed. He was not a particularly smart writer either, which led me to believe he was hired only because of his penchant for suspenders, pinstripe shirts and horn-rimmed glasses. Frank looked exactly like the kind of person who would work at *The Capitalist*, and you should know that editors sometimes experience these lapses in judgment, and recruit as if casting a film instead of running a magazine.

'Morning, Tom,' he said.

'Frank.'

'Have a good weekend?'

It wasn't the question you understand, it was the *tone*. His tone. Oh yes, he had seen the papers.

'Fine, thank you.'

I was brief and to the point. I opened the *New York Herald* and started with the foreign section. I read that the Russians had embraced capitalism so heartily they had dispensed with the economics of the white market and gray market, moving directly to the black. Inflation in Moscow had become a problem so fast, the Russians hadn't even found time to invent a word for it. They called it *inflatzia*. I seriously wanted to read on, but Frank couldn't leave it at that.

'Tom, I have to tell you, buddy...'

Buddy? He was my buddy? I was his buddy? Well, this was interesting.

'You've certainly raised a few eyebrows about the place this morning.'

'Really?'

'Oh, come on. Don't act surprised. We all saw the papers.'

'I see.'

'Well, out with it, then. What's the deal? How did you meet her? Are you really dating her?'

Frank had never asked so many questions of me so eagerly. Suddenly I enjoyed the thought of denying him any response.

'Frank. I really can't talk about her. Or us. Sorry.'

This was the first time I joined Mr Wilkes and Alexandra in the lie they had assembled. I admitted there was an 'us', just as had been reported, and I still don't know what made me do it. Yes, I do. It was the idea of sending Frank Wicker-Smith III completely crazy.

'What's the big secret, buddy?'

'No secret. None at all. It's just that, well, Frank, I have never discussed my private life with you before, so don't you think it would be a little strange to start now?'

Frank's finer breeding kicked in at this point. He backed off, for WASPs hate nothing more than to be told they lack manners. The conversation was over before it began anyway, for I was saved by the bell. A phone call from Louis's secretary, Marlene, summoned me to his office. Immediately. As I breezed past her, she smiled at me, displaying all her teeth. Like a horse almost. I was not dreaming. Marlene, who everybody agreed wore skirts way too tight, had never acknowledged me like this before. She told me to go right in.

Louis was in fine form. Grinning like the cat who ate the canary. Chewing on a bagel, clutching a styrofoam cup of coffee with his chubby little fingers, he didn't even bother with greetings. He motioned for me to sit down and, with a mouth full of food, started in.

'Tommy, I can't tell you how many calls we had this morning. About you. About the magazine. I hope you don't mind, but I talked to some of the reporters. The TV guys want to film pieces

121

outside the building. What could I say? It's a free country, right? I didn't tell them anything incriminating, so don't worry. Just that you worked here, I respected you very much, as did everybody, and that you were a very private, intense guy. Right? Because you are, right? I told them to make sure they mentioned *The Capitalist*. Hope you don't mind.'

'No, I don't.'

What else could I say?

'Listen, Tommy. I never meddle in the lives of my writers. Live and let live, right? Right. I don't care who you sleep with, Alexandra West or the lady who cleans my house. I really don't. But I have to say, I'm glad it's not the lady who cleans my house. The publicity for us has just been unbelievable! Incredible! Could boost sales. I mean, you understand I had to talk to the guys who called, don't you?'

'Oh, sure.'

'Tommy, listen to me. What you do in your own time is none of my business. But I have to ask. You don't have to answer. Where did you meet her? I mean, we're talking Alexandra West here! This is the big time, Tommy. That calendar of hers, whoa! She's an industry. Anyway, that's besides the point now. Tommy, I hope I don't offend you when I say she doesn't seem like the kind of woman you would date.'

'No offense taken.'

'I mean, I know your wife left you and all, and when that happens some guys just spin out, but, you know, I don't know. Tommy, I've got to tell you, I opened the papers yesterday and I thought I was back in college smoking pot.'

I had to laugh. I liked Louis, I always had. He was larger than life, never without a cigar or a bagel held captive in his hands. He loved money, loved Wall Street and got excited in a way that most men save for the bedroom when the stock market took a huge dip, or a mogul got indicted. When Simon went down, Louis had an orgasm.

He was amiable, but, make no mistake, he ran our office with an iron will. I saw Louis Goldberg as the Wall Street counterpart of Louis XIV. *L'état c'est moi*, the French king famously once said. *I am the state*. In our office, Louis Goldberg (sans the silly wig) was the state too. He made the laws, we followed them.

I always thought Louis liked me. Ten years is a long time to work for someone, but even so, we had never been so chatty before, so buddy-buddy. It seemed his respect for me had grown overnight, that he felt wrong to have pegged me as quiet, reserved and predictable. I always felt, of course, that these were my finer qualities, but they do not get you invited into the editor's office on Monday morning to shoot the breeze. Nor do they get secretaries in skirts two sizes too small to bat their eyelids in your direction. Nor do they make your colleagues sit up and notice you for the first time in years. I have to say, I was kind of enjoying the attention. Oh, what the hell. I was completely enjoying the attention.

'Louis,' I said.

He stopped chewing, as if I were about to divulge some top-secret information.

'If you promise not to say anything...'

'Sure, sure.'

'Well, I'll tell you this much.'

'Tommy, it's none of my business. Whatever you want to say, fine. If you want to say nothing, fine with me too. Whatever.'

He tried to act casual, but his body language gave him away. He couldn't stand it anymore and leaned across his desk. I had to tell him something, and as Mr Wilkes had failed to provide me with a decent story to explain our meeting, I realized I would have to invent one myself. There was no time like the present, and I could in fact test it out on Louis. If he bought the story, I would simply retell it. Now I just had to figure out what it was. Believe me when I tell you I was making it up as I went along.

'It's not as serious as the papers say, Louis. You know how they always go overboard.'

'Oh, sure. Sure I do.'

'In fact, we met only a couple of times before the film premiere.'

My first lie.

'We met through her publicist, Michael Wilkes. He used to be in public relations for one of the studios (God, I hope he doesn't ask me which one) and we talked a couple of times a month. He would give me background for stories on movie deals, studio mergers, stuff like that.'

'Sure. Sure.'

My God, I think Louis is buying it.

'Then he went into business for himself two years ago, representing actors. More money in it, he told me. Anyway, we lost touch, you know how that happens, then a couple of weeks ago I was jogging in Central Park and we met up again.'

So far so good, although Louis did look me over to see the results of the jogging. He could find none.

'Alexandra moved here from Los Angeles, she was sick of all the trashy movies they put her in, and she became his client. And then this premiere thing came up, and she and her boyfriend just split, and she didn't want to go alone.'

'Of course not.'

Louis not only bought my story, he was most sympathetic.

'She was complaining that there were no decent guys out there, and he said, well, you know, I just ran into one a few days ago. He meant me.'

My third lie.

'Of course he did.'

'He told her that I was this solid, serious guy who never misquoted him, always played fair with the facts. Said I was a real Southern gentleman.'

'So?'

Louis was now egging me on. I have to admit I was rather enjoying myself.

'So she asked to meet me. When he called, I thought it was a joke. But it wasn't. We had a drink one night after work, and then she called and asked me to the premiere. That's it. End of story.'

Fourth and biggest lie. It really wasn't a great story but given the time I had to prepare, I thought it went over pretty well.

'So all that stuff about love and marriage and ...'

'I don't know where they got that from.'

'But you do like her?'

'Who wouldn't?'

And that was the truth. Who wouldn't like her? Barbie dolls traditionally were not my type, but he didn't have to know that.

'So, what's she like?'

Louis was practically foaming at the mouth.

'Nice. Really nice. And very different to what you would expect. Smart. Well read.'

I thought if Alexandra wanted to use me to realign her image it was my solemn duty to help.

'So is it official? Are you dating?'

Now that I couldn't answer. I couldn't say no because Louis would have been crestfallen. This guy suddenly knew someone who dated a movie star. He was enjoying being associated with me just as much as I was starting to enjoy the association with her. People did treat you differently when they thought you were somebody. I was starting to sense this now. I couldn't deny him his little fantasy then and there. Nor could I tell him the entire date was a set-up, which he would soon read about in *The Vulture* some months hence. I doubted once the magazine hit the stands, complete with our conversation regurgitated for the piece, our future would be quite so cordial.

'I think that's all I want to say at this point, Louis.'

'Sure. Sure. I understand. Hope it works out for you, Tommy, I really do.'

He rose and I rose and we walked to the door.

'You're not offended, are you?'

'Offended?'

'All that stuff I said about my thinking I was on drugs when I read you were dating her. Now that you have explained to me what she is really like, well, it's not a shock anymore. But you, serious guy that you are, in the beginning the idea of you two together just didn't, you know, fit.'

Oh, Louis, I wanted to say. If you thought the pairing strange, you should only know what I think. Instead I said nothing and returned to my desk. I checked my messages. Nine calls in ten minutes, including two from Jake. The rest from tabloid news reporters. Newly confident after my dress rehearsal with Louis, I was now ready to take on Jake, *mano a mano*.

'It's me,' I said as he picked up the phone.

'Jesus, Tom. Did you know your phone is out of order? I called all night but the exchange said the line was down.'

'It wasn't down. I ripped it out of the wall.'

'Why?'

'Reporters. Wanting to talk to me.'

'Well, they're not alone. Do you want to tell me what's going on? I mean, I thought I was your best friend, for crying out loud.'

Well, I mused, maybe we should amend that title slightly. Are you my best friend? Best friends do not steal each other's wives. You are still my closest friend, but I'm not sure you're the best.

'I can't talk now. Meet me for lunch at the Blue Moon at one.'

'Tom, I'm sure there is a really great story to all this and I can't wait to hear it.'

'I'll fill you in on everything,' I promised.

Yet there was one matter I had to deal with before hanging up.

'Jake, just tell me this. What did Elizabeth say?'

'Who?'

'Elizabeth. My wife. Your girlfriend. Remember her?'

'She . . . she . . . Tom, I'd never seen her like that before.'

'Like what?'

'Like, she didn't stop talking about you all day. She kept hassling me to call you. She was mad. It was like she hadn't given you permission to date anyone else and was furious that you had.'

'Okay. See you at one.'

I was purposely cool in response, but what I really wanted at that moment was to jump into the air and scream, Yes! She was mad! She was shocked! She was jealous! Yes! Suddenly, for the first time in months, I felt so happy, so elated, so, I don't know really how to describe it, I thought, I suspected, like Louis the day before, drugs were involved.

The second I put down the phone it rang again. Marlene of the short, tight skirt was on the phone. She said I was to drop into the photo department 'when you have the chance, Tom' to have a photograph taken. From now on Louis would no longer simply run my byline with my column, but a photograph of me as well. This was a canny move on his part. Instead of informing your readers that a column they are digesting was written by a faceless, if well-educated writer, why not point out the guy also takes bubble baths with a celebrity blond?

Louis's brain had gone from first gear to fifth in an instant. Shrewd and lewd, but you can't fault his style. *The Capitalist* was a magazine that made money telling other people how to make money. Now presented with an opportunity to make more money, it would be sacrilege to ignore it. Later that day I would also learn that my column would be bumped further forward in the magazine, and that my name would also appear on the cover. 'Tom Webster – the Insider' it would tease.

It was the royal treatment for a guy who writes 800 words every week on whether interest rates will rise or fall. It was, in short, ridiculous, destined to create enemies among my colleagues and uncalled for. But it was, come to think of it, the most fun I'd had on a Monday morning in ten years of coming to work.

Chapter 16

Even the guys at the Blue Moon looked at me differently. Jealousy, a new-found respect, I couldn't be sure. The waiters smiled at me with an enthusiasm above and beyond the usual. I arrived early and, after slipping into a booth, witnessed a cook emerge from the kitchen, stare at me and retreat. The Mexican busboy winked as he placed water on the table.

Jake arrived clutching the previous day's papers. I have no idea why he needed to bring evidence. I was there and knew exactly what had gone on. Maybe he felt I would be unable to deny it when faced with proof. We ordered and Jake immediately got to the point.

'I'm not saying anything. The stage is all yours. Talk. Now. Go.'

Quickly I rattled off the identical story I had delivered to Louis. With the second telling I became more bold and confident, even embroidering here and there. But in essence it was the same tale. We met through her publicist. She complained bitterly about the dearth of nice guys on the planet. He introduced me to her to prove her wrong. We had drink, we clicked. Then she asked me to the premiere. No, we are not in love, although there is a connection there. No, we are not getting married. Yes, she is as beautiful in person. Yes, they are implants. Yes, she does read books and is on the whole far more intelligent than given credit for. I had told the truth and lied in equal measure.

'Okay. I'm fine with all that. Now do you want to tell me why the secret? I didn't even think you were dating anyone, and then I find out you are, and it's with her! A movie star! Why couldn't you tell me? Tom, I was really hurt I had to read it in the papers.'

I'm sure he was, but Ms MacDowell had absolutely forbidden me to speak to him. His reaction, I wanted to tell him, which I was currently filing for future reference, was absolutely crucial to the piece. Ms MacDowell had decreed that fame changes not only the subject, but those in their immediate orbit.

'Jake, I'm sorry. I really don't know what to say. It happened very fast. She called me about the premiere with hours to spare. You were in Philadelphia with Elizabeth. I couldn't exactly call you there and say, guess where I am going tonight?'

'Okay. But what about the drink? You had a drink with her and never mentioned it.'

'Well, for one thing I didn't think you would believe me.'

'Sure I would. Why wouldn't I?'

I was struggling here. Jake was getting angry, turning rather prosecutorial in tone. Why had I not mentioned the drink we had enjoyed? Well, in part because it never happened. I ploughed on and hoped my flimsy excuse would stick.

'Jake, the truth is . . .'

'Yes.'

'She asked me not to.'

'What do you mean she asked you not to?'

'She asked me not to talk to anyone about our meeting. She said she was sick of having an innocent drink with a man and reading overblown gossip about it the next day. So she made me promise to tell no one.'

'I'm not no one,' he shot back. 'I've known you since the second grade. We went to camp together. We smoked our first cigarettes together. I was best man at your wedding.'

He was indeed my best man, though I failed to see him in the same light since he absconded with my bride.

'She made me swear I would say nothing. I was going to tell you, I guess I felt strange about it. I'm sorry. I didn't mean to put you in an awkward position.'

'Awkward! Man, Elizabeth was convinced I knew about this whole thing and picked the biggest fight with me, accusing me of hiding this from her.'

Oh, so they had fought over me. Elizabeth loves a good fight too. She can argue until the cows come home, change for dinner, put on fresh clothes, and then go out again. I'm sure she gave him hell. I'm sorry to say, that news made my day, more than Marlene in the short skirt smiling at me, more than Louis putting my photo in the magazine. I made them fight. Good! Good. Good. This fame stuff wasn't as bad as I thought.

'Tom, I gotta ask. Did you . . .'

I knew what he was getting at. Sex. Did we have sex? I don't know, *did we*?

'Everything but,' I answered. 'I let her sort of lead, if you get my drift. And she stopped me there.'

'Man. Man, oh, man. I can't believe this. I just can't fucking believe this. You made out with a movie star. How can you sit there and be so calm?'

I just shrugged.

'So when are you seeing her again?'

Here came the big lie.

'Can't say. I'll let you know.'

I knew it was over, but I couldn't admit that to Jake, in fact I almost couldn't admit it to myself.

'Well, you will let me know, won't you? Promise me that.'

'Sure.'

He was still steaming when I left. I knew he would calm down, he always does. He throws these little tantrums, then apologizes later. Sometimes we fight about baseball and it gets so heated you'd think something momentous was at stake. He's been like that since he was a kid, and was not about to change now.

Back at the office I wasted the afternoon taking calls from the usual suspects. Public relations people hawking new books, lunch invitations, business conference invitations, the norm. No one, however, failed to mention my date.

'Saw you in the papers, Tom, nice photo.'

'What's she really like?'

'The breakfast is at seven, and the speaker will begin around seven-forty-five. Hope you can make it. Also, Mr Webster, I liked the photo of you in the paper.'

'You know, Tom, if you ever want to write a book, you know,

about finance or something, I'm happy to set up a meeting for you.'

Most of the callers complimented my hitherto unknown hidden talent for taking photographs. A book deal was suggested, a first. Even though you couldn't see them, you could sense they were both stunned and smirking on the phone. Frank Wicker-Smith III behaved impeccably and did not ask me another question.

The day finally concluded. Heady stuff. I planned to run home and write it all down. Grabbing my jacket the phone rang again. I debated ignoring it, but grabbed it when Frank shot me an evil stare. It was Mr Wilkes. He asked that I come to his office after work. His company was in midtown, and gave me directions. He had something he needed to discuss with me that couldn't be done over the telephone. Then he asked me how I was holding up. Under the circumstances, I said, I thought fairly well.

'Is it what you expected?' he asked. 'The attention, the chaos?'

'No. I have to say no.'

'It never is. Still, are you enjoying the ride?'

'The jury is still out on that one. It's not as bad as it was yesterday.'

'And tomorrow will even be better. You adjust and people adjust. You'll see.'

'I expect I will.'

'Just think of it this way. The worse it gets, the better your article.'

'That's the only way I have come to think of it,' I told him.

'Well, gotta fly. See you later, Tom.'

'Sure. See you later.'

I sat back in my chair. Something was afoot. The Riddler was not quite finished with me yet. This I did not like.

His office was impressive. Everything was expensive, the furniture, the paintings, the whole package. Now at eight p.m., his staff, whoever they were, had left for the day. It was me and Mr Wilkes as he ushered me in and asked me to sit.

'I'll get straight to the point. Tom, I can't tell you how great the fallout has been.'

'Fallout?'

'From your date. The press. Even I didn't think we could turn Alexandra around so quickly.'

'She's been turned around?'

'Well, not completely, no. But partially. It seems her dating you has really impressed people. They really think if a guy like you falls in love with her, she must be deeper than people thought.'

'But I am not in love with her.'

'Of course you are. Everyone is.'

'I'm not.'

'Tom, listen to me. We had magazines calling today to do pieces on her that wouldn't touch us with an electric cattle prod before. In fact if they wrote about Alexandra, it was only to hold her up to ridicule. And two calls today from independent film directors who want to send her scripts.'

'Thurgood?'

'No. But it's only Monday. He'll bite. What I am saying is this. The publicity for us has been incredible. Better than we could have imagined. And that Marilyn Monroe—Arthur Miller angle all the papers went on was brilliant. And I didn't even feed it to them. Those airheads in the press thought that one up themselves.'

'Yes, I was kind of intrigued by it too.'

'You're a good-luck charm, Tom. Of course I am pleased this all worked out for you too. That goes without saying. I'm sure the article will be great.'

The man was a snake and to his credit he didn't even pretend to keep his fangs hidden from view.

'Mr Wilkes, why did you tell them we were in love? That I had known her three months?'

'Oh, that. They needed something to go on, Tom. I mean, in a sense I did it for you. For your article.'

Oh, he did it for me. How thoughtful. How kind. The man was a boa constrictor.

'Tom, I'd like to ask . . . Well, Alexandra would like to ask . . . We both would like you to keep this up just a little more. The affair. Your affair. It's too good for us to let it go now. Go out with her again. And this time you can talk to some media guys if you want. Tell them how smart she is, how people have misjudged her, how a serious guy like you would never date a mattress.'

In other words tell them all the lies he already told them.

'I don't know.'

'Tom, think of your article. The more you see her, the better it gets.'

'Mr Wilkes.'

'Please, Tom, call me Michael.'

'Michael, you cannot imagine how disruptive this publicity has been to my life.'

'Tom, I can. You forget it's my business to disrupt people's lives using publicity.'

'Yes, but all of them come to you willingly.'

'So did you.'

'But I was different.'

'How so?'

'It was an experiment. I asked for one date. Then I wanted to disappear.'

'It's too late, Tom. Even if you crawl back into the woodwork now, you'll always be Alexandra West's ex.'

'But we were never an item.'

'Sure you were. I read it in the papers.'

He had me cornered. He was good and he knew it. They wanted one more date. One more public outing of Mr Serious and Ms Bimbo.

'We helped you, Tom, now you help us. Not many celebrities would have agreed to your little scam in the first place, but we did.'

'Because there was something in it for you too.'

'Sure. I'm not denying that. We just want a bit more. One more date. Just to convince the people out there you guys are an item.'

'One more and then it's over, right?'

'I promise.'

'I want it in writing.'

'Oh, Tom, can it really have been that bad?'

I had to admit actually it hadn't. That the premiere was kind of fun, watching my colleagues sit up and my editor grovel was highly enjoyable, and hearing that Elizabeth got jealous was close to orgasmic.

'It's been interesting.'

'Sure it has. Well, we just want it to get more interesting. See?'

The Riddler was hard to resist. Besides, I rationalized, I could use a second meeting to raise some questions about my experience with Alexandra. We could compare notes. We could discuss celebrity and how it alters everything. Surely she would have some thoughts on the issue. Okay. You win.

'What would you like me to do?'

'Edgar's. Take her to Edgar's on Saturday night. Everybody will be there, the place is always crawling with media and movers and shakers. Everyone will see you.'

I had never been to Edgar's, although it was an institution in New York. If memory served me correctly, it was on the east side of Manhattan, and I restricted my dining to cafés around Wall Street and the Chinese take-out joint at the end of my street.

'What do I have to do once I get there?'

'Nothing. That's the beauty of it. Order dinner. Make conversation. Act like you and Alexandra are discussing politics, the economy, the space program, I don't give a shit.'

'You know, last week a reporter followed me into the bathroom.'

'Sure. It'll probably happen again. Just be polite. The competition between the tabloids is a fucking bunfight. It's nothing personal.'

'After this date what happens?'

'Then you're off the hook. I'll feed them a story how you two have stopped going out in public because of all the attention. Then in a few more weeks I'll let it out that you broke up because she had to go to Europe to do a movie or something. Leave it with me.'

'Promise?'

'I promise. Listen, Tom, relax. Enjoy it.'

'I have enjoyed it in a way. I just don't want it to get out of hand.'

'Hey, admit it. It's not such a bad life, is it? Having people smile at you all day, guys in the office a bit jealous, secretaries flirting with you.'

'How do you know that happened?'

'It always does.'

'Really?'

'Oh, sure. Bet your life on it.'

The deal was struck. One more date. At least this time I knew what awaited me. The stares. The knowing looks. The shock at me, the nerd from Wall Street, with her, superbabe from Hollywood.

Arriving home, Hector was waiting. He informed me more reporters had cruised by asking questions. By my estimation he had pocketed enough money to trade in his beat-up car for a Porsche. He swore black and blue he told them nothing. Nothing but yes, I did live in the building, and no, Ms West had not come by that day. I thanked him, though doubted the sincerity of his story. To take my mind off the new bargain I had just struck with the devil, I headed for the bookshelf and scanned my library. *The Knights of the Round Table. The Crusades. The Civil War.* I was not in the mood for a civil war, particularly when in truth it was anything but civil. I settled on a book about the passengers aboard the *Mayflower*. I had already read it, but I had already read everything on my bookshelf. Starting again, I traveled back 400 years to meet a people clinging to Puritan values so earnestly they had to leave their homes behind in order to establish peace in their lives. Maybe when this was all over, I would have to move to Plymouth too.

Chapter 17

As each day progressed, the interest in me lessened. My feeling was the office staff had adjusted to the situation, though there were minor rumblings when it became known my name would now be splashed across the cover of the magazine. I did not speak to Alexandra the entire week, which I found quite odd, but convinced myself those in the public eye do things differently from us mere mortals.

My mother called twice from Houston to inform me reporters from *Celebrity Scene*, *The Eye*, and papers in New York and Houston had called and asked for family photographs and a copy of my senior yearbook. I instructed her that no photos of me were to leave the house, on pain of death.

'Oh, but, Tommy darling, they said they would return them.'

She still called me Tommy even though I was forty-three years old. In her eyes I was still four.

'Mom, no. N-O. Do you understand? I don't care if they promise to return them with a big bow and a bunch of flowers.'

'But, Tommy, you were such a cute little boy. I have a lovely photo of you at Disneyland when you were ten. Gosh, time flies. I remember the day your father and I brought you home from the hospital. Mickey Mouse is in the photo too. He has his arm around you.'

Clearly Mom was enjoying the break these reporters had injected into her routine, which consisted of shopping in the morning, soap operas in the afternoon. She watched them all in succession just as the network people dreamed their viewers would, and, given the similar storylines, never actually knew which character belonged to which program.

This drove her best friend Edie crazy when Edie called to thrash out a character's next move following an abortion, marriage or divorce. Edie always liked to play fortune-teller and predict what would happen next. But Mom never knew whether Thorn, the resident heart-throb in one show, was married to Rose from a second or Lily from a third. Edie said it was Mom's inability to concentrate on the finer points of the soaps that drove her to Valium. Mom said it was Edie's good-for-nothing, cheating-heart husband, Big Ben, that put her on tranquilizers, but never mind. They were like Jake and me, those two. Hung on through thick and thin, good times, lean times. Edie, however, never ran off with my father, though I heard Big Ben once made a pass at Mom. But she later told me Big Ben hit on anything breathing, so she dismissed his kind offer. She never told my dad or Edie, although I think they both probably knew.

So not only was Mom enjoying a little attention right then when this thing exploded, Edie was too. She was sitting in Mom's kitchen when the papers started calling, and as such felt she was part of the deal. Edie suddenly found herself a bit player in a minor soap opera and couldn't believe her luck. She was no longer plain Edie, wife of Big Ben, but Edie, best friend of the mother of the man who dates that movie star.

'Betsy, no.'

I always called her Betsy when I was angry. That was the sign I was serious.

'Not even the one with Mickey Mouse?'

'Especially not the one with Mickey Mouse.'

'All right, Tommy. Whatever you want. But they were very nice when they called.'

'Betsy, you've been warned.'

'Fine, son. No photos.'

Jake and I spoke every day and it was clear he was still angry. He was short and guarded on the phone, demanding to know my every move in between asking whether I intended to see

Alexandra again. 'And I hope I don't have to read about it in the papers again, Tom.' I was then made to swear black and blue that if anything happened, he would be the first to know.

The wonderful thing about the celebrity industry is that it is so damn huge. Bigger than the Commerce Department, probably bigger than NASA. There are so many famous and wannabe famous out there now, you have to take your turn getting noticed. You can be all over the papers one day and non-existent the next. Unless Alexandra did something which was in their opinion gossip-worthy, she disappeared off the radar. So in the following days, the space once occupied by us was earmarked for others. Sportsmen cheating on their wives with hookers, actors eating at their own restaurants, new clubs opening that were so 'underground' you needed a road crew to help you dig your way down there.

I began to study the daily gossip columns with a new-found intensity. I learned that sightings of supermodels, what they wore, ate and who they slept with, often garnered more attention than decisions on foreign policy. Stories about actresses working out in gyms were also popular, and the copy invariably mentioned the star was fatter and less toned in person than their photographs suggested.

This constant delight in taking people down a peg or ten permeated the pages, and as I had never read these columns before Sunday, I was receiving an entire education. Now, six columns later, I was a devotee. I was searching for her name, I was searching for mine. And, I have to say, I did not like the attention, but I did not want to be ignored either. I felt by the end of the week like a cheap one-night stand. Thank God it didn't last long.

The supermarket tabloids hit the streets on Friday. Presumably they were so packed with news about the celebrity merry-go-round one needed to set aside the entire weekend to get through them. I could joke, but these journals had circulation figures quadruple those of *Time*, *Newsweek* and *The Capitalist* combined. *Celebrity Scene*, the magazine that conducts exclusive interviews at urinals, had a huge color photograph of me and Alexandra, along with a headline that read: HE'S A NERD AND I LOVE HIM ANYWAY.

Following this massive ego boost was a lengthy article in which a multitude of sources had told *Celebrity Scene* that Alexandra and I were madly in love. She in particular had long been searching for a man to discuss politics and philosophy with, and finally she had found him. She was, apparently, also fascinated by the inner machinations of Wall Street, and I was helping her invest her millions in the stock market. The Marilyn–Arthur angle reared its head again, which gave the article reason to rehash their entire affair, and draw comparisons with us.

By the time I had finished the article I had learned this about myself. I was a quiet, private, dependable guy according to my co-workers, but a genius with a keen understanding of the financial world. I had gone to Yale, which I appreciated their mentioning. I was separated from my wife, who had run off with my best friend. I loved that they mentioned that. I was alternately described as a Wall Street nerd, a player, an opinion maker, a history buff and 'one of the most respected financial writers in New York, according to investors'. I was? How nice.

But more importantly, who had been their sources? Louis? Marlene of the short skirt? Frank? By contrast, every sentence that mentioned Alexandra also contained the words buxom, beauty, blond, tantalizing, ravishing, sex symbol and, for the *pièce de résistance*, 'If Marilyn Monroe had a daughter, she would have been Alexandra West.' Well, goodness. Talk about taking genetic liberties here.

Not to be outdone, its arch rival, *Starscene*, also splashed *moi*, Alexandra's new man, over two pages. The headline hurt: BEAUTY AND THE BEAST: HOLLYWOOD DISH FALLS FOR DORK NEXT DOOR.

But worse was the fact that details of our affair occupied page ten and eleven, and that pages one through nine were devoted to others considered more worthy of immediate attention. This would not ordinarily have offended until you learn what beat us to the punch. Recipes from a cookbook entitled *Are You Hungry Tonight? Elvis's Favorite Food*, were on page four, complete with an interview with his private chef. All the recipes appeared to involve peanut butter and bananas, which didn't sound like there was a great deal of cordon bleu cooking going on in Memphis to me. Still, I always rather liked the King, so resolved not to hold him personally responsible.

Spaceships were landing on the Canadian border on page two, and customs officials were most angry the little green men had not organized the proper visas. A televangelist who had fallen from grace by cheating on his income taxes was also ahead of us, as was the basketball star who left his wife for her best friend. This article I read with particular interest. There was a composite page of gossip on page five, and page six concerned itself with TV stars bickering on the set of a sitcom I never watched. On a separate page there were just photographs of celebrities, in which I noticed most of the women looked just like Alexandra. She later told me they all used the same plastic surgeon, which cleared up that confusion.

Getting over the hurt at being relegated toward the back of the magazine, I read for the tenth time about my apparent likeness to Arthur Miller. That I had never written a play or he never worked on Wall Street was beside the point. Presumably the fact I had studied *Death of a Salesman* in school was enough to establish a link. All Arthur's traits were immediately transferred to me, and I was subsequently discussed as being as brilliant, bright and brainy as he was. Their talent for alliteration was astounding. Buxom, Bouncy, Beautiful Alexandra was attracted to my Brilliant, Bright and Brainy conversation in the same way as Marilyn had been drawn to Arthur.

He had the grace to take Marilyn seriously, to look beyond the blond hair and breathy voice. So did I. This time Alexandra was quoted personally in the piece, though I doubted she spoke to them. She said it was early days yet, which was true, but her feelings for me were very intense. That I had only seen one of her films, that I barely knew who she was when we met, and I was a complete Southern gentleman.

'Every man just wants one thing from me,' she was quoted. 'Tom doesn't. He just wants to talk to me. I can't tell you how refreshing that is.'

Well, I cannot tell you how refreshing the rest of the article was to me. She went on to add that you shouldn't judge a book by its cover. She had dated gorgeous, good-looking guys in Hollywood and they were all bores, preoccupied with their careers. They were men who never met a mirror they didn't like. And she hinted they were useless in the bedroom. I, by contrast, was Casanova on heat.

'Looks aren't everything. Besides, I have always had a thing for short, intelligent men. I think they're sexy. I think Tom's sexy.'

The closing line was devoted to Alexandra alluding to the fact I was a demon in bed. Her 'friends' said she had never been so satisfied sexually and couldn't rip my clothes off fast enough. I was living proof that when you kiss frogs, they really do turn into princes. And not only was I a prince. In the bedroom, I was king. Now this kind of publicity I could handle. If this story didn't make everyone forget about Elvis's penchant for peanut butter and banana sandwiches, nothing would.

Friday morning I was at work, absorbing the news of my new-found sexual prowess, when Alexandra called. I didn't recognize her voice at first.

'Hey, lover boy.'

'Excuse me?'

'How you doing, boyfriend?'

'Who is this?'

She squealed and I thought I recognized the laugh but still was unsure.

'Sorry, Tom. It's me. Alexandra. Just a little joke. Didn't mean to scare you.'

'Hi. No, you didn't scare me. Well, okay, just a little.'

'How you doing?'

'Fine. And you?'

'Brilliant, thanks to you. I can't believe what has happened.'

'So Mr Wilkes said.'

'Incredible, right? I mean, we had to practically beg to get a piece about me in *The Vulture*. Michael had to promise them one of his other clients if they would write about me. Now all those serious guys are chasing me for articles. People are calling with scripts. Good scripts, Tom. Parts where I don't have to take off my clothes.'

'Great. I'm really happy for you. But, but do you really think it's all due to this? I mean us? I mean the idea we are involved?'

'Must be. When a smart guy like you comes out and says I have brains, people buy it.'

'Glad I could help.'

'Yeah. And thanks for coming out again tomorrow. I really appreciate it.'

She had me in the palm of her hand and she knew it.

'Seen the tabloids?'

'Just reading them now actually.'

'Trust me. I never spoke to any of them. Neither did any of my so called "friends". It's all made up. I never told anyone we were having sex or any of that stuff in *Starscene*. Oh, yeah. Sorry about the headlines. I feel bad they described you as the dork next door.'

'Don't worry about it.'

'Yeah, well, it wasn't nice.'

'I'll be honest, Alexandra. I don't normally read these supermarket magazines. Are you in them often?'

'Every week.'

'Every week?'

'Yep.'

'Doesn't it drive you crazy? I mean, do you ever talk to them?'

'Sometimes. Most times they just make up any old stuff they want.'

'Why don't you sue?'

'What for? It's harmless. I'm going to sue them for calling me beautiful and sexy? Are you going to sue them for saying you are a fantastic lover?'

'I suppose not. But what about the lies? I mean, all that stuff about us was untrue. Fortunately they were nice lies. What about when they get mean?'

'Oh, they do. They'll turn on you in an instant. They write that you're sleeping with some guy you never met and you're breaking up his marriage. It's infuriating, but in the end I just gave up. I mean, once the entire world has seen you in *Playboy*, it's not like you have a whole lot of secrets anymore.'

'It's amazing to me you take it so well.'

'Hey, I just look at it as something to show my kids one day. You know, look, kids, see when Mommy was a star. The thing is, right now they're pretty good to me. In ten years they'll be writing how I lost my looks and I'm over the hill. They give actresses over forty a really hard time. I know it's going to get worse, so I am enjoying it while I can.'

'I guess.'

'Anyway, about tomorrow. Thanks again for doing this. You'll have fun, I promise. Come to the Waldorf about seven. You know the room number.'

'What do I wear?'

'Whatever you like.'

'A suit?'

'Sounds good.'

I had other questions to ask, but she said her goodbyes and hung up. In the brief time I had known her, I could not fault her ability to take the good with the bad. Trading privacy for fame was a deal Alexandra had long made peace with, and I liked her attitude. Besides, she was right. Would any man sue a magazine that dared to suggest he was the second coming of Warren Beatty?

I had one last order of business. I had deliberately avoided telling Jake about my dinner date with Alexandra all week. I didn't want to be interrogated again, I didn't want to have to make up more lies. Saturday morning I called his apartment. Elizabeth answered. Now this would be interesting.

'It's me. He home?'

Normally all I heard was her passing the phone and mumbling, 'It's for you.' That morning was different.

'*Well, aren't we moving up in the world?*' she said caustically.

'Are we?'

'Oh. I. Think. So. You started with a school teacher but threw her over for a movie star.'

'Liz, if memory serves me correctly, I threw you over for nobody. You threw me, remember?'

'It was nothing personal, Tom.'

'Well, neither is this. I mean, did you really expect me to sit home reading history books for the rest of my life?'

Actually, that had been *my* plan.

'No, but I didn't expect you to take up with a trashy bimbo like that Anita West either.'

'Alexandra. Her name is Alexandra.'

'I don't care what her name is. I just think it's pathetic, Tom. A man like you going out in public with someone like her. Aren't you embarrassed?'

Well, she had a nerve. She was also angry and jealous and I was beside myself with joy.

'Why should I be? Appearances are deceiving, Liz, she's much smarter than she appears.'

'I'll bet. I'm sure she's home reading Plato's *Republic* as we speak.'

'Maybe she is.'

'You know they're not real.'

'What?'

'They're implants. You did know that, didn't you?'

'Frankly, it has never come up in conversation.'

'Tom, I'm glad I have you on the phone. Reporters have been calling me, asking about our marriage. I'm hanging up on all of them. One turned up at school on Thursday and I threatened to call the police if he didn't leave. I see in those trashy magazines today they have me painted as the Wicked Witch of the West for leaving you.'

'I'm sorry about that, Liz. Truly. I never spoke to them. Neither did Alexandra. They make it all up.'

'Whatever. But people read it. All week at school I had teachers whispering behind my back. Students were asking me to ask you for Alexandra's autograph.'

'I can get it for you if you like.'

'No, I do not like,' she bellowed. 'What I would like is for you to ask these reporters to leave me alone.'

'Now, how am I supposed to do that? They are probably picking through my trash right now while I'm talking to you.'

'Why are they going through your trash?'

'It's better you don't know. Is Jake there?'

'One second. He's coming.'

Our first conversation since she left was not a resounding success. She in particular was less than polite. But her tone didn't sting the way I thought it might. In fact, I rather enjoyed making her as angry, hurt and bewildered as I had been one year before. Jake took the phone. I told him Alexandra and I had dinner plans for that evening, a last-minute thing. He thanked me for telling him, then hung up. He was stunned. He had nothing left to say.

Chapter 18

I had never dined at Edgar's, but I knew, the way you know these things, that Edgar's was *it*. The place to be. The place to go in New York to be seen by those who need to see you. For those of you from out of town, let me fill you in as to the seating arrangements.

The bar is the domain of reporters. The front tables belong to the B-list celebrities, the back room to the A list. Alexandra said she loves Edgar's because everyone leaves you alone. Waiters asking for an autograph is a no-no. Deals are struck and phone numbers exchanged but never in an obvious fashion. If you wanted to strategically place your name in the papers, Edgar's was a handy accessory to the crime.

This was all explained to me in the car. I was wearing my number-two suit again, and hoped Alexandra didn't notice she had seen it before. She was wearing, well, my God, you should have seen what she was wearing. A black T-shirt three sizes too small that I believe showed off her mammary assets to great effect. It was tight as a bandage around an Egyptian mummy. This T-shirt, she informed me, cost $300 at Gucci. Translation: it cost her nothing, but mere mortals paid that amount. It was paired with a black leather miniskirt, also Gucci, that was so short, one more inch up and it would have been a belt. The heels were incredibly high. Manuelas, I think she called them.

As I took in the big picture, she assured me she was really a jeans and T-shirt kind of gal. But if she dropped in to Edgar's dressed like a college student, she ran the risk of anonymity. The outfit, she explained, was chosen very carefully. While she demanded privacy once seated, she had to ensure that everyone knew she'd arrived. It was the, hey-everyone-I'm-here-but-don't-come-near-me approach to dining out.

She was right, of course. She walked in and all heads turned on cue. And when I say turned, I mean the kind of action that sends most of us to chiropractors for realignment. Whispers began immediately, as spotters at the door passed the word Alexandra had arrived. I followed, and more neck-craning followed me. So it wasn't a stunt, you could see diners saying among themselves. They really are together.

Alexandra gently took my hand in hers. We remained wrist-locked while the maître d' led us to a table. It was interesting to note the looks we received from the room as we breezed past. The reporters at the bar looked up, and you could sense their relief that they would have a story for the following day. Women stared straight at Alexandra's face, checking for signs of wrinkles and aging. Men by contrast stared straight at her chest. Unless rebuked by wives or girlfriends, most men stayed there. A few went further south to her hips, but you could count them on one hand.

Alexandra smiled around the room, making eye contact with everyone. She was good at this, and she knew it. I'm gratified to say they acknowledged my presence just as eagerly. Women threw me surreptitious smiles, signaling their approval. They seemed to say they understood what Alexandra saw in me, that still waters run deep, that sort of thing. Men, on the other hand, shot me down with looks of pure envy. Envious that I was dating her, envious that she had chosen to bestow her love on me, envious that I apparently performed gymnastics in bed they had failed to master. The maître d' seated us.

'Well, that went great,' she said.

'What did?'

'Our entrance. Everyone saw us. Everyone.'

'Well, it would be hard not to.'

'You never know. When the place is packed with stars, you can get lost in the shuffle.'

I found that a near impossibility. The only people who would miss the entrance of a tall, platinum-blond movie star with enormous breasts would be those eating in the restaurant next door, or possibly Europe.

'Would sir care to order some wine?'

It took a minute to realize the waiter was talking to me. Well, actually sir would be happy to oblige and order some wine. I asked him to recommend a white, and whatever he selected, that was what I ordered. Though the food here was five star and I should have used the opportunity to go on some gastronomic discovery tour, I was worried about the bill and ordered the cheapest thing on the menu. It was, would you believe, pasta with tomato and mushroom sauce for $32. (Ravioli with fresh truffles and spinach clocked in at $42.) I guessed the raw ingredients in my dish would come to about $2, and made a note to come back in my next life as a restauranteur. Making 1,500 percent profit on a dish is not daylight robbery, it's genius.

I felt less overwhelmed than at our previous meeting, but still nervous. I wanted to ask her so many questions, but in between bites people kept dropping by to say hello and introduce themselves. They were all in the industry and Alexandra could afford to ignore no one. I was up and down like a jack-in-the-box as she introduced me to people and I rose to shake their hands. When our entrées were over, I saw a window of time and thought I would climb through it.

'Alexandra?'

'Hold my hand.'

'I want to ask you a couple of things.'

'Hold my hand. We're in love, remember.'

'Sure, I'm sorry.'

I extended my hand to take hers across the table. She shot me a huge smile.

'I have to ask you . . . when you started becoming well known, before you got to where you are now . . . did you enjoy it?'

'Enjoy what?'

'Fame. Recognition. That fact that everyone suddenly knows you.'

'I can't remember anymore. I forget what life was like before.'

'My friends are acting kind of funny.'

'That'll happen.'

'My ex-wife is really mad at me.'

'Really? Well, good. She left you, right? So now it's karma time.'

'Colleagues at work are acting strange.'

'Probably jealous. Probably shock. I remember now when I had my photo in a magazine for the first time, some of the girls at school got pretty bitchy.'

'Why do you think that happens?' I asked. I genuinely wanted to know. 'I mean, in my article I would like to explore more of what happens to people around you than what happens to you. I mean, me.'

'Well, I guess it's because... Hang on.'

She then moved her chair around to my side of the table. Suddenly we were sitting together as opposed to across from each other. Waiting until she could sense a large portion of the room were looking-but-not-looking, she kissed me. On the lips. A few times. My response was that of a department-store mannequin. I sat ramrod straight while she endeavored to devour me.

'Kiss me back, Tom.'

I did as instructed, albeit tentatively, and found I thoroughly enjoyed the experience. After that brief liplock she dragged her chair back to its original position. A waiter approached with dessert menus. We agreed to order one slice of apple pie and one slice of cheesecake and share them. I wanted an answer to my question, but Alexandra was bored with the subject and wanted to know more about Elizabeth and our marriage. When the dessert arrived we ate half of our portions and then I suggested we switch plates as planned. Alexandra had other, far more newsworthy ideas.

'Feed it to me.'

'What?'

'Feed me. And I'll feed you.'

Feeling like a complete idiot, I followed her instructions to the letter. Reporters were taking notes without taking notes, if you understand. I rose to go to the bathroom, turning to see if anyone would follow. Nobody did. But when I returned a reporter was seated in my chair, chatting to Alexandra.

'Tom?'

'Yes?'

'Bill Carlton. *New York Review*. Nice to meet you.'

We shook hands.

'And you.'

'I read your columns all the time. Best finance analysis in the business.'

I bet he had never read one, and I would bet my apartment and my lips sofa too.

'Thank you. Thank you very much.'

Now I sounded like Elvis.

'I was just chatting to Alex here about the two of you. It seems serious.'

'Oh, it is,' she purred.

Oh, oh. Here we go. More lies.

'Can I ask, any plans? Wedding bells?'

'I think that's a little premature, don't you?'

'Well, it has been three months,' he said. 'I know people who get married after three days.'

Actually, Mr Carlton, it was one week since we first met, but what's eleven weeks between friends?

'No. No plans. Just friends.'

Oh, he loved that. The old, we're–just–friends line.

'Alexandra was telling me that it seems to be a bit more than just friends, Tom.'

I grinned. I wondered what else she had told him in my absence. As I would read in the paper on Monday, it was in fact quite a lot.

'Alexandra's a big girl. She can say what she wants. My story is that we are just friends, and for the moment I'm sticking to it.'

Carlton winked and nodded. He knew the drill. I didn't, but was learning fast.

'Have it your way. Enjoy your evening.'

When he was out of sight, I asked Alexandra what she told him.

'Nothing really. Okay, I said we were really happy together and I was glad I had finally found someone who saw through the blond hair. I told him everything off the record.'

'So he won't print it?'

'Oh, sure he will. He just won't say where he got it from. He'll cover my tracks.'

I felt nauseous. There are, I believe, two kinds of people on the planet. Those with academic smarts and those with street smarts. Rarely do they coexist in the same individual. Alexandra had none of the former, but harbored the latter in spades. She was people savvy and confident and knew how to manipulate circumstances with a finesse I would never acquire if I spent my entire life trying. She didn't know who Caesar or Napoleon or Henry VIII were, but I envied her all the same. She could pull strings with ease. This was fine for her, but I was suddenly feeling trampled. I suggested, since this was our second and last date, maybe things were getting a little out of hand. Alexandra disagreed.

'It's gotta look real, Tom. People in the biz have to believe I'm serious about working here.'

'But you are.'

For someone who fell into the business by accident, she had found her calling. Funny how ambition rears its head that way. Pushed into the race, she discovered she liked running. Alexandra's tone told me she was prepared to fudge any lie, fix any story, in order to get ahead.

'Yes, I know that, but they don't. With you around, well, you make me look smart.'

'But the way you dress, that skirt... I mean, you... you make yourself look dumb,' I blurted out, sorry the minute I had.

'I know. But that's all taken care of. In fact I have something to tell you. Are you ready? I'm toning down the hair.'

Well, I doubted she was splitting the atom.

'Really? Well that's a good idea.'

'And I'm getting glasses. Those little turtle ones.'

'Tortoiseshell?'

'Yeah, those.'

'I didn't know you were short-sighted.'

'I'm not.'

Of course not. What a stupid comment.

'And the miniskirts are going soon too. I'm getting into pantsuits. Armani. Less flash and trash, more class, you know? Michael has it all planned.'

Of course he does. I knew his fingerprints were smeared all over this, but wondered if anyone else suspected. I would find out soon enough. Alexandra refused the offer of a second cup of coffee, and I followed her lead as instructed. She grabbed her handbag and announced we were leaving.

'Never stay too late anywhere, Tom. A party, a launch, even dinner. Always leave them wanting more.'

There were those street smarts again. See, I would have had two more coffees and probably more wine and stayed the entire evening. Alexandra rose.

'Wait, I have to pay the bill,' I said.

'Oh, Tom, you're so sweet. You don't have to pay. We're being comped.'

'Oh, right. Like last time.'

'See, you're catching on.'

Damn. If I'd known tonight was gratis, I would have had the $98 seafood platter. On our way out Alexandra stopped at every table where she knew someone to say goodbye.

Back in the car I was utterly frustrated. The evening for me personally had been a success if you looked at it from the perspective of heart palpitations per minute. The week before my blood pressure had been stratospheric. That night it was much more calm. Darwin was right. Evolution worked. I was adapting. I certainly wasn't Joe Cool, but I wasn't Joe Nervous Wreck anymore either. But Alexandra had revealed little of her own feelings on the issue of fame, though I tried hard to draw her out. Either she didn't think about it or the entire subject bored her. I made one last attempt in the limousine back to the hotel.

'I never asked you about your interview with *The Vulture*. How did that go? They're a pretty sophisticated magazine. Were the questions very different to what you usually get?

'No, thank God. I was really nervous when I went in to see them too. Like you said, they're not *Celebrity Scene*. I even read the newspaper that day so if they asked me any questions about current affairs I could answer. And Michael made me memorize a list of books I had recently read in case they asked me about that, because of where we shot the photos and all.'

'Really? A book list? Do you remember what was on it?'

'Um, Shakespeare, because you know I had really read that one...and...'

'Which one?'

'What?'

'Which one of Shakespeare?'

'*Romeo and Juliet.* We did it in high school.'

'Did you like it?'

'Sort of. That old English is really hard to understand. I liked the movie better.'

Of course she did.

'What else was on the list?'

'Um, a book about this woman who falls in love with a man but she tells him she can't marry him.'

'*The Bridges of Madison County?*'

'No. No. It's set in England. I saw the movie of that one too, but I didn't watch it all the way through. It was in black and white and I hate movies in black and white. I mean, there are so many colors out there, why limit yourself?'

Why indeed?

'Do you know who the author was?'

'Yes, hang on. I remember. Elliot Brunting.'

Never heard of him. Must be some author you buy at the airport to help you kill time in the clouds between peanuts and the movie.

'No. Wait. Emily Brunting.'

'Emily Brontë?'

'That's it.'

'*Wuthering Heights?*'

'God, you're smart, Tom. That's it. *Wuthering Heights.* Have you read it? I bet you have. What a stupid question. Is it good?'

'It's a classic.'

'That's what Michael said.'

Of course he did. I was positively dying to know what else he had told Alexandra she had read, but squeezing one title out of her left her so exhausted, I opted to leave it at that. I wondered, however, if I could include this little revelation about pre-interview coaching in my own article. Possibly telling readers that Alexandra was forced to memorize book titles would be too cruel. Still, Ms MacDowell wanted everything in the piece. She was certainly paying for it.

'And they never even asked you what you read?'

'No. Which really surprised me. Surprised Michael too. And they didn't even ask about what I read in the paper either.'

'Do you read the newspaper every day?'

'Sure, if I'm in it. I bet that sounds vain to you, doesn't it, Tom? I bet you read the paper every day whether you're in it or not.'

I smiled.

'I read a couple actually. It's my job.'

'Wow.'

'So what did they ask you?'

'All the usual stuff. No big surprises. How I felt about turning thirty. Why did I move to New York? Did I really think I could shed my image and start over? They only asked a couple of questions. They took a lot more time with the photo shoot.'

Then I learned something that to me was so delicious, so ironic, I nearly lost my eyeballs as they rolled around in their sockets. The photo shoot, clearly engineered by Mr Wilkes, was conducted at the New York Public Library, in the great, cavernous, hallowed reading room. This is a room so sacred, so silent, the smell of leather bound books and the wisdom of those who wrote them seep out of the walls.

You can hear brains ticking over as students and scholars soak up information. The place positively buzzes with intelligence. And into this literary cathedral they shot Alexandra, after hours, seated at a desk poring over an ancient text. She was wearing a ballgown, bedecked in diamonds, she told me, and the idea was to play up the incongruity of the setting and the sitter. Who would have thought an action-adventure babe would visit a library? It was brilliant! Mr Wilkes deserved a medal. He clearly hoped that subconsciously the pictures would plant that idea that books and Alexandra were not such a weird match after all. Now her association with me was only reinforcing that notion. I could barely wait until *The Vulture* hit the streets.

At the hotel, Alexandra motioned for me to stay in the car, while she made moves to get out. The driver would drop me home. She did not ask me upstairs to see her etchings and fool the public, as it were, explaining that Mr Wilkes had decreed the idea of my staying over *verboten*. He wanted people to think she was staying at my place when we were together, though a cursory search through my garbage would squelch that idea. She thanked me again for playing along in her own little movie.

'No, thank *you*,' I said.

'You've been a good sport. I can't imagine it was easy.'

'No, it wasn't.'

'You're a good actor. Maybe you should think about the movies,' she joked.

'I don't know. Somehow I doubt I'm what Hollywood is looking for.'

'Don't put yourself down, Tom. You're a nice guy.'

She extended her hand to shake mine.

'Well, thanks again. I'm sure I'll see you around. New York is a small place.'

'Yes. It's a small place.'

She left me alone in the back seat. That was it. After one week of attention, phony affection, dinners, premieres and people thinking I was sharing her bed, it was all over. Although I couldn't wait to be where I was now, suddenly I was sad. It was over so quickly. And she was quite nice really. Harmless. Naïve in one sense, yet she had a savvy about her I admired.

The chicken and the egg dilemma occupied my thoughts as the driver spun us around to head for my apartment. How to explain her push to reinvent herself when already so successful? Did she always want to be a celebrity? Had she chased it all along and feigned surprise when it materialized? She insisted the spotlight was thrust upon her before she knew what was happening. But does there not come a point where ignorance turns to acceptance turns to fulfillment?

She said she never wanted to be a film star. Now she wanted it bad, while demanding to change the terms of the contract she had signed with the public. They wanted skin. She wanted clothes. It would be a difficult stunt to pull off, and, frankly, why bother? I had never been satisfied with her original answers and resolved to call her in the morning and put some more questions to her. This she could not deny me. Hey, we were friends now. In the meantime Hector awaited me at the door. Did this guy never go home?

'Evening, Mr Webster.'

'Hector.'

'Have a nice night?'

And just who wants to know? I wanted to ask.

'Yes, thank you.'

'See Ms West again?'

I smiled broadly.

'Good night, Hector.'

'Good night, sir.'

By the length of his smile I guessed by now he had put a down-payment on a condo in Florida.

The papers on Monday outdid themselves. Mom even rang to say Alexandra and I had made the *Houston Chronicle*. At home I was considered the local boy who made good. Real good. Going to Yale and writing a column in *The Capitalist* were never considered good, or good enough to garner me a mention in the Houston papers. But dating a movie star was. Mom said a number of friends had called. Neighbors asked questions when she ran into them at the supermarket.

'What do I tell them, Tommy?'

'Nothing. Tell them nothing.'

'But that's rude. I have to say something.'

'Tell them we have been on a couple of dates and so we'll see where it goes.'

I hated lying to my mother, but when this was all over, she of all people would understand.

'They're still calling asking for photographs.'

'We've been through this, Mom. No. No photos.'

'Fine, Tommy. Whatever you say.'

My colleagues greeted the news of a second date without as much fuss as the first. Though stares and raised eyebrows still greeted me, they were becoming almost jaded. Even Mr Pinstripes, Frank Wicker-Smith III, grunted hello but didn't request any additional information. I hadn't sighted Louis yet, but guessed he was thrilled the relationship was still on life support. The articles played up exactly what Alexandra knew they would.

That we fed each other dessert was missed by no one. Neither was our smooching at the table. What she wore received a lot of attention. The end result was that we were pronounced a serious item, as evidenced by our clear passion and respect for each other.

Alexandra, they noted, appeared happier and more relaxed than she had in a long time. I was said to be guarding her privacy 'jealously' and would not talk to reporters. But the general consensus was that I allowed Alexandra to reveal her true self. With me she could abandon the dumb side and let the hitherto unseen genius shine through. For her part, she had ended my self-inflicted depression following the break-up of my marriage. One newspaper noted that I had become the patron saint of ordinary Joes everywhere who believed mega-babes were out of their league. The patron saint stuff made me laugh. I, of course, knew something nobody else did. My days as a saint were numbered. This time it was really finished.

Monday mornings in the office I follow the same pattern. Open the mail, read the competition, mull over column ideas, then call contacts to get their predictions for the week ahead. It's what Mom would call housekeeping, but I find it nothing but irritating. All these little tasks and nothing to show for it at the end of the day. I called Jake to meet me at the Blue Moon at one.

'No. Too busy, Tom.'

'But it's Monday. You're never busy on Monday.'

'Can't do it.'

Or won't do it. He was mad, or so it seemed to me. But I had told him about the second date. I had warned him.

'Not even for half an hour?'

'Up to my neck in work.'

'Have it your way. Tomorrow, then?'

'Possible, but I can't say.'

'Have a good weekend?'

'Not as good as yours, I see.'

He was mad. I wasn't imagining this. Why was he mad?

'Jake, you angry?'

'No.'

'You sound it.'

'Sorry. Just stress. Gotta go. Speak to you later.'

But it wasn't stress. He knew it, I knew it and he knew that I knew. My dating Alexandra was really getting under his skin. Why?

156

Because it was against the law for guys like me to get involved with girls like her and I was screwing with social convention? Because people were asking him questions at work that he couldn't answer? Because Elizabeth was making life difficult for him at home? I felt sad Jake was so upended by this and decided a second call was in order.

'It's me again.'

'Yes.'

'Half an hour. Come on. I didn't talk to you all weekend.'

'Well, that's not my fault. Somebody was too busy with Miss Movie Star at Edgar's.'

'Please. Last chance to change your mind.'

'Sorry. No can do.'

Well, screw him, I thought. He'll come around. I did my best.

Tuesday he blew me off as well. Another excuse about an excruciating workload. In all the years Jake had been managing other people's money, I could not recall him ever working that hard. I knew the excuses were lies but was prepared to wait him out. Wednesday he finally agreed to dine with me. Clearly he had calmed down, and besides, there was a ball game on TV that night that we had to discuss before the first pitch.

Three days after he ran off with my wife I was sitting in a diner with him discussing a ball game, and now he would return the favor. Despite upheavals in our personal lives, all was suspended when the Yankees were involved. This was an immutable law. If it ever turned out that Jake had secretly collaborated with the Russians during the Cold War, I would be crushed, but still go to games with him. If you love baseball, you understand. So imagine my horror after pleading and begging and groveling for two days, in finding I suddenly had to cancel our lunch. On the eve of a big game too. I was disappointed, but he, oh Lord. When Jake learned exactly why our bagels with cream cheese were sidelined, he was not disappointed. He was ready to kill.

She arrived unannounced. But when you are wearing a pink T-shirt that stops just above the navel, black leather pants that look as if they have been shrink-wrapped around you, and you shimmy through a magazine newsroom where everyone is clad in navy-blue suits, you don't really need announcing. I heard murmurs and gasps before I looked up to see what was coming toward me. It was Alexandra. She slowly walked through the office while watching out of the corner of her eye as advertising executives came out of their cubicles to get a better look. They say bad news travels fast, but I think news about blond bombshells in the office travels faster. Louis came out of his office grinning and sucking twice as hard on his cigar. Alexandra ignored them all, though she knew she had their undivided attention. As she neared, all eyes shifted from her to me. She leaned over my desk and kissed me. When she started to speak, it was not human speech but purring that came out.

'Surprise,' she whispered.

Well, she got that right.

'What are you doing here?'

'I thought I'd take you to lunch. A surprise lunch. On me.'

'You could have called,' I said, still stunned she was there in the flesh.

'But it wouldn't have been a surprise then.'

'How did you get past security?'

'Easy. I just told them you were expecting me. Are you coming?'

I grabbed my jacket in a state of complete shock.

'I thought we were finished. I mean, Mr Wilkes said . . . I mean, what are you doing here?' I whispered.

'I'm here to take you to lunch. Why can't you believe me?' She smiled, but this time turned to acknowledge everyone in the room, throwing them a major-league grin.

The only thing I now recall is that Frank Wicker-Smith had stopped blinking at this point, his eyes dialating with shock and desire. I bundled her out of the newsroom as fast as I could. Then just as we were leaving the building I remembered Jake. I grabbed a phone in the lobby and called him to cancel. Urgent meeting with the editor, I said. Louis had no other time but lunch, I said. But what about baseball? he asked. I'll call you later, I promised. He seemed to buy it.

On the street I started to hyperventilate. Alexandra was still enjoying the ruckus she had caused inside, and the stares she was getting outside. The security guys from our building and those neighboring all left their posts to get a closer look. If terrorists had wanted to enter the place laden with explosives, then would have been a good time.

'So where to?'

'I thought you were taking me to lunch?' I said.

'Sure. Yes. But I mean, I don't know any places around here.'

Suddenly a man of around sixty approached and asked Alexandra if she was indeed Alexandra West. When she confirmed his suspicions, he asked for an autograph for his teenage son. When he left, she laughed. She indicated they used that line, but the autograph was in fact for themselves. He would, she guessed, probably return to his office and show it off. I thought autographs were stupid and told her so, but Alexandra said they confirmed that a meeting between a celebrity and the hoi polloi had occurred.

I was tired of standing on the street as everyone stared.

'Can we please just start walking?'

So we did. Alexandra asked me where I usually went for lunch. When I told her it was the diner down the block, she insisted we eat there. It had been a long time since she dined like regular people, and became extremely excited by the prospect. I could not imagine the looks that would greet us there, but decided I couldn't worry about that now.

Arriving at the diner, we were seated immediately, although with the commotion we caused you would have thought Elvis had returned from the dead. Waiters fought among themselves to serve us. Cooks, busboys, cleaners, dishwashers all raced out of the kitchen. Other diners dropped their forks. Hiding behind two giant menus, we tried to grab a minute of privacy. It was during this minute Jake arrived. I forgot he often ate there alone. As the menus lowered and he found that I was there, who I was with, his face turned white. He was seated at a single booth quite near ours and if looks could kill, I could have started working on my eulogy. Out of the corner of one eye I watched him order his usual. Out of the corner of the other I watched the entire room stare us down.

'I think we should leave. Maybe this isn't such a good idea.'

'No. I love it. It's been so long since I ate in a diner. They have side orders of french fries. I'm not supposed to eat them, but I'll order them if you don't tell Michael.'

'I won't tell. I think we should go.'

My cries fell on deaf ears. Bagels with cream cheese were ordered. Diet Cokes. A side order of french fries, extra crispy. Salad without dressing because she was on a diet. Alexandra told me to relax. Easy to say but hard to achieve. How could I explain my best friend was sitting nearby eating alone because I was supposedly in a meeting with my editor? From his body language it appeared Jake was considering voodoo dolls and pins for dessert. After his initial glare, he never acknowledged me again. I constantly glanced in his direction, hoping to signal an apology, but it didn't work. He ate, paid and bolted.

'You're not eating your bagel.'

'I'm not that hungry,' I said. It was the truth.

'I'm starved.'

'Alexandra, what are you doing here?'

'Oh, okay. I guess I should tell you what I need to talk to you about.'

'I didn't think you just wanted to eat lunch.'

'See how smart you are? You knew there was something else on my mind.'

I was angry she had put me in this terrible situation with Jake. On this occasion flattery would get her nowhere.

'Well?'

'Well.'

'So?'

'So. So, Tom. You know how I've been living at the Waldorf?'

'Yes.'

'Well, I've got to leave. It's costing a fortune and anyway there is only so much luxury and room service you can take before it gets boring.'

'I have never found luxury and room service boring.'

'Well, it is. Trust me.'

'So you want me to help you find an apartment?'

'No. I have already found one.'

'Great. Where is it?'

'Upper West Side.'

I relaxed. She had come to tell me we were to become neighbors. She wanted to warn me I might run into her in the neighborhood, and we should plan some strategy in case we do.

The woman had brains after all.

'Where on the Upper West Side?'

'Well, that's what I have to tell you. The apartment. The one I'm moving into. *It's yours.*'

She stuffed four fries into her mouth, awaiting my reaction. It was not long in coming.

'Mine! This is a joke, right?'

'Wrong.'

'Alexandra, I'm not following. Why don't you explain what's going on? I think I heard you say you wanted to move into my apartment, but I'm sure I heard wrong.'

'No, you didn't. I want to move in with you. You're a single guy now. You have space for me. We are dating after all. I think it's time we took this relationship to the next level.'

She was serious. She was crazy. No, she was serious.

'We are not dating. This relationship is not going to the next level. It doesn't exist! I thought I would never see you again.'

'Yes, but you have no idea what has happened.'

'Try me.'

'See, when we first went out, there was talk it was a set-up. But after the second date the talk changed. People think it's serious. Tom, I can't tell you how you've helped me. I've had A-list directors call me and offer me parts. Small stuff, but good stuff. You're my good-luck charm. I can't let go of you now.'

'Alexandra, I'm honestly happy your career has taken off in New York. But these people would have called anyway. It has nothing to do with me.'

'Michael thinks it does.'

I wanted to scream. Waiters and patrons, however, had us locked in their gaze, so I resisted the temptation to have an instant nervous breakdown.

'This is his idea, isn't it? That you move in with me.'

'No. It was both of ours. I've been looking for an apartment but haven't found anything I like yet. Then we thought, why don't I move into your place? I'm not just thinking of myself, Tom. I'm thinking of you. This would be great for your article.'

Oh, how noble of her, thinking of me as well.

'Alexandra, this is madness. Insanity. No.'

'But if we move in together, the industry will know it's really, really, really serious between us, that I wasn't just trying to scam anyone.'

'Why don't we just keep dating, then? Wouldn't that be enough?'

'Tom, as far as people know we have been dating three months. It's time for us to move in together. We're madly in love.'

'But we haven't been dating three months and I don't love you! I'm sorry. I didn't mean for that to sound so harsh. You're actually a nice person. It's just that this idea is ridiculous.'

'It worked for Marilyn.'

'Marilyn?'

'Marilyn Monroe. When she married Arthur Miller, everyone looked at her differently.'

'We are not getting married.'

'I'm not asking you to. I just want to move in.'

'No.'

'Please.'

'No.'

'Pretty please.'

'I think you and Michael are placing far too much emphasis on two dates and a little bit of noise about us in the newspapers. Those directors would have called anyway, don't you see that?'

'Maybe they would, and maybe they wouldn't. I'll never know. But this I do know. Since you've come into my life it's just getting better and better.'

'I am not in your life. This was an experiment.'

'Sure. It started off that way. But now it's different. Tom, please. I'm very tidy. I'm hardly ever home anyway. I promise to get my own phone line.'

'No.'

'Will you just think about it?'

'No.'

'Give me a reason why not?'

'No.'

I was a man of few words that day.

'Can I say anything to change your mind?'

'No.'

'Michael thinks . . .'

'No.'

She shot me one of those smiles that make most men go weak at the knees and hard in other places. It would have worked on me too had the circumstances been different.

'Check, please,' I yelled at the waiter.

'No. My treat,' she said.

I didn't think so. Lunch was not a treat. It was not a good time had by all. It was a nightmare. I put her in a taxi but before doing so apologized profusely and told her I hoped she understood. I could not have her move into my apartment, my life. Already the relationship had created problems between myself and a number of people. This would only exacerbate them. Though disappointed, she listened and seemed to indicate she understood that what she was asking was an imposition. She kissed me again and asked merely that I think about it some more.

'You don't have to make a decision like this immediately, Tom. Sleep on it.'

Famous last words.

To say I returned to the office completely undone would be an understatement. So I didn't realize at first why everyone was smirking at me on my return. Within minutes, however, I figured it out. Nobody had bought the story about lunch. They believed, because they wanted to believe, that we had run to some nearby hotel and had sex. Jealousy has its own scent, and it was one that keenly pervaded the length and breadth of the room. Little did they know my loosened tie and exhaustion were due to vastly different circumstances.

The rest of the day I spent in total silence. The only decision I made was that I would call Mr Wilkes that evening and demand that he and his client get out of my life. The deal was over. I had ample material for my article. I thought about calling Jake but realized any apologies would be futile. I would wait another day, possibly two, before explaining the situation. On the subway home I thought people were staring as if they recognized me from somewhere, but then dismissed it as paranoia. Boy, was I relieved to be home, I thought, as I turned the corner into my street. Boy, was I wrong.

There appeared to be a commotion going on. A crowd had gathered around a truck unloading something. Then I spotted the television cameras. Reporters clutching microphones started racing toward me. Flashbulbs went off. What the hell?

'Tom! Tom! Tom!' they yelled at me.

Getting closer, I found the truck was a moving van, and it was parked right in front of my building. Men whose muscles had been honed lifting pianos were hauling piles of clothing out of the truck and heading into the lobby. I knew what was happening there and then, but I prayed that I was wrong. I was not. Alexandra was standing inside my apartment, coordinating the moving men as if directing traffic. Mr Wilkes was there too, sitting smugly on the lips. As I walked in he bolted upright, aware both he and she had been caught mid-crime.

'What the hell is going on?' I bellowed.

'Tom, darling, I knew you'd change your mind, so I thought I would just move in.'

'Who called the television people?'

'I don't know,' she said.

'I did not change my mind.'

'But in time you would.'

'I wouldn't, Alexandra. I told you only hours ago I wouldn't and I haven't. Please pack everything up and leave. I'm serious.'

I turned to Mr Wilkes.

'I hold you responsible for this. She's not smart enough to think this one up on her own. No offense, Alexandra.'

'Tom, calm down,' Wilkes said.

'I will not calm down. I have just come home to find a woman I barely know moving into my apartment. And how did you get in anyway?'

'Hector let me in,' she said.

My God, she already knew his name. Alexandra must have charmed him to death.

'Please. I don't want to appear unreasonable, but you can't stay. I'm sure you understand.'

Alexandra shot Wilkes a look that could have been interpreted many ways. It was that raised eyebrows what-do-we-do-now look that indicates Plan A has backfired but no one has worked out Plan B. Alexandra moved into purr mode again.

'Tom, it's late. I can't ask the guys to pack everything up now.'

Suddenly for the first time I looked around my apartment and saw boxes everywhere.

'I'll call them in the morning and they can come and get everything, okay? Just let me stay the night.'

It was late. And they were practically done.

'Can't you go back to the Waldorf?'

'I checked out.'

'Well, check back in.'

'I can't. Everyone thinks I've moved in with you.'

'Everyone? Who's everyone?'

'The papers, the TV guys. They're outside. It will be everywhere by tomorrow.'

Oh, my Lord. How to undo this mess? The papers and TV guys were outside, no doubt summoned by the Riddler. The news would be everywhere tomorrow. The whole world was soon to learn that Alexandra West and I had moved in together. This is what Mom would call a daymare. That's a nightmare you have during the day. I couldn't kick her out right then. I had to let her stay at least one night. I would do what she had suggested and sleep on it, hoping that reason and a solution would come to me in the dark.

But one thing I had already learned. In every relationship there is always a power imbalance. Elizabeth and I had it, Jake and I have it, and I think it's normal. Under perfect circumstances, it shifts so continually that one partner never feels at the mercy of another. It ebbs and flows according to moods and maturity, and extraneous things such as jobs and success. But in this relationship, though highly artificial, the power imbalance was monumental.

I thought because I had initiated everything, it had in fact rested with me. I could call the shots, I could have her do my bidding. But standing in the middle of my apartment, surrounded by her shoes, her old copies of *Vogue*, her clothes and make-up, I saw for the first time that I never had any power, that she had it all. She always did. And the problem with power (I mean, just look at Napoleon), whether in a relationship with one (Josephine) or 1,000 (the French army), is that those who yield it only want more, and those who wield it rarely exercise caution.

I had been warned.

Chapter 19

I recall very little now of her first night in my apartment, except that I tossed and turned like the proverbial yacht in a storm. After Alexandra sent the moving men on their merry way and Wilkes disappeared into the darkness, we were left staring at one another, and for a second she looked genuinely apologetic. But it was only a second, for then she announced she was going out and asked if I had a spare set of keys. Though stunned and angry, I had little choice but to hand them over. She kissed me softly as she departed, hoping that would somehow calm me down. It did not.

Instead, left alone to my own devices, I went to my alcohol cupboard and poured myself a brandy. I could think of nothing else to do under the circumstances, and sank into the lips to throw it back. Instantly I realized brandy was the perfect antidote to what I was feeling, and poured myself another. I turned on the baseball game, which I would be watching alone. Jake had left a message on my machine that he was 'busy' and could not make it watch the game. Busy, I guessed, was a euphemism for furious. At me.

When the brandy was finished I switched to Scotch, and after that I don't remember. Though there were no witnesses, I can safely say by the time Alexandra returned I was so drunk I had passed out on my bed. I never heard her return, in fact I doubted if I would have heard a nuclear device being detonated in Central Park or in Mom's kitchen in Houston for that matter. When my alarm rang at seven the following morning, I thought a computer chip simulating a jackhammer had been implanted in my brain.

To this day I don't know what was the bigger shock, the intensity of the headache or the sight of a naked Alexandra West sprawled under a sheet, asleep on the lips. My living room was chaos, but in the midst of it all lay this sleeping Venus. She woke on hearing me shower and shave, and when she sweetly wished me a good morning, I grunted in response. Dressed and clutching a briefcase, I sat down next to her. She had wrapped the bed sheet loosely around her, leaving little to the imagination.

'I'm really in no mood to talk. I've got . . . I've got . . .'

'A hangover?'

'A busy day at work ahead. A lot on my mind.'

'And you've got a hangover.'

'Is it that obvious?'

'Well, the empty bottles on the kitchen sink sort of give it away, and you do look kind of green. Can I make you some coffee?'

'I don't have time. I'll grab some at work.'

'Aspirin. Really helps.'

'Thanks for the advice. Now, about this living arrangement.'

'What about it?'

'I don't think I need to repeat how I feel about this. Nor do I care to. You promised you would move out today and I hope, I hope when I come home this evening you will be gone. It's nothing personal. You're very nice. I even have to say there are worse things that can happen to a guy than to wake up and find a movie star asleep in his living room. It sort of made my morning. I'm sure it's something I'll tell my grandchildren, if I have any. But that's besides the point. You can't live here. You have to go. You promised. You did promise to leave, right?'

'Right.'

I thought she was going to cry. I felt bad even though I was the victim in all this.

'You have to admit what you and Wilkes did was really unfair. Below the belt.'

She sat there pouting like a sad puppy. Weird, because I had always considered her rather feline to that point.

'Tom, you're my good-luck charm, I told you that.'

'Yes, well. I am very flattered, even if it's not true. If you like, we can keep dating, even though by the terms of our agreement we are officially finished.'

'But if we kept dating, we would move in together eventually anyway. This just moves things along a little.'

'Alexandra.'

'Michael will be really angry.'

'Listen, Michael needs you more than you need him. You know that. If you move out this afternoon, what is he going to do? Seriously?'

'I don't know.'

'Alexandra, please. You promised. Call the moving guys, go back to the Waldorf.'

Silence.

'Alexandra?'

'If that's what you really want.'

'It's the only thing I want.'

'Fine. I'll go.'

'Promise?'

'I promise.'

'Swear on a Bible?'

'I swear on a Bible.'

I, of course, was thinking about *the* Bible when I said that, the one written by God and his prophets and assorted holy men. Alexandra I now see was thinking in terms of her bible, which could be *Vogue* (her fashion bible), *Variety* (her film bible) or *Starscene* (her gossip bible). Clearly our understanding of taking an oath on a bible did not mesh. In other words, when I returned home that evening, she was not gone. Nor had she made the slightest attempt to leave. She was right there where I left her. Well, at least her belongings were. She had left a note informing me she was in the gym. She signed it Alexandra and then three kisses. Nor would she leave the day after that, or for many days in fact. She was, I had concluded, Napoleon with implants. She had all the power. She made all the decisions to suit her. And when she launched an invasion, the territory in question stayed invaded until she chose to decamp.

That morning I went to work and grunted at everyone. The entire office had read in the papers that Alexandra had moved into my apartment. I think Frank Wicker-Smith was actually close to being hospitalized on digesting the news. Again he tried to ask me some vague questions, but I was in no mood.

'Tom.'

'Yes, Frank.'

'Congratulations.'

'For what?'

'Well, on moving in together. It's a big step. Must be serious.'

'Must be.'

Frank, still showing his impeccable WASP breeding, which I think is encoded in his DNA, realized he was to back off and, mercifully, he did. Louis, however, was another matter. Instead of getting Marlene to call me into his office, I was summoned by our leader himself.

'Tommy, get in here when you have a minute,' he barked down the phone.

'Sure, Louis.'

I sauntered past Marlene, who was wearing another form-fitting dress. There must be a store somewhere in New York that sells skin-tight clothes, and I figured she had an account there. She flashed me a huge grin and told me to go right in.

'Tommy, sit down.'

I sat.

'Tommy, I didn't know it was so serious. I mean, moving in together. Wow. You really got us there, buddy.'

You don't know the half of it, Louis.

'I see.'

'Some TV people called me today, asked me for an interview about you because they say you won't talk to them.'

'I won't.'

'Not a problem. Of course. And why should you? You're a private guy, right? But, Tommy, I have sales to think about, you understand that. Any chance I have to push the magazine, well, you know. I've got shareholders to worry about.'

That was true, but I think Louis wanted to grab his fifteen minutes of fame while there was still time.

'I won't bore you with the details. The upshot is some crew is coming here in the afternoon to shoot footage of the newsroom, then I'll give them some soundbite, probably two minutes, on how you are the most valuable financial columnist I have, I really respect you, blah, blah, blah. You okay with that?'

'Louis, since you're asking, I'd rather you didn't.'

'I understand. You fall in love and can't believe the whole world wants to know about it. I respect your privacy, I really do, Tom. But you have to see my point. Shareholders. I'm doing it for them. This will give us a big push in circulation.'

'Louis, you can't really believe that. You can't think people will buy *The Capitalist* because one of its columnists is involved with a movie star? It's ludicrous.'

'Ludicrous shmudicrous, Tommy. You haven't seen the new circulation figures. Up this week. Up last week. Up every week since your name hit the papers.'

'But why?'

'Curiosity, Tommy. People want to find out what she sees in you. No offense.'

'None taken.'

'Since you won't talk to the press, people are reading your column to get a sense of who you are. It's brilliant.'

'It's insane.'

'Tommy, I don't care how insane it is. It's working. Also, while we are on the subject, NBC called and asked if you were available to join a new program on money and investing they're starting up. Give a five-minute commentary at the end of the show.'

'Louis, are you serious? That's hilarious. How could they think I would be able to do that? I'm no expert. I just interview experts and write what they think. You know that. That's the beauty of it. I don't have to have any opinions myself.'

'I told them yes.'

'Louis, how could you?'

'Listen, nobody understands the market, so whatever you say, nobody will know that it's wrong. Just rehash your column on the tube. Piece of cake.'

'I can't do it.'

'Sure you can. Look, I'd love to do it. I've been trying to get a shot on those shows for years. But they want you.'

'They wouldn't want me if it wasn't for Alexandra.'

'Who cares why they want you? The fact is, people are going to tune in to get financial advice from the guy sleeping with Alexandra West. These guys are starting a new show and, you know how it is, they need instant ratings or they'll disappear. Television is brutal, Tommy. You're a drawcard.'

'They told you that?'

'Basically. And of course they think you're a smart guy. That goes without saying.'

'Louis, no.'

'Think about it.'

'I have.'

'Think some more. Just think. TV! Wow. I'd love to be on TV.'

'Then you do it.'

'Tommy, with pleasure. Only snag is, they want you, buddy. They want you.'

Indeed they did. And they were not alone. That day a lot of people wanted me. I went from the guy my wife didn't even want, to the man everyone couldn't live without. The producer of the show in question, *Your Money*, called and welcomed me to the cast. It was to start up a month later and run on Sunday mornings after the political pundits had argued themselves hoarse. He said they hoped the audience who watched the media equivalent of Ferdinand and Isabella on *Meet the Inquisition* would then stay on the couch to learn what to do with their money. I was to appear at the end of the program and suggest a stock tip, working in a comment about current government policy.

I didn't want to ruin his morning then and there, so rather than informing him I had no intention of working on a show called *Your Money*, *My Money* or even *Money 'R' Us*, I asked if I could be sued for giving bad advice.

'Sued?'

'Yes, sued. Could I be held liable if I recommend a stock and it plummets and people go bankrupt?'

'God, I never thought of that,' he said. 'I'm just the producer. Last show I worked on was *Live at Five*. I personally know jack about money, Tom. I'll check with the legal boys and get back to you. I'm glad you brought it up. Shit, the last thing we want is a lawsuit.'

Good. That bought me some time. And now for the rest of the offers.

To summarize. An offer to write a book from a big, big, big publishing house. Any topic you like, Tom. Finance. Swimming-pool maintenance. Dog-grooming. I got the distinct impression they didn't care what I wrote about as long as Alexandra would come on the book tour.

A weekly spot on a financial program on talk radio. A major Internet conglomerate called wanting to know if I wanted to start my own website. Excuse me? Me? What for, I asked them? Dispensing financial advice, they told me. I could be www.TomWebster.com, they said. They promised that with the right marketing, which I assumed meant if Alexandra mentioned it every time she went on a talk show, we could be drawing thousands of hits a week. I am not making this up. I thanked them for their offer and said I would get back to them. (In their dreams.) I then wondered, if Attila the Hun or Alexander the Great were alive, would they be on the web? Would they be dispensing battle plans on www.AlexanderTheGreat.com? Could I email Attila.Hun@Pentagon.Usgov.org with some invasion queries? Was www.TomWebster.com an inevitability?

There was an interview request for a feature on men behind famous women and how they cope. And calls galore. From my mother. From corporate publicists asking if they could put me on more mailing lists. From tabloid reporters wanting to know the wedding date. My mother again. More tabloid reporters. TV reporters. But no Jake.

I was determined to call him that morning and apologize profusely, but in between all the other calls and faxes, I never found the time. Instead, at one I headed for the Blue Moon, hoping he would be chowing on a bagel and cream cheese. He was. I sat down in his booth. He said nothing. I said nothing. It was like a scene from a Spaghetti Western where the good guys and the bad guys stare each other down. I really had no plan, other than I felt I owed him some explanation.

'How you doing?'

'Fine.'

His tone was so abrupt, his look so mean. In all the years I had known him I had never seen Jake this angry. Never.

'I guess you read she moved in.'

'I guess I did.'

'It wasn't my idea. Honest. I was just as surprised as you are. I came home and there she was.'

'You don't expect me to believe that?'

'It's the truth.'

'Right. She just moved in. You had no idea.'

'None.'

'Tom, don't bullshit me.'

'Jake, I'm not. She asked me if we could move in together and I said no, I wasn't ready. I thought she understood that. Jesus, I really hardly know the girl. Next thing I know she's in the apartment.'

'And I suppose you asked her to leave.'

'I did.'

'Tom, people don't move into your apartment against your will.'

'I didn't think so either, but I was wrong.'

'Right. The papers say it's serious. Is it?'

This was my cue. Do I break down and tell him the truth? About the money, the magazine article, the date, the entire set-up? It would certainly diffuse the situation, probably save our friendship in the process. But I couldn't. Partly because of Ms MacDowell, who would have me drawn and quartered. But partly because, in among all his anger, I kind of enjoyed watching Jake react to the idea that I was dating Alexandra, enjoyed causing friction between him and Elizabeth at home. I had gone too far to turn around now.

'No. Well, not serious in the true sense.'

'In what sense, then?'

Good question.

'In the sense that any relationship can be serious when you have only dated a couple of weeks.'

'The papers say three months.'

'I told you already, that was a lie.'

'Tom, I don't know what to believe anymore. I can't believe you have conducted this entire relationship behind my back. You have no idea how I feel.'

Then something happened that was completely unexpected. I let loose about his running off with Elizabeth, something I had never done before.

173

'Well, you have no idea how I feel about you running off with my wife!'

I was hollering. Me. I never holler. What was happening to me?

'That entire relationship began behind my back also if you remember. I might be dating a movie star but you stole my wife, goddamnit.'

Jake was stunned. I hollered at him. He had seen me shout at baseball, he had seen me shout at games on television, but he had never seen me shout at him. I mean, really yell. His eyes dialated and his eyebrows rose to meet his scalp.

'I thought you had dealt with that.'

'Oh, did you? How could you think that? We never discussed it.'

'Sure we did.'

'Elizabeth informed me she was leaving, then she left. When we met the next day for lunch, and in fact we were sitting in this very booth as I recall, you mumbled an apology, then we talked about baseball and we never brought it up again.'

'I didn't know you were so mad.'

'Of course you didn't. You've never been married, so nobody has ever stolen your wife from under you. It was pretty low, you know. I never talked about it with you because for the first six months I was so stunned I couldn't speak.'

'I'm sorry, Tom. Really. I thought the marriage was over before I came into the picture.'

'And what made you think that?'

'Elizabeth said it was.'

'Well, maybe for her. Not for me.'

'I'm really sorry, Tom.'

'Yes, well . . . given the circumstances I don't think I owe you any explanations about Alexandra, or her moving in with me or anything. I'd say we're about even right now.'

I was so mad I couldn't believe it myself. I drank a glass of water and stood up to leave like a gunslinger.

'We still going to the game Saturday?'

'Oh, sure.'

'See you then, if I don't speak to you before, Tom.'

'Yep. See you then.'

I had just given my best friend a serve that would probably be clocked at over 100 miles per hour on any tennis court in the country. The funny thing was, I didn't feel bad. I didn't feel happy. I felt powerful, and now I knew why Alexandra and Wilkes and Alexander the Great loved running their own little show so much. Power is a fine feeling. Yes, sir. That it is.

Chapter 20

I returned to work to find a note on my desk to call Jeannie in advertising. Jeannie was the office bombshell, *The Capitalist's* version of Alexandra. She was not as beautiful as Alexandra, but she was striking in her way. Though she was married with children, it was said Jeannie had a problem with fidelity.

Jeannie told her victims she had a surplus of sexual energy and needed to roam outside the bonds of marriage to satisfy her needs. Apparently her husband understood this, but I doubted it. My guess was her husband had no clue his sweet demure wife, who kissed him goodbye every morning, went to work and then embarked on a search for other men to kiss as well. Jeannie had clearly divided the office into desirable and non-desirable men, and she busied herself hitting on the former and ignoring the latter.

I was, I knew, on the non-desirable list, although Jeannie was always perfectly pleasant to me. She tried hitting on Frank once but he rebuffed her advances. I doubted it was because it was beneath him to have an affair, but suspected he slept only with women who went to his country club. Even while cheating, to Frank breeding was paramount.

So when she left a message to call her, I assumed naturally it was work-related. I was wrong. Jeannie was calling, she said, to say hi, so I said hi in return. Then she got to the point, which was, as points go, rather sharp.

'Tom, can you talk?'

'For a minute.'

'You know I've always liked you, Tom.'

'Thank you.'

'No, really. I know we never really talk much at work, but I always had you pegged as one interesting guy.'

Liar.

'I just thought you might want to have a drink after work. Sometime this week?'

I nearly fell out of my chair. Why is that women want you only once you're unavailable? Technically, of course, I was available, but this information was not public. As far as Jeannie was concerned, she wanted to sleep with the man who sleeps with Alexandra West, and I learned, as the days stretched on, she was not alone. A number of women made passes.

An intern left her phone number on my desk. I could make a bunch of intern jokes at this point, but I think you've heard them all. Suffice to say interns never spat in my direction two months ago. Letters started arriving for me at *The Capitalist* from completely strange women, informing me they were 'big fans of mine'. They wrote they thought I was hot. Attractive. Couldn't believe how lucky Alexandra was to have nabbed a solid guy like me, when there were so many weirdos out there. Can you believe that? Big fans of mine! Incredible. Some even sent photos of themselves. In bikinis. And worse.

Around this time I also started getting emails from female colleagues in the finance game that were, and I am not imagining this, work-related and then some. They actually began flirting with me over the Internet. After that tabloid story that had me pegged as a sexual acrobat, people let their imaginations run wild.

'Jeannie, I'll be honest. I don't think so. I have a girlfriend and, well, aren't you married?'

'My husband is out of town.'

How convenient.

'Well, my girlfriend isn't.'

'Gee, is she lucky or what? To have a man like you. Stable, dependable. I bet you really love her.'

'Jeannie, I can't really discuss this right now.'

'Of course not. That's why I'm suggesting a drink.'

'Thanks, but no thanks.'

'Think about it. You don't have to answer me now.'

That appeared to be the catchphrase for the day. Think about it. Don't make any decisions. The book deal, the radio show, the television spot, the website, they will still be here waiting for you tomorrow, Tom. So just think about it. But don't forget, we want you on our team, Tom. Not only that, they wanted to pay me money too. After you did the numbers, I could get rich. In her own way, Alexandra was doing for my career what I was doing for hers. Making me respectable. A player. By the afternoon I was over my disgust at how fickle people were and beginning to enjoy my new-found clout.

So what if I didn't know anything about the stock market? Louis was right. Nobody did. I thought I'd quite like being on television once a week. That way Mom could see me in Houston. That way Elizabeth would see me whether she liked it or not. I'd have to buy a new suit, of course, but with the extra money I could afford it. Radio? Well I'd just recycle my television spot. A book? Truth is I always wanted to write a book, now I had an offer. How could I turn it down? I couldn't really. It might never come my way again. The only thing I didn't want was Alexandra in my living room naked under a sheet when I got home.

My phone rang. I debated whether to answer it. What if it was more women in the building trying to bed me? What if it was another publisher trying to lure me into their arms? I didn't think I could take much more of this adulation. But Frank shot me a filthy look each time I let the phone clock another ring, so wearily I answered it. Well, what do you know. Oh. My. Lord. Finally.

'Tom.'

I know this voice.

'Hello, Elizabeth. How are you?'

'Tom, I can't believe you.'

'Why can't you believe me?'

'Letting that tramp move into our home.'

'Our home? You left "our" home a year ago, Elizabeth.'

I could see Frank pretending to be busy, but hanging on every word.

'It's still our home, Tom.'

'It's my home now, Liz, and I can move anyone in I want.'

Little did she know I would have traded Alexandra for her in a minute.

'I'm so disappointed in you, Tom. I just don't recognize the man I married.'

'This is why you called? To tell me what a failure I am in your eyes? You said that when you left. Don't you remember?'

'My, we are getting big for our boots, now that we are moving in different circles! Look, I called because reporters and photographers are still bugging me day and night and I want you to get them off my case.'

'And how do you expect me to do that?'

'Can't that bimbo girlfriend of yours do anything?'

'Such as?'

'Tom, they are making my life hell. They wait for me at school. They got my email address and now they bombard me day and night for interviews.'

'Liz, look, I am sorry this has happened to you, but it's happening to me too, and much worse, I might add.'

'Oh, please. You asked for it, Tom! You're going out with her! You're sleeping with her in our bed! I didn't ask for any of this! You have to make them stop calling me.'

'Liz, I'm not a magician. They will sniff around you as long as they think there's a story there.'

'I'm not talking to any of them. They don't want to hear my side of the story anyway. All they want to do is paint me as a witch for leaving you.'

God, hearing her sooo mad made me feel sooo good. I'll leave it to the Freudians among you to work out why.

'Liz, ignore them. Call Joe – he's our lawyer – and get him to do something.'

'What can he do?'

'I have no idea. But I'm guessing more than me.'

'Jesus, Tom. This is just…I mean…I just hate this, Tom. I HATE YOU!"

She slammed down the phone.

While Liz was yelling at me I vaguely remember a television

crew passing through the office, so I should have been prepared. I wasn't. Instead, that evening Mom called to tell me I was on television. An entertainment program called *Hollywood Update* had scrambled together a segment on my relationship with Alexandra. Mom said she was upset I hadn't combed my hair and that my tie was askew. Apparently they had shot some footage of me arriving home the day Alexandra moved in and used that, along with me on the telephone in the office to illustrate their story.

Alexandra had not granted them an interview either, so they resorted to stock footage of her, of which there is caseloads. At the end of the piece Louis appeared, and talked about me as if I were about to win the Nobel for economics. Mom said aside from my untidy appearance, she was very proud. She had started to become a mini-celebrity too, the mother of the man who was sleeping with that Hollywood star. The show aired at seven in the evening and then was rerun at eleven. I caught the rerun, and cannot tell you how utterly disconcerting it is to see people you have never met weigh in about your life as though they were experts. Here is a sampling.

Reporter: 'Things are hotting up for Hollywood sex kitten Alexandra West and her plain-Jane boyfriend, finance guru Tom Webster.'

Now I was a *guru*.

Reporter: 'Yesterday Alexandra moved in with the shy, brainy columnist for *The Capitalist*, and friends say it's only a matter of time until wedding bells start ringing. A source has told *Hollywood Update* that Alexandra considers this a trial marriage, and if it works, next on the list are children. And not just one! Alexandra wants six! Her favorite show when she was a kid was *The Brady Bunch*, and a source tells us she wants her own Brady Bunch. And this man [intercut footage of me on phone] is her Mike Brady.'

At this point I nearly lost consciousness, but stayed glued to the set, for the next face belonged to Louis.

Reporter: 'Louis Goldberg is the editor of *The Capitalist*, the man behind the magazine that probes the world of the rich and famous. He hired Tom Webster ten years ago, and says he always knew the quiet, thoughtful history buff had a secret side.'

Cut to Louis.

'He's very deep. I think you can gauge that from his columns.

He's very smart. Very bright. Impressed me from day one. Serious, stable, happily married until . . . well, until it broke up. Which, by the way, was a complete shock to him, as it was to the rest of the office.'

Reporter: 'Tom Webster also thought he was happily married until his wife, Elizabeth, a school teacher in the Bronx, ran off with his best friend.'

Cut back to Louis.

'He seemed very sad after that. So we were all thrilled when he started dating again. Not that we had any idea who it was. We were all flabbergasted, but really happy. If there is any guy out there who deserves the attentions of a movie star, it's Tom.'

By then Louis was flirting with the camera so aggressively it qualified as sex with an inanimate object.

Reporter: 'Time will tell if this Hollywood bombshell can make it work with her bookish boyfriend. Some say they are the Marilyn Monroe and Arthur Miller of our time, but, unlike Marilyn and Arthur, Alexandra wants a happy ending. We'll keep you posted. Back to you in the studio, Steve.'

As I was digesting this insanity I heard the key in the lock. For a second I thought it must be Elizabeth, for I was so used to her coming home late after PTA meetings. Then I realized it was Alexandra. She was dressed casually, which indicated to me she had not gone out anywhere special. She hadn't. She had gone to Michael Wilkes's apartment for dinner, where I guessed they continued to plot her career with General Patton precision.

'Tom.'

'Alexandra.'

'I haven't gone yet.'

'So I see.'

'Look, I thought about leaving all day. I even started packing. Really. But, Tom . . .'

She came to sit next to me on the lips. She grabbed my hands in hers and did her sad puppy routine again.

'I think it looks bad if I move out twenty-four hours after moving in. For you too. We need to think this through. Just give me until the end of the week. Then I'll go. Promise. Anyway, it will make your story better. Just give me until Saturday. Sunday. Please. Pretty please.'

I was too exhausted to argue. Whatever.

'They did a story about us on *Hollywood Update*.'

'Did they use the line about the Brady Bunch?'

'How did you know that?'

'I was there when they called Michael for background. He made it up on the spot and bet me lunch at Balthazar they would use it. I said they wouldn't, it was too corny.'

'Michael set that story up?'

'Tom, who else?'

'Why? He knows I want you to leave.'

'Well, he does, sure, but his job is to keep my name out there. And when those reporters call, if you don't tell them something, they just make it up.'

'But Michael just made it up.'

'That's different.'

'How?'

'Well, when we make it up, it's a strategy. When they make it up, you threaten to sue. Tom, in this game you have to call the shots, not them.'

She really was Napoleon, with implants.

'Even if the shots are a total fabrication?'

'Why do you look so surprised? You're in the media, you know how this stuff works.'

But the truth was I didn't. I spoke to government analysts and Wall Street stockbrokers all day, and they talk a language called statistics. They didn't lie to me, because they couldn't. The practice of capitalism is nine parts mathematics to one part the whim of those stupids in Washington. You can't make up the math. It either adds up or it doesn't. Your country either has a deficit or a surplus. Your company is running at either a profit or a loss. You can't tell me your shares are valued at $100 and expect me to print it when the market values them at $10. I had no idea in the entertainment world publicists would feed the media stories that were total fantasy. I was naïve, a fool, and Alexandra clearly thought so too.

'Honey, don't feel bad. They would have predicted we were going to have kids even if Michael hadn't mentioned it.'

'But we're not having kids.'

'Of course not.'

'You're leaving by the end of the week.'

'That's right.'

'You are leaving, aren't you? I mean, really leaving. Not just saying you might.'

'Really. I'm really leaving.'

'And how will Wilkes explain that to the press? I mean, today I'm about to father six children, tomorrow we break up?'

'Oh, you don't worry about that. Michael's real smart. He'll think of something.'

That's what terrified me.

Chapter 21

It was *déjà vu* the next morning, for there I was wandering into the bathroom bleary-eyed, and there she was naked under a sheet, asleep on the lips. For the first time I noticed a pile of scripts on the floor. These must be the infamous scripts that had been offered since we became an item, movies that would, she hoped, remake her career. I wanted to take a look, but I resisted approaching because I didn't want to wake her. My plan was to leave and avoid any social contact. No luck. By the time I had showered and dressed, she was up and in the kitchen making scrambled eggs.

'Morning, Tom.'

'Morning.'

'I'm making breakfast for us.'

Indeed she was.

'I picked up some things yesterday at that store on the corner. You bachelors are hopeless. There was nothing in your refrigerator except for six boxes of frozen lasagna. That's hardly food, Tom.'

God knows what a commotion she must have caused dropping into the Korean deli to pick up some groceries.

'I order in a lot since Elizabeth left.'

I heard toast pop in the toaster, so for a second I was distracted from the big picture. I thought Elizabeth had taken all our appliances. Apparently not. Then I saw it. Her. In my kitchen. She was wearing a T-shirt, an apron and nothing else. And she was playing Suzie Homemaker. It was quite a sight.

'Sit down. It'll be ready in one minute.'

I sat as instructed. She had laid the table and even poured orange juice. I must say, having a Hollywood bombshell cook you breakfast is not a bad way to start the day. She placed scrambled eggs in front of me, then a plate for herself, and sat down. She buttered my toast and placed it on a second plate. In all the years of our marriage Elizabeth never buttered my toast.

'*Bon appetit*, Tom.'

'Yes, *bon appetit*.'

I started to eat. Boy, a homecooked breakfast sure beats a donut on the run. She was a good cook. If her career ever took a dive, she would definitely find work at the Blue Moon.

'Alexandra, I have to tell you, I've been, I've been...'

'What, Tom?'

'I've been getting all these offers. It's incredible. It's amazing. Book deals, TV spots, websites...'

'Oh, sure.'

'You thought that would happen?'

'Of course. You're my boyfriend. You're a somebody now, right? Isn't that what you wanted for your article? Everybody wants a somebody on their team.'

'But three weeks ago I wouldn't have been offered a deal if my life depended on it.'

'Well, I'm glad I could help, Tom.'

'Yes. I guess I should say thank you.'

'See, you help me and I help you. It's great, isn't it?'

'Speaking of that, how's the career thing going with you? I saw some scripts over there.'

'Amazing, Tom. Simply amazing. I have an audition this afternoon with a director who a month ago wouldn't even spit in my direction.'

'Who?'

'I don't know his name, or his films. But Michael said he's a really big player in the independent market, and if you work for him, it tells the industry you're serious.'

'And he just called?'

'Yep. Called my agent, said he wanted to meet me. Just like that. And it's because of you, Tom. You're my good-luck charm.'

'Alexandra, if you had stayed in New York long enough this would have happened anyway. Maybe I just accelerated things a little.'

'No. Michael says you're the reason. The word is, and Michael relies heavily on the word, if a serious guy like you hangs out with me, then I'm more than just a sex kitten. I mean, Tom, you look like a professor. So if you think I'm intelligent enough to hang out with, I must be, right?'

'But it's all hype.'

'The entire world is hype, Tom.'

'Well, that's very exciting, then.'

'And he's not the only one. Everyone's been calling. I didn't get this much attention even after I did *Playboy*.'

'So how do you think everyone is going to react when it comes out this entire relationship is a sham? When my article is published, it could ruin everything.'

'I'm not worried. By then I'll have a couple of deals stitched up. Michael doesn't think it will affect me at all. He thinks I'm blameless. But he thinks it might really hurt you.'

Hello.

'He does?'

'Yeah, well, me, I'm a movie star. People expect us to do off-the-wall things, publicity stunts, all that stuff. But you, you're a serious financial guy, right? When you admit to scamming the public all these weeks, Michael thinks your reputation might take a beating. All those people who signed you up for book deals and whatever, they're going to feel pretty stupid. But then again, maybe not. Don't worry, Tom, it'll be fine in the end.'

But I was worried. Sitting there at the table I had an instant anxiety attack, complete with palpitations, sweating and shortness of breath. Michael Wilkes had a point. Things had gone way overboard. My social experiment had crossed the line I initially drew in the sand.

If I start milking all these opportunities, the television spot, the book deal, even my new expanded column in *The Capitalist*, once everyone learned they had been conned, they were going to be pretty mad. Really mad. Frank Wicker-Smith would go back to loathing me, and I preferred our relationship now, with him insanely jealous of me. And what if Louis fired me? What if the TV show offer was pulled? I made a note to call Ms MacDowell when I got to work and discuss these concerns with her. Wilkes was right. The way things stood now, I could get badly burned. Alexandra would rise from the ashes intact.

'Alexandra?'

'Yes.'

'I've made a decision.'

'Yes.'

'You can stay here if you want. You don't have to move out on Saturday. I have to sort out this mess. I think Michael might be right. If we split up suddenly and it comes to light the entire thing was a hoax, my reputation could really suffer. I could be ruined. I can't believe I'm saying this, but I'd like you to stay until I can talk to the people at *The Vulture* and sort some things out. This affair thing has gone way overboard. I should never have agreed to a second date. I don't know how I can write this article now and come out the other end with my reputation intact. I mean, for better or worse, I'm Tom Webster, financial columnist with a public face. I have commitments. Deals. People are paying me money for my opinion. It's not what I expected, you understand, but it happened and now I have to deal with it.'

'So what you're saying is I can stay?'

'Yes. Until I make some decisions. I mean, I think it's best as far as the public is concerned that we continue this charade.'

'If that's what you want, Tom, I'm glad to help.'

'I mean, we will break up, but in a while, not yet.'

'Of course not. Not yet. When you say.'

'So I guess you can unpack all those boxes and cases in the living room.'

'Sure. Good. Whatever you say, Tom.'

'I've got to go to work. I'll see you later. Thanks for breakfast.'

'Oh, Tom.'

'Yes?'

'We're going to an art show in SoHo on Saturday afternoon.'

'Right. Okay. That sounds good. No. No, it doesn't sound good. No. I'm going to the baseball game with Jake.'

'The guy that stole your wife?'

'Yes.'

'Well, I don't get that at all. Not at all, Tom. If somebody stole my husband, I'd hire a hitman.'

'Well, it did cross my mind. But we have gone through too much to let the whole friendship slide just over Elizabeth.'

'Too weird.'

'I know. Sometimes I can't believe it myself. Did I tell you she called me again yesterday?'

'No shit. She's mad, right?'

Alexandra was beaming.

'Furious. How did you know?'

'Tom, you're dating me. Alexandra West! Of course she's mad. I mean, I wouldn't want my ex-husband dating me.'

There were those smarts again.

'Anyway, about Saturday, you have to come to the art show. If we don't show together, people will think the relationship is in trouble.'

'Jake will be furious.'

'Jake can go screw himself. Listen, you don't owe him a thing. That creep ran off with your wife.'

'He's not a creep.'

'He is, Tom. It's really low to do that to your best friend. If the press finds out you went to a game with him instead of out with me, the fallout will be terrible.'

She was right. Sitting there in her T-shirt and masses of blond hair, the vixen was making total, perfect sense. Terrible sense. I couldn't fraternize anymore with Jake in public. What kind of man still hung out with the guy who ran off with his wife? Surely not a smart, intelligent, financial guru. And what man would go to a baseball game when they could be dating Alexandra West? She really was on the ball. I had to hand it to her.

'Fine. We'll go to the gallery. I'll cancel Jake.'

'Now you're thinking, Tom. I was a bit worried there at first, I didn't know if you'd catch on. But you have. You learn fast. I'm proud of you.'

I rose and she rose and straightened my tie, just the way Elizabeth used to. I thought she was going to kiss me goodbye but she didn't. Instead she started to load dishes in the sink.

'Have a nice day, Tom,' she purred in that voice that made me turn to mush.

'Yeah. Thanks. You too.'

I left the house racked with anxiety about my future. Pull yourself together, Tom, I heard a voice in my head say. Look in your books for the answer. And so on the subway I told myself I would take a page from the pilgrims during the Crusades. Things got tough marching from Europe to Jerusalem (as they will, it's quite a walk), but nobody packed it in. They soldiered on. And that is what I would do. That is who I would be. Tom Webster. Crusader. Soldiering on.

Oh, heaven help me.

Chapter 22

At work my voicemail was full and it wasn't even nine a.m. There were calls from newspapers in London and Germany wanting to talk about Alexandra, there were editors at publishing houses who'd heard I might write a book and wanted to make counter-offers, there were invitations to business conferences.

It was insane, and I was flattered and offended in equal measure. One day nobody wants you, next day they can't live without you. The idea of me, ordinary Joe, capturing the heart and body of Alexandra West so intrigued and titillated the world, everyone wanted in on the act. Intellectually I was starting to understand this. Emotionally I was exhausted, and realized I wanted some time out. I left a note on my desk that I would be going on an interview and would not be returning the rest of the day.

It was an outright lie, but I needed to think, and the office was no place to find peace and quiet anymore. Too many colleagues spent their precious available moments throwing me knowing smirks, too many secretaries flashing lascivious smiles. God knows what they were saying behind my back. Probably a combination of 'lucky bastard' and 'Why him?' According to Mom they were even saying it in Houston. She called to say the 'People' page in the *Houston Post* had taken to calling me the poster boy for every man who had sand kicked in his face at the beach. The reason Mom called was not because she wanted to repeat the news, but because she was angry. She was hurt they were calling her son ordinary. She was mad they headlined another story 'Beauty and the Beast'. She told me she loved me, and while I wasn't Robert Redford, she thought I was very handsome and wanted me to ignore all the newspaper reports.

'Please let me send them some baby pictures, darling. You were so cute as a little boy.'

'Mom, we have been through this before. I said no.'

'Well, let me speak to them, then. They call every day.'

'No.'

'No one?'

'Mom.'

'All right, Tom. You're the boss.'

But I wasn't the boss, and she made that quite clear when she finally caved and spoke to the *Post*. A gossip reporter called Dixie Lee had called every day since the story broke, asking what Mom thought of my new relationship, and she would very politely thank Ms Lee for calling but refuse to comment. But wound a mother's pride, insult her offspring, and you are asking for it. After three weeks of boiling, the kettle whistled loud and clear.

Tom Webster, the local boy who stole the heart of Alexandra West, has never talked publicly about his relationship with the Hollywood megastar, but his mother, Betsy, finally broke her silence today. She told us she's hurt media columnists continue to express shock over her son's attachment to the bombshell.

'They keep saying they don't know what Alexandra sees in him. Well, if you knew Tom, you'd understand. He's a very kind, loving son. He's very smart. He's not like those people she probably ran with in Hollywood who drive fast and do drugs and God knows what else. Tom isn't like that. He reads a lot of history, he's a good son. He never forgets my birthday and on Mother's Day he always sends flowers.'

Mrs Webster said she hadn't met Ms West yet, but guessed Tom might bring her to Houston for Christmas.

'We haven't discussed it, but he always comes home for the holidays, and if he would like to bring her, I would be thrilled.'

Mrs Webster admitted she had never seen an Alexandra West movie, but was planning to go to the video store this week and rent one. Nor was she aware until we mentioned it that everyone knew exactly how lucky Tom was because they could see what he was getting in the pages of *Playboy*. Mrs Webster seemed a little shocked. She said she didn't know Ms West had done the layout and had no interest in looking at it.

After that little interview with the *Post*, Mom called me just as I was planning to escape the office.

'Tommy, it's Mom. I didn't know she was in *Playboy*.'

'Yes, she was. But it was a long time ago. She regrets it now.'

'Good. I'm glad to hear it. I don't like those magazines. You never read them, do you, darling?'

'No, Mom.'

'You're a good boy and I love you, Tom.'

'You too, Mom.'

It's funny going home in the middle of the day, back to your own apartment. You feel like you are doing something illegal, and in a way you are. You are a fugitive from work, and you know it. But I needed some down time, some privacy, some headspace. Hector was stunned to see me. I was deeply suspicious of him now, convinced he was on everybody's payroll. Every story that Wilkes didn't plant somewhere, I was sure bore Hector's imprimatur.

'You just missed them, Mr Webster.'

'Just missed who?'

'A bunch of people. Tourists. Fans. They were standing outside the building taking photos. They wanted to know if Alexandra, er, Ms West, was home, and I told them she wasn't.'

'Have they gone?'

'Yes, sir. But they said they would come back tomorrow. They all had pens and books, so I guess they wanted autographs.'

'Thanks, Hector. Look, I'm sure this new development, Alexandra moving in, has been a huge strain for you. I'm sorry about that.'

'No, sir. You don't know how boring it is standing here all day. Since you got together with her, I enjoy coming to work.'

'You mean normally you don't like your job?'

'No, sir.'

'Can I ask why?'

'Too much sitting around and doing nothing. And the uniforms itch in summer.'

'I see. I'm sorry to hear it.'

'So the job is great now. I've talked about it with all the guys. Alfonso, Rick, all of us, we all feel the same way. Since she moved in, it's never a dull moment.'

'Well, I can't argue with that.'

'One man yesterday asked me for my autograph.'

'What!'

'That's what I said. But he said he collected autographs of the doormen who stood guard at the buildings of famous people. He said people laughed but his collection would be really valuable one day.'

'And you . . . and you gave it to him?'

'Sure. And you know what? I felt like a movie star. It was great. I told him, anytime.'

Good Lord. What next for Hector? A sitcom? A book deal? Uniforms from Brooks Brothers?

'Is everything all right, sir?'

'All right?'

'You're home early today.'

'Right. Right. Working at home today. Too much chaos in the office. Too many phone calls.'

'Of course.'

'Listen, if anyone asks, I'm not home.'

'Of course not, sir.'

Yesterday Hector signed his first autograph. How many more would he sign before this was over? I couldn't wait to tell Ms MacDowell. I think when your doorman starts signing autographs, it's a message from the gods the end of civilization as we know it is coming in on the next train.

Inside, I loosened my tie and walked into my bedroom to hang up my jacket. It's an old habit Elizabeth drilled into me. In the early days of our marriage I used to come home, tear it off and throw it wherever, which drove her insane. She would start ranting and raving, and in the end I learned it was better to hang it up than have a fight. The habit is now ingrained. So that day I opened my closet, but couldn't find my clothes. Instead I found hers. Piles of them. Gowns and skirts and everything French and very expensive hanging where my clothes used to be.

I had to search right back to the end of the rack before I found my suits and shirts compressed and buried in some dark netherworld of the wardrobe. My shoes had all been given the same treatment, while endless pairs of stilettos were on my shoe rack. Opening my drawers, I found my socks, underwear and ties had been amalgamated into one drawer, while her stockings, underwear and such claimed all the space. Nor did it end there. Dinky little boxes covered in pictures of angels and cherubs were on the dresser, and inside were hairclips and jewelry and Lord knows what else. I know I had told her to unpack, but not to pack me up in the process.

The bathroom was ten times worse. My shaving things, deodorant, all my guy stuff was squished onto one shelf in the cabinet atop the bathroom sink, while masses of make-up, lipsticks, eye pencils, foundations, lined the shelves. Hot rollers and blow-dryers and brushes sat on the laundry hamper. Pink fluffy towels hung where my blue less fluffy towels used to reside. Newly washed bras hung over the shower rail. My bathroom looked like a bordello. Whatever instinct drove me home now made me want to go back to the office. At least there nobody tampered with my desk, or its contents. Until she took over my job as columnist, at least I knew at work I was safe.

There were fourteen messages on my answering machine, and they were all for her. A masseuse confirming an appointment. Her agent calling to ask if she had read a specific script. A secretary to a hairdresser rebooking an appointment for a cut and color. Reporters from a multitude of tabloids. I thought they were only supposed to talk to her through her publicist. Then I realized my number was in the book, and this would only get worse unless I changed it. Michael Wilkes calling about an interview request from a current affairs program preparing a profile on the new clout of independent film directors. I copied down all the messages, exhausted by the end. I had no idea this so-called career of hers required so much upkeep. Then I called *The Vulture*. Ms MacDowell came straight on the line.

'Tom, my God. Who would have thought? You're a genius, do

you know that? Every day I pick up the newspapers and it just gets better and better. At work, you are all we talk about. When I say we, I mean only the people here in on the secret. Please don't feel the entire office is talking about you. Tom, I had no idea things could get this big. It's fantastic. I can't wait for your story.'

'Ms MacDowell, I'd like to meet with you to discuss something.'

'Please, call me Jamie. And the answer's no. We can't be seen in public together or even have you come to these offices anymore. You're recognizable now.'

'Well, can we talk on the telephone?'

'I have ten minutes before my next meeting. Shoot.'

'Jamie, you just said you had no idea things could get this big. Well, neither did I. But this is not big. This is out of control. Big I think I could handle. This is chaos.'

'That's fame for you.'

'But you don't understand. I wanted one date. Somehow that became two, then three, now she's in my apartment!'

'I know. It's fantastic!'

'It's not fantastic, it's a nightmare.'

'Which is the point I was making when we first met.'

'No. The nightmare is that she is now using me, manipulating me somehow to further her career in a way I never anticipated.'

'She's a smart cookie that one. You'd never think it to look at her, would you? I wrote her off as a ditz, but the way she is working your relationship is incredible. I give her three gold stars.'

'Jamie, that's the problem. She wants the relationship to go on.'

'Good.'

'No. Not good. The longer it goes on, the more famous I get and...'

'And the more famous you get, the better your piece.'

'No. The more famous I get, the worse it is going to be for me when it all comes to a sudden halt.'

'I don't think so, Tom.'

'Jamie, I'm close to a book deal. A TV show. For some reason people think I'm a financial whiz. When the article is published and they learn they were conned, I could be in deep trouble. I will be in deep trouble. Some people might sue. Fraud. I don't know, they'll find something. I might lose my job. These people I'm dealing with are offering me good money. They are not going to appreciate being taken for fools.'

'Brilliant.'

'Excuse me?'

'Tom, listen to me for a minute. Hear me out. Say, just say, hypothetically, of course, the worst-case scenario happens. Say all these new deals unravel when the piece comes out. Say they exile you to social and professional Siberia, we'll publish a follow-up piece a month later where you can chronicle your descent into hell, pointing out how fickle the whole process is.'

Oh, my Lord. She saw my fall from grace as an opportunity for a sequel.

'Jamie, I am not interested in writing a follow-up article about my life as a pariah. I would like to act now before we get to the pariah stage. I would like to practice some kind of disaster aversion, and I was hoping you could help.'

'No can do. This is out of my hands. We paid you for an article on overnight fame, and that's what we expect you to write. As to the consequences of your actions, well, they are certainly extreme, but I did warn you. Shit happens, Tom.'

'Is there nothing we can do?'

'Tom, I think you are panicking before the fact. I admit some people might be a little ticked off when they realize the relationship was a hoax. But their anger will last a week, two max, and then they'll get over it. Plenty of relationships in Hollywood are set-ups. Everybody knows and nobody cares.'

'Jamie, I want out. I'll give you back the money. I can't write the article. It will ruin me.'

'If it wasn't for the article, you wouldn't be the recipient of book deals and TV offers in the first place. If you want to keep your commitments to them, you have to keep your promises to us.'

'Why?'

'Because we have a contract with you, that's why. Now, Tom, please be reasonable. You're upset. I can see that. But for all the people who will think what you have done is low and conniving, there will also be others who'll see it as brilliant and incisive.'

'I doubt that.'

'Tom, I have to go. I expect the piece on my desk in a month. Good luck.'

She hung up. I was more upset now than ever. I could have cried, except I was distracted by the buzz of the intercom.

'Yes.'

'Sir, it's Hector. I know you said you are not home but there is a delivery man here with flowers for Miss West. I didn't think you would mind signing for it.'

'No, of course not. Send him up.'

It was the biggest flower arrangement I had ever seen. Given the timing and the way I was feeling, I chose to look at it as a funeral arrangement. Plus it came with a basket of fruit that could have fed a Third World nation. Technically she was my paramour, and being so pissed off and annoyed, I felt no guilt about opening the card. It was from some director or producer welcoming her to New York. Clearly they wanted to work with her, and this was stage one of a full-pronged attack to romance her.

I had one option left. Mr Wilkes. The guy was not a brilliant public-relations maven for nothing. An expert at damage and spin control, if there was a way for me to fulfill my obligations without tarnishing my reputation, he would know it.

Otherwise, well, otherwise I really didn't know if there was an otherwise. I called his office and left a message. The day so far was not among my happiest. In the morning a beautiful movie star cooked me breakfast. In the afternoon I contemplated suicide. There's a saying that some guys have all the luck, and earlier in this mess I was actually starting to believe I might be one of them after all. I was wrong.

I called a couple of government contacts in Washington to sound them out about some new bills introduced into Congress that would make donations to museums, galleries and theater companies tax-deductible. The idea was to reward people who gave to charity with more than just plaques, with refunds. My sources said there would be the required bunfight before the bill wormed its way through Congress, because some bleeding-heart liberal was sure to rise up and cry about yet another tax dodge for the rich. The sooner these liberals figure out everything is a tax dodge for the rich, the sooner they can quit complaining and go about fixing the country. I also thought it might be a good idea to sound out some people at this art gallery I was going to on Saturday about the idea. Maybe it wouldn't be a waste of an afternoon after all.

Rob, my source on the Hill, said he would get back to me with some firm figures regarding how much money the government thought museums would realistically haul in from the new law, and how much the government would lose in taxable income. Normally at this point he would have hung up, but not that day.

'Tom, gotta tell you. Your friends down here in DC are pretty impressed by the new girlfriend.'

'Thanks, Rob.'

'Man, who would have thought? No offense.'

'None taken.'

'How's it? I mean, how's it going and all?'

'It's going fine.'

'Sure looks like it.'

'Well, good.'

'Gotta thank you, Tom. You're making all us pinstripe hacks look sexy for once. I'll see if I can't organize someone down here to organize a Congressional Medal or something.'

He laughed uproariously and I tried to join him. But all I could think was that Rob was another friend who would be mad as hell when the truth came to light.

'But I'll only get the medal thing happening if you promise to bring her to the ceremony.'

'Sure, Rob. Consider it done. Talk to you next week.'

In fact I learned that afternoon as I placed a few more calls that every source made a point of mentioning Alexandra, inquiring into the welfare of our relationship like concerned parents. All of them expressed complete surprise that we had become an item, and many thanked me for giving them hope. One on the Budget Subcommittee said he told his wife as a joke if she didn't treat him better, he would leave her for a movie star. 'And I said to her, if Tom Webster can get Alexandra West to move into his apartment, us finance boys are hot stuff. If you don't start doing more cooking and cleaning around here, I'm off to Hollywood to get me a trade-in.'

The buzzer went again. I really should have stayed in the office. More flowers, but no fruit. Clearly these guys didn't want her as badly as the previous suitors. I placed them on the floor next to the first bunch. One more bouquet like this and I really could have held a funeral. I then called Jake. This I knew would not be easy, and it wasn't. I canceled the game and, armed with a new bravado, I actually told him why. Alexandra, I said, had already committed us to attend an art show. I was sorry, I said, but you understand that the only thing more important in life than baseball was women. He did understand that, didn't he? Not quite. He was silent at the other end. Then he started begging, cajoling me to change my mind.

'But you don't know anything about art. Why do you have to go?'

'Alexandra said we'd be there.'

'Tom, get real. It's the Yanks. We have tickets. You can't blow me off for some art crap.'

'Sorry. I've got to go.'

'You've changed, you know that.'

'No, I haven't.'

'Yes, you have. You would never dip out on a ball game before now. It's her. She's changed you.'

'Look, she just said it wouldn't look good.'

'What?'

'Me and you. At the baseball game.'

'I don't get it.'

'She asked what I was doing hanging around with the guy who stole my wife.'

'Why the hell did she ask that?'

'I don't know. Just did. She thinks it's strange we still hang out.'

'What do you care what she thinks?'

'She's got a point.'

'I don't believe this. She's brainwashing you.'

'I don't think so, Jake.'

'My God. It's pathetic. She's got you under her thumb. Do you have to ask her permission to watch television too?'

'Jake, please don't get angry.'

'I'm not angry. I'm pissed. There's a difference. We have a deal, Tom. No matter what's going down in our personal lives we never miss a game. It's a deal that has worked fine for thirty years. Now she comes along and the deal is finished.'

'I could go to games with you before, because nobody knew who I was. Now if someone spots us at the ballpark it will be in the papers the next day.'

'So what do you care?'

'I don't care.'

'But you just said you did. Jesus, Tom. Listen to me. Snap out of it before it's too late. I mean, sure, you probably really like her and everything, but how serious is this? Is it going to last? Come on. You're not trashing our friendship over her?'

'I would never do that, Jake. Just right now I can't be seen in public with you. It reflects badly on me, and her too.'

'You what? We can't be seen in public together? What am I? A serial killer?'

'Jake, calm down.'

'I am calm. I'm pissed. There's a difference. Tom, I'm hanging up and I sincerely hope you call me back before Saturday and tell me you changed your mind.'

But I wouldn't call him back. And I wouldn't change my mind. Alexandra was right. What was I doing hanging out with the guy who walked off with Elizabeth? Didn't I have more pride? Yes, I did, thank you very much. Anyway, last time I went to an art gallery was in ninth grade on a school excursion. It was time I went back. My mind was made up. And to think I even considered suggesting the four of us might get together for dinner. Not anymore. I doubt he wanted to meet her, although I would have loved rubbing his nose in it. And just at that moment, Alexandra walked into the apartment. She completely ignored the flowers, though she must have realized they were for her, kicked off her shoes and sat down next to me on the lips.

'You're home.'

'I live here.'

'But I thought you would be at your office.'

'I left early.'

'Right.'

'You have messages on the pad over there and the flowers are for you too.'

'Thanks.'

'Why do they send flowers?'

'Oh, just, you know, to say hi.'

'Why don't they just call and say hi?'

'That's not the way its done. You have to send flowers.'

'So . . . what did you do today?'

'Met with people. Directors. Went to the gym. Meetings. My life is all meetings, Tom. No fun. Just meetings.'

'I told Jake I couldn't go to the ball game on Saturday.'

'You did. Really?'

'You seem surprised.'

'Well, I thought you'd chicken out.'

'I thought I would too, but something happened when we started talking. I played our conversation over again in my mind and I thought you had a point. What am I doing hanging out with him?'

'Exactly. Mind you, this art show is going to be dullsville, so don't get your hopes up.'

'We sort of had a fight.'

'Sorry to hear it. Was a bad fight or a good fight?'

'There's a difference?'

'A good fight is where you clear the air about stuff that has been bothering you for a really long time and at the end you kiss and make up and stay friends. A bad fight is when everything ends badly and you don't know what you are going to say to them next time they call.'

'I think it was a bad fight.'

'Ow. But you know, Tom, you have to stick up for yourself in life. I always used to make a point of only having good fights with people. Especially in Hollywood. I would argue with a director but always made sure it was smoothed over by the end, because otherwise they spread rumors about you and ruin you. They run to the press, tell everyone you're difficult, and half the time it's because you wouldn't sleep with them.'

'I don't want to sleep with Jake.'

'But then I started having bad fights with people too.'

'Why?'

'Well, I don't know really. I think in the end I got sick of being

Miss Goody Two Shoes. I got tired of always worrying what they would do to me if I didn't play ball. Then one day some director asked me to strip in a scene which wasn't in my contract, and I thought, to hell with you. By then I was too famous to fuck with anymore, and I won. I figured out that people needed me more than I needed them, and if we had a bad fight, they came crawling back, not me.'

'But I am not in that position. I'm not famous. If I have a bad fight with someone, it stays bad. Nobody comes back at me to smooth it over.'

'You're wrong, Tom. You are famous.'

'I'm a famous boyfriend. That's not the same.'

'It's all the same, Tom.'

'Jake was furious. He says I've changed.'

'Don't worry. I promise you when he calms down, he'll try to fix things, you won't have to do a thing.'

'How do you know?'

'Trust me. You're famous, Tom. He's just a famous guy's friend. You have the upper hand.'

I told her Ms MacDowell had refused to bail me out of either my depression or my untenable situation. Alexandra commiserated but reiterated that the entire scenario wasn't as bad as I was forecasting. Again she insisted I was putting the cart before the horse, and people forgive and forget, or at the very least forgive. I told her I also wanted to talk to Michael about some sort of damage control we could manufacture to downplay the revelation the entire relationship was a scam. She promised if anybody could tinker with any problem and solve it, he could. Somewhat calmed by her reassurances, I began to relax.

I started to feel really comfortable with Alexandra in my home. It was nice to have someone to talk to, and she wasn't the ditz I assumed she was. I mean, she would never make it into Yale, but with that face and body, who needs Yale? They invented Yale to help people with my face and body get a break. Not her. Even without all the make-up and skimpy clothing, she was a knockout. Then and there I found myself sizing her up in a way I never had before, more aware of her body, her perfume, her everything actually. The walk, the mannerisms, they were all so feline, so sexual. Probably calculated too, but it had an undeniable effect on me. I think I was, in some ridiculous way, falling for her. Not in the truest sense, but in the I-wouldn't-mind-sleeping-with-you sense. I was ashamed of myself for even thinking it.

'Tom, I'm staying in tonight, I hope that doesn't clash with anything you have going.'

'Clash? What would I have going?'

'I don't know. That's why I am asking. You might want to have some friends over or something.'

'No. Actually, since the separation I never really have anyone over except Jake, and we're not talking right now.'

'Well, I'm beat. I just want to watch some TV and hit the hay.'

'I thought...'

'You thought what?'

'Nothing.'

'You thought I go out every night to parties and premieres and dinners. You think I'm a social slut, don't you?'

I smiled. She had me. It was true. I did think that.

'Well, that wouldn't have been my choice of words, but your picture is always in the papers.'

'That's Michael. He does that, organizes all that stuff. Truth is, when I'm shooting I'm in bed every night at nine, because I have to be up at five, and if I don't get any sleep, I look like shit on camera.'

'So are you shooting something tomorrow?'

'Photo shoot for *Vogue*. If it's decent, it might make the cover.'

'I see.'

'Oh, hey, did Michael call you about Tommy?'

'Tommy?'

'Tommy Hilfiger called Michael about you.'

'Am I supposed to know that name?'

'Oh, Tom. You really don't live in this century, do you?'

'Not if I can help it.'

'Tommy is just like one of the biggest designers out there. He dresses *all* the rock stars.'

'So what does he want with me?'

'He wants to give you clothes, dummy! He asked Michael for your number. All the designers want to dress the boyfriends or girlfriends of celebrities now. It's not brain surgery, Tom. Haven't you noticed that every time we get our picture in the paper, they write about what we are wearing?'

'But all I wear is my Macy's suit.'

'Exactly. They've noticed you're no fashion plate, which means you're ripe for the picking.'

'Ripe for the picking?'

'For a makeover, Tom. I mean, you're a finance guy, of course you wear suits, but now that you're my boyfriend, they figure you might want to get hip on the weekends.'

'I might want to get hip on the weekends?'

'That's what the people from Tommy told Michael.'

'Alexandra, I can understand them wanting to dress you. But me? It's idiotic. It's up there with pet rocks, it's so stupid.'

'Tom, I keep trying to tell you. They think we're lovers. They think we might get married some day. You're on their radar now. If you wear Tommy Hilfiger to the gallery on Saturday, he'll get a shitload of publicity. You're good for business.'

'I believe you, Alexandra. But why does he think I want to dress like a rock star?'

'Why wouldn't you? Everybody else does, Tom. Hey babe, it could be fun. Do you want me to tell Michael you're interested?'

'Absolutely not.'

'I think you're making a big mistake.'

'How so?'

'Well, first of all, they are going to give you a truckload of free clothes. And second of all, I've looked through your wardrobe, Tom, and you're not exactly Mick Jagger when it comes to style. And third of all . . .'

'I own an Armani suit!'

'And third of all, it could be good for your article.'

I keep telling you, she has these flashes of brilliance that just astound me.

'You're right. It could make it interesting, couldn't it? Me dressing like a rock star on Saturday. I mean, totally ridiculous, but interesting.'

'See, Tom, now you're getting it. Just relax. Enjoy the ride. You and I both know it's not going to last. When this is over, you'll have all those Tommy clothes as a souvenir.'

'Okay, fine, tell Michael I'm interested.'

She beamed again. The smile was so high-wattage it could have lit a night game at Yankee Stadium.

So this was how far I had come. I was ditching Jake and a game (never before in my life, not even over Elizabeth) so I could dress up like Mick Jagger and take Alexandra to an art show. I just hope they don't ask me to sing.

Chapter 23

So that night I stayed home with a movie star and watched TV. I know. Unbelievable, right? But that's what happened. We ordered Chinese food from the little place on the corner and read our fortunes out to each other at the end of the meal. Mine said the future was pregnant with opportunity, which Alexandra said was a sign things would all work out in the end. Hers said all things come to those who wait, which she interpreted as a sign her born-again career would take off.

We watched an old Hitchcock movie on cable, and opened a bottle of wine. She was utterly engrossed in the film, taking careful mental notes of the lighting, what the actresses wore, which profile they turned to the camera. About the dialogue, story or direction she cared little. She often pointed out when the continuity went awry, when a hairstyle from one scene didn't match that of the next. She looked at the movie rather than to it, seeing only appearances, no depth. Her attitude, I thought, was a perfect paradigm for her own career and life.

When the film ended we were both tipsy and tired. I have no idea now how what happened next happened next, but I leaned over and tried to kiss her. Maybe it was the wine talking, maybe I felt I had to inject some sizzle into the article, but if truth be told it was simply hormones. I'm not asking forgiveness, only suggesting it's a rare man who spends the night with a blond bombshell in his very own apartment eating Chinese food and downing white wine who doesn't try something.

Alexandra looked hurt first. Then shocked. Then she pushed me away. Then came the lecture.

'Tom!'

'I'm sorry.'

'What are you doing?'

'Trying to kiss you, I think. No. I'm sure of it. I was trying to kiss you. I'm sorry. I'm not like this normally. It must be the wine.'

'Tom. No. Gotta be "Victor".'

'Excuse me?'

'You've got to be Victor.'

'Who's Victor?'

'Mature. Victor Mature. You know, the actor.'

'I know the actor.'

'It was something my dad made up. He was always telling us to act mature. And so he would say like, "Alex, I want you to be Victor about this and see my point of view. You are not going to that party." Or whatever he wasn't letting me do. When he wanted us to be mature about things he would always say, "Be like Victor. Be mature."'

'I see.'

'So that's what I'm telling you, Tom. This was a business arrangement. That's it. No offense, but you're not my type. You're very nice, just not my kind of nice. Not the nice I'm attracted to. In a way I wish you were my type, cos you're solid. All the men I go for, well, anyway, doesn't matter.'

'Alexandra, I'm sorry. I never intended to, you know, make a pass. It was just the moment.'

She didn't seem to accept either the apology or the feeble excuse that went with it.

'Tom, you know what I liked about you? In all the time we have been dating you never tried to hit on me. Every man does, and you didn't. You were so respectful. Shy, in fact. I really appreciated it. And now you've wrecked everything.'

'How could I wreck everything? There is nothing to wreck. We are not dating.'

'But you tried.'

'I tried to kiss you. I wasn't trying to sleep with you.'

'Oh, come on. Where do you think kissing leads?'

'Alexandra, I'm really, truly sorry. I feel I have offended you and that was not my intention. The kiss wasn't planned.'

'Well, I don't know. Just make sure it doesn't happen again. Got to be Victor, Tom. Remember that. Now I'd like to go to sleep, please.'

'Of course.'

Her tone was unmistakable. I was being banished from my own living room. I went to my bedroom as instructed and picked up a book. I read the same page at least six times before tossing it on the floor. I felt like that time when I was ten and got caught playing baseball inside the house and was sent to my room until dinner. It was the exact same feeling, except now I was older and wiser and felt far more stupid. Wasn't this my house? Why was I in hiding? So I tried to kiss her? Shoot me. Hell, she could understand that? The whole world thinks we are having wild sex anyway.

Maybe she couldn't understand. Maybe she didn't comprehend the effect she had on men. Garbage, of course she did. I'd seen her work that charm, turn it on whenever she needed it. And here I was, after having attempted a humble liplock, in exile. I heard her brush her teeth, make up the bed and turn out the light to go to sleep. Waiting fifteen minutes, I then rose, tiptoed around my own house, used the bathroom, my bathroom, like a criminal on the run. I guessed there would be no scrambled eggs, no buttered toast the following morning and I was right. Nor was there orange juice or a sexy smile awaiting me. Just a quick hi, good morning, got to run, see you later, and she was gone. Damn. And I was hungry too.

Bruised and shell-shocked, I somehow found my way to work. My fellow pinstripes of course were still in awe of me, their respect having grown in leaps and bounds and still multiplying. If only they knew. That afternoon messengers delivered contracts from *Your Money* for my television spot and a formal offer from a publishing house for a book deal. If I accepted it, I would have to get an agent, and, having no idea about such things, thought this would be something else I could raise with Mr Wilkes. Even though the car may have stalled with Alexandra, the wheels were certainly in motion on all other fronts.

That evening I met with him at the Blue Bar in the Algonquin

Hotel for a drink. I laid out the scenario as I saw it carefully and methodically. Even though it was he who predicted the negative fallout, now he appeared unmoved by my plight. I then opened my briefcase, searching for props to make my arguments carry more weight. Contracts for television shows and book proposals were placed on the table. I was, I pointed out, on the verge of signing, committing to people who believed I was Alexandra West's boyfriend. When they learned I wasn't, I could be skiing downhill awfully fast. He listened intently, then in response ordered another beer and grabbed a handful of pretzels.

'You're overreacting, Tom.'

'I don't think so.'

'Look at it from my perspective. Trust me. This is my business now, my territory. When the truth comes out, sure, there will be some initial shock, surprise, maybe a little backlash. But you must understand, the deals, the people who are signing you up, when they think it through, hey, you're still the same guy. You might not be Alex's boyfriend, but you're still qualified to give financial advice, write that book, make that speech. You never misrepresented your credentials, you just lied about your love life.'

'These people are going to feel like they have been taken.'

'Not necessarily. Not if you write the article carefully enough. Not if you chart your rise to where you are now, include some witty anecdotes, kiss up to everyone who really pissed you off, then humbly apologize to everyone you lied to, appealing to their intellectual instincts.'

'I don't follow.'

'Well, first write the article about your overnight success. You understand that part, don't you?'

'Sure. But it could hurt a lot of people. Co-workers. My boss. My best friend. Mind you, that friendship is already a train wreck. If I write about their reactions to what happened . . . I mean, some of them were just mean. Not to my face, but I know what they were saying.'

'Hey, they were saying it to me too. If you think it's hard to date Alexandra, you should try explaining to columnists and reporters how it happened she's in love with you. I had to lie big-time.'

'Thank you, I think.'

'But we did it, Tom. We have them all fooled.'

'Don't you worry what this will do to your reputation too?'

'Tom, I'm a publicist. I have no reputation. We are right up there with lawyers and used-car salesmen. It's ironic, but publicists have the worst PR in the business. We should hire someone to do public relations for us, but nobody wants the job.'

I actually felt kind of sorry for him at that instant. Then I forgot about him and continued to feel sorry for me.

'So what are you saying?'

'I'm saying write the story. You have to. Then at the end, grovel to everyone you scammed. Ask them to look at things from your perspective, appeal to their egos. Tell them there was no intent to hurt them personally. Ask them to look at the entire incident as a serious attempt to unmask the hype of celebrity in our culture, blah, blah, whatever. Then thank them, really thank them, for actually playing a part in your movie. Suggest they were integral to a story that the whole of America is now going to be talking about. Then take a vacation. Disappear for one or two weeks, then come back. It will all be over.'

'You make it sound so simple.'

'It is. Trust me. Look, the most important thing is not to panic. People, I find, have a huge capacity to forgive and forget. Well, forgive anyway. Nobody forgets.'

'I don't know. I'd rather give back the money and cancel the whole thing.'

'Too late, Tom. Too late. Know what I think?'

'What?'

'I think on top of these deals, you'll get more, including a book deal to expand your article and include all the detail you left out of the *Vulture* piece.'

'That's insane.'

'No, it's not. People are fascinated by stuff like that. Every guy in America would kill to date Alexandra West for a month, have her move into their apartment. You did it! So it was fake. Big deal!'

Well, that was one book I would never write. The article was punishment enough.

'You sure this will work? If I just write the piece carefully enough, I could avert disaster?'

'Tom, if you think you're famous now, wait till the article comes out.'

'You didn't answer my question.'

'The answer is no problem. This is not a disaster. It's all fixable. Trust me. Look what I have done for you so far. I won't desert you now.'

'Fine. Thank you. Now I can go home and sleep tonight.'

'Ah, Tom. Speaking of going home to sleep.'

'Yes.'

'You are intending to sleep alone, aren't you?'

He knew. He must. Jesus.

'Of course.'

'I mean, sorry to bring this up, but I heard you tried something the other night.'

'It was a mistake. I was a little drunk. Hey, you can't blame me, huh?'

'Right. But don't try it again. Remember, Tom, this is business. This relationship doesn't really exist. Gotta be Victor.'

Chapter 24

I was out of the doghouse by the following evening. Alexandra returned home late and threw me one of those smiles that suggested everything was forgiven. Good. So now I wouldn't have to sneak around my own apartment like a burglar. I was going to bring up the fact I did not appreciate being moved out of my own closets, but since the kiss fiasco, thought better of it. But the real sign I was now out of Château Bow Wow was when Hector buzzed at seven a.m. while she was cooking me breakfast again. This I liked, and realized I would seriously grow to miss once she had up and left.

'Sir, it's Hector. I just want to let you know your wife is on the way up.'

'She's downstairs?'

Alexandra spun around from the stove and threw me a wicked grin. Her eyes widened like saucers.

'No, sir. She's on the way up. She didn't want me to announce her, but I thought you would want to know.'

'Thanks, Hector. Good work.'

Alexandra launched into action. I mean, she was brilliant. She raced to the lips, ripped off all the bedding and bundled it into a closet. If the world thought we were sleeping together, Alexandra certainly was going to play her part.

I had barely put down the intercom when there was a knock at the door. I was in boxers and a T-shirt. Alexandra was in panties and a T-shirt. Without realizing it, we had dropped all formality when it came to dress, and in the mornings ate breakfast garbed as though we were really lovers.

I opened the door. Elizabeth, clutching a briefcase, was dressed for school. Oh, Lord. This was going to be interesting. I mean, interesting like the Mexicans storming the Alamo. I could smell blood.

'Hi. This is a surprise.'

'Can I come in?'

'Why didn't you call?'

'I don't think I need to call to come to my own apartment.'

'Well, I have got someone staying here.'

'Yes. So everyone keeps reminding me.'

At this moment, if there was an orchestra in my living room, I would have had them play the theme music from *Jaws*. Alexandra came out of the kitchen, acting completely innocent.

'Honey? Honey, who is it? I heard someone at the door.'

Elizabeth was rendered speechless. She just stood there as Alexandra approached and extended her hand. Alexandra towered over Elizabeth, her five feet nine to Elizabeth's five feet two. I was so tense I didn't know where to look. But Alexandra was just loving this moment, and she worked it.

'Hi, I'm Alexandra. Sorry I'm not dressed. I wasn't expecting anyone. Nice to meet you. And you are?'

'Elizabeth Webster.'

'Oh. Oh. Hi. Oh. Right. Elizabeth. Well. God. Good to meet you. Tom's told me so much about you.'

'I'm sure he has.'

MEEEOOOW.

'Well, Elizabeth, what brings you here so early?' I said.

'I need to talk to you, Tom. *In private*.'

'Oh, I hear my cue.' Alexandra giggled. 'I'll go take a shower.' Then she moved in real close to me and kissed me softly on the lips.

'I'll miss you, baby,' she purred.

Elizabeth was dying. She was turning beet red. Watching her so mad was better than the sex with Alexandra I never had.

'Well, I guess you two would have met eventually, so why not now?'

Elizabeth walked in and sat down on the lips.

'She's not exactly your type, Tom.'

'This is what you came over to tell me?'

'No. But now that I have seen her in the flesh, I can't imagine what you two talk about all day.'

'You'd be surprised.'

So would I, actually.

'I can't imagine she would be interested in the Lincoln presidency, unless of course she could play the role of intern.'

'She's an actress, Elizabeth, not a porn star.'

'How can you tell?'

My, my, she was catty for seven in the morning.

'Elizabeth, why are you here?'

The truth was, I knew why. I saw why. The curiosity was killing her. She had to see if we really had set up house together. So she came. She saw. She got insanely jealous. I had Alexandra West naked in a shower in the next room, and my wife in front of me having a breakdown. I thought I would explode from happiness.

'I came because I just can't take this anymore. You have to do something.'

'Can't take what anymore?'

'This. You two. The press are driving me crazy. I got home last night and a camera crew was waiting for me. The kids at school are driving me nuts. People are talking behind my back.'

'Liz, I told you when you called last week, there's nothing I can do.'

'Break up with her.'

'What!'

'Come on, Tom, you know it's going to go nowhere. Look in the mirror. Haven't you asked yourself what she's doing with you? A big movie star like her? It's laughable. I don't know what she's up to, Tom, but it's going to end, so why not do it now? I want my life back.'

God, what cheek. Alexandra thought so too, for at that juncture she came out of the bathroom looking totally sexy, wrapped in the smallest towel.

'I'm sorry, Elizabeth, but I couldn't help overhearing. You want Tom to break up with me because people are giving *you* a hard time?'

'Oh, come on, Alexandra, we all know this isn't going anywhere.'

'Gee, you've got a nerve coming here, telling Tom who he can and cannot sleep with. I don't care what you think, lady, but *I love Tom. I do.* For your information this relationship is going somewhere. Hey. Why do you care so much anyway? You didn't want him anymore.'

Elizabeth was dumbfounded. But she regrouped in a flash.

'I don't care who he sleeps with! I just want the press to go away!'

'Sounds to me like you're jealous.'

Oh, you go, girl. Give her the old left hook.

'Don't be ridiculous. Me? Jealous of a woman like you? Huh!'

'And just what is that supposed to mean?'

'Tom knows what it means.'

Liz grabbed her briefcase.

'Goodbye, Tom.'

Liz stormed out. I looked at Alexandra in amazement.

'You are a brilliant actress,' I said without a trace of irony.

'Well,' she said purring, 'it *was* a great part.'

Chapter 25

After the prizefight between Elizabeth and Alexandra, the rest of the week was uneventful by comparison. I went to the Tommy Hilfiger showroom with Alexandra, and a special consultant to the stars greeted me as if I *were* Mick Jagger.

'Oh, Mr Webster, Tommy is just thrilled to have you on board!'

I wondered whether Tommy would be *just thrilled* when he found out I wasn't who he thought I was. After an hour of trying on a number of items that I would not normally be caught dead wearing at gunpoint, we decamped with a pair of black pants that sat on my hips (I don't really have hips so it was quite an ordeal to find a pair), a pair of plaid pants, a deep-purple velvet jacket, a plaid jacket, a pink shirt with oversize cuffs, a blue shirt with an oversize collar, and a very psychedelic tie. It was Tom Webster does Mick Jagger by way of Austin Powers. Even Alexandra thought so.

'You looked fab in those clothes, Tom,' she said in the cab back home. 'Really. I'm not just saying it. You looked... *shagadelic.* Elizabeth is going to have a fit.'

Oh, she was right about that, and I have to admit that was 99 percent of the reason I was going along with this nonsense. Pressing all Liz's nerves was causing me more joy than I can articulate.

Bouquets of flowers continued to be delivered by all and sundry in the film business and by Saturday my living room resembled the

White House rose garden. It also had turned somewhat into the local post office. Michael had brought around a few bags of fan mail, which Alexandra suggested I read, thinking it might add spice to my story.

It was all so similar, all so adoring. They wanted pictures, or better yet dates. Some even made reference to me in their letters. They hated me for stealing Alexandra's heart. I must admit, between the letters arriving at *The Capitalist* from women professing their love for me, and now garnering a mention in her mail as the target of their envy, I was getting quite an ego boost.

There was one letter, however, I felt we should turn over to the police, from a man who said if I didn't leave Alexandra alone, I might go scuba-diving in cement flippers. I had seen enough mob movies to know what he was talking about. Alexandra promised to turn that letter over to the FBI.

'I can't believe all these people write to you. I mean, I'm getting letters, but this is unbelievable.'

'That's nothing. There are bags more in LA at my fan mail service.'

'How does that work?'

'Well, once you get to be a really big star, you pay people to open and answer your mail for you. They sort through it and only send the good stuff to me.'

'What do you consider good stuff?'

'Letters from people in hospital wanting me to visit. Letters from little kids with drawings, I love those. And the letters from kooks so we can call in the police.'

'And when they write you from hospital, do you visit them?'

'I can't. If I did, it wouldn't be fair. If you visit one, you have to see them all. But I always send a photo and a note. A couple of times I've called them up to offer support, you know.'

That was really nice of her. I was actually impressed.

'But mostly the mail is guys asking for dates. Some propose. Some send rings in the mail, can you believe it? Diamond rings. I could die. I return them all. Some guys send naked pictures.'

I dug through her mail and picked one at random.

Dear Alexandra,

You are the best, best, best, best, best, best, best, most beautiful, beautiful, beautiful, sexiest, sexiest, sexiest movie star in the whole world. I love you more than my wife, but please don't tell her that. I think about you when I am with her. I would leave her to be with you. Now that you know this about me, would you go to dinner with me? My number is —

Yours in eternity,
Tom in Texas

Another Tom from Texas interested in Alexandra West. Maybe he thought since she is currently dating a Tom, he had a chance. I asked Alexandra what she would do with the letter.

'Send him a photo. I mean, the guy's married, for chrissakes. He should know better.'

Indeed.

Saturday morning I was banished from own apartment. Alexandra asked me to leave because a hairdresser, make-up artist, manicurist and stylist were coming over, and they wanted free run of the place. It was, I thought, a gargantuan effort just for an art show, but Alexandra said we would be greeted by full court press, plus the movers and shakers who would be attending needed to be dazzled. I think her exact words were, 'I want to charm the pants off them, Tom,' and I had no doubt she would achieve her objectives. Team Alexandra arrived around ten and began setting up to begin her transformation.

Donning my Yankees baseball cap to give me some kind of protection, I made myself scarce with a trip to my local bookstore. Brighton Books was an old-style store that I feared would soon be squeezed out of business by the Godzilla-sized superstores springing up in the neighborhood. Brighton Books played classical music, had attentive sales staff who sent you little postcards about new releases, and a fabulous history section. Even though the superstore was cheaper, I felt duty bound to patronize Brighton Books to support the dying concept of personal service.

They also had the softest, biggest, plumpest armchairs in Manhattan, and you could sit in them all day reading and nobody ever moved you on. I hadn't been there since the entire drama with Alexandra unfolded, and hoped that this would be the one place the staff would not make mention of it. Deeply buried in literary journals and the like, Brighton Books employees would rather have root canal than read *Starscene*. Or so I thought. Presumed. Alas, even bookworms have their weaknesses and supermarket tabloids were one of them.

As I walked into Brighton Books, John, the manager, looked up from the register and did a double take. He blurted out something about not seeing me in a while and welcomed me in. They had a slew of fresh releases on the shelves, he said, and there was a new biography of Eleanor of Aquitane he thought might be of interest. As I made my way to the section, he stepped out from behind his bench to follow me. Finally he approached, as I stood perusing the dust jacket proclaiming the virtues of Miss Aquitane.

'Haven't seen you in a while, Tom. Thought you forgot about us, or worse, abandoned us for the gorilla up the road.'

'Oh, I would never do that, John. I've been busy.'

At this point that smirk that I have been getting from a lot of men lately unfurled across his face.

'So I noticed.'

'Yes.'

'You're a lucky guy, Tom.'

'Thank you.'

'Though I have to say, I never pegged her as your type.'

'Well, neither did I before I met her.'

'They say she's really quite smart. The blond hair and all, that's just an image.'

'It's true.'

Oh, God. Back to lying again.

'You should bring her in here sometime, Tom. If she likes to read, I'm sure there is something here we could fix her up with.'

And so I learned that even serious, horn-rimmed-glasses wearing New York bookstore managers turn to jelly when thinking about blond busty actresses with tresses of hair. In a way I liked John better now. He was always so serious, and he ran the store as if he were a librarian. Now he seemed more human, more approachable. I could also see where this conversation was going, and realized I wanted to exit pronto. I bought the book and fled the place to stroll the neighborhood. Now here was another person who would be mighty angry when the truth came out. What if the staff of Brighton Books were so disappointed in me, so upset I had sunk so low, they never forgave me? Never sent me little notes in the mail again?

When I returned home Alexandra was sitting in a chair in the center of the room, being primped, pampered and blown dry.

'Darling, is that you?'

I sheepishly made my way into the living room.

'I missed you. Was your shopping expedition a success?'

I held the book over my head like a trophy.

'Went very well.'

'Darling, come here.'

She leaned forward to kiss me while everyone else moved back in unison and watched. When the kiss was over they moved back into position around her.

'He's just so divine,' she said to no one in particular. 'I can't get over how lucky I am. Tom, darling, what do you think of the color?'

'Color?'

'My hair?'

I stood back and took a look at her hair. My God. Alexandra was no longer a platinum blond. They had changed her hair color to a much calmer version. In the light it was almost red.

'I've gone strawberry blond. Do you like it? It's part of the new me.'

I did like it and said so. Making her hair darker raised her IQ twenty points immediately.

'Lean forward,' said a tall man drying her hair.

Alexandra then tossed her head down again. Realizing my presence was no longer required, I retreated to my bedroom to get dressed as a rock star.

The only way to do this, I told myself, was to pretend it wasn't happening to me. I chose the purple velvet jacket because it was the most subtle thing they gave me, and I could pretend I was King Henry VIII, who wore a lot of velvet for special occasions, like weddings and beheadings. I paired it with the pink shirt, and donned the black pants that were still looking for the hips they were supposed to rest on. I finished the entire scenario off with a pair of black lace-up shoes I had bought years ago with Elizabeth, which to my amazement Alexandra told me were now back in fashion.

I couldn't bring myself to put on the neon tie, so opted to go without. I dressed without looking in the mirror. Frankly it was too painful, and I decided I would only look once everything was in place. Then, when finished, I spun around to get a glimpse of the new me.

I think there is only one word to say at a time like this, a word you know I would never normally use.

Fuck.

I looked like Jimi Hendrix if he had been white, short and fat. I checked again just to make sure I wasn't seeing things. No, there I was, looking positively, as Alexandra had predicted, *shagadelic*. There was no way I was leaving the house.

'Tom, can I come in?'

Alexandra didn't wait for an answer. She barged right into my bedroom.

'Wow! Wow, Tom. Look at you!'

'I can't go out like this. I look beyond idiotic. I'm getting changed.'

'You can't get changed, Tom. You promised the Tommy people you would wear their clothes this afternoon.'

Again, the mattress was right. What I didn't realize about this celebrity business, but which now rang loud and clear, was how many people you get into bed with. There is no such thing as a free ride, even when you are famous. The clothes might technically be free, but they still cost. The price I was about to pay was looking like the secret lovechild of Keith Richards and Queen Victoria.

'So how do I look?' she asked.

As opposed to me, she looked, well, unbelievable. Wearing a black cocktail dress and her hair now piled high on her head, she was doing her best impression of Alexandra West meets Audrey Hepburn in *Breakfast at Tiffany's*. The effect was stunning.

'Chanel. It's their Little Black Dress. Also part of the new me. No more trash and flash. I'm going uptown, Tom.'

'You look like Holly Golightly,' I said.

'Who?'

'*Breakfast at Tiffany's*. Audrey Hepburn played Holly Golightly.'

'Oh, God. I've never seen that film. You must think I am so stupid.'

'No, of course I don't think you're stupid.'

Actually I did. Any actress who hasn't watched the entire Audrey Hepburn oeuvre and taken copious notes doesn't deserve a career.

'You look beautiful, Alexandra. You deserve a better-looking guy than me to take you there.'

'Tom, please don't talk like that. Now you're not Tom Cruise, you're still Tom Webster, you're looking very hip right now, and after living with you for a week you I can say you are very appealing in your own way. Quite sexy, I think.'

I blushed. And not just a pink blush, but a red, fire-engine blush.

'Thank you.'

'You're most welcome, Tom.'

She just called me 'quite sexy'. You heard her. *Alexandra West called me Quite Sexy.* On reflection, it proved to be quite the day of transformations for both of us. My wardrobe went hip, her wardrobe went classic, my ego expanded and her hair changed color. Tell me, who needs to go to the baseball game?

Chapter 26

We took a limo to the art show. When it stopped in front of the gallery, I could see photographers, assorted television crews, and even quite a considerable crowd of onlookers. I hadn't spotted Charlie and his gang, but assumed he was there.

The yelling began immediately. 'Alexandra!' 'Alexandra!' 'This way.' 'Over here.' Nobody called my name at first, but then I heard it. 'Tom.' 'Tom.' 'Over here.' I followed Alexandra into the gallery like an obedient border collie, taking all my cues from her. She stopped and posed for the paparazzi for a few minutes before rushing past them. Always leave them wanting more, she whispered to me.

Inside it was another world. The chaos on the street was soon forgotten as perfect-looking waiters roamed the room handing out champagne. Alexandra said they were all actors waiting to happen and I did not doubt it. I felt sorry for them, forced to serve and smile at people whose jobs they coveted. There was a lot of air-kissing going on, and Alexandra instructed again to stay cool and smile a lot. People rushed to her to say hello, and she introduced me as, 'This is Tom, the love of my life.' This gave many people an opportunity to size me up in the flesh, and I wondered what they were thinking. Today we were not Marilyn and Arthur, we were Holly Golightly and George Peppard doing Hendrix. No matter, the crowd still registered various levels of disbelief and I knew it.

'Alex!' shrieked a tall, striking brunette who rushed at us from the other side of the room. She was wearing a dress cut so low and so short I wondered why she bothered. She was, like Alexandra, somewhat surgically enhanced. I thought for a minute I heard an accent, but couldn't be sure over all the noise.

'Don't move, darling. I'll be right there. I'm just going to get another champagne.'

I looked at Alexandra with the kind of stare that demanded an explanation in twenty-five words or less. She mimed putting her fingers down her throat, and, following that, I needed nothing more.

'I hate her. Don't be nice to her.'

'Who is she?'

'You don't recognize her?'

'No.'

'Rachel Carter-Brown. English. Used to be on a soap over there. Came to Hollywood and milked all that sophisticated British stuff to the hilt. You know, talks with a plum in her mouth even though she's not really upper class. She and I often go up for the same parts, mostly action adventure, although I can't understand how anyone could choose her over me. Michael says it's the idea that she's British and sexy that some directors go for. Look at that dress. She looks like a hooker.'

That she did. The differences between them were all the more striking now that Alexandra was dressing like a CEO.

'I heard she's thinking of moving out to New York after seeing what it's done for me. If she does, it's war. This is my turf now.'

'But if she is successful in Hollywood, why leave?'

'Because she wants to make my life a misery. I don't know. Probably same as me. Sick of being thrown out of burning buildings and getting rescued by he-men toting machine guns.'

'Is she any good at what she does?'

'No way. She couldn't act her way out of a paper bag. Look at that body, would you? All surgery. And the name's fake too, you know. It's really just Brown. She added that Carter to make people think she was royalty or something.'

I didn't think this was the time to point out to Alexandra she was not exactly Katharine Hepburn herself, or that she had similarly improved on Mother Nature via a surgeon's scalpel. Silence sometimes is indeed golden.

'Here she comes. Remember, don't be nice to her.'

'Alexandra!'

'She's always spreading rumors about me. That I slept around to get parts. Like she's a nun.'

I was quite enjoying myself now. I was about to witness, well, I hoped I was about to witness, some fireworks between two women who were declared rivals. I had so enjoyed the spat that had taken place in my apartment earlier in the week, I was pumped now for round two. But it was not to be. People who hate each other in Hollywood pay no homage to the William the Conqueror art of war. They never attack offensively, but defensively. They never knife you in the chest, but in the back, right between the shoulder blades. Nor do they act during daylight hours. Rumors and gossip are spread late at night, via telephone or email, and enemies always, always, cover their tracks.

'Alex, darling,' said Rachel in a voice which made me think of Margaret Thatcher addressing Parliament. 'So I finally get to meet him. He's adorable. So cute. The pictures in *Starscene* don't do him justice. Wherever did you find him? Love the jacket.'

'Tommy Hilfiger,' Alexandra informed her.

On the surface, they were as pleasant as could be. The undercurrent, of course, was palpable, but onlookers would never have guessed. Alexandra dutifully, begrudgingly, introduced me to Rachel. We shook hands. She told me how lucky I was to find a girl like Alexandra, and I agreed.

'She's just the sweetest girl. Not like some people in La La Land,' she said.

I could see Alexandra was thinking, yes, not like you. After some carefully calibrated chit chat about my work, which clearly bored her, she turned all her attention to Alexandra. They talked movies for just a minute, as neither wanted to reveal what they would be working on next. Alexandra said she was sorting through offers. Rachel responded she was too.

They discussed London, Hollywood and New York, and Alexandra cooed and gushed about her new home state. I was never once asked about my opinion. All I was required to do was stand there holding Alexandra's hand like a store dummy. Occasionally she leaned her head on my shoulder, as if to signify how close we were. For a pair of second-rate actresses, they were actually putting on quite the show. They even posed together for a photograph when a camera was thrown in front of their faces, placing me in the middle like a kind of Berlin Wall. Then suddenly my prayers were answered. It turned nasty, as I hoped it would.

'You're looking well, Rachel,' said Alexandra finally. 'But different somehow. Your face looks different.'

Oh, the claws were coming out now.

'No. No different to when we last met. But speaking of changes, you're eyes are looking great. What make-up are you using to cover up those little lines you have?'

Saucer of milk for the brunette in the heels, thank you, waiter.

'I don't use make-up to cover up my lines because I don't have any lines, Rachel.'

'Oh, so you had surgery, then? I heard you did. Well, it came out great. Good move. Don't worry, I won't say a thing. Our secret.'

Alexandra was furious and squeezed my hand. I spoke up for the first time, realizing it was now expected of me to intervene and implement some crisis control.

'Alexandra, I'm starved. Let's go find some food.'

'Let's,' she said firmly, scowling at Rachel. But she was not finished yet.

'I have not had my eyes done and if I hear you starting rumors that I have, I'll tell people about all that liposuction you had on your thighs.'

'Girls, please,' I said.

Rachel Carter-Brown stormed off. She was steaming. Alexandra was steaming. I grabbed her and walked her toward a buffet. It took us twenty minutes to get there, in between stopping and air-kissing more people, posing for more photographs, walking the walk and talking the talk, as they say. Finally we had a minute to ourselves.

'I'm sorry, Tom. I didn't mean for you to see that.'

'Do you always fight with her?'

'She started it.'

'You kept it going.'

'Whose side are you on?'

'Sorry.'

'Imagine saying I had eye surgery for lines. The nerve.'

'She was rather catty.'

'She's always like that. Always has to take a shot. I hate the English. There should be a law. They shouldn't be allowed into the United States. I'm glad we threw their tea in the harbor. I'm glad we kicked them out of the country.'

So she did know some history after all. Very impressive.

'Calm down. She was trying to needle you. The thing to do now is act like it didn't affect you one bit.'

'Eye surgery. That bitch.'

'Exactly. And you know it's not true, so don't let it worry you.'

'But it is true.'

'What?'

'I did have surgery to remove some lines. On screen everything is huge. Your face is enormous. Crow's-feet look like roadworks. They had to go.'

'But you are just barely past thirty.'

'Yeah, I know. If I had had them done at twenty nobody would have noticed. Now everyone can tell.'

'I really don't think it matters, Alexandra. Nobody cares.'

'She's going to tell everyone. I'll tell Michael. He'll plant a story about her. She's going to pay for this one.'

I was staggered. All this anger spewing with volcanic force just over a few facial lines. It was on her fortieth birthday that Elizabeth first started looking in the mirror and crying about aging. Then again Elizabeth only had to face thirty students every day whose chief mission was to finish class early and get to the mall. They neither cared nor worried that Elizabeth was losing her youth. I actually found the little lines developing around her face rather beautiful, though I failed to tell her so. Maybe if I had... Forget it. It's too late now.

'Alex, let's look at the paintings. That is why we're here.'

As if to rub her nose in it, the paintings were nothing but lines also. Lines seemed to be the theme of the day. Huge white canvases with lines drawn on them, sometimes a splash of red right down the middle, sometimes a diagonal line in blue and purple. The paintings all had pompous titles like *Destruction* and *Eclipse*, and I didn't know whether to laugh or cry. The price tags started at around $10,000 and a number of paintings already had been tagged with a red sticker, indicating they had been sold.

'What do you think?' said Alexandra, somewhat calmed.

'I think it looks like lines to me. I think Michelangelo spent eight years on his back painting the Sistine Chapel and this is how far we have come? Take me back 500 years any day of the week, Alexandra.'

We continued to stroll the gallery, moving politely from one canvas to the next, as if we did this all the time.

'Looks kind of dumb to me too.'

'Well, that's modern art for you.'

'I know I shouldn't say it, Tom, but I bet I could do this.'

'No, you shouldn't say it, but I think you're right.'

As we hit the corner of the room Alexandra drew me closer to her. She instructed me to nuzzle her and I did as told. She also made sure it went on long enough that everyone got a full view. There would be no mistaking this was one sizzling romance. Hey, even at a tony art show, the papers would say, we couldn't keep our hands off each other.

'Quick, we better go say hello to Roger.'

'Who?'

'The artist, dummy.'

'Who is it again?'

'Roger Corbett. The actor.'

'Who?'

'God, Tom, I don't believe you don't know this either. Roger Corbett. You know, he played the detective in *Trackers*, that movie about small-town cops who outwit the FBI tracking a killer.'

'Never saw it. Give me the plot just in case.'

One thing about Alexandra, she was good at summarizing events, people and emotions in thirty seconds or less.

'What happened was, this killer goes berserk in a small town in the Midwest. Three farmers are found dead in their cornfields, and the FBI come on the scene. And so the small-town detectives get their noses out of joint because they think they were doing a good job on their own. Well, the FBI tell the local police to back off, but they keep searching anyway, and now there's a race to see who can find the killer first. And the local boys win. Made over $100 million. Corbett played chief of the FBI team.'

'Who was the killer?'

'That was the best part. It was the wife of the local police chief. The guy is living with a murderer except he doesn't know it. She was this quiet, sweet, country wife, but underneath she was this wild child. Turns out she had affairs with all of the victims, then poisoned them so they wouldn't talk. The scene when he realizes he has to set a trap to capture his own wife is amazing.'

'Sounds like a great film.'

'It was. Won Oscars and everything.'

'I'm sorry, I know I should know this stuff.'

'Forget it. I don't have a clue about Wall Street, so I guess we're even.'

Suddenly Roger Corbett approached. He was handsome in a graying executive kind of way, very debonair. He did not look like an FBI detective, and I later learned although he was nominated for a Best Actor Oscar, he did not win. He lost it to the actor who played the head of the small-town cops, the guy who had to arrest his own wife. Them's the breaks.

'Roger!' Alexandra gushed. 'Fabulous. Fabulous. I had no idea you were so talented.'

He beamed.

'Roger, this is my boyfriend, Tom Webster. Tom, Roger Corbett.'

'Webster? Any relation to the dictionary people?'

Here we go again.

'No, sorry, although I do know some interesting words.'

He laughed. The joke was so tired but it never failed me. Thank God. I felt I should say something nice about the exhibition, but the only thing I could think of was that Roger Corbett was no Michelangelo. Some people should really stick to their day jobs.

'The paintings are wonderful. Truly. I find them very interesting. Challenging.'

He beamed again.

'Yes, well, people think they are just lines, you know, that it's easy to paint them, but they haven't got a clue, have they? They think I do it all in ten minutes. I get really upset when they don't get what I am trying to say.'

People like me. I was dying to know what in fact he was trying to say, because to me all his work said was that he could draw straight lines. Instead I opted to change the subject.

'I loved *Trackers*, thought it was one of your best performances.'

My God, I was becoming such a great liar.

'Thank you. Thank you. Bitch about losing that Oscar. I mean, I really thought I had a shot. Anyway, Martin deserved it. I'll give him that.'

'Next time,' I reassured him.

'From your lips to God's ears.' He laughed.

By now my mind was starting to wander. Glittering people, catfights among rival actresses, overstretched canvases covered in straight lines, none of it makes up for an afternoon with the Yankees. I was dying to the know the score, but realized nobody at the shindig would either know or care. They were too busy checking out who else was there, what they were wearing, handing out cards, making plans to do lunch and posing for photographers. In the center of all this social swirl I stood saying nothing, but taking it all in. Eavesdropping, I learned all the actors present bitched about their agents, other actors, demanding directors and 'the system', whatever that was.

Apparently there was consensus that 'the system sucks' and the 'system works against us'. There was also much discussion about 'the loop', as in who was 'in the loop', 'out of the loop' and how there was even a loop within the loop, a subloop, in which those on the triple-A list got their hands on everything first. I made a mental note to ask Alexandra if she was in the loop, and if not, why not.

The crowd I estimated to be roughly 50 percent Hollywood and film industry friends of Roger Corbett and 50 percent art world types. I have to admit, sartorially, though I felt like a complete joke, I fit right in. I actually looked like I belonged. A lot of men were wearing velvet, and even more were dressed in pink shirts. Okay, the actor types were wearing pink. The SoHo crowd, they were all wearing black, and seemed to be completely awed by the sprinkling of stars in their midst. By contrast, the actors in pink totally ignored the artists, having decided that on the what-can-you-do-for-me scale their value was nil, and concentrated their efforts on shmoozing each other. The New York artists, meanwhile, actually discussed the work adorning the walls, and whether out of competitive jealousy or genuine intellect concluded they were garbage.

'If he wasn't Roger Corbett, the only place these works would be hanging would be in his basement,' sniped one man in black.

'This stuff couldn't get hung in an abattoir,' said another.

Just for the record, the papers the next day gave the show a lukewarm review, which Alexandra informed me would have been a negative for anybody else.

'The fact that he is a star helps,' she said. 'Write that in your article. All those reviewers think, well, for an artist he's not good, but for a great actor who paints on the side he's not bad. Michael says they always go easy on stars who sing or dance or paint. They can't forget who they are.'

I found this idea completely idiotic.

'Do you mean to tell me that if you decided to paint some pictures this week, exhibit them and call the press in, they would be too scared to pan you?'

'Yup.'

'I don't believe it.'

'Ask Michael. He's repped a number of actors who also sing. He says they shouldn't even be allowed to sing in the shower, but they all get record deals because they're big names.'

'But surely market forces come into play here. If you don't mind me theorizing for a minute, if the record doesn't sell, they never get another deal.'

'But they do sell.'

'But you just said the records they make are terrible.'

'They are. Just like Roger Corbett's paintings weren't any good. Stuff sells because the celebrity sells them.'

I was confused and shocked and horrified, because somewhere in the depths of my being I knew she was right.

But back to the party. Clinging to Alexandra like the proverbial leech, I shuffled around with her for two hours. We met a lot of people whose names completely escape me, but I always knew who was important to Alexandra by the way she gave me a gentle dig in the ribs. Those whom she considered bores or useless professionally warranted no digs, and I learned we were to chit and chat for but two minutes before moving on.

Those potentially useful, such as magazine writers and editors, producers and studio executives, received the full Alexandra West treatment. The pouting lips, the outward thrust of the breasts, the dazzling smile. A number of people commented on her new look. They loved it. Alexandra told me she couldn't wait to tell Michael.

It was interesting again to note how many men could not hide their surprise at our coupling. A number of women flirted with me, which, I cannot deny, I seriously enjoyed. Some people had already heard about the book deal and television spot, and wished me well. I gathered up quite a collection of business cards, and handed out my own in equal measure, still unsure why I would need the services of a independent film producer or antiquarian-book seller. No matter. People's attitudes toward me ranged from polite to obsequious, all due, I knew, to the fact I was Alexandra's boyfriend. But I admit one thing. Despite the lights, camera, action, tone of the entire affair, despite the phony air-kissing and missing the Yankees, I found myself having a fine time by the end. What had started out as a chore and a bore ended as one of my better social encounters. Probably the best, if you don't count my wedding. At the gallery women had fêted, fawned and flirted with me in constant succession, and this kind of treatment works wonders on a fragile spirit. Dating a movie star does have its fringe benefits. Of course, I know to everything there is a downside, I just didn't know I would learn its exact nature so soon. But I would. I always did.

We left the party and returned home. In the limo I admitted to Alexandra I rather enjoyed myself, while she declared the entire affair to be a thorough bore.

'I'd much rather go shopping.'

Actually I had no real idea of what she liked to do in her spare time, and thought this was a good opportunity to ask her.

'Well, I don't normally have spare time. If I do, I like to, you know, hang out. Shop. I love to shop.'

I must explain shopping for her is not like shopping for you and me. She goes to a designer, tries on clothes she likes, and then walks out with them gratis, or at the worst pays about 20 percent of their retail value. She'd spent, I discovered, two hours at Chanel choosing clothes the day before, and had an appointment with some guy called Richard Tyler next week to get some pant suits.

'Richard Tyler makes the best suits out there. Very elegant. I never used to wear him, but he's now going to become a big part of the new me.'

I made a note of it.

'And where do you go when you hang out?'

'Restaurants, clubs, bars. But I'm always working. When you have to get up at five a.m. every day, you don't go out.'

'Ironic,' I said.

'What is?'

'We think all everyone does in Hollywood is party. Now you're telling me all they do is work.'

'Yes. And they only go to parties to meet people who can give them work.'

'Really?'

'Or get drugs, or women. I'd give anything to go to a real party one day.'

'Hey, if we're still together at Christmas, I'll take you to *The Capitalist* office party. You'll see how the other half lives.'

'What happens?'

'Nothing. That's the problem. Everybody gets drunk, some people disappear and make out, somebody else ends up sitting on the photocopier Xeroxing their butt, and then you go home. Mind you, if you came, it would certainly liven things up.'

Alexandra laughed. She still knew the boys in the office were digesting her first visit to the newsroom.

That night I stayed home. Alexandra went out for a quiet dinner with a girlfriend called Penny, her oldest friend from high school. Penny and her husband lived in New Jersey and drove in for the big event. I read about Eleanor of Aquitane while watching the baseball highlights on television. It was actually rather a great day but for the fact Jake wasn't speaking to me. The Yankees beat the Mariners 3–1, even without my cheering them on from the stands. Exhausted, I was considering going to sleep when Alexandra returned home. It was still quite early and I commented on the hour.

'Yeah, well, they still had the drive back, so they had to leave.'

'You don't sound like you had the greatest time.'

'Yeah, well …'

'Did something happen?'

'No, just the usual.'

'Which is?'

'You meet up with friends from high school, from home, wherever, and you have all these high hopes for a great reunion, that you will talk forever, and it's never that way.'

'How long hadn't you seen Penny?'

'Years. We talked on the phone occasionally. Sent Christmas cards. But we lost touch basically. Then when I moved out here I called her and suggested she come into the city and I would take her and her husband to dinner.'

'Where did you go?'

'Josephine's.'

'And?'

'And I thought they would like a really fancy New York restaurant, you know. I mean, I doubt they eat out a lot. He's a mechanic. She's home with three kids.'

'But they didn't like the food?'

'I think the whole place freaked them out. The menu was in French, for starters. Everyone was dressed, well, you know, very New York, and they weren't. I think they felt very self-conscious.'

'And?'

'And after about half an hour we ran out of conversation. They asked me a couple of questions about Hollywood, I saw pictures of their kids, and we kind of ate in silence. There was a lot of silence. Tom, it was horrible. I'm exactly the same Alexandra she went to school with, but she was treating me like we never met. Like a stranger.'

I truly felt bad for her.

'I'm sorry it didn't work out. Listen, if it makes you feel better, it's not just you. Happens to everyone. When I go back to Houston to see my mom, I run into old school buddies and you never know which way the wind's blowing. Some of them you really connect with, some of them, well, nothing to say.'

'Really?'

'Oh, sure. Though with you it's a bit different. You're a celebrity. I think that probably makes it harder for them.'

'So what do you think will happen to you when you go home now?'

'What do you mean?'

'Well, you're a celebrity now too, Tom. And once you go on TV, that's a whole other world. People at home will handle you differently too.'

Again, the dumb blond who was not so dumb had a point. What would happen when I went home this year? If it was anything like what was happening with Jake, I could wait to find out.

Chapter 27

There was a very famous social experiment conducted a number of years ago, and at the time I remember reading the results and dismissing them in haste. But act in haste, repent at leisure, said a wise man eons ago. The time had arrived for me to repent, as the results I discounted now had me firmly in their grasp. In short, a university professor wanted to ascertain what impact men with money and position made on women.

Six women were shown photographs of six men, ranging in looks from absolutely average to downright ugly. They were asked to rate them on a scale of one to ten and then answer a number of questions, a rating of one being truly ugly, ten being devastatingly handsome and sexy. They were also told the men were all uneducated and working class. Without exception the women thought the men looked unremarkable, averaging a score of around three. They added that the men all appeared to have dull personalities and no sense of humor. (You can get all this from a photograph? Who knew?) When asked if they would be interested in dating any of them, all replied in the negative. No surprises there.

A second set of six women were then ushered into the room. They were shown the same photographs, but this time they were told the men were all millionaires, captains of industry, college-educated and commanding much respect in their communities. Well, guess what? These same guys climbed upward along the handsome-o-meter in leaps and bounds. They were all rated as nines and tens, good-looking, sexy and eminently datable. In particular, the psychologists noted, the ugliest male in the pack was described as rugged, aggressive, smart, strong-minded and beguiling.

Interesting that, among the first poll group, they opined the only way they could have sex with Mr Seriously Ugly would be with two paper bags on hand. One would be placed over his head, and the second over hers, in case his fell off. The upshot of the entire study? Money and glory turn ugly into beauty. Fame and fortune erase flaws all us working stiffs possess, like average looks and quiet personalities. Yes, folks, clothes may make the man, but it's the perception others hold of you that gets you the girl.

I now saw myself as living proof of the aforementioned experiment. Initially, when the press caught wind of me, the little gossip items referred to me as the beast to Alexandra's beauty. I took no offense at the description, for I understood they needed a catchy phrase to garner attention, and this was it. But when they got tired of that one, they consulted their dictionaries and new phrases appeared, including, in no particular order, nerd, nerdmeister, intellectual, tweedy, bookish, plain Jane and, my personal favorite, Napoleonesque.

I enjoyed being compared to Arthur Miller and, not to diminish Mr Miller's achievements, I relished the idea of being considered Napoleonic. I suspected the phrase was employed not due to any belief I had invaded France or freed its peasants from tyranny, but rather because I was shorter than my paramour, Alexandra, whom they now implied bore a resemblance to his love, Josephine. The very idea made me laugh uproariously, and I enjoyed the entire affair.

Then something changed. Around the same time women started hitting on me in the office, around the same moment females would approach me when Alexandra was not around and suggest a quiet drink, gossip columnists started singing a different tune as well. The old experiment results were coming home to roost. Now famous, elevated from the perch of anonymous finance columnist to guru status, basking in the reflected glory of a movie star stapled to my arm, I too suddenly appeared to the world greater than the sum of my parts.

If Alexandra considered me attractive, by God, I must be, right? And I was smart to boot. According to some of the hype, I was the second coming of Einstein. Soon they stopped writing that I was nerdy, bookish or unremarkable. In their place were phrases like financial maven, hot-ticket columnist, Yalie boyfriend and, my all-time favorite, 'Tomcat'. Now that was just too fabulous for words, and I have no doubts as to how it started. After all the stories in the supermarket tabloids about what a sex machine I was, 'Tomcat' was only fitting. It suggested a sly, cunning, promiscuous male, roaming the night for fresh feline prey. A veritable sex king of the animal world, and surely a perfect partner for a sex kitten. Frankly, I didn't think it could get any better. But once again, I was completely, utterly and totally wrong.

Sunday morning I was woken from a deep sleep by the doorbell. Rick, the relief doorman, probably on somebody's payroll too, announced that Michael Wilkes was on his way up. I looked at my watch. Eight a.m. Now what did he want that couldn't wait an hour, or at least be accomplished by a phone call? I threw on some jeans and ushered him in. Alexandra woke up at this point and excused herself to the bathroom. Wilkes was grinning and I didn't like it one bit. Oh, Lord, I thought, what now? He waited for Alexandra to emerge before announcing we had made the cover of *The Eye*, this glossy weekly magazine that covered celebrities, assorted individuals involved in rescue missions, lottery winners, heart-rending love stories and scandal.

Reasonably well written, it was color from cover to cover, living a few rungs up from the tabloids. While Britain's royal family dominated their covers, they also loved celebrities battling illnesses, bitter divorces and tearful confessions from the famous about plastic surgery gone awry or careers come unstrung due to drugs and alcohol. Alexandra was a regular feature on the fashion pages and occasional inside story, but only made the cover once, three years ago. And that privilege, I learned, she had to share with two other busty, action-adventure accessory actresses (yes, including her arch nemesis, Rachel you know who) in a feature story about the private lives of busty, action-adventure accessory actresses. Now she had a cover all to herself. Well, nearly.

I was on it too.

Wilkes pulled the magazine, of which he had obtained an advance copy, out of an envelope with the flair of someone unveiling a precious Renoir or Picasso.

'We did it! We did it!' he gushed.

I thought he would start dancing around the room at any moment, and wondered if I should put on some music.

'Look, guys, we did it! We made the cover of *The Eye*.'

I assumed Alexandra had given them an interview and was momentarily sidelined by thoughts of what lies she had concocted this time. But no, she assured me, she had not spoken to them despite their requests. This was, I discovered, all very calculated. The magazine had been angling for an interview for some time, but Michael wanted to wait until Alexandra had serious work stitched up before giving *The Eye* access to his client. He considered the story of her relocation to New York old news, and told them they could have Alexandra exclusively around Christmas time, when there would be more news to report. (And better-selling issues chock full of advertising.) Besides, she was about to appear in *The Vulture* and *Vogue*, and he, more than anyone, knew the value of keeping Alexandra a hot commodity. Overexposure is the enemy of celebrity. And then, of course, there was me. They wanted to write an article including our relationship, and this was really why he put his foot down. He said exposing me to an interviewer for any length of time made him too nervous. What if I slipped up and revealed the hoax? If my behavior was a little suspicious, this might send reporters on some Watergate-like investigation, he said. (I mean, he had a point, but drawing parallels with Watergate?) Appealing to my better instincts, he announced he didn't think I would want to subject myself to any pop-culture analysis of our affair, and he was right. So, it appeared, unable to wait, they had gone ahead without us.

Despite Michael Wilkes's inability to control the situation, and, like all good control freaks, he would have a nervous breakdown over it later in the day, right then he was pleased as punch. So how do you write an in-depth article about a relationship between a movie star and her Citizen John boyfriend without speaking to either of them? You talk to everyone around them, from their doormen to their dentists, from their editors to their ex-wives. And you talk to their best friend, the person they normally go to baseball games with, the person they trusted with everything, including their wife. And then you talk to his wife. And you learn, as I did, that they have plenty to say about you. Plenty to say.

The cover photo was taken from the film premiere. The headline, TOMCAT AND THE KITTEN, was followed by '*The Eye* probes the inside story of the bombshell and the brain. Are Alexandra West and Tom Webster the Marilyn and Arthur for the 1990s?'

The article ran over six pages, with various photographs of us together, along with some cheesecake shots of Alexandra taken from *The Devil and The Deep Blue Sea*. There was also a photograph of Marilyn and Arthur shortly after their marriage, driving home the point we were Monroe and Miller reincarnated, if anybody had any doubts.

Rehashing old news about us, the piece did, however, attempt to inject some context. The writer noted that Alexandra was not alone among beautiful women seeking out serious, non-flash boyfriends, and cited a number of candidates currently walking in similar shoes. Credit was given to Marilyn Monroe for starting the trend, but five gold stars were handed to Alexandra for rekindling it. A celebrity psychologist weighed in that my appearance on the scene was a classic move undertaken by a beautiful woman who had had enough of being objectified by men. He also suggested I had given thousands of men everywhere hope they too could date 'up', which he described as a 'social earthquake of sorts... Tom Webster is redrawing the terrain for all men this decade.' Well, nice to know and I'm glad to do my part. The article also revealed women were now asking themselves to look again at the guy they once refused to date. Still waters run deep apparently, at least according to Alexandra West.

I would calculate half of the story was a regurgitation of what already had been written. The other half was the stuff of which cardiac arrests are made. In a separate page entitled 'Who is Tom Webster really?' there was a detailed analysis of my personality from the perspective of a number of on the record and off the record sources. According to those who chose to remain anonymous, which I assumed meant my doormen and co-workers, I was indeed quiet, contemplative, serious, hard-working and a bit of a loner. For those dying to get their names in print I was far more interesting copy. My editor, Louis, hailed me as a future Secretary of Commerce. My old high-school teacher Mr Parks declared I was an excellent student, with a passion for history. My dentist, Dr Shomberg, revealed that I once took his son on a tour of *The Capitalist* newsroom when I learned the kid was thinking about becoming a journalist. The fact they had contacted my dentist took me aback, but at least he didn't hand over my dental records. Overall the comments were flattering and mild.

Except.

Except that Jake had felt it time to vent in public what he had obviously been feeling in private. And boy was he angry. And boy do angry people deliver the best lines to reporters hoping to beef up what could have been a fairly ordinary biographical rundown. Oh, yes, they do.

I'm still too distraught to recount the full gist of his comments in great detail, but I'll try to give you the guts of it. After detailing all my achievements, the writer saved the best for last. A sampling:

Not everyone, however, has unreserved admiration for Alexandra's new love. Jake Gissing, Webster's best friend since second grade, is no longer speaking to his long-time buddy. Gissing said Webster's infatuation with West drove a wedge between their friendship that seems to be permanent.

'He's changed. He's not the Tom I used to know. He used to laugh at and about the very people he now socializes with. And particularly her. He would rather go to the electric chair than date someone as stupid and vacuous as Alexandra West. Suddenly he's going to film premieres and art openings? It's just laughable.'

Gissing revealed that once Webster split from his wife, Elizabeth (see main story), and they set up house together, he and the finance wizard remained close friends.

'Tom was totally understanding about the situation. I considered his easygoing nature his best feature. Now he hasn't got time to take my calls, cancels plans we made months ago to go to ball games, lies to me. He's turned his back on all his old friends. It's like he traded us in because we are not good enough for him anymore. We're not Hollywood.'

He didn't stop there. He went on and on. A complete laundry list of complaints, and with each sentence he just became more and more angry. He complained I believed all the hype, the book deals and TV deals were going to my head. When he was finished, Elizabeth weighed in. She wasn't angry, however. She was vicious. She informed millions of readers she left me because I was boring, our marriage stuck in a rut and I preferred books to sex (I have already told you, that's not true).

'Tom's led a very sheltered, dull life. He has a good heart but he doesn't express his feelings. My life was going nowhere with him. I think the only reason Alexandra likes him is that he will never overshadow her. I think people with big egos can't survive in a relationship with someone similar. Well, Tom is the polar opposite, believe me. He'll never steal her thunder.'

Elizabeth then continued by saying she wished me well (oh, yeah, thanks a lot), but was embarrassed to admit we had once been married.

'I think he's just been seduced by that whole Hollywood thing. I mean, I thought Tom had some class, but clearly he doesn't. You can live with someone ten years and they still shock you. What self-respecting man would go out with somebody who looked like that?'

I was seriously enraged when I finished the piece and so was Alexandra.
'That bitch.'
'She's just jealous,' I said.
'Good,' she said.
'Hey, guys, let's concentrate on the good stuff,' said Wilkes. 'The inside story is great. Really positive and upbeat. We should get more offers now because of this.'
They were thrilled. I was not. The story indeed made Alexandra

look great. It was terrific public relations for a star who lived for terrific public relations. For me it was another matter entirely. My ex-wife and best friend had come forward to take turns at humiliating me. They couldn't just stick the knife in, they had to twist it too. Very nice. *Et tu, Brute?*

No need for an encore, in case you're wondering, Jake. I mean, I cancel one ball game and the guy goes off the rails. So now the gloves were off, hardening my resolve to write the *Vulture* article and reveal the entire scam. Boy, would Jake and Elizabeth feel stupid when the truth was out and plain as day for all to see. I'd make them grovel back, if I accepted their apologies at all. The nerve, suggesting I had no class. Prefer books to sex. I was going to make them grovel all the way home, just like those three little pigs. Grovel, grovel, grovel, grovel.

In hindsight, *The Eye* was tame compared with what was coming. But at the time I was hurt beyond compare. My first instincts were to ring Jake and Elizabeth and thank them sarcastically for their wondrous contributions to journalism, but I thought better of it. I would display the class they suggested I lacked by ignoring the both of them. I hoped they felt some catharsis by going public with their complaints. I, of course, would soon have my turn at bat. And when I did, I planned to hit the ball so far past the stands only outfielders standing in Canada would catch it.

By Sunday night I had calmed down somewhat. Sensing my hurt, Alexandra and Wilkes took me out to dinner at a small, pricey Italian place that had just opened up. Even though it was a sham, Alexandra was very affectionate toward me, and I sensed there was more to it this time than mere acting. She genuinely felt bad Jake and Elizabeth had attacked me in print, and said so a number of times that night. Even at home she asked if there was anything she could do.

'I'm happy to call them and give them hell,' she said while I was in the bathroom brushing my teeth.

'No need,' I yelled through the door. 'I think when *The Vulture* article comes out they will realize the error of their ways.'

'No, but I mean, now. Why wait? Let's give them a serve now.'

I came out of the bathroom.

'I'd rather you didn't.'

'All I'm saying is, if a friend of mine treated me like that, I wouldn't take it lying down. Your ex-wife, well exes fight, that's not news. But after the way you forgave him following her leaving, for him to treat you like this . . .'

'Alexandra, I'll handle it.'

'No, you won't. You'll wimp out.'

'Thanks for your support. Are you saying I'm a wimp?'

'No, I'm saying the magazine hits the streets tomorrow and you should strike while the iron is on.'

'Hot.'

'What's hot?'

'The expression is, "Strike while the iron is hot."'

'Whatever. Stop trying to change the subject.'

'I appreciate your concern, but I'll handle Jake my way.'

'I think it's pathetic. You went to the baseball with him after he stole Elizabeth, now he assaults you in *The Eye* and you say nothing.'

'I'll have my turn.'

'Well, don't waste it. That's all I'm saying.'

'Good night, Alexandra.'

'Good night, Tom.'

Once I was in bed, reading the books I apparently prefer to sex, Alexandra knocked on the door.

'Tom?'

'Yes.'

'Can I come in?'

'Sure.'

She came in and sat on my bed.

'Look, I didn't mean to get mad. I didn't mean to insult your friends. I don't want you to think that.'

'I don't.'

'I don't think you are a wimp. I know this has all been a very strange and weird trip for you, and I bet you never expected your friends to turn on you.'

'No, I didn't.'

'Well, they do. When I hit it big my friends went to the press too. They said the same stuff. I had no time for them anymore.

Complained I got too big for my boots. It hurts, I know. I just
don't want you to take it lying down.'

'Did you?'

'In the beginning.'

'Then what?'

'Then I started calling them up and asking them why they were
talking about me in public. Oh, you should have heard them, all
sweet and sorry. If you don't tell Jake and Elizabeth to go take a
hike, they'll do it again.'

'Alexandra, I told you. My turn is coming.'

'Okay, Tom. You're the boss.'

Chapter 28

And I believed my turn was coming, so I had no need to panic. But first it was someone else's turn. The tabloids. All of them. And hell hath no fury like a tabloid newspaper competing with another to sell copies at the checkout. No fury. None.

Monday morning walking to the subway I saw them. Hanging off a newsstand, gently waving in the wind. How I had missed them Friday I'll never know. The two best-selling tabloid rags in the United States, *Celebrity Scene* and *Starscene*, both had pictures of me on the cover. I cannot tell you how the sight of your own face adorning a national magazine, no matter how dubious the quality, brings your recently digested breakfast almost back to the table.

Trying to keep my head down, I purchased them both, then, nimbly walking behind the stand as if waiting for someone, I took my first real hard look at them. In short, the tide turned this way. First I was a curiosity. Then they loved me. Now they hated me.

ALEXANDRA WEST AND PROFESSOR BOYFRIEND TO SPLIT! barked *Celebrity Scene*.

HIS CHEATIN' HEART — BANKER BEAU CHEATS ON ALEXANDRA WEST, AND IT'S NOT THE FIRST TIME . . . EXCLUSIVE, cried *Starscene*.

If these stories were news to readers, they were not alone. They were news to me too. Big news. In *Celebrity Scene*, readers learned my relationship with Alexandra was under intense pressure and we were on the verge of a break-up. Why? Because I apparently couldn't handle sharing my love with thousands of other men in private and on screen.

'A source close to Webster says the relationship turned sour after he made demands of Alexandra to stop wearing sexy clothing in public.'

This apparently explained away her recent switch from blond hair to red, and those business suits replacing miniskirts and halter tops.

'He also suffers fits of jealousy anytime they are out in public and another man so much at looks at her,' said the source.

'Webster has given the sex kitten an ultimatum, "Obey me or we're finished!"'

Reading on, I learned Alexandra told her friends that she was puzzled and hurt by my aggressive behavior. 'He's suffocating me,' she said. 'But I love him and I don't know what to do.'

I had also forbidden her to pose for *Playboy* ever again (I did?) and, here's the kicker, asked her to give up her career following our impending nuptials.

West told friends her brainy boyfriend told her after they were married he wanted her to get out of showbusiness and be a stay-at-home mom to their brood.

But Alexandra, who met the finance whiz three months ago after moving to the Big Apple to tune up her career, says she has no intention of changing diapers and baking cookies for the rest of her life.

This conflict, then, was set to destroy us. I had fallen in love with a free spirit and now wanted to rein her in. I wanted to take Alexandra out of the public domain, away from her fans, and lock her up for my use exclusively.

'At first it was nothing but dinners and sex,' said our source. 'But now all they do is fight.'

Celebrity Scene then printed a number of photos of Alexandra recently, complete with newly dyed reddy-blond hair and her new CEO power wardrobe, comparing them to cheesecake shots of old. The sartorial switch was at my insistence apparently. Basically, in this little play I was cast as the villain locking Snow White in the dungeon. I had no idea how this article came to be, but doubted even Wilkes would sink this low. I was right. Later I learned he was as shocked as I was. Planting rumors of a split was not part of his plan. Yet. He said this was something that had to be done, but not until Alexandra's deals were set in cement.

Starscene also featured a photograph of us on the cover (amidst other assorted celebrities), this time taken at the art show opening. The article inside, describing my alleged indiscretions both past and current, would have been fascinating if I were not its subject. In HIS CHEATIN' HEART! I learned I was anything but the intellectual financial guru, bookish, rock-solid boyfriend the world thought me to be. Another source, refusing to unmask his or herself, presumably because, like Deep Throat in Watergate, national security was at stake, said I had been a serial cheater throughout my marriage, and was well known at a number of escort services in Manhattan.

'Oh, sure, we know Tom,' gushed one prostitute by the name of Passion to the rag. 'He's one of our favorites. Likes to play rough, that one.'

Another lady of the night echoed Passion's sentiments. 'I see Tom real regular,' she said. 'He's a bit kinky, you know, but a real gentleman. Not like some men, who act like total animals.'

Readers learned I always paid in cash so my indiscretions could not be traced. Now if you want to say I was a Casanova in a past incarnation, it would not be true, but I am not going to complain. But hookers? Prostitutes? Kinky sex? Please. I'm not judging anyone who does that sort of stuff, I'm just saying it's not me. Definitely not me.

'Oh, don't let those serious faces and tweed jackets fool you,' a 'close friend' is quoted as saying. 'He cheated on his wife all the way through their marriage. Secretaries, colleagues, anyone who was willing.'

Starscene went on to suggest, no, insist, that even though I had one of the sexiest women in the world on my arm and in my home, the indiscretions hadn't stopped.

'He's cheating on her now,' the source said. 'And she has no idea.'

Neither did I, so that made two of us.

'He's sex-crazy,' said another source. 'Tom has a classic lion personality. He loves the hunt but is bored after the kill. He always needs to move on to fresh prey.'

So do I sing the theme from *Born Free* now or what?

I had read enough. Stuffing the rags into my briefcase, I kept my face to the ground and hit the subway. On the train I began to fume. Okay, I said to myself, let's stay calm. What would George Washington do? And then I realized George Washington wouldn't have had a plan either, because, lucky for him and Martha, there were no supermarket tabloids back then. People were too busy writing the Declaration of Independence to pen drivel like this.

I was stunned. I was going to force Alexandra to stay home and change diapers? I was cheating on Elizabeth for ten years? I paid for prostitutes? I mean, for crying out loud, I was a serious financial journalist, with a column and TV spot and book deal, and whether I deserved them or not, they were now mine. I wanted people to respect me, I needed people to respect me. This garbage could ruin me. It could kill my career. What if the TV people call and cancel? What if they say, 'Tom, we are a program appealing to the rich family man, and this hooker stuff, well, we can't use you anymore. You're not credible.' What about my friends? Family? Would people in Houston read this and believe it? I was hurt and mad and confused, worried that even after *The Vulture* article, some of this stuff would not go away. If you throw enough mud at a wall, no matter how slimy, some of it always sticks.

Coming out the other end at Wall Street, I rushed into work, hoping to buy a few hours of peace. The tabloids are not considered a must read at *The Capitalist*, so I figured I had time ahead of me until someone saw a copy and brought one in. To my absolute horror both tabloids were waiting for me on my desk, atop faxes and reports and all my mail. Placed there no doubt by any number of co-workers delighting in my humiliation. If they had run a cover story leaking that I was about to win the Nobel Peace Prize, the tabloids would not have been on my desk. But that I was cavorting with hookers demanded my immediate attention. Nobody rushes to give you good news, but bad news they hand-deliver. Frank Wicker-Smith was buried in the *Wall Street Journal* and did not dare make eye contact with me. Nobody did. I threw the rags in the trash and dialed Wilkes.

'Have you seen the tabloids?'

'Yes. Actually, Tom, to be honest, I saw them Friday.'

'Friday!'

'Yes. But I, we, didn't think you could handle them and *The Eye* cover story, so we thought we'd just show you *The Eye*, and let you discover the tabloids on your own.'

'So Alexandra saw them too?'

'Yes.'

'I don't understand. What do you mean I couldn't handle it all?'

'We thought having your best friend and your ex-wife trash you in print would be enough of a blow for one day. The tabloid stories are absolute garbage and we knew you'd see them and just brush them aside.'

'Well, thank you for treating me like a complete baby.'

'Tom, calm down.'

'Anything else you've been hiding from me?'

'Nothing, Tom. Nothing. Don't get upset. I can hear you're upset. The tabloids, those stories are absolute crap.'

'I know that. You know that. But if it's in print, people believe it.'

'Anyone who knows you won't buy it for a second.'

'What about all the people who don't know me? Right now a lot of guys on Wall Street are enjoying a good laugh at my expense.'

'I doubt it.'

'You have an answer for everything, don't you?'

'Tom, please.'

'Just tell me you didn't plant these stories.'

'Tom, I swear, I'm as shocked as you. Listen, let's have lunch. I'll explain a few things.'

'Fine. Where and when?'

'You choose.'

'Somewhere dark. Somewhere they won't recognize me.'

He laughed. I did not feel inclined to laugh along with him.

'Okay. There's a nice little place down near you called Forbidden City. Great Chinese food and bad lighting. I'll meet you there at one.'

He did not lie. It was dark, and we sat in the back hidden from view. Even though I had no appetite, Wilkes insisted I eat, as the food he swore was terrific. He was right, it was good, and it was a pity I was in no mood for gastronomic delights.

'Tom, I'm glad you came,' said Wilkes as the waiter poured us wine.

'I'm very upset, Michael. Very upset.'

'I know.'

'Do you? Have you ever been humiliated like this? Your best friend? Your ex-wife? Hookers you have never met? You must admit this three-pronged assault is quite impressive.'

'It's par for the course, Tom.'

'What? You mean to tell me you knew this was coming?'

'Let's just say I was not surprised.'

'So why didn't you warn me?'

'Why worry in advance about things you can't control?'

'But what about you? Isn't that your job, to control this sort of nonsense?'

'Tom, I'm flattered you have so much faith in me, but there are even things Michael Wilkes can't control, and the tabloids are one of them.'

'But surely you know people on these papers?'

'Well, I'd never admit it in public, but I have spoken with them from time to time.'

'So?'

'So basically they are a beast of their own making. I can plant stories with them, but they also fabricate whenever they feel like it.'

'Surely I can respond?'

'Of course you can. You can sue.'

'Good. Let's sue.'

'Not so fast. It's not like you decide to sue today and tomorrow you're in court. These things take years to put together, and by the time your turn in the witness box comes up, everyone has forgotten it. The court case just dredges it all up again. I've found suing is pointless.'

'Michael! My reputation is right on the line here. Right on the line! They wrote that I see hookers regularly. I've never paid for sex in my life. I went to a Catholic school. The nuns are going to disown me.'

'We could threaten to sue and ask for a retraction.'

'Good. We'll do that, then.'

'Won't work.'

'Why not?'

'Rarely does. A retraction is an admission of guilt. The tabs would rather die a thousand deaths than admit their sources don't exist.'

'Speak to me in language I can understand. Where does this leave me?'

'Honestly?'

'Honestly.'

'Nowhere. Just grin and bear it. Next week it will be all forgotten. Next week they'll skewer someone else.'

More food arrived. As we ate, Wilkes tried again to placate me.

'Tom, I think you have to understand something. It's not you. I mean, it is you technically, but it's not you personally. It's what you represent. It's what all celebrities represent.'

'I don't follow.'

'When it comes to celebrities, the media work on a theory we call SKD.'

'Which is?'

'Search, Kill and Destroy. Search for fresh talent, kill them with kindness, put them on a pedestal, then destroy them when they start getting too successful.'

'And this applies to me?'

'Precisely. When you hit the scene you became the poster boy for average guys everywhere. The press lapped it up. This quiet guy snags a movie star. You couldn't write a better movie.'

Okay, so what was his point?

'People loved the story. It sold magazines. Then along with the recognition came the deals. The TV spot, the book contract. Then Joe Public, who initially lived through you, got a tad jealous. Do you follow?'

'Keep going.'

'Here's the thing. They loved you in the beginning because you represented them. And women thought you were sexy because you personified all the qualities they are looking for in a man. Solid, serious, all that junk women go for. But at a certain point when the public perceive you as too successful, enjoying it all a bit too much, they start to hate you for exactly the same reasons they liked you.'

'So they hate me now?'

'They don't hate you. They're jealous. Of the seven deadly sins, Tom, envy is the most insidious. Trust me, I handle enough stars to know what I'm talking about.'

'So how does this explain the stories about me with hookers?'

'If you commit a sin, you have to suffer. Your sin was success, celebrity. Even celebrity by association, as you call it. I told you. The public let you enjoy it for a short time, they even encourage you. Then they say, enough's enough. All these men start to say, hey, it's not fair. This guy dates a bombshell, and I am still home alone at nights eating TV dinners.'

'So they do resent me?'

'In a way. And so the tabs take the pulse of the country and sense the party's over. They start to attack you. Reveal a flaw. Cut you down to size. Make the public think you are suffering. That's why all the stories about affairs and imminent splits. I know those articles are pure, 100 percent crapola. But people read them and feel better. They go back to their little lives and say to themselves, that Tom Webster is not as great as he thinks he is. He's got a dirty little secret and now we all know it.'

'This is ridiculous. You're making excuses for this. For them.'

'I'm just telling it the way I see it. I'm not making excuses for the tabloids. There is no question if we sued them, we'd win. They could never produce any hookers in court who know you.'

'No, they couldn't!'

'But they have papers to sell. They build you up and then they have to cut you down. The readers demand it.'

'Well, I am very happy to appease the readers, Michael, but in the meantime my reputation is in the toilet.'

'You're taking this too personally. I promise next week nobody will remember.'

'Bullshit. My entire office now thinks every time I say I'm going out for lunch I'm going to some seedy motel. Help me, Michael.'

'You want help? Here it is. Smile. Smile and say nothing. Rise above it. Your time is coming, Tom. Remember that. Get-even time is coming. No celebrity ever gets the chance you're about to get.'

'I hope you're right, Michael.'

'Tom, not to sound like an egomaniac, but I'm always right.'

Chapter 29

President Kennedy was right when he said anger was a wasted emotion. I think the exact phrase was, 'Don't get mad, get even,' which I now adopted as my mantra. Previously, in situations that tested my patience, my reaction would have been muffled rage. Getting even just wasn't my style.

Elizabeth hated this about me. Hated the lack of emotion or resolve to right perceived wrongs. Hated the fact we never fought like, quote, ordinary couples, unquote, whatever that was supposed to look like. She read somewhere that the louder the fights, the better the relationship, as apparently this was a sign the air was being constantly cleared. I believed the louder the fights, the richer the divorce lawyers, and whenever I said this she reprimanded me for being flippant. I liked my drama in history books, not real life, although of late I'd had my fair share of both, as you can see.

So the idea of revenge through *The Vulture*, getting even via the written word and not the spoken, appealed to all my fighting instincts. I rued the day I ever called Ms MacDowell and tried to extricate myself from the task of penning the piece, and thanked her for insisting I make good on my promise.

Of course her interest in doing this was wildly divergent from my new resolve to deliver, but no matter. She had a magazine to sell, advertisers to placate. I now had scores to settle, explanations to reveal. I also had, I believed, some insights to impart to a public, ready or not, on the nature of my experiment and the very notion of fame. As Mr Wilkes intimated, the best-case scenario would be that everyone forgave my behavior and applauded my audacity. The worst-case scenario was that, well, what was the worst-case scenario?

I believed it might be that I would lose all the advantages that had since fallen across my path, the TV show, the book deal, the column in *The Capitalist*, the attention from women, and return to my former life consisting of dinner alone, baseball with Jake and my history books. I would, of course, have some interesting clothes, which once I reverted to Tom Webster, Mr Nobody, I could wear on Halloween.

I heard little in the office that week concerning the tabloid reports that 'Tomcat' Webster and his 'kitten' were on the outs. Thank God people were either too embarrassed or too polite to raise the subject, although I knew they had seen the articles, and they knew that I knew. Even Louis, not exactly Mr Subtle, thought better than to mention them. Frank Wicker-Smith, now too terrified to ask me any questions vis-à-vis my personal life, was, I suspected, enjoying my public humiliation as much as I had once reveled in his envy of me.

In Houston, Mom told me I was the hottest topic of conversation since the last space shuttle came back safely. I was going to call her and warn her about the tabloids, only her regular as clockwork Monday morning at the supermarket beat me to it. She read all the stories at the checkout, unable, she said later, to look the cashier in the face while handing over the money. Horrified, she loaded her groceries into her car and raced home, breaking the speed limit. She was so upset she left her milk, bread, eggs and melting ice cream in the trunk and charged into the house to call me. After assuring her the stories were all nonsense, she made me promise on my father's memory I had never visited a prostitute.

'We didn't raise you like that, Tom,' she said.

'I know and I didn't go to one, Mom.'

'Now I know we were not perfect parents...'

'You and Dad were great parents.'

'No. We made some mistakes. But you see, Tom, that's the way it is. It's all trial and error. But still, not this. We taught you to respect women and respect yourself.'

'Mom, I swear on ten Bibles, I never hired a hooker. The stories are false.'

'Promise?'

'Yes.'

'Promise me again.'

'I swear.'

'So how can they write those things? Evil people!'

'I don't know, Mom, but they do.'

'Can't you sue?'

'It's very complicated. It's not a good idea. It just reminds everyone of the original allegations. I've been advised to keep my chin up and weather the storm.'

'What did Alexandra say?'

'She said she was very sorry about it, but that was the price of living in the public eye.'

Actually Alexandra hadn't said anything as yet, but I am sure that would have been her response and saw no reason not to interpret it for Mom.

'Are you still happy with her, darling?'

'Yes.'

'You don't sound it.'

'Mom, I'm as shocked as you about the tabloids. That's all I can think about right now.'

'Darling, you know I don't like to pry, but is there going to be a wedding? I mean, the papers last week all seemed to think so.'

'No, Mom. They made that up too. We're still getting to know each other.'

'But you are living together.'

She had me there.

'Mom, I have to go.'

'I love you, Tom.'

'Love you too, Mom.'

God bless her. She would be the one person who would truly understand when the hurricane blew over. Until then she was in for some sideways glances from friends, behind-the-back sniping from neighbors. For that I was truly sorry. I didn't deserve this treatment, but I had brought it on myself and had to deal with the dice as they rolled. She did nothing to warrant this feeling of shame, for, as she said correctly, she did not raise her son to socialize with women who charged by the hour. Thank God I had *The Vulture* card left up my sleeve.

But first I had my future to plan. The producers of *Your Money* had called me to a meeting with the entire staff of the show. I believed now this would be my first and last meeting with the team, for I was sure I would be shown the door. Since the most recent tabloid revelations, I would understand if they declared I was no longer a credible electronic columnist. But I underestimated the very people who would be contributing to my mortgage payments.

Ushered into a small meeting room on the tenth floor, the new executive producer, a man whose name was Charles but who insisted I call him Chuck, gave me a firm handshake and motioned for me to sit. My stomach was doing somersaults as I waited for the inevitable speech about budget cuts or whatever other excuse they could have dreamed up in so short a window of time. Instead he offered me coffee, juice or alcohol, and I declined all three. I was having a sixteenth-century England, Anne Boleyn kind of moment. If they were going to put me on the block and cut off my head, I would just as soon get on with it.

'Tom, before we go in to meet the team, I wanted to have a word alone,' said Chuck.

'Sure thing,' I replied, wondering whether in his day Charles II of France would have instructed his staff to call him Chuck too.

'You understand what we want you to do, don't you?'

'Yes, of course.'

'I just want to go over it once more. You appear at the end of the show, talk about some burning issue in Washington that will impact on Wall Street. Make it light, tight and breezy, and then sign off.'

'Can I ask a question?'

'Shoot.'

'A lot of burning issues, as you call them, often take more than three minutes to explain, let alone link up to more burning issues on Wall Street. If I need more time, do I get it?'

Chuck rolled his eyes, as if I had asked for a private jet to take me home when the meeting was over. Heck, all I wanted was more time, a request, I later realized, made every day by every living, breathing person who ever worked on the tube.

'In short, no. Tom, that's what I thought I would have to go over with you so I'm glad you brought it up. This is television. Never forget that. No matter how complex the topic, you get three minutes every week. So my advice is, keep to the simple stuff and save the serious shit for your column or the boys on the *Journal*.'

'I see.'

'We often have this problem when the print boys come over to TV. They write scripts that run forever. Well, don't even think about it. Remember, light, tight and breezy.'

'But fiscal policy is anything but light, tight and breezy.'

'No shit. But your job is to make it so.'

'Got it.'

'Tom, everyone reacts the same way. The print boys move into electronic because the money is good, then spend all their time bitching about how shallow the medium is. Take my advice, get over it now. Just do your bit, take the money and run. Any hand-wringing or philosophizing is a complete waste of time. This is a program about money for people watching in their pajamas. They want tips, advice, they want to get rich. And nobody has a clue or gives a shit how Washington works, so even if you tried to explain it, they wouldn't listen. What they want to hear every week is this. Interest rates are going up. Interest rates are going down. Put your money in computer stocks. Put your money in foreign markets. Buy bonds. Don't buy bonds.'

'I hear you.'

In all, he delivered a multitude of instructions. I now saw exactly what I had let myself in for, but remained thankful for two things. One, they were paying me a bucket of money, and I mean a bucket. Two, Chuck had not mentioned the tabloids, so obviously thought little of their veracity or ability to affect my contract, which, incidentally, had still not been signed.

'If you just wait in here a second, I'll get my secretary to go get your contract.'

The man was reading my mind. He returned to his office waving the contract like a cheerleader.

'Got it.'

'Good.'

I wanted to sign it before anything else could go wrong. Chuck produced a pen from his top pocket with all the flourish of a magician turning his wand into plastic flowers. I was about to sign when Chuck asked if I had read it.

'Yes, I went over it in my office when your secretary sent me a draft.'

What a liar. They did send me a copy but I never did anything much with it beyond pulling it out of its envelope. The deed was done. I was now officially on the team. When the ink dried I decided to broach the topic of the tabloids.

'Chuck?'

'Yep.'

'I just want to say I really appreciate you not mentioning my private life just now.'

He grinned. It was not an understanding grin, but one far more salacious. Clearly he had read the tabloids even if he possessed the grace not to mention them.

'My wife reads that garbage, I don't. I mean, I heard about it, sure, but figured it was bunch of crap.'

'It is. Believe me. I lost my lunch reading those stories.'

'So you and her are still an item, then?'

'Me and Alexandra? Yes.'

Well, technically we still were.

'I have to admit I was rather worried how it would, well, you know, go down around here. The stuff about hookers, I mean.'

'Tom, we know those rags for what they are. Besides, if anything, they are good for the show. Sorry to have to tell you, but it's the truth. The more your name gets out there, the more people will tune in when we launch.'

I was now really sick to my stomach.

'But I want them to watch for my advice,' I cried out. 'I don't want them to tune in to see the guy who cheated on Alexandra West with hookers!'

'Did you?'

'No!'

'So you have nothing to worry about.'

'But you're telling me that might be why some people tune in.'

'Tom, I can't lie to you. A little scandal might help us the first week. But if the show doesn't cut the mustard, the viewers won't come back, doesn't matter who you are sleeping with. Nobody here believes those stories, trust me. If we did, we wouldn't have had you sign that contract right then, would we?'

'But Mr and Mrs Viewer don't know that.'

'I don't know what Mr and Mrs Viewer think, nor do I give a shit. I just want them to tune in, buy a shitload of cars and software, and stop flipping during commercials. If they watch you because you're the guy who's doing Alexandra West, well, so be it.'

'That's why you hired me, isn't it? Well, not you, but whoever is really running this thing.'

'Sorry, Tom, I don't follow.'

'There are plenty of guys out there who are better-looking, who could deliver your three minutes of financial advice. You wanted me because I'm a movie star's boyfriend.'

'Now wait a second. We wanted you because you're a smart guy, you have a column, and, okay, you're a movie star's boyfriend. I can't lie. You were on the cover of *The Eye* last week, Tom. We can't buy that kind of publicity. It all helps.'

Five minutes later I was ushered into a second room on the same floor, where I shook hands with about ten people whose names escape me. I do remember they all smirked and smiled and made me feel paranoid. We were informed we would shoot a pilot episode the following Sunday, but as the show was a done deal, we would get a slot in the coming weeks. While the team would work all week on the guts of the show, I was required to appear only on Saturday to write my speech and rehearse its delivery. Chuck thanked everyone for coming and then cleared the room.

On my way out I was stopped by a woman who introduced herself as Lucy.

'I'm the line producer. Glad to have you on board.'

'Thanks, err, Lucy.'

She batted her eyelashes at me. My God, she was flirting with me. I am not making this up. This is not wishful thinking undertaken by a forty-three-year-old man concerning a cute brunette at least ten years younger who would not ordinarily give him the time of day. She was flirting with me, plain and simple.

'You going out?'

'Yes.'

'I'll walk with you.'

And she did, asking me all sorts of questions about my job at *The Capitalist*, never once mentioning Alexandra or the tabloids. This I appreciated.

'See you Saturday, Tom,' she said.

'Looking forward to it,' I replied, and it was not a lie.

I was. This fame stuff did have its upside, and I saw now that it came in two colors – blond and brunette. I was living with one, and soon to be working with the other.

Go on. Hate me. I would if I were you.

Chapter 30

I thought nothing else of my role on *Your Money* that week. Other events conspired to demand my full attention. Predominantly they involved having Michael put out press releases on Alexandra's behalf denouncing the tabloids and assuring them our relationship was rock solid. She was no country gal but she was sure singing 'Stand by Your Man'.

Despite celebritydom taking up more and more of my time, work that week was all-consuming, and I had a number of calls to make to shore up both my column and my TV spot. Contacts in Washington all made cracks about the hooker stories, and I tried to laugh them off, but deep down they hurt. Sure, people who knew me realized they were fabricated, but there would still be many who didn't know, and didn't want to know.

They chose to believe them because they were far more amusing than the truth, which was that I was a one-woman man during my marriage, and in fact I was a no-woman man since my separation, given that my current relationship was a total con.

Wednesday night I resolved to go home, unplug the telephone and collate all my notes, journal entries, newspaper clippings and attempt to begin to form them into the *Vulture* article. Though I had time, I saw more chaos ahead, not less, and thought I better get started. Plus I was in the right mood. I was mad and hell hath no fury like someone wrongly accused who needs to rewrite the history books.

But it was not to be. Alexandra arrived home and insisted we go to a movie. I had not seen her for a few days, as she had risen early and returned late, busying herself with whatever kept her busy, doing whatever it is celebrities do. I don't know if she was trying to avoid me, or was working on a project of some sort, but as I was in no mood to socialize, I hardly cared our paths failed to cross.

'Hey,' she said as she walked in the door.

'Hey.'

'Busy tonight?'

'Yes, actually. I'm going to get started on the article.'

'Oh, screw it. Let's go out. I haven't been to the movies in ages. I bet you haven't either.'

'I don't think so.'

It was at this point the kitten curled up next to her Tomcat on the couch and began purring. As I said before, this approach is next to impossible to resist.

'Please.'

'Well . . .'

'Good.'

And suddenly we were out the door. We bought pretzels on the street, doused them in mustard, and joined the line at the cinema. Fellow movie-goers could not believe their eyes. Here was Alexandra West, arm in arm with guru Tom Webster, eating pretzels, on line. No pushing to the front. No demanding star treatment. It was all they could talk about.

'Look, it's them. Don't look now. Now look. Just over there.'

'They are not pushing in or anything.'

'No, it is them. Look. It is.'

Alexandra winked at me and said nothing. We approached the window, bought our tickets and still had fifteen minutes to kill, so went straight to one of those Seattle-inspired coffee bars in the neighborhood.

'I'm sorry about the tabs. Michael said you were real upset.'

'I wanted to sue.'

'I know how that feels.'

'But like this? I mean, Alexandra, this stuff about hookers . . . I'm so embarrassed. I'm a laughing stock in the business community.'

'I'm really sorry, Tom. Try to forget about them. I know, I know, easy for me to say. But just think of it this way. When the *Vulture* piece comes out, everyone will know the truth.'

'Will they?'

'Sure.'

'Alexandra, the people who read *The Vulture* are not exactly the same people who read about Martian landings in the Iowa cornfields.'

'Point taken. But people who know you will know the truth, and that's what matters.'

The bombshell made sense, as she did more and more.

'So where have you been the last couple of days?'

'I got a new personal trainer. He has me up at six to meet him at the gym at six-thirty. The man is a complete maniac. You'd think I was in training for the Olympics.'

'Why do you need a trainer? You look fine to me.'

'Everybody has one. You just have to, that's all.'

She then lowered her voice.

'Look, Tom, I'm not a spring chicken anymore.'

'You're just past thirty.'

'Yes, and there are seventeen-year-olds and twenty-two-year-olds auditioning against me. You don't get it, you're not a woman. Women can never get old on screen. Men can. If you are a guy and you turn gray or get fat, you're distinguished. If I put on a pound, I'm out of work. Michael says now is the time to take care of myself. No more cruising, relying on Mother Nature to do it for me.'

'So, is this trainer guy any good?'

'Brilliant. I think. I mean, I don't know because I just started with him, but he says in six weeks I'll look like that statue, the Venus and Milo.

'Venus de Milo.'

'Right. The Greek one.'

'You know she has no arms.'

'Who?'

'The Venus de Milo.'

'What do you mean?'

'When they discovered her she was in perfect shape, just no arms.'

'Did someone cut them off?'

'They don't know.'

'Well, if someone did, that was stupid.'

'Not as stupid as the medieval puritans who covered the genitals of naked statues with fig leaves because they thought nudity offended God.'

'But we were born naked.'

I could see the conversation was getting too intellectual for her liking. Her eyebrows were starting to knit, and she looked confused.

'We better go. Movie starts in five.'

We found seats and sat down before I realized I had no idea what we were seeing. The movie was in French, made by some new, hip French director whom, Alexandra informed me, she also wanted to work with some day. French movies were currently more trendy than American movies, principally because, I think, they were in French. Just reading the subtitles made you feel sophisticated, made you feel like putting on a beret. It was not a bad film, I recall, a love story between fifty-somethings whose '*amour*' had thoroughly upset the children (isn't it always the way?), though I confess the *madame* and *monsieur* did not have my undivided attention.

Alexandra busied herself for one and half hours snuggling up to me, stroking my hand and generally cooing in my ear. This treatment escaped no one, even in the dark, and I realized she was doing it with both eyes on the newspapers, who would report it in the following days. This was her way of dismantling the tabloid rumors, proof positive were still an item.

Hector the doorman was on late duty, and bowed and scraped like a courtier on our return. This I was beginning to enjoy. At home the answering machine was blinking like a maniac, and, twelve messages later, I found they were all for her. The trainer called. A hairdresser, an agent, a friend from LA informing her he would be in New York and wanted to have lunch. Wilkes, Wilkes again, and Wilkes a third time. I wondered what he wanted. I gave Alexandra the laundry list of callers, and she threw it on the table.

'Screw them now. It's too late. I'll call them tomorrow.'

She entered the bathroom to brush her teeth and do whatever

she did with all those little tubes of cream that lined my shelves.

'So what's the story with James?' she asked through the door.

'James?'

'Your friend. The wife-stealer.'

'Jake.'

'Right. Jake. You talking yet?'

'He hasn't called me and I haven't called him.'

'Jesus. Sounds serious.'

'He shredded me in *The Eye*. I'm supposed to forgive him?'

She appeared in the doorway with her face covered in thick white cream.

'Exactly. I can't believe you ever hung out with him after he ran off with you know who.'

'So you keep saying.'

'Babe, the guy's scum. I'm sorry it's like this, but now you see him for who he is.'

'You know, Alexandra, you're right. And wait till the show starts. I'll be on TV Sunday mornings, and he'll still be home in his apartment slicing a bagel. That'll drive him crazy.'

'Good. I hope he chokes on it.'

You had to hand it to her. For a non-girlfriend embroiled in a nonexistent relationship, she was constantly loyal.

Chapter 31

Or so I thought. Friday morning is usually down time for me, as the column has been turned in, the magazine is already at the printers and us pinstripes sit around trying to look busy to justify the paycheck that arrives Friday afternoon.

But I had that day whipped myself into a frenzy, nervous about my first rehearsal as a high-powered TV financial guru the following day. I had decided to follow Chuck's advice and keep it simple. My topic would be the bond market, and whether people with a couple of thousand to invest should put their money in it or in stocks. I planned to quote a source at the Federal Reserve who had told me interest rates would probably be lowered, making bonds the place to be.

I tried writing this down in a chatty way, and found it was a skill I did not yet possess. I then worked and reworked this speech as if it were the Gettysburg Address. Suddenly I was interrupted by a feeling, a sensation that something was happening in the newsroom. I heard gasps and saw heads turning, and concluded the police had arrived to arrest someone for insider-trading. I then heard the chairs all turn on their swivels. But this was no insider-trading scandal.

This was Alexandra West, entering the newsroom again, sashaying between the desks, looking determined and keeping her eyes forward, marching toward me. Though it had been at least five weeks since the first time she tried this, the reaction had not muted any. You get a bombshell to parade down the middle of your office on a Friday, even with strawberry-blond hair and wearing a pants suit (Calvin Klein, she told me later), and watch your colleagues' eyes dilate.

She parked, if you can call it that, at my desk, leaned over to kiss me, then positioned herself atop it.

'Let me guess. Another surprise lunch date?'

'Oh, Tom, you're so smart. You should be on *Jeopardy*.'

'So what gives?'

'Well, I thought, he's had a rough week. A surprise visit from *moi* and a nice lunch wouldn't hurt.'

'Alexandra, I don't have time. Seriously. I've got to write this piece so I'm ready for the TV bit tomorrow.'

'Hey, it's three minutes. It's a snap. By the way, you're not going to wear that on TV, are you?'

'What? This suit?'

'Yep.'

'Well, I'm not wearing the Tommy stuff.'

'No, you don't have to, but you can't wear that either.'

'What's wrong with it?'

'Gray. Never wear gray on TV, washes you out. Makes you look like a corpse.'

'But I just bought this.'

I had indeed just spent more money than sense on a new Italian gray suit which the man in the store assured me was top of the line. Unless forced, there was no way my Hendrix attire was ever going public again. Chuck had not issued any warnings against gray suits, and Elizabeth always liked me in gray.

'Take it back.'

'I can't. In case you hadn't noticed, I'm already wearing it.'

'Change it for one just like it in navy. Gotta wear navy blue on TV.'

'Who says?'

'Michael.'

Well, he would know. He does seem to know a lot about a lot of things. Right then I needed to know more about his theory concerning navy blue versus gray, but was interrupted by a number of colleagues who had summoned up the courage to

269

approach Alexandra and ask for autographs. They all lied like rugs and insisted they were for teenage sons and cousins. Alexandra turned on the charm and I sat back and watched them salivate. They gushed about her talent, her movies, her looks. She was dripping sex appeal. I mean, it was oozing out of her pores. She winked at me, and this time I winked back. It was amusing to say the least. When the autograph hounds returned to their desks, Alexandra motioned that I should rise and follow her.

'I don't have time.'

'I don't care. Get up.'

Now I should have dug my heels in, but when a movie star who looks like the reincarnation of Marilyn, Jayne Mansfield and Rita Hayworth barks an order, and your colleagues are taking notes, one has little recourse but to obey.

'We are not going to the diner. Jake will probably be there.'

'Don't worry. Michael booked a table at a nice little bistro around here.'

'He did? Does he book all your lunch dates?'

'Oh, Tom. You really don't like him, do you? He's just helping me out until I get to know the city better.'

'You just love walking through my office making a scene, don't you?' I said on our way out.

'Hey, your friends look kind of bored around here. I'm just doing my bit to brighten up their day.'

'You certainly are.'

Wilkes's choice was on the money. It was a nice little bistro, quiet and cosy, nestled in a tiny alley in the financial district. It was called Raphael's, and the cuisine was Italian, in deference to the painter's home country. I noticed a number of older businessmen with beautiful young women as their dining companions, and guessed these women were not their wives.

'Michael says this place never leaks.'

'I don't follow.'

'Very discreet. They won't call the press after you leave. A lot of famous men, you know, judges, lawyers, politicians, bring their mistresses here. The staff are sworn to secrecy.'

Well, I didn't think it was father-daughter day.

A waiter approached. He either had no clue who Alexandra was or was doing the best acting since Orson Welles in *Citizen Kane,* for he pretended not to know. We ordered pasta, red wine, salads. Being taken to lunch by Alexandra West on Friday afternoon after she has already knocked the socks off your entire newsroom is kind of nice in a way.

'Tom, you've had a hard week.'

'Well, it's over now. Although I have to tell you I feel really bad for my mom.'

'They giving her a hard time in Dallas?'

'Houston. She lives in Houston.'

'Right.'

'She's too careful to say if they are. She indicated she was not thrilled about the tabloid stories. Begged me to promise they were not true.'

'I feel bad for my folks too when they spin all the crap around me.'

She had never really discussed her parents and I was hoping this could be an opportunity to glean some information, but it was not to be.

'You don't seem to talk about them much. Your parents, I mean. I never see you calling them.'

'Yeah, well, we don't really get on. There's no icky secrets or anything, they're good people, just, you know...'

'No, I don't know.'

'Religious.'

Ah, so that was it.

'Catholic?'

'Yep. Think Hollywood is Sodom, wanted me to be a nurse. Didn't exactly do jumping jacks when I appeared in *Playboy.* If you think your mom is upset, my dad had to go on heart medication.'

'I see.'

'So it's better this way. We talk once a week. I love them, but we don't connect. They want me to go back to Jersey, marry an accountant, have kids and go to church on Sundays.'

'That's not a terrible life, you know.'

'Yes, but it's not my life anymore.'

'Got it.'

The food arrived. It was great and I had no idea how hungry I was. As I dug in, Alexandra suddenly turned very serious, leaned in and suggested I keep eating as she had something to say.

'Tom, there's no way to do this nicely. So, I am just going to come right out with it. I'm breaking up with you. The movers are at your apartment right now packing my stuff. When you get home tonight, I'll be gone.'

I choked.

'Excuse me? What? What? Why? I mean, I don't get it. You're joking, right?'

'No.'

'Yes, you are.'

'No, Tom.'

I choked some more and downed a glass a water really fast. It didn't help.

'I thought you wanted us to stay together until all your deals were signed. And my deals were signed. Right? Right?'

'Come on, Tom. You knew this wasn't going to last forever. Even Elizabeth said as much.'

'Of course not . . .'

'Well, it's over.'

'Just like that? So sudden? No discussion?'

'I'm afraid so.'

The kitten was not in evidence at that moment. I was dealing with a tiger, huge teeth, giant claws.

'Can we just discuss this, please? Alexandra, I know this was not a permanent deal. But right now, with all the allegations about me, I need us to present a united front to the world. If you leave now, it could impact on my book deal, my, my, my everything. My credibility. Please, just hang around until *The Vulture* article comes out. I mean, this is for your benefit too, right? The longer you stick around me, the more directors and producers think you're serious, smart, all those things you want them to think, right?'

'No can do.'

'Could you explain why?'

'There are a couple of directors in town, I don't want to name them, well, they intimated that if I wasn't in a relationship, they would like to take me out.'

'You mean sleep with you.'

'Your words. Not mine.'

'So why don't you? I mean, it's not like you have any real obligation to me.'

'It's them. They say they can't risk their reputations on unavailable women. These are serious-type guys. Older. Don't want to be branded home-wreckers.'

'And if you sleep with them, will that assist you in getting parts?'

'I never said I plan to sleep with them. I would like to date them, however.'

'Pathetic.'

'What is?'

'They take the moral highground when it comes to dating, but use the casting couch when it comes to auditions.'

'Let's just say, it would be to my advantage right now to be single and available.'

'But I thought you needed me to restyle your image.'

'I did. And you were great. But it's done. Michael said it's complete. It worked.'

'And so you don't need me anymore.'

'Right.'

'I don't know what to say.'

'I'm sorry, Tom.'

'Where are you going to live?'

I pushed the plate away. My mind was racing in twelve different directions. This wasn't so bad, was it? I would get my life back, my closets, my bathroom. I would never have to wear purple velvet jackets and pink shirts again. I could go back to corduroy. I had ample material for my article, and this would actually make a nice closing paragraph. I wondered if Wilkes had thought that part through. No, this wasn't the end of the world. But then maybe it was. I think it was. Yes, it was. No longer her boyfriend, my currency in the market would float down to zero.

The book deal would probably be canceled. Chuck would fire me from *Your Money*. Nobody wants to take advice from a dumped boyfriend who no longer sleeps with the woman of their dreams. Women would no longer flirt with me. My doormen would no longer grovel. I was no longer Alexander the Great. I wasn't even

Alexander the Good. I was Napoleon at Waterloo. No, wait. Wait. I was Lincoln, and she was John Wilkes Booth, the actor killing me with a single shot. The assassination of Tom Webster, just like Honest Abe, had been in the offing for weeks. The only difference was that Wilkes had an audience, while Alexandra preferred to do her killing in private.

'So what is Michael going to tell the press? About us? Why we broke up?'

'We have that all worked out. He's going to release a statement saying that it was a mutual decision based on, you know, the fact that I am going to be traveling all the time to locations, and some stuff about how you found life in the spotlight too much and needed time out. How we are still great friends, but moving in together was a mistake. But we still love each other dearly.'

'You and Michael seem to have thought this through all the way to its logical conclusion. Can I ask just how long this break-up was in the works?'

'Couple of weeks. Two, I think.'

'You knew all the time and yet you continued to live in my apartment, take me to the movies, to dinner, as if nothing was on the horizon.'

She tried to look sorry but I wasn't buying it.

'So this is it?'

'This is it, Tom.'

We didn't leave together. She said she had to run and would pick up the bill. I continued to sit a little while longer. I felt exactly like when Elizabeth left, but I didn't understand why. Elizabeth I love. Or loved. I don't know anymore. Alexandra I didn't. How could being dumped by someone you care so little about hurt so much?

I returned to work a shaken man. The afternoon was a blur, and that evening when I returned home Hector shot me a look of concern and sympathy as I made my way to the elevator. Despite my irritation at her presence, her absence was equally hard to take. After weeks of no room, I now had so much space to myself it was awful. She moved out lock, stock and barrel, and the lack of lipsticks lining my bathroom shelves was actually depressing. On the table was a note.

Tom,

It was great. Really. No hard feelings? Good luck with the article.

Alex.

P.S. I'll call in a few days with my new phone number. I'm not hooked up yet.

So it had all boiled down to this. By now I guessed word was out we had broken up. I was no longer Tom Webster, boyfriend of the sex symbol, but Tom Webster, divorced shy guy, eating microwaved dinners on the lips, reading history books. I felt like garbage. At least Elizabeth would be thrilled.

Chapter 32

I said nothing on Saturday at the TV studio, and nobody said anything about Alexandra in return. It was all very businesslike, with the flirtatious Lucy helping me with my script, and assuring me a gray suit was an excellent choice. I practiced reading my piece off the autocue a number of times before they rolled tape. What staggered me was not how uncomfortable I felt proffering my opinion to the electronic eye, but the contrary. I loved it when that little red light came on, the camera focused on me and I became someone other than who I really was.

For three minutes I was Tom Webster, finance guru, business whiz, the man who knows. I delivered my piece and then watched the video in playback. Television is a cruel medium, and now I understood why it pays so well. The salary is compensation for the fact that you look like the Michelin man. I did not like the way television made me look, but I loved how it made me sound. Important, imposing, smart. I was told to return on Sunday for a taping, and dutifully I did. Except for one thing.

By Sunday, the New York papers were full of our break-up. How the moving vans came and packed Alexandra up, how upset she was, no, make that devastated, by the state of affairs. She was devastated? Wasn't it mutual? Apparently not. The statement Wilkes leaked to the press read nothing like what Alexandra promised. No mention of me hating the spotlight, her going on location, or our rushing the decision to move in together. And not a word about our still loving each other dearly, but needing time out. Instead, wait for this, Wilkes – well, I assume it was him – told the Sunday papers that Alexandra was shattered by the tabloid stories linking me to hookers, and when she questioned me about them, I confessed they were true.

I did?

A source tells this column that at first the Marilyn lookalike dismissed the stories of her brainy boyfriend cavorting with prostitutes as jealous talk planted by rivals. But after confronting Webster with the goods, he fessed up it was true. He was a serial romancer, and had scored with millions of women, both during his marriage and while dating West.

My face turned purple.

Our source says West ordered a moving van minutes after his confession, and was out the same day. When it comes to Webster, it appears still waters don't just run deep, they run around. West was seen sobbing while packing up her belongings and friends say she is crushed by the split. Webster, meanwhile, has parlayed his relationship into a deal-a-thon of books, television and radio. Some guys have all the luck.

Some do, but I wasn't one of them. To their credit, the *Your Money* staff kept to the business at hand on Sunday too. I donned my suit and we ran through the entire show from opening to closing credits. Lucy stood on the sidelines with a stopwatch as if monitoring a shuttle countdown. The host of the program, Carol Owens, was one of these smart, I've-got-a-business-degree-and-great-legs kind of women born to be on television.

Cleverly they did not put her behind a desk, but perched her in a chair designed to showcase her short skirts. In truth, she didn't have to do much, just introduce pieces that had been taped throughout the week, like a newsreader. In the final three minutes she said something in the order of, 'And now for investors, stock tips from *The Capitalist*'s man inside Washington, Tom Webster.'

And then the little red light went on, and I made some of that

TV small talk I always thought banal when I was a viewer.

'Thank you, Carol. Great to be here.'

'Great to have you on board, Tom. Any tips for our investors out there, Tom?'

'You bet, Carol.'

So there you have it. I was turning into one of those television Ken dolls I so despised. But Lucy insisted we have ten seconds of small talk to drive home the idea we were not just reporters, we were family. Right.

After Carol threw me a cheesy smile, I threw one back. Oh, us finance reporters. We are just so happy and smiley. Yes, we are. The camera then went in for one more close-up of her legs, and I was off and running.

'In Washington this week the Federal Reserve hinted they may lower interest rates when they next meet. What does this mean for you the investor? Well . . .'

Lucy gave me the thumbs-up. And then it was over. Everyone clapped, and we were notified the show would be shown to the network, the research boys, and then given a slot.

And then I did the most dishonorable thing I could. I fled the studio. Did not stick around for the post-mortem, did not thank Carol or her lovely legs. Made a feeble excuse of having an appointment and bolted to lick my wounds in the comfort of my own home. I was defeated, just like . . .

No matter the truth, Lucy, Carol, the world now believed I had cheated on Alexandra West. Here I was, so greedy that, despite dining nightly on gourmet food, I needed continuous side orders of fries. At home I called Wilkes and left a message that I was furious about the negative publicity regarding our so-called break-up and demanded he rectify the situation. He never called back.

I knew Elizabeth and Jake had probably opened some expensive champagne by now to celebrate my downfall. I could picture them laughing over the pictures of me in my Austin Powers get-up (which ran alongside a lot of the stories), rolling their eyes over what a fool I made of myself.

I needed comfort and called Mom. I explained that the break-up was real, but the reasons given were not. Again, the woman was a saint, the only person who made me feel better.

'Darling, don't worry. I believe you if you say it was mutual, and that's what I will tell everybody.'

'Mom, it's a waste of time. If it's in print, people believe it. I know. I work in print. Remember?'

'Tommy, darling, now that it's all over, I think I can tell you something. I was always worried it wouldn't last. You two seemed to come from different worlds. I was happy you were happy, and it was nice for you after that awful business with Elizabeth, but maybe this is for the best. Maybe it's better you find someone more like you. You know, a more quiet girl.'

I had to laugh.

'Sure, Mom. A more quiet girl.'

'Remember this, Tom. Broken hearts mend in time. She wasn't the right one for you but there is someone out there who is. I know it.'

'I do too, Mom.'

Mothers. Don't you love them?

Chapter 33

'Sorry to hear you two lovebirds broke up,' said a voice as I arrived at the office.

It was the detestable Frank Wicker-Smith III, attempting to provide sympathy but loving every minute of my agony.

'Morning, Frank.'

'Morning, Tom.'

'Just for your information, the split was mutual. I never confessed to cheating on Alexandra because I didn't. Those stories are garbage. I don't cheat. Not like some people.'

My God. I couldn't believe how nasty I could be at nine a.m. on a Monday.

'Of course it was mutual,' said Frank smirking. 'Did I suggest anything else?'

And with that he didn't speak to me for the rest of the day. Boy, was he going to get it in *The Vulture*. Frank aside, the day was a success, contrary to my expectations. Even at this late stage I learned a very valuable lesson, one I hadn't counted on. If celebrity makes people sit up and stare, notoriety makes them stand and applaud. Now that the Sunday papers had given credence to the tabloid stories, they were considered gospel truth. No longer the paramour of a famous flame, I now had another feather in my cap, this commodity they call 'an edge'.

My colleagues winked at me all day, as if admitting me to some secret society to which they had long belonged. More women approached me, not less. I learned a good boy linked to a bad girl is not as exciting as a naughty boy linked to no one. I elicited sympathy over the break-up, and also admiration for my errant behavior. Any man who had the guts and gumption to cheat on Alexandra West must have private parts the size of Alaska, they thought. I suppose now they expected me to go out and buy a motorbike and leather jacket. Even Louis was impressed. He intimated as much when he called me into his office for another Monday morning chat.

'Tommy, boy, gotta tell you. I had my doubts. Never thought it would last, but I hope you aren't taking it too hard.'

'Well, no, actually, because she didn't leave me. It was mutual.'

'Of course it was.'

'No, really, Louis. It was.'

'Say no more. I believe you.'

But I doubted it. Still, either way, Louis didn't seem to care.

'Just wanted to let you know the break-up doesn't affect your job around here. The column is staying up front. We are getting good reaction to it, advertisers are asking to be placed around it.'

'But what about all these allegations of my hanging out with, you know, prostitutes? Does this not affect how people view me? I mean, the business boys must be laughing from here to Washington.'

'Bullshit. Everyone cheats, Tommy. You just got caught. They feel bad for you. There but for the grace of God...you know...'

'But I didn't cheat.'

'Of course not.'

'No, really, Louis. You have to believe me.'

'I do, Tommy, I do.'

He didn't. And the reason he didn't was that he liked the bad-boy image this latest flap had now created. If I had an edge now, the magazine, always regarded as pinstripe and stuffed shirt, had an edge by association.

'How's the TV thing going?'

'Taped a pilot yesterday. It's not brain surgery, but I'll go back.'

'They mention *The Capitalist* when they introduced you?'

'Yes.'

'Good. Make sure they keep the magazine name out there.'

'Sure thing, Louis.'

That afternoon I fielded more phone calls in two hours than I'd had since the entire ball started rolling. Gossip reporters wanting my version of events. I insisted over and over the split was a mutual decision. I knew they were rolling their eyes at the other end as this did not constitute the sexy answer they needed. A number of magazines wanted interviews. Another radio station wanted to sound me out about financial commentary. An afternoon talk show was assembling a panel on former boyfriends of the stars, would I be interested? No, I told them, I would not. A news magazine program offered me $10,000 to give my version of the break-up, and I hung up. It was insane, and never-ending.

Gossip columnist Dixie Lee called from Houston and asked perceptively if I ever considered that Alexandra used me to retool her tawdry image. Good question but one I refused to answer. No, I said, it was love on both parts, we just moved too quickly. Finally the book editor with whom I was negotiating regarding a tome on government fiscal policy and the consumer called. I held my breath, waiting for him to drop the ball.

Au contraire. He wanted to deal. I asked whether recent stories dragging my reputation through a volcanic mudslide had worried him at all. The response was a hearty laugh. No, I was told, it will only sell more books. In fact he wished the book was already written so they could capitalize on the publicity. I should have been shocked, but had ceased to be some weeks before. He wanted a ten-page proposal by the end of the week, after which an advance for $60,000 would be drawn up if the proposal passed the test.

'Have no fear, Tom,' he said. 'Nobody cares what you do in your spare time. If you have girls on the side or wear a bra under your clothes to work, it's all noise, and as long as it's something, the book will sell like hotcakes. And that's why we are in this game, right?'

'Right,' I said. 'Right.'

Two more calls that day would cause my head to rotate. The first came from the elusive Ms MacDowell. She was whispering and I whispered back, as one does in these situations.

'How's it going?' she asked.

'How do you think?'

'Oh, Tom, I'm sorry they butchered you like that.'

'Me too.'

'Your article should go a long way to squaring things. You see now why you have to write it?'

'Jamie, I can't wait to write it.'

'Good. I'm calling because we need to set up a photo shoot with you.'

'Me alone? Or me and Alexandra?'

'You alone. We are going to use paparazzi shots of the two of you, and we have stuff left over from a shoot we did with Alexandra.'

'Fine.'

'I think I should mention we had a meeting and decided to move you from an inside story to the cover.'

'Excuse me?'

'Well, the story turned out much better than we could have anticipated. It's too good to waste on the inside. We think the fallout will be huge.'

'Jamie, I just want to tell you, for what it's worth, I never cheated on her.'

'Of course not, Tom. Of course not. I never thought anything else.'

And then she called. The other vixen. The woman from the gallery opening, Rachel Carter-Brown. The brunette version of the blond version of whatever version was Alexandra West. Said she was coming to New York for a movie premiere, didn't know many people in town, and would I be her date? A ridiculous offer to be sure, but one I couldn't refuse. I could see what she was up to, but I didn't care. Rachel had no idea she was about to help me as much as she planned to hurt Alexandra, but she was. Oh, yes. Her wanting me meant Elizabeth would not have the last laugh. I would.

I told Rachel I would be honored to escort her to the premiere. She assured me she checked, Alexandra had not been invited, so there was no fear of a run-in. And then she asked if it was really over between us.

'I don't want to move in on someone else's property, Tom.'

Like hell she doesn't.

'It's over. Really.'

'Good. Frankly, I never knew what you were doing with her anyway. She's so plastic.'

Funny, I once heard someone say the same about her.

'I'll call you when I hit town,' she said. 'Can't wait to hook up.'

'Me neither. Can't wait.'

With the deadline looming, and no Alexandra to distract me, I threw myself into penning the article that ignited this entire mess in the first place. Re-reading my journal entries, it was impossible to believe so much had happened in so short a time.

Using my living-room floor as a drawing board, I laid out all the magazine articles I clipped, notes, diary entries, etc. Jamie MacDowell was right the first time we met. Step into the system and it works like a charm. Too well, actually, which, she said, was the entire point.

I had expected the writing of the piece to be a long, hard road, but in fact it was just the opposite. Sentences and paragraphs rushed from my head to the computer screen in rapid-fire sequence, fueled by anger and memory. I resolved the format would be in the mode of a letter, addressed to Jake, whom I was now seriously missing in my life. Baseball is no fun when you go alone. Nor is life. It's essential that we each have but one friend out there who totally understands and appreciates us, and, spouse-thievery notwithstanding, he was the one. Friendship, like marriage, often comes with conditions insisting you stick around for better or worse.

By the end, the article was long, very long, though Jamie instructed I write as much as I felt appropriate and they would make cuts at her end. I tried to be amusing yet honest, describing the various emotions that accompanied my ascent of Fame Mountain. Shock at the loss of privacy, hurt due to reactions of co-workers and friends, the betrayal by Jake, the rage of Elizabeth, the ego gratification that women saw me as something other than what I was, and finally acceptance.

I then confessed I enjoyed being famous, for it gave me financial and professional leverage I otherwise never would have been granted. As Wilkes emphasized over and over, it's not who you are, it's who people think you are. And for a number of glorious weeks people thought I was the love of her life, and they wanted a piece of the action, which meant a piece of me.

The article began thus:

Dear Jake,

You have been my best friend since second grade, and few people can claim to still connect with someone thirty-seven years after an initial meeting in a sandbox. But for the last few weeks you have refused to speak to me. Why? What possibly occurred that could abruptly curtail all talk of baseball playoffs, daily lunches, nightly phone calls, if my wife leaving me for you didn't? I'll tell you what happened, though I ask nothing but your patience, for this may take some time.

I became famous. You became jealous, and a wise if calculating man told me recently that of all the deadly sins, envy is the most insidious. You thought I was in love with a movie star, a woman clearly out of my league. You were shocked and hurt to think she loved me back. But most of all you were confused. You, my mother, my ex-wife, my co-workers, my editor, all made adjustments to accommodate my celebrity into their lives. So did the press. The public. And it was all for naught.

All the tears, the gossip, the hurt, the I-can't-believe-it backstabbing. Jake, I never loved her. She never loved me. It was all a game, a set-up, an elaborate sham conducted in the name of social science. Sadly, it worked. Beautifully. You bought the idea, along with millions of men who believed, because they wanted to, that quiet nerdy guys could become Tomcats overnight if given half the chance. Now hear this. In the real world, there is no chance. How many people win the lottery? Really win the lottery? How many of us middle-aged, out-of-shape men truly find ourselves in bed with a movie star? None, and that includes me.

From our first date to our last, the entire proceedings were heavily scripted, although I must point out a lot of rewriting occurred without my knowledge or consent. What you are about to read, Jake, is a journey I undertook motivated by money, boredom, mid-life exhaustion and anger that you took Elizabeth from me. If you can't believe I would do such a thing, you are not alone. Neither can I.

What followed was a detailed description of the first furtive phone call from Ms MacDowell, her offer and my acceptance of it, my misfired attempts at achieving overnight fame, and my approach to Alexandra with an offer of my own. I left nothing out, including what is commonly known in journalism as the juicy bits. The shell-shock of my first premiere, the false affection we displayed toward each other in public, the reactions of waiters, doormen, her fans (I gave Charlie a big rap for persistence) and the paparazzi, my sartorial make-over care of Tommy, her make-over care of an army of stylists, the hell of becoming tabloid fodder, the joy of being touted as a sexual acrobat, and my new career as a finance guru.

I noted the reaction of my pinstripe colleagues as Alexandra made successive trips to the office, and my own feelings about having her move into my life while mooching off my reputation. I felt no duty to protect Alexandra after her insistence our split was due to infidelity on my part, and assured Jake that she was using me as much as I her. I explained her publicist, Michael Wilkes, had devised the entire Marilyn–Arthur Miller strategy, and I complimented him on his genius.

All efforts prior to my arrival to convince those 'in the loop' that Alexandra was greater than the sum of her parts had, for various reasons, failed. My offer was manna from heaven, and, understandably, if I wanted to exploit her fame to create my own, she expected something in return. Who says you can't buy respectability? Not Alexandra West. To her credit, I explained she also loved the idea of the article. Her own transition into the public eye had been invasive, full of tabloid rumors, professional jealousy and obsessive fans. If anything could be done to shed light on the phenomenon, she told me, she wanted in. Sure, I can hear you saying, he's kidding himself. I was not. I knew her primary purpose in entering this agreement was selfish and self-serving. She needed me to give her credibility. Pure and simple. But as the drama unfolded she enjoyed having a front-row seat, and did provide genuine sympathy in some difficult times.

I wrote probably way too much about Alexandra, when the article was supposed to be about me. But I couldn't help myself. I figured when a Marilyn lookalike moves into your apartment, cooks you breakfast, people want to know what went on. I admitted I failed to crack the veneer of Alexandra West, who, I felt, was spectacularly unintelligent but extravagantly street smart. For this reason alone I admired her. She barely read, but knew a hell of a lot. Mostly, for someone who wound up a celebrity more by accident than by design, she was a quick study. True, she was alternately cruel and kind toward me, and yet I liked her. And I liked living with her. Who wouldn't? Away from the cameras she was softer, more pliant, there was clearly a heart there. Was she aggressive and competitive? You bet.

I couldn't help myself and threw some history into the mix as well. I explained that whenever things became too chaotic, I sought refuge in my beloved history books, drawing comfort from my heroes, from tales of their courage in the face of enemy attack. I also pointed out that Alexander and Napoleon and Honest Abe had earned their fame, while I had done nothing to merit mine. And I said by the time she left me I saw Alexandra as a combination of Empress Theodora of Byzantium, an actress (yes, even in the year 527 actresses were trying to bed royalty) who married a weak king but was so smart she ran the empire from behind the scenes, and Lucrezia Borgia, a vixen who hooked up with a slew of smart men, only to use them, then kill them when they stood in her way.

Then I addressed the big question of S-E-X. Did I sleep with her? I tried. Was I successful? No. And I made a point of emphasizing that rumors she left me due to my predilection for hookers were false. There were none, I protested. And I prayed they believed me.

I then found myself following Wilkes's advice slavishly. I thanked everyone who played a part in my story for their contributions to my tale. Louis, Frank Wicker-Smith III (who did not emerge smelling of roses, let me tell you), Alexandra, Wilkes, all the television, radio and book people who waved cash under my nose, the tabloid press, the paparazzi, the videorazzi, the website people, everyone. Jake, my mother, Elizabeth. I felt like I was at an awards ceremony.

Then I groveled for their forgiveness, hoping once the initial burst of anger over the con had lifted, they would see things from my perspective. How I was conducting the great social experiment at the dawn of a new century. How their participation was key to its success. How together we lifted the veil on fame, unmasked its shallow core in all its hype and glory. And then I begged them not to dispatch me to social Siberia after reading the piece.

I then handed the piece in to Jamie and waited. Nervously. Anxiously. I continued to sign myself up for radio spots and other assorted professional activities, as one thing inevitably leads to another. Once one person wants you, everyone wants you. After publication, however, I believed no one would want me.

Boy, was I wrong. Would I never learn?

Chapter 34

Jamie sent me an advance copy of *The Vulture*, which bore my face on the cover, along with the headline: THE MAGIC MAN – TOM WEBSTER CONJURES HIS OWN CELEBRITY.

Inside, the article was reprinted pretty much as I had written it, with a few cuts made for space. Jamie wrote in a note that no advance copies would be provided to the media, despite this being the usual deal. Though getting your magazine mentioned in the pages of another was considered a coup (read: free publicity), Jamie had decided a better strategy would be to build a wall of secrecy.

To that end she informed the usual suspects that advance copies of *The Vulture* would not be available because the cover story was so explosive its power would be diminished if a trail of bread-crumbs were left along a path. Instead, a complete loaf would be for sale for everyone on Monday morning. She insisted that withholding the magazine would drive reporters more crazy than handing it over. I believe she was right, for I learned later, on Sunday night, every reporter in town was trying to get a copy. Jamie said if you whip people into enough of a frenzy, sales double. I think she and Louis were probably married in another life.

I read the article twice, then felt the honorable thing to do was provide Alexandra with a copy. I called Wilkes and offered to fax him the piece, but there was no need. Jamie had already sent him one, and he professed to have loved each and every word of it. In fact, not only did he gush, he asked if he could visit later to discuss something. My curiosity was so aroused I couldn't say no. Later, in my apartment, he refused beer or coffee, and got straight to the heart of the matter.

'Your story is going to rock the planet.'

'I doubt that.'

'Trust me. It was pretty impressive.'

'Didn't mind that I called you a snake? The Riddler?'

'Are you kidding? I loved it.'

'Can I ask why?'

'Publicity. I'm going to get more clients out of this.'

'Even if my perception of you was not exactly positive?'

'You painted me as someone who would do anything for a client. They love that.'

'I guess.'

I hadn't realized Wilkes would view this as a personal victory too. Impossible to foresee all the ramifications.

'Anyway, enough about my career. Tom, you realize when this hits the streets you are going to need a publicist.'

'I am?'

'My God, you still don't get it, do you?'

'What, you mean for mop-up and damage control?

'I mean, for offers. Book deals, movie deals, interviews.'

'Michael, I hardly think the offers are going to be pouring in after everyone realizes they have been scammed.'

'I bet you 100 bucks, no, make it 1,000, they do.'

The man was serious. A thousand bucks was not spare change. Maybe he did know something I didn't.

'You want to bet me $1,000 they are going to want me more after this, not less?'

'Yep.'

'Okay, forget the bet. You win. Even though I refuse to believe you.'

'You're going to need someone running interference between you and the monster. Up until now you did it all yourself because it was intermittent. But it's really going to power up, and I'd like to apply for the job.'

'Well, this is ironic.'

'What is?'

'The man who stabs me in the back one week wants to dress the wound the next.'

Wilkes laughed.

'Tom, I always said this and I'll say it again. It's nothing personal. It never is. It's business.'

The man was too good to let go, and he knew it. So did I.

'Mr Wilkes, I think you just signed your next client,' I said, extending my hand.

The snake grinned, baring his fangs.

'Welcome aboard, Mr Webster. Welcome aboard.'

Wilkes stayed another half an hour, suggesting that I inform *The Capitalist* switchboard all calls regarding *The Vulture* article were to be handled by him. He advised me to change the message on my voicemail at work, my answering machine at home. I found this all highly dramatic, but promised to obey his commands. Though I was thoroughly sick to my stomach worrying about the reaction, Wilkes was in party mode.

When he left I called Mom in Houston. The jig, as they say, was up, and she had a right to know the truth. I explained everything from start to finish as best I could, asking her to forgive me for lying to her all those weeks. Despite my inability to see her facial reactions, I could sense them from her voice. Alternately shocked, surprised and delighted, she refused to wait until the magazine went on sale the next day, and insisted I read the entire piece over the phone. Almost an hour later she was, I believe, speechless. This was news in itself, as my mother could talk under water with a mouth full of concrete.

'Darling, I don't know what to say.'

'Don't say anything, Mom. I just want to say thanks for always being on my side, and apologize for any grief I caused you.'

'Grief? What grief?'

'Well, reporters calling up. Neighbors talking behind your back. It couldn't have been easy.'

'Tommy, you know what? I kind of enjoyed it. Not the bad talk, of course not. But in the beginning. A little attention never hurt anyone.'

I couldn't believe she was taking it so well.

'I love you, Mom.'

'I know, darling.'

As we talked, for more than two hours in the end, Mom was as worried about my future as I was. Would Jake read the piece and forgive me? Elizabeth? Louis? Would the deals fade away? I assured her my newly hired publicist, Michael Wilkes, insisted the fallout would be only positive. Mom had her doubts. So did I. We were not related for nothing, you know. Exhausted but unburdened, I hung up and went to sleep. Or tried to. I was up every hour on the hour, and the following morning experienced what I am sure was jet lag. Never mind that I hadn't gone anywhere, I felt, and looked, like garbage.

The fallout began raining down the minute I entered the newsroom. For the past weeks I had been greeted by smiles, admiration and envy. Now everyone either didn't look at me or went out of their way to scowl. By ten a.m. it seemed everyone, even the cleaning staff who spoke no English, had read the article. I saw copies of *The Vulture* everywhere. My colleagues, who, I think I explained, are uptight pinstripes, were furious.

The attacks started on the inter-office email. At least fifteen messages from colleagues telling me how low I was, how rotten it was to drag them and *The Capitalist* through the mud. They did not, they said, enjoy being conned by either me or Alexandra, no matter how noble my intentions.

Then magazine shareholders began emailing. One left a particularly vicious message, informing me I had risked *The Capitalist's* reputation and share price, making the publication a laughing stock by conducting a stupid, self-serving experiment. He said I was a pathetic fool, having a mid-life crisis, and should be ashamed of myself. He suggested I start packing up my desk, because I wouldn't be a *Capitalist* employee by the end of the day. He would call the chairman of the holding company and see to that.

I looked around the room, desperate for support, please, just one smiling face in my direction, but it never came. Frank was out on an interview, but I already knew what his reaction would be. People hissed all morning as they walked by. In response I chose to keep my head down, stay at my desk, do my housekeeping. By noon you could have felt the chill in the air from Delaware.

Actually the last part is a lie. I wasn't doing my housekeeping, I was sitting there eating antacids as the pit in my stomach grew larger by the second. What I had convinced myself of last night, that my grand experiment would be greeted with praise by all and sundry, appeared a gross miscalculation now. By making a fool of myself, I had made a fool of them. Of course they hated me. Did I really think they would buy me a drink when *The Vulture* hit the streets? Actually, I must confess, I thought they would.

I wondered whether Jake had seen the magazine, or Elizabeth. If my colleagues' reactions were anything to go by, I could forget ever getting Elizabeth back, and baseball with Jake was out of the question. Once I had been the guy who couldn't be seen in public with him, because he absconded with my wife. Now he would be the one who couldn't be seen in public with me, because I had humiliated him with my con game.

The more I thought about it, the more I felt I would vomit. I told myself to calm down, but have you ever tried to tell yourself to calm down? It never works. So I reminded myself to look to the past, to think of all my heroes and how they had their backs to the wall but kept on marching. And that is when my heart just sank like a stone. That is when a feeling of shame so enveloped me I wanted to cry.

I had, for one minute, maybe two, convinced myself that fame was fame, earned or manufactured, it didn't matter. Conquer an empire or date an actress, what's the difference, right? It's all about people remembering your name. Well, there is a big difference, and the truth, which I knew, but recently, conveniently, chose to ignore, devasted me.

I wasn't Cleopatra or Alexander or Honest Abe, and if I were to have lunch today with any of them I would die of shame. I had my face on the cover of *The Vulture*, but I had as much right to sit at their table as the busboy clearing the plates. They did it the hard way, the right way. They were leaders, they fought wars, they paid in blood, they changed civilizations. I went to an art show dressed like a fat Rolling Stone. Oh, yes, Abe Lincoln would have been really impressed.

The phone rang. It was the publishing executive who romanced me like a lover when he thought I was the finance guru boyfriend of the world's biggest sex symbol. Only weeks ago he told me what a genius I was, how the book on economics I would soon be writing for him would revolutionize Wall Street. The ego massage he gave me was so intense it practically had me sexually aroused. But now, unmasked as a loathsome con artist who merely masqueraded as a player, he wasn't quite so hot at the thought of getting into bed with me. Cold actually.

'Have to withdraw our offer, Tom. You understand. There are big issues here management aren't happy about. Fraud. Misrepresentation. Personally, I thought your story was kind of clever. But the big boys upstairs are furious. Furious. I'll be frank, Tom. The company guards its reputation like a bulldog, you know that, and they just can't do business with the guy who took the public for a ride with a stunt like this.'

'I understand. Please tell your superiors I am sorry if they are upset,' I said sheepishly.

'Will do, Tom. Got to go. I'll send round some paperwork clarifying our position so you have it in writing. Take it easy, buddy.'

So here it was. The beginning of the end. How many other deals would be canceled by day's end? I guessed all of them. Who would want to be in bed with a scam artist? I wouldn't. I was most empathetic to their situations. Given what was going on, I saw there was no way I could stay at *The Capitalist* now either. By noon I thought the honorable thing to do would be to resign. Just as I began typing up my resignation letter, Marlene called and frostily summoned me to Louis's office. Good, I thought, I won't have to resign. Louis is going to fire me. She didn't wink at me on my way in.

Well, it was nice while it lasted.

Like a man walking to the Tower to be beheaded, I lumbered slowly to Louis's office. If the morning so far was anything to go by, I was expecting him to bellow, bark and show me the door. When Louis got angry, it was a sight to behold. But I was not to behold this sight. What I beheld was a man bouncing in his chair with glee. Rubbing his chubby fingers together with glee. He was as happy as a kid on Christmas morning.

'Unbelievable! Tommy, unbelievable!'

I said nothing, thinking my best approach would be to let him take the stage.

'Un–fucking–believable. I read your story twice. And I'm going to read it again to make sure I wasn't dreaming the first two times.'

I smiled. This was the first person who didn't want me drawn and quartered all day.

'Why you had to write the best article of your career for another magazine, I don't know.'

Still smiling, but nodding as well.

'Jesus, Tom, you could have let me in on it.'

'I didn't even let my mother in on it.'

'Point taken.'

'Louis, thanks for taking it so well. Frankly, I thought you called me in to fire me. The shareholders seem pretty mad. I just had a book deal canceled, and the staff, well...'

'Fire you? Are you nuts? Tom, I think you're a fucking genius. Why would I fire a fucking genius? Screw the shareholders. I'll handle them. So tell me, how were you coping when it was all going down?'

'I wasn't really. It's sort of like being tied to the tracks and watching a train come toward you.'

'I'll bet.'

'No hard feelings?'

'Are you kidding?

In truth, Louis had little reason to complain. I had been kind to him in my story, because he deserved it. He was honest from the word go about his intentions to capitalize on my celebrity, but never made a move without consulting me first. I appreciated that.

'Tommy, I'm so happy I could pee my pants, and I haven't done that since summer camp when I was six and saw a snake. You're a fucking Einstein, you know that? This is going to sell *The Capitalist* even more. I'm ordering another print run.'

I loved Louis. Everything you did in life was a potential business deal. If you couldn't turn an opportunity into money, it wasn't worth discussing.

'One more thing. I've had a ton of calls already. Given some quotes to the papers, you know, about how I had no idea, I wasn't in on the scam, but yet I think it's the work of a master. Some TV crews want soundbites, they are coming in later.'

'Fine. Whatever you want, Louis.'

'Listen, Tom, you're not going to leave us, are you?'

'Leave you?'

'With deals, movies, I don't know what else around the corner, you're a big shot now. Probably figure, I don't need this little column anymore.'

'Louis, I'm not leaving.'

'Because if it's a matter of money . . .'

'I'm not going anywhere.'

'Just checking, Tom, just checking. Didn't think you were.'

So Louis was going to get his stab at fame, and he was as excited as a rooster in a henhouse. Me, I could take it or leave it, although I was bound by the terms of my contract to do some post-article publicity and I would not back out now.

'Hey, Louis,' I called out, just as I was leaving his office.

'What?'

'Who do you want to play you in the movie?'

'Movie? There's going to be a movie?'

'Well, not yet, but my publicist bet me 1,000 bucks there would be.'

'You want to know who should play me? Why not me? I can play myself better than anyone can play me, right? Tell those Hollywood boys they don't need to call De Niro. I can play myself just fine.'

And you know what? He was right. Nobody could play Louis better than he could.

I returned to my desk to find Frank was back. I was buoyant after my meeting with Louis, but Frank's arrival meant that feeling wouldn't last. I braced myself for him to let me have it.

'Tom, I, I . . .'

'You're in shock.'

'Total.'

'Well, don't be. At least now you know what you were thinking all along was right. You couldn't understand how a guy like me could be dating her, and now you know.'

'Hey, look, I'm sorry if you think I have an attitude.'

'Excuse me?'

'You wrote that I am a snob. You said I was rude, unable to hide my horror at your new elevated status.'

'I never wrote that.'

'You insinuated it.'

'I merely said your reaction was one of incredulity, which it was.'

'Well, I'm sorry.'

Excuse me? He was proffering an apology? Now this just plain stunned me, knocked my socks off, as they say. I thought Frank would be livid and he had every right. Instead, he was asking forgiveness.

'Frank, if you want to be pissed at me you have my permission.'

'I'm not angry, Tom. Hurt maybe.'

'I see.'

'I must say, Tom, you had me fooled. All of us.'

'That was the general idea.'

'For what it's worth, I really enjoyed the piece. Except, of course, the parts where I am mentioned.'

'I never wrote you were a snob.'

'But I am a snob, Tom. I think it's actually one of my better qualities.'

I laughed. So did he. The man was nothing if not honest. I extended my hand and he shook it.

'No hard feelings?'

'None.'

'Thanks, Frank. I never thought I would say this, but you have been one of the kindest people to me all day.'

'Boys not taking it well?'

'They want my scalp.'

'They'll cool off.'

Have to say, never thought I would be so happy to see that WASP breeding come through.

'Oh, Tom. One more thing.'

'Yes?'

'My wife just called. She wants your autograph.'

I was just about to step out for lunch, hoping to catch Jake at the Blue Moon, when Wilkes called. He was so breathless you would have thought he was on the phone while running the New York marathon.

'Tom, you there?'

'Yep.'

'Unbelievable! Fucking unbelievable! Never seen anything like it!'

'What?'

'You! That's what. Everyone wants you!'

'They do? I doubt that. You should see what greeted me here this morning. And I just had a book deal canceled . . . and I suspect there is more coming.'

'Which book?'

'The economics book.'

'Oh, fuck them. Do you really care? You don't want to write a book like that anyway. Who gives a shit about economics? It's so not sexy. Tom, listen, I've got book deals coming in for you in just the last hour that will make you wet your pants. And shit, newspapers want interviews, television want interviews, Hollywood want to talk to you about a movie. I told you.'

He was delirious.

'You're making this up.'

'Not a chance. You should come down here. Place is a madhouse.'

'Really?'

'Tom, get a pen. I've booked you and Alex to do some television together. A couple of tabloid news shows, talk shows, even the nightly news. Jesus, Tom, we made the news.'

'We did? Is this good?'

'Oh, you're a real joker. Also you two are doing some breakfast television tomorrow morning, but we can talk about that later. I've got crews coming over to *The Capitalist* at three to do interviews with you.'

He listed even more calls and opportunities that had presented themselves in the last hour. The book deals to pen the story of the story of how I became the story. Movie deals to be made of the book deals. Advertising companies wanting me to endorse artificial sweetener, only fitting for an artificial celebrity. Wilkes was drowning in offers, and the man was like a junkie on a high. Thank

God I had hired him. He promised to call me back, and we could discuss the offers in more detail. Before he hung up, he explained again what I had refused to believe when he had suggested it weeks before. Forget my colleagues, he said, who cares what they think? Outside of the office I was being a hailed a genius, the Einstein of the media age. The double-headed monster of the public and the press, the beast I had much maligned in my article, had performed a 360 degree turn and returned to worship me. As the boyfriend of a celebrity I was a story. As the faux boyfriend of a celebrity I was a bigger story. Go figure.

He then put Alexandra on the phone. She only wanted to know one thing, what I would be wearing on TV so she could coordinate. I promised to wear navy, which thrilled her, as she said it gave her the greatest number of options for contrast. I truly loved Alexandra. She didn't want to appear on television to discuss the deeper ramifications of the exercise she had participated in, she wanted to look hot.

I couldn't get out of the damn office. Jamie called to see how I was coping, and I assured her I was hanging tough. Mom called within a minute of Jamie to ask the same question. To her I admitted I was little overwhelmed. Would I never get out of here? The phone rang again. This time it was Jake. Finally. He sounded stunned, and asked if we could meet at the Blue Moon for lunch. I told him great minds think alike, because I was just going over there to find him.

Chapter 35

At the Blue Moon, the waiters looked pleased. It had not slipped by them we had had a huge falling-out. Now we were back in our usual booth, eating our usual bagels with cream cheese. I thought they might applaud our reconciliation, but they restrained themselves. I'm not going to lie, sitting with Jake was really uncomfortable at first, and there was about three minutes of silence where we both read the menus as if studying baseball stats, all to avoid each other's gaze. When the waiter approached we ordered our usual, making our research into the day's specials clearly redundant. He took the menus out of our hands, leaving us to face each other. I smiled then, and suggested Jake take the floor.

'I don't know what to say.'

'That seems to be a recurring theme today,' I said.

'What, the guys at work?'

'Stunned. All of them. Like deer in the headlights.'

'Well, count me in, then.'

'You're counted.'

Another sixty seconds of silence.

'Tom. I, I, I'm sorry things got so bad between us.'

Hello. He was apologizing? Jake was apologizing? Now this I didn't expect.

'Hey, I'm sorry too. Really. More than you can imagine.'

'No, you don't need to say that. Look, I took your wife, I trashed you in print, I don't blame you if you never speak to me again.'

'Well, too bad. I intend to. And I think we should go to the game Saturday as well.'

Jake beamed. All was forgiven, though I must say it would take a while for all to be forgotten. The truth was, I missed him, and knowing what my future might be like, I needed a buddy by my side.

'That was some piece of work, Tom. Jesus Christ. You certainly had us all fooled. What the hell were you thinking when it was happening?'

'You know, when we started dating, it all happened so fast I never had time to think, just react. Writing the article was the first time I got to crystallize my thoughts at all.'

'And me? You must have thought I was complete bastard.'

'I thought, I thought... well, I was hurt. We've known each other a long time. I never thought there could be situations in life where your closest friend could turn on you over a woman. I mean, I forgave you over Elizabeth, and here you were, steamed because I was dating a movie star.'

We laughed, but Jake was clearly ashamed of his behavior.

'What can I say? I'm sorry. I really thought you were tossing our friendship into the trash over her.'

'And you thought I was turning into one of her pet poodles that did everything she commanded?'

'That was Elizabeth's theory.'

'Speaking of whom...'

'I called her to tell her to buy the magazine. I haven't spoken to her again today...'

'Do you think she'll speak to me? I mean, not that she did since she left, but now I've really done it, right? I mean, here she is marching over to the apartment at seven in the morning demanding I break up with a woman I'm not really seeing. She's going to hate me for the rest of my life.'

'Yep. I'd say that would be accurate. We both know Liz has a temper.'

Lord. I didn't know what would be worse. Her silence or her fury.

'Hey, Tom.'

'Yes.'

'I know you wrote you never slept with her, but still, must have been pretty cool having her live in your house, right?'

'Jake, that was the best part. Going out in public with her, I was too nervous. But waking up and finding her sprawled on the sofa, Jesus, I had to pinch myself every morning. It was pretty cool.'

'So what's she really like?'

'I never really figured that part out. She's no rocket scientist, but she's no dummy either. Very calculating. Street smart. Really understands the system and how to work it.'

'And she got what she wanted, right? These directors and producers she was hoping to meet, she met them?'

'Bingo. Offered her roles, the works. She got what she wanted from me.'

'And you got what you wanted from her.'

'Money-wise, you could say that. But I could have done without the guys sorting through my trash and interviewing me while I was in the bathroom.'

'That stuff cracked me up.'

'Might make amusing reading, but you should experience it. Pretty humiliating.'

'You know which stuff I liked the best?'

'No.'

'The moment the press stopped writing about you as a nerd and started talking about you as if you were some big deal. You know, the part where you wrote they thought you were sexy, the poster boy for every man who had sand kicked in his face. And I loved it when women started hitting on you.'

'It all happened. Just as I wrote it.'

'I loved it. I mean, I hated it when it was happening, but I love it now.'

'Anything else you want to know?'

'Yeah. What's it like? Being famous?'

'Good and bad. I liked being treated well. I liked the women flirting. I felt powerful. I liked the leverage. Hated the intrusion. And I hated the nastiness of it all. The lies. That hooker stuff really threw me.'

'You know, I never believed that. Even though I thought you had changed, I never bought that part of the story.'

'Thanks.'

I would have to say, Jake was reveling in it. And in his new status as the best friend of the guy who pulled off the scam of the week. I reminded him that next week it would be old news, and we could all return to our lives and routine. At least that was my hope.

'Tom, don't be so naïve.'

'About what?'

'About all of us going back to our old lives. This thing has changed everything now. You're famous. Whatever the reason, however it happened. I'm a famous guy's best friend. You said yourself. You have all these deals now.'

'True. But I would like to retain some semblance of privacy.'

'Good luck.' He laughed.

'Hey, after what I have already been through, it couldn't get any more intense.'

Again, I, Tom Webster, was as wrong as wrong could be.

Chapter 36

The following three days I took off from work, as I conducted my whirlwind tour of the big three and the small 100 television networks. I sat on the couch in the morning opposite cheery hosts, I sat in a chair in the afternoon opposite cheery hosts. Everyone is just so damned happy to be on TV, just like we are on *Your Money*. I did live satellite links with local shows in Houston, touted as the hometown boy who taught those slick New Yorkers a lesson. Alexandra and I appeared on a number of tabloid shows, and I was told over and over by reporters off camera how much they admired what I had done. This in spite of the fact my efforts had made them look exceedingly stupid. Trees were felled and newspapers printed which devoted sections to *The Vulture* cover story, followed by detailed explanations as to what-it-all-meant.

Everyone had a different take on the story, but seemed to follow the we-have-abandoned-God and replaced-him-with-the-cult-of-celebrity line. I was asked over and over what I believed the moral of my story was, and while I spoke from the heart on the first day, I found as time marched on I became a broken record. By the end of the week my answers were so carefully calibrated and rehearsed I could have just mailed them in.

Even so, a sampling from the breakfast show *Good Morning, New York* will provide a solid example of the week's events. Seated opposite the ever cheery Monica Martin, I was interviewed at 8.07, right after the news. I have to say I always liked watching

Monica in the morning, so it was a treat to meet her.

'Two days ago the latest issue of *The Vulture* hit the streets, and since then it has been almost impossible to buy a copy. Why? A cover story that has the whole country talking involving a movie star and a finance journalist who dated for a couple of weeks. Now they confess the relationship was a complete scam, undertaken, they say, to test the waters of celebrity, to see how deep they run. Today we are lucky enough to have the author of that article, Tom Webster, here now to explain it all. Good morning, Tom, and thank you for being here.'

'Morning, Monica,' I said.

'Tom, let's start at the beginning. You attached yourself to Alexandra West, for want of a better word, to see how long it would take for you to achieve celebrity status of your own.'

'Right.'

'And it didn't take long, did it?'

'No, Monica, not long at all. From our first date the media were all over me, digging up my past, cornering me in restaurant bathrooms. And when I wouldn't speak with them, they made things up.'

'Well, Tom, speaking as someone who lives in the public eye all the time, I can tell you printing lies about people is an industry.'

'So I learned.'

'Now, Alexandra agreed to undergo this experiment with you for reasons of her own, did she not?'

'Yes, Monica. She moved to the East Coast to restart her movie career, but found nobody wanted to take her seriously. She thought that attaching herself to me would transfer to her what I had, a serious side.'

'And it worked, didn't it?'

'Not instantly. At first people were dumbfounded, but over time they believed it. Alexandra started fielding offers from the movie producers she wanted to work with.'

'And now? What do they think of her now?'

'You mean since the article hit the streets?'

'Yes.'

'They love it. If anything, she has received even more calls in the last three days. Everybody now wants her in their movie. As I wrote in my article, Alexandra is genuinely a nice person, and much more sensitive than her bimbo image suggests.'

'But she was the one who initially traded heavily on that image.'

'Yes, Monica, she did. But one reason she agreed to date me was to see if she could change that perception. And she did.'

'And what about you? How did this all affect you?'

'Well, Monica, I'm still recovering. It was very overwhelming, very intrusive.'

'But you did have a movie star move into your apartment for a few weeks. That must have been interesting.'

'It was. But you can't get too upset about your clothes being moved out of your closets, otherwise you would never make it through the day.'

She laughed so hard you would have thought I had told the joke of the century.

'I understand your colleagues are all a little angry, also stunned, Tom.'

'I think everyone, including me, is a little stunned right now, Monica. Everyone is digesting this.'

'And your best friend, Jake, to whom you addressed the article in the form of a letter?'

'We have talked it through and made up.'

She beamed. Everyone loves a happy ending.

'Last question before we break for a commercial. You wrote in your article you didn't want to weigh in and philosophize about what this says about American culture.'

'No. I thought I would just pen my journey as it happened, and leave it for others to decide how to interpret it.'

'And what have you found?'

'Pretty much what I expected. I think it's a very complex issue, but most commentary seems to lament our obsession with personalities. I mean, if you can turn somebody who is dating a star into a star...'

'Right. Then where does it end, Tom?'

'That I don't know, Monica.'

And I didn't. The interview was over. Monica did not ask me how I had parlayed the event into my own series of deals, but others did, and I felt in the interest of full disclosure I had to outline every business opportunity I had signed. Throughout the entire week, Wilkes was in a constant state of joyous hysteria. Actors were calling, begging him to take them as clients. For him, this was as close as he would get to hitting the lottery. Alexandra's career boomed, as she too was hailed a genius.

She did her own fair share of television appearances, regurgitating my article 99 percent of the time. She was always extremely sweet when talking about me, and for that I shall be eternally grateful. She gushed what a relief it was to move into my apartment for those few weeks, to live among 'normal' people. And she reiterated how awful she felt watching the media tear me apart for their own amusement and circulation.

We spoke nightly throughout the week, discussing strategies, what we would be wearing, and which reporters asked the most intelligent questions. Alexandra said she was enjoying the fallout from the article far more than she had ever enjoyed her career, for she was being asked what she thought about something other than her beauty routine.

Together we covered all the major news outlets in the country. And it didn't end with us. Wilkes appeared on a number of programs, billed as the mastermind behind the Marilyn–Arthur strategy that reeled the public in. Mom was interviewed. Jake finally capitulated, assuring everyone the feud was genuinely behind us. Louis grabbed his fifteen minutes of fame so aggressively I think by the end he had clocked up about seven hours. Even Mr Detestable, Frank Wicker-Smith III, was quoted in a few papers. Reporters contacted Simon Burke in prison to get his take on the story, as he technically set it in motion.

And yes, Hector the doorman. Quoted in *The New York Review*. Initially I had made myself famous, but by the end of the game the whole team had been anointed. It seemed everyone who had been mentioned in *The Vulture* had something to say, and a tape recorder to say it into. Except Elizabeth. She was conspicuous by her absence from the ensuing circus, even though she must have been contacted. She never called me, and while I was dying to know what she thought, things between Jake and myself were still rather tender, and I thought it best not to bring her up. The curiosity was killing me but ultimately I would not die from it. Why?

Here's why.

Chapter 37

On Saturday, a full five days after the article hit the streets, she appeared. In the flesh. In my apartment. Our apartment. She still had her keys, so when I arrived home from a television appearance, she was waiting for me. Sitting on the lips. She looked good too. Really good. My jaw hit the floor, nevertheless.

'Shocked to see me, Tom?'

'That would be an understatement, Liz.'

'We need to talk.'

'Sure.'

I put down my briefcase and noted the place was chaos. I had not cleaned during the week because of the demands on my time.

'After all the years I nagged you, you still don't put away the dishes. Just leave them out on the sink for all eternity.'

'I'm a single guy now, Liz. And one of the joys of living alone is that you can leave dishes on the rack forever and nobody complains.'

'Well, that's what I want to talk about.'

'The dishes?'

'Your status. You being a single guy.'

'Go on.'

As she started talking I put on the kettle and made coffee. I needed an activity because I felt too thrown to just sit down next to her.

'The divorce isn't coming through for another four months, you know.'

'I know. Bet you can't wait.'

'Actually, I can.'

'Excuse me?'

'I want us to try again.'

My jaw, already on the floor since her arrival, now crashed through to the apartment below.

'What?'

'I'm leaving Jake. It wasn't working. I see now it was just some textbook pre-menopausal mid-life thing. I'll be blunt, I want you back.'

'Hang on a minute here. This isn't some kind of April-fool joke, is it?'

'Do I look like I'm kidding, Tom?'

'You want me . . . us . . . to get back together?'

'Yes.'

'What does Jake say?'

'I spoke to him before I came here. He's in shock. But he'll get over it.'

'And so let me hear this again. You want us to reconcile?'

'Right.'

'Can I ask why? You haven't spoken to me for almost a year except to tell me you hate me.'

'I'm sorry, Tom. I really am. But those reporters made my life hell too, you know.'

'I know, and I told you I was really sorry about that.'

'Apology accepted.'

'I'm speechless.'

'I understand.'

'Liz, what happened? Why now?'

'I realized I still love you.'

'All of a sudden?'

'Not all of a sudden. While this whole Alexandra West thing was happening. I mean, I thought I was over you, but when you started dating her, I was jealous. I was. And then they wrote about how smart and sexy you were and I thought, it's true. I can't believe I didn't see it before. And then when women started flirting with you, I thought, hands off him, he's mine. Ten years of marriage, Tom, you can't just throw it away.'

'You did.'

'I'm sorry. I don't know what else to say.'

'Have the media contacted you?'

'I'm not talking to them.'

'I thought you must have given them their marching orders. You're the only holdout, you know. Even Hector is giving interviews.'

We both laughed. It was the first time in a long time the icy air that blew between us melted somewhat. I was dumbfounded, to say the least. She wanted me back. She wanted our marriage back. This was a conversation I had fantasized about for so long, and now, confronted with it, I couldn't believe my reaction. Yes, I still loved her. But it was over. For better or worse, I couldn't go back to her. I couldn't return to our old life. So even she had swallowed Michael Wilkes's bait. She left me having declared I was a crashing bore. Now I was sexy and desirable. The irony would have been delicious if it had not hurt so much.

'Liz, I'm sorry. I don't think we can start over. Too much has happened. You know. Water under the bridge and all that.'

'What are you saying? That you can do better than me now? You're too famous to have a history teacher for a wife anymore?'

Well, I did have a date with Rachel Carter-Brown next week.

'Don't be ridiculous. It's just that, I don't know really. My life now is about moving forward. Going back to us would be going back to...'

'Do you even love me anymore?'

'Of course I do. But I was so broken when you left, you can't expect me to just pick up a year later as if nothing had happened.'

'But you did with Jake.'

'Jake's different. I never vowed to love, honor, obey and the rest of it with Jake. I never had sex with Jake. I never took out a mortgage, bought china or looked to Jake after my father's funeral for comfort. That was all about you. And you just upped and left. I don't have the heart to go through it all again. What if you leave again?'

'I won't.'

'There are no guarantees, Liz. You said that when you were leaving. You said, Tom, there are no guarantees our marriage would last forever.'

'I did say that, didn't I?'

'I love you, Liz. I'm just not in love with you anymore. I'm sorry.'

I felt like a character from a daytime soap opera as I said that. Funny how scenes from your own life can sometimes contain all the corniness and cliché of a television program. Elizabeth began to cry and I put my arms around her.

'What are you going to do?'

'Find an apartment. Start over.'

'I'll be earning a lot more money now. I can help you out, you know that. I think we should sell this place and each buy our own.'

She gathered her things, and stood up. I walked her to the door, we hugged, and she left. I could not believe what had just transpired. She wanted me back and I said no. I really did. Only one thing to do. I called Jake. He was feeling bruised, but my news cheered him somewhat, as horrible as it sounds. We talked about the ball game the next day, how we still planned to go. And then I called my mom, to tell her that I loved her, and all about Elizabeth's visit.

'You know, Tommy darling, I suspected she might resurface.'

'You did?'

'Mothers know these things.'

'And?'

'I'm proud of you.'

'You are?'

'Yes, I am. I know I always taught you that everyone deserves a second chance, but the woman who walks out on my son isn't getting one from me.'

'Mom, I had no idea you felt this way about Elizabeth.'

'Well, I do. I can forgive her but I won't forget.'

'I feel the same way, Mom.'

'You can do better now, Tommy. You can find a girl who'll love you more than she did. I know it.'

I knew it too. Mom was reiterating something Elizabeth had said not moments before. The ugly truth was, I was famous now. Me. Tom Webster, famous. I could shoot Abe Lincoln in a crowded theater and everybody would know who I was. They would say, Tom Webster shot him, officer, we'd know that face anywhere.

I know this isn't nice coming from a nice guy like me, but when you're famous, you can upgrade your women. I *could* do better than Elizabeth. I could get me anyone I wanted. Alright, within limits. I'm not fooling myself. I'm not Alexander the Great, Napoleon or Julius Caesar. In the great scheme of things, I am no hero. But today, right now, I am Tomcat Webster, the sexy guy who preys on all and sundry. I am a financial powerhouse whose opinion is sought after, valued, repeated. I am the guy who convinced the world I was somebody, and then became somebody because I pulled it off.

Who would have thunk that in three short months I could go, as they say, from zero to hero? Not me. Not anyone. But there you have it. They were wrong. I was wrong. Boy, was I wrong.

Boy Oh Boy Oh Boy Oh Boy.